BLACK RIVER

NILANJANA ROY

PUSHKIN
VERTIGO

Pushkin Press
Somerset House, Strand
London WC2R 1LA

Black River was first published in India by Context, an imprint
of Westland Books, a division of Nasadiya Technologies Private
Limited, under the name Nilanjana S. Roy, in 2022

First published by Pushkin Press in 2023

1 3 5 7 9 8 6 4 2

ISBN 13: 978-1-78227-943-3

Designed and typeset by Tetragon, London
Printed and bound by Clays Ltd, Elcograf S.p.A.

www.pushkinpress.com

For Tarun Roy (1939–2021)
father and friend
who always let me raid his bookshelves

Contents

Reasonable Doubt

Inquiries

Reckoning

TEETARPUR, 2017

Blight

Munia's eighth birthday falls on the hottest day in June, with the smell of burning cane scenting the air. She forgets the heat in her excitement over the slice of cassata her father has brought all the way from Teetar Bani, the main town. Chand had ordered the precious gift from the only shop in the town that possessed a freezer, and carefully packed it in a tin pail filled with jute sacking and ice purchased from Raju Golasharbatwala's cart.

The cassata melts, a puddle of bright colours. She eats it slowly, bending her head to the dented tin plate and lapping up the last delicious drops of strawberry. It is a rare taste, a flavour she has not encountered before. Her father asks, 'One more slice?'

She nods, but halfway through, she holds out her plate to Chand, presses the spoon into his hand. 'You also eat. One spoon for you, one for me.' He takes tiny bites.

❦

There is nothing Teetarpur is famous for. The older residents say proudly that their village is not known to have inspired a line in a film song or even a mithai, has never produced

so much as a celebrity or a famous politician. They cherish
its anonymity, though the younger generation would have
preferred a more rousing history.

Chand's hut, and his brother Balle Ram's equally modest
establishment, are almost the last houses in the village.
They are set on a slope just before the soaring forests arc
upwards on the first hill of the Aravalli range. A canal
flows behind Chand's home, opening out onto untended
fields.

Their huts are about an hour's walk from the tumbledown
police chowki that marks the start of Teetarpur, a fifteen-
minute ride on Chand's ancient Rajdoot 350cc bike. In
their boyhood, the two huts were part of a dozen-strong
cluster, but most of their neighbours had moved to the
village proper, disliking the isolation, the dark shadows
cast by the forest at night.

Balle Ram and Chand stayed on after their father's
death, unwilling to abandon their ancestral land. Chand
plants a few food crops in the field near his hut and leaves
the trees to flourish as they please. Balle Ram and he reap
fair harvests from their other fields, which are a long walk
away, part of the patchwork of village lands that lie behind
the police chowki.

Chand's only other neighbour is the richest man
in Teetarpur, Jolly Singh, who brings some of Delhi's
briskness with him. Jolly Villa rose brick by brick fifteen
years ago, its brightly painted gates and balustraded roof
one of Teetarpur's wonders. It rests like a gaudy crown on
a low ridge, looking down at Chand's hut and the village
below.

In the mornings and early evenings, pilgrims pass by
Chand's hut to pray at the shrine of an animal-loving

sage who lived high up on the first of the great hills of the Aravalli range. But they are otherwise undisturbed. During the day, only peacocks and snakes travel up the hill to the quiet shrine.

Chand has grown to cherish their isolation and independence, though he tells Munia many tales of Delhi, of other faraway places they find in her school atlas— the Arabian Sea, the winding silver ropes of the Yamuna, the Ganges, the towering snow-covered ranges of the Himalayas. She has hazy memories of the capital, which she had visited once with her father when she was just five years old.

'An ocean of cars and a sea of houses,' Chand says to Munia. 'At first you put your hands over your ears because of the noise from the traffic, but you liked Delhi after a while. We'll go again, someday.'

'But I like it here the most,' she says firmly. 'I don't want to go anywhere else.'

'When you're grown up, you'll want to see the capital. Everyone does.'

'I want to see the Himalayas.'

And Chand says, delighting Munia, 'Some day we'll take the Rajdoot, you and I, and we'll go all the way to the mountains, you'll see.'

～

Chand's fields, the trees and the mehendi bushes that surround them, are set down from the road, hard to see even from Balle Ram's home. Chand knows that when he leaves to farm his other fields, this small patch of earth becomes his daughter's private kingdom.

He has seen Munia whirr across the ragged green carpet of the cowpea fields when she thinks no one is watching. Her thin, sunburnt arms, speckled from the sun, and bare feet put him in mind of the tiny brown bird she's named after.

Munia is quiet with strangers and with family, rarely speaks in front of Balle Ram or his wife Sarita. She is an explorer at heart, fond of illicit excursions, absorbed in the games she invents, and plays with birds and insects.

She talks only to her father. Him she tells everything, the conversations she overhears, stories she has made up. Her piping words patter as rapidly as monsoon rain against a thatched roof. She tells Chand about the four men hanging at a steep angle off bamboo scaffolds that appear to be anchored in the sky itself, stringing long ropes of lights like twinkling green stars in Jolly Singh's massive farmhouse, and about the new carp pond there, gleaming with fat red-and-gold fish. About the bus that collided with a truck at the crossing up ahead, both drivers unwilling to be the one who braked first, and how the loosely packed sacks of marigolds, the truck's cargo, had burst and spilt in an orange river across the road.

That time, she had carried one of the marigolds back home to show him, allowing him to cradle her in his arms as he inspected the small, crushed petals. 'You smell of woodsmoke,' she had said to him. 'I smell of mud and sweat and dirt,' he had replied, but his daughter was already asleep, her head a tired smudge against his checked kurta.

❧

Every summer, the heat grows more fierce. The dhak trees in the forests that the villagers have protected and held sacred for centuries shrivel in this furnace. Even the peafowl that roam the slopes are too listless to call out to each other, and the silence in the forest settles heavily around Chand and Munia.

As the temperature soars, the red rot spreads across Chand's land. The blight races from field to field, no matter how diligently the farmers of Teetarpur uproot the infected clumps of sugarcane. The stench—fermenting, gangrenous—rides across the fields along with the smell of burning crops. Bugs fatten on the spoils and white grubs scuttle out of the way of the flames, fastening onto new stands. The rot takes hold easily, the land smoulders.

Smoke from the cane fires hangs thick and acrid over the village. Chand has to leave Munia behind when he sets out to tend his sugarcane fields. He ignores his daughter's pleading eyes, even though it's her birthday week, gently turns down her soft demand to be carried there on the high throne of his shoulders, to be included as an essential part of his working life.

Chand tells her, 'You're eight years old—all grown up now. Don't give your aunt any trouble while I'm away. You promise?'

She nods reluctantly.

Munia's silent prayers work. Her aunt leaves to collect wood for the stove. In a flash, she is out, exploring.

The sun leaves thorny prickles on her skinny, bare legs as she steps into the cool grey mud where her father had watered the plants that morning. She likes the way it squishes up between her toes, a friendly massage from the earth. A strip of sun-baked earth, powdery and ferociously hot beneath the soles of her feet, spans the gap between the bund and the neem and jamun trees. The thin silver chains of her anklets set off a faint carillon as she fits one foot, and then the next, into the wide cracks in the scorching earth. She shudders at the delicious change in temperature, the coolness secreted away deep inside the furrowed land.

Placing her cheek against the bark of the trees, she feels the difference between smooth bark and scaly bark, the texture of each tree as singular and well known to her as her own family's faces: her uncle's rich dark skin, her aunt's papery, delicate skin, the comforting touch of her father's rough-skinned, gentle fingers.

She walks warily over the fallen nimbolis, careful not to tread on the green berries, hard as stones. It is quiet in the orchard, with no spring breeze to cool the air, only the first heavy stirrings of the summer heat rising up from the dust. A worker's scaffold, the shape of a swing, lies at the foot of the tree, anointed by a thick coil of rope. A leftover from the construction on the Lovely Pure Veg Bhojanalaya. She has seen her father use it to repair the roof thatch.

She ducks beneath the jamuns. Their slender, long-fingered branches reach out and brush her tangled, sun-browned hair.

Munia has plucked a skirtful of berries when she sees the man. He is in the nearby plot, leaning back against the makeshift planks of cart wood that wrestle the thorny bushes into a low fence. Strangers rarely come through these parts. There is nothing to tempt them in this untended plot of common land that separates the fields from the forest soaring above. But this man is no stranger.

~

The heat dries out the sugarcane leaves. They thrust upwards into the sky, black against the harsh white glare.

Chand squats in the mud, sees the grey mould sprayed across the sugarcane stems, the bruises on the stands of cane. Inhales the sour, fermented air, the kind of stench that rises off the skin of alcoholics drunk on the hooch sold in plastic packets up and down the length of the state. The exhalations from the sugarcane on this side of the fields seem almost human. He probes the stem with his cane knife.

The stem splits easily. Inside, there's discolouration, and Chand has to turn away, take a breath of fresh air before his nostrils inhale the red rot again. He sights along the line, along the stands. An untrained eye would see little—just a hint of grey fuzz on the stems, a few black spots here and there. But he knows what he will find inside: red bruises, maroon discolouration. The damaged cane reminds him of the fragility of pulped flesh and broken bones. He brushes the thought away.

Chand stands at the edge of the fields. He is covered in the dust scattered by the wheels of trucks on their way to the stone quarry, masking the summer tan of his skin, turning him into a ghost. The trucks link Teetarpur with the brisk rumble of the new industries springing up around the Aravallis, and the elongated mansions where they grow only trees and flowers but no useful crops.

From the stench across the embankment, Chand guesses that many will have no sugarcane crop at all. This, in a year when many of the villagers have been selling their land, some for money, some because their children no longer want a life tied to farming.

Chand walks home as swiftly as he can, ignoring the scorching sun, harsh on his back. Munia hates it when he stays out in the fields too late. She likes to tell him about her adventures, real and imaginary, in these quiet evening hours. The sweat pools and prickles between his shoulder blades, and he quickens his step, glad to be returning to his daughter.

The Man in the Field

Munia considers the man gingerly, as she would assess a battle-scarred bull monkey for malevolent intent.

He closes his eyes and wipes the sweat off his brow with a cotton scarf. Not a local red cloth but a fancier printed city towel. He tips his head back, his eyes closed.

Munia inspects the jamuns gathered in her skirt. They are squashed and not as purple as she likes them to be, but when she cautiously bites into one, the flavour explodes on her tongue.

She looks over at the man. He has his eyes open, and his head tilted, and he is watching thick grey puffs of smoke from the chimneys of a faraway brick kiln drift by across the blinding hot blue of the sky.

The girl shuffles back through the cool, sticky mud, holding her skirt like a bag around her knees. The munias start to call, their high, plaintive voices plinking far above her head.

She hears a laugh, the rustle of long skirts over the scrub and rock, and looks over, losing her fear. Munia understands illicit meetings. She is a brown scrap, so easily overlooked. Hidden in the branches, she has seen lovers come up to the mandir, taking selfies, seen them look around and go behind a bend in the road.

The jamuns, sun-ripened, fill her mouth with sweet, purple juice. The man stretches and leans towards the woman, swinging her around lightly so that he stands facing in Munia's direction, the woman's back to her.

'You never have time for me these days,' the woman says. 'Is it the factory that keeps you busy or is it those famous sluts from your infamous city?'

'Too much work,' the man says.

Her voice hardens, business-like. 'Did you bring it?'

'Yes,' he says. 'But later, no? First some masti.'

She says, 'The full amount?'

'What you asked for. Yes, I brought it. But no more after this, okay?'

She says, 'First you beg for a taste, then you don't want anyone to know what you've been sticking where. Don't worry, baba, I won't tell anyone about us. You can run back to your family and pretend you never met me. Wait, I'll do it, don't rip my blouse, it's new! You're so impatient!'

'You're so tempting,' he says. 'And we'd better be quick. We might not be easy to see from the main road, but someone could take a shortcut along the canal and spot us. You like this? And this?'

Munia glances idly at them, admiring the woman's tight pink-and-green blouse, the silver ribbons she has plaited through her thick, long hair, the vivid patchwork green of her swinging lehenga. The woman has her head down, shy, but the skirt is bolder. It swings towards the man and strokes his ankles, then he moves a hand, and magically, the skirt lifts, higher and higher, and Munia hears the woman gasp as the man's hand disappears under the bold, flirtatious lehenga, which is rucked up to her waist now.

The sun is directly over the man's head, but she is close enough to see him close his eyes, and she watches, casually interested. The woman is shuddering, her long hair in disarray, still moaning, still murmuring endearments.

He raises his head and looks in Munia's direction. She doesn't think he has seen her, but she shrinks back, just in case.

The man removes the gaudy towel from around his neck. It is patterned in browns and purples; shimmering butterflies, their outlines shaky, their eyes a glaring orange, are printed in vivid deep dyes across the length of it. The colours—the strutting blues, the garish golds—dance before Munia's eyes, even at that distance. She watches in fascination as the man uses one hand to twist it into a rope, expertly, stroking the woman's hair with his other hand.

He twirls the towel. The colours go round and round, a rope of blue and gold butterflies. The woman looks up at him, and he slams the flat of his hand across her windpipe. Munia hears the choked-off beginnings of something that might have been a scream, and involuntarily raises her own small hand to her neck. The woman sags to one side, like a sack of crumpled clothes for the dhobi, and the man moves with swiftness, slipping the towel around her neck so gently that he might be garlanding her.

The woman sighs loudly, breath leaving her body in a long exhalation, her generous bosom heaving, and Munia recovers from her fright. It is a game between them then. The butterflies flash in the sunlight, dancing. The man kneels beside the woman, his hands moving deftly.

Munia can see him looking with tender care into the woman's face. Then he laughs and picks her up like a bundle, something darkening at her throat. Her long hair flutters over his elbow like a flag. He carries her down, weaving through the scrub, out of sight, towards the straggling dhak trees.

⌒

A pair of green bee-eaters settles on a low branch, and Munia stretches up to watch them. One of the pair has caught a wasp, and it dashes the insect against the bark, smashing the wriggling yellow creature until it hangs limply from the bird's beak. Chand had once told Munia that bee-eaters are cleverer than people. They take the sting out of the wasp, just like he carefully extracts the rough stone from mangoes with his thin-bladed knife before giving the fruit to his daughter to devour.

Munia turns to go back home.

The man is right there, smiling, squatting so that he looks straight into her eyes, the towel slung carelessly around his neck. He has circled around and returned.

'Were the jamuns sweet?' he asks. 'It's all right, you can talk to me. I know your father, and your uncle, Balle Ram.'

Munia relaxes. The man speaks differently from them, his Hindi smooth and citified. But he has the soothing tone of a person used to gentling startled animals, or shy children.

'You're not scared, are you? I think you're too grown up to be scared of anything,' he says, voice pitched low. 'Only small girls get scared. You're a big girl, aren't you?'

Munia nods, a quick, bird-like movement of her head.

'If my friend was here,' the man says casually, 'she would have given you a toffee. You saw her, didn't you? The woman who was with me?'

The girl nods again. She looks hopefully at the man, who smiles, and like a magician, pulls out a fistful of coins. Her eyes widen.

'Which ones do you like?'

She points to the ten-rupee coins.

'And this?' he says, bringing out a five-rupee coin.

She wavers. The ten-rupee coin is worth more, she knows that, but the five-rupee coin is shinier, prettier.

'Here,' he says, before Munia can decide, 'take them all.'

She holds the coins in her hands and closes her eyes, feeling each separate one like a treasure.

'Do you like swings?' he asks her. At last, she smiles.

'I can make good swings,' he says. 'When I was a boy, we used to make rope swings and tie them to the branches of trees. Have you seen that type of jhoola?'

Munia shakes her head, no.

He picks up the scaffold and expertly tosses the long, fat coil of rope over the thickest part of the branch. Glances around to check, but they are alone, the man and the girl, invisible from the road. He makes a double loop and beckons Munia closer. She comes up, clutching her precious coins in both fists.

'That'll hold,' he says, pleased. 'That's done the trick.'

He produces a handkerchief, a striking navy blue. Ever so gently, he prises the coins out of her hands, ties them in a bundle, ties the corners of the handkerchief to her skirt. 'There,' he says. 'So that they don't fall out.'

She crinkles her eyes, not seeing a swing yet. 'This is how you make a swing,' the man explains as he kneels on the ground. 'You tie a thick knot and then you make a loop. Come, I'll show you.'

She draws a circle in the dust with her left toe, suddenly shy. Then she makes up her mind and steps towards him, putting up her purple-stained hands, allowing herself to be lifted onto his knee, watching as he knots the rope. 'It's a shame,' he says softly. 'That you were playing here today. That you saw.'

He gives her a tight, encouraging smile. 'Swing, little one. Swing.'

Munia in the sunlight, smiling up at the man, the noose around her thin, unresisting neck. The peacocks take wing, vivid green streaks over the trees. They are finally calling, three-note shrieks that rend the air, but there is no one to hear.

The Weight of Rope

A sound draws him to the back, that is how he finds her. As he is about to step into the hut, Chand hears a man sobbing, such an unexpected sound. He jams his tired feet back into the worn leather of his jootis and goes around to check.

He sees a bundle hanging from a tree limb like a discarded shawl. The sun is directly in his eyes, its white light blinding, black shadows and shapes shimmering when he blinks. A second huddled form on the ground. Sweat in his eyes. He blinks it away.

Then the disparate shapes, the harsh sobs, come together, like one of those puzzles they sell at the fair, where black cardboard pieces suddenly come together to form a bird, a star. Or a tree, a girl with a rope around her neck, her feet dangling far above the earth, hanging from the jamun's thickest branch.

He tries to call her, Munia, Munia, but his mouth is dry from shock and from the heat. He forms the syllables of his daughter's name and whispers it into the heavy air.

A man kneels on the ground, his white salwar streaked with dust and mud, holding on to Munia's limp feet, crying like a child, his breath rasping and hard.

The girl's eyes are closed, her lashes resting lightly on her cheeks, purple stains on her curled fingers. She could be holding her breath, except for the tilt of her neck, the coil of rope, the swing dangling at a crazy angle, a heavy wooden counterweight.

She will open her eyes, her father thinks, she will smile at me and put out her arms to be helped down, and then I will carry my Munia inside one more time.

The man in his torn white kurta, his mud-streaked salwar, puts his hands to his head, keens, a long, low sound. When his elbow hits the child's feet, she spins slowly, turning in a wide circle, her toenails ringed with dried mud. Chand sees the livid discolouration around her neck.

The man begins to crawl towards him on his knees. It takes a moment for Chand to recall his name: Mansoor Khan. He had wandered into their village some months ago, one of the drifters who sometimes passed that way in search of shelter.

A quiet man with pain-filled eyes, dignified and private. He carried a bag of carpentry tools, but was not fit to work. He often wrapped his hands in cheap white muslin to cover some old injuries, the frayed ends of the cloth giving him a spectral air. From time to time, he walked with a purposeful tread around the fields, muttering gibberish rhymes to himself. He survived on alms and the kindness of the local farmers. Chand too had put small packets of atta and dal, tea leaves and crumbling brown molasses in Mansoor's frayed cloth bag, as they did with holy men and the occasional harmless lunatic.

Mansoor is plucking at his sleeve, saying, 'Chand, Chand, I didn't do it, I was crossing your fields for the shortcut. I did nothing, I saw her hanging in the tree, it wasn't me, it wasn't me.'

Chand slaps his hand away, can barely make sense of Mansoor's babbling. 'I have to get that rope off her neck, it's too heavy for her,' he says.

He can't take his eyes off his child, her small body slowly twirling like one of those painted wooden puppets from Rajasthan, dancing at the end of a string. The sun beats down. He is shivering.

Night Duty

Ombir Singh feels a red, throbbing knot of pain tightening at the back of his skull. Twenty hours is normal, thirty-six doable. He'd once gone seventy hours without sleep: noises sharpened, colours brightened till they were painful, the floor and the roof swung around him.

Forty hours since he left the Teetarpur station house in Bhim Sain's charge, and he hasn't managed even a short nap. Sweat and dirt stiffen the collar of his uniform, his back muscles are on fire from the long ride on his Bullet to Faridabad and back.

He shoulders his fatigue like a heavy, familiar backpack and steps inside the station house. The evening is falling swift. Inside the station house, two hurricane lanterns cast a warm glow over the register, and lizards scurry up the painted brick to the straggling thatch of the roof. Outside, sequestered in the pound, he hears the hobbled cattle snort, adding their odour to the ammoniac smell rising from the grey gutter that bisects the thana's main room.

Bhim Sain is asleep at the desk, his head resting on the pages of the station-house register, his jowls sallow and sagging like an old dog's. A strip of his heart pills have fallen out of his pocket to the floor. Near his outflung hand, Ombir sees a paper plate rimmed with leftover grease from the pakoras he buys by the dozen from Lovely Bhojanalaya. Ombir slides a hand under Bhim Sain's cheek, lifting his jowls an inch so that he can extract the register, then places the sub-inspector's head gently back on the rough wooden table that serves as their desk. He will take an hour to catch up with the paperwork. Then he can wake Bhim Sain, get in the four or five hours of sleep he has been craving all day.

Ombir is scrutinising the day book when he hears the bike. Bhim Sain's snores stop—the sub-inspector is able to cross from deep sleep into instant wakefulness at the first hint of a disturbance. The engine skips a beat from time to time, and Ombir recognises the arrhythmic signature of Dilshad Singh's sputtering Yamaha.

By the time Dilshad arrives, Ombir is at the gate, raising his torch in the twilight so that he can see their visitor's face more clearly. Green-eyed, his face and stylish beard as chiselled as any film star's, the young man moonlights as a police photographer. He had honed his trade taking portfolio pictures for women who were determined to make it some day as local pop singers, and wedding troupe dancers who posed as deities for calendars or as porn stars for the cheaper magazines. The work sharpened his eye for detail, made him useful at crime scenes.

'Thank God you're back,' he says. 'What a calamity! They're all there, I told them they must wait until you two reach.'

Ombir says, 'Wait. Take a deep breath. Calm yourself down and then explain properly.'

'Chand's daughter has been murdered. I took photographs before Balle Ram and he brought her down from the jamun tree. And they've caught the murderer already.'

Ombir says, 'Munia is dead? The little one?'

He has known Chand for many years, and was glad to see him return from the big city to his family and his lands eight years ago. Every morning, if his work isn't too demanding, Ombir walks the length of Teetarpur village, and up the main road towards the forests. The village lies at the edge of the Delhi–Haryana border, an hour's drive down silent, forested roads covered in powdery summer dust. Its soul has remained half a century behind the capital. Delhi's frenetic, relentless activity is not to the taste of most of Chand's generation of villagers.

Meanwhile, Teetar Bani grows steadily, like a concrete wasp's nest, sandwiched between the highway and the stone quarries that stubble the rolling hills, the first swell of the Aravalli range. The village, Teetarpur, is over a hundred years older than the town, but much smaller and set farther back from the highway, close to a belt of sugarcane factories and oil mills. It is a modest settlement of barely two hundred huts and single-storey brick homes.

The brothers' huts are at the far end of his beat. He has watched Munia grow up, become a quiet child with large, curious eyes who kept to herself.

A memory from two days ago: the girl watching him solemnly as he went about his rounds. He had gone up towards Jolly Villa, and when he came back, she was imitating a policeman's slow, deliberate walk. He had laughed. She stopped, stricken to be noticed, then gave him a shy wave before running away.

'We'd better get there before they take matters into their own hands. Who's the bastard who did this?'

'Mansoor,' Dilshad says.

Ombir frowns, and Bhim Sain says, joining them, 'Must be some mistake. Mansoor wouldn't harm anyone. And why would he hurt Chand's daughter? They used to let him sleep in the field some nights, gave him tea, and a meal also.'

'Mistake or not, we should hurry,' Ombir says, kickstarting their unreliable Bullet. 'Angry men don't stop to think.'

~

The flaring light of petromax lanterns illuminates the scene. Mansoor kneels on the ground, his white kurta torn, his black salwar streaked with dust and mud.

Balle Ram and a score of villagers surround him. In the centre, Chand, bowed over the body of his eight-year-old daughter. Dust on her skirt and face, livid rope marks where the noose has slackened on her neck. Ombir looks around—fifteen men already, some with scythes, others with axes. And he and Bhim Sain with only one revolver between the two of them, because Bhim Sain's revolver is with the gunsmith for a faulty front sight.

Chand's brother is the one to handle, he decides. If he can calm Balle Ram down, he has the crowd. If not, his record will show that he couldn't prevent a village lynching, and that might hold up his overdue promotion even longer. He is relieved when Bhim Sain does the right thing. The sub-inspector kneels by Chand's side, gently puts a hand on the man's shoulder, speaks a few words of comfort.

Ombir holds up his hand for silence. The crowd quietens, its attention held by Balle Ram and Chand, grief softening the edges of vengefulness in the atmosphere.

Balle Ram steps forward. 'This is our business, Ombir-ji. Not yours. This man came into my brother's fields, he killed my niece, he took her from Chand. Leave him to us. I told Dilshad not to interfere.'

Ombir says, 'Where was she found?'

Balle Ram points to the jamun tree.

'I have photographs,' Dilshad calls.

Ombir scans the ground rapidly, playing his torch over it, his heart sinking. Of course Chand's family and the rest of Teetarpur would have crowded around without a thought to footprints or any other signs left behind by the murderer. He will have scant evidence to present. And even if Mansoor confesses, the courts rarely trust a prisoner's confession without eyewitnesses to the actual murder. So easy to beat one out of a man.

He flashes the light full on Mansoor's face. Usually, Mansoor has a gentleness about him. Ombir thinks of him as one of God's children, one of the imperfect pots baked from the Almighty's clay, with a crack running through. In Teetarpur, he had received the respect due to all madmen, until this day.

The man whimpers. Ombir holds his torch steady, letting them see what they've done already, the bruises rising blue and livid on the carpenter's skin, the blood dripping from his forehead onto his kurta.

'And who found him?'

Chand raises his head. His deep-set eyes are filled with stunned anguish, his face gaunt and lined.

'He was clasping her feet when I arrived,' Chand says.

'Your daughter was already dead?'

'Yes.'

'He didn't try to run away when he saw you?'

'No.'

'Did Mansoor say anything to you?'

Chand blinks, recovering himself with an effort. 'He said he'd taken the shortcut and seen her. He said he didn't kill my girl. He was crying.'

'He's a madman,' Balle Ram says. 'They don't behave the way we do.'

Ombir looks around at the men and says, 'Please lower your weapons. Give me one chance to settle this. We also knew Munia. We also care about Chand. I know him personally. Only one chance, that is all I ask.'

Bhim Sain picks up the cue. 'Give them some space,' the sub-inspector tells the gathered men. 'I want photographs of the area without all of you crowding around. We'll need them for our files.'

Two more men arrive in a tempo, carrying thick slabs of ice covered with gunny sacks against the heat. Ombir is glad for the distraction. Bhim Sain organises some of the men, helps them carry the slabs into Chand's hut.

Ombir feels Mansoor's trembling hands clutching at his ankles. He ignores the man, pulling away. If at all he can help it, Ombir doesn't want to draw the crowd's attention to the poor lunatic. He sits down on the ground, a few paces away from Chand, and motions to Balle Ram.

The man hesitates, then reluctantly walks over and sits down. One small bit of ground gained: always cut the leader off from the mob. Ombir can speak more privately despite the circle of watchers.

'For almost three years,' he says, keeping his voice so low that Balle Ram has to lean towards him, 'I came by this way, passed your brother's hut most days. I saw your niece grow up. She has been taken from all of you in the most cruel way possible. Balle Ram, Chand had his daughter, and he had you. Now he has only you. My question is, will you help him or make it worse for him?'

'How can anything be worse than this? She was ours, too. We loved her like our own daughter. My wife—she's at home, she can't even speak without breaking down.'

'Yes. And it would be the easiest thing in the world for me and Bhim Sain to leave this man with you tonight.'

It's the truth. All he has to do is not file a report, to warn Dilshad that, for the official record, he never took any pictures, never came to the station house. He could so easily look away while their rough justice takes its course. But questions may be asked. The paperwork will come around to him, in time. And there is one other matter, a minor detail but important to him, which he wants to turn over in his mind later.

'Why are you wasting time, Ombir-ji? Give him to us.'

'Because of Chand. For his sake.'

He waits, but Balle Ram is silent and confused.

'The man has lost his child. In the heat of this moment, he and you could do anything at all. No one in the village will question your right. But the murder of a young girl— it's not so easy to cover up. It hasn't happened before in Teetarpur. Drunks and junkies, pimps and whores, their bodies turn up from time to time. This is the first time that one of our own has been killed, that too in such a terrible manner. Look around you. There are too many people here tonight. If it was only you and Chand—well … That might have been different. But this is a sizeable crowd. Someone will talk. They promise they won't, but they always do, and then what? Then this case won't be handled by us, Balle Ram, it'll be handled by the CID.'

Balle Ram says, 'What do we care? Let them come.'

'You don't care? When it's over, when your brother can't mourn in peace because there is an inquiry, when policemen who don't know the two of you drag him away to the big station in Faridabad to ask questions, you'll care. If there's a court case, you'll care. Is he in any shape to manage all of that? Think, Balle Ram, set your own loss aside and think. You are all your brother has left. Will you protect him, or will you shove him into harm's way? I can't protect him once there is official involvement.'

He waits, lets his words sink in.

'And the department will be involved. Chand's home is next to Jolly-ji's farmhouse. There will be a thorough investigation. Balle Ram, please try to understand. I cannot let anything happen until Jolly-ji himself is made aware of this terrible situation, but I am with you. I will stand with you and Chand. All I ask for is time. Only two weeks.'

Balle Ram shakes his head, bewildered. 'Two weeks? For what?'

'Allow me to conduct an investigation. If they send officers from Faridabad, I'll be able to manage it. We'll make sure we find out if it's Mansoor who did it or—'

'Chand shouted out for me, I came running. We both saw him, how can there be any doubt?'

'I don't doubt you,' Ombir says, soothing the man. 'But I have to be certain. It's the law. Give me just a handful of days, Balle Ram. After that, I promise, you will have your justice.'

'Where will you hold Mansoor?'

'I'll make sure he's held right here, in our lock-up.'
Ombir is fairly certain that this will be the case. The central
jail and the district jail are both overcrowded, and it will
take time to arrange the prisoner's transfer.

'All right,' Balle Ram says. 'But only one week, not two.
After that, no matter what you say or what the law might
do, he is ours.'

'One more thing,' Ombir says.

'What?'

'Munia. We have to take her body to the morgue.'

They both look at Chand. His craggy face is almost
serene. He holds his daughter to his chest, his eyes closed.

'Tomorrow morning,' Balle Ram says. 'Tonight, let us
take care of her.'

Ombir gives in. He has Mansoor, he'll see to the rest
later.

Watched by the knot of men, Bhim Sain helps Mansoor
to his feet, makes him hold out his shaking hands, takes
him formally into custody.

'It wasn't me,' Mansoor says suddenly. 'Chand, I would
never hurt the little one.'

'Get on the bike,' Ombir says. He tells Bhim Sain to tie
Mansoor securely to him, and to follow on the back of
Dilshad's Yamaha.

The Bullet roars to life, chugging fitfully. Mansoor Khan
feels the handcuffs, tries to shake them off, submits. From
time to time, he jerks his wrists, like a cow attempting to flick
away flies. But he seems to feel protected by Ombir Singh's
presence, calms down as the bike leaves the mob behind.

At the station, Ombir leads Mansoor Khan to the grey-
painted storeroom at the back of the thana. He places an

earthenware ghada of water on the floor, a steel tumbler, then brings in a charpai, its coloured strings sagging.

'Sleep, I'll bring you some food later,' he says. 'If you have to shit or piss, call me. We won't make you do it in here.' He places an empty Dalda tin under the cot, just in case the suspect needs it.

In the station house, he listens to Bhim Sain giving the Faridabad station-house officer a full report. Ombir pushes away thoughts of sleep, buzzing at him like insistent mosquitoes.

His eyes close briefly even so, against his will. And the image of Mansoor's hands returns, demanding attention. He had taken a good look at them twice, once when the man was on the ground, once when he had got onto the bike, his feet slipping off the guard. There were a few drops of blood, presumably Mansoor's own, on the gauze that wound around his hands. But nothing else. No bark, no dried leaves, no twigs, no purple stains from the jamun berries, nothing to testify that he had indeed touched the tree or the girl. It doesn't prove anything, but it does arouse Ombir's curiosity.

From behind him, Bhim Sain says, 'They're taking the case seriously. I spoke to Bhadana also.'

'Jolly-ji's manager? Is he here?'

'No, he's returning tomorrow, and Jolly-ji himself will return as soon as he can. They said he's attending to business in the city. But Bhadana promised they would give us all the help we need, and the SHO at Faridabad said they'd send an officer. A big officer, top one. Haryana cadre, but my friends say he grew up in Delhi and has uncles in politics over there. He's not like us.'

Ombir stares at the worn desk. 'When does he reach?'

'The day after tomorrow,' Bhim Sain says. 'First thing in the morning.'

Ombir wishes he could put his head down and sleep until the Delhi boy arrives. But a day is very little time.

'Suspects,' he says. 'We'll need more suspects.'

Ombir takes a sip from the glass of water. It tastes stale and foul, as if a lizard has pissed in it. 'There was only one clear footprint at the base of the tree. From a fancy shoe, not from a plain jooti, not chappals or sneakers. No one out there tonight was wearing that kind of shoe. And Mansoor's hands, his bandages—there wasn't a shred of bark from the tree on them.'

'Are you saying he didn't kill that poor girl?'

'What do I know? Maybe he goes around the country pretending to be mad and killing innocent children all the time. Maybe he's speaking the truth and he was in the wrong place this evening. That's not important. When the Delhi boy arrives, he'll want a list of suspects, they always do. So we'd better find him some.'

Bad Characters

A dust storm blows his daily newspapers and a few loose sheets from open files off their desks, covers his charpai in a thin, persistent layer of grit that Ombir can feel on his skin hours later.

Bhim Sain had quietly taken his shift. 'Rest is essential to work,' he had said, quoting one of his favourite gurus, a charlatan who had been drummed out from Punjab for sleeping with his disciples but found a fitful celibacy and a new ashram in Haryana. 'Without a well-rested body, the mind becomes weaker and more prone to takeover by demons.'

Grateful, Ombir plummets into sleep, but an hour later, he is wide awake. His eyes feel raw and shrivelled, scorched by the heat.

He closes his eyes, takes refuge in pranayama, trying to still his thoughts. And fails. On the in-breath, he sees the branches of the jamun tree. On the out-breath, he sees Chand.

Suspects, their names and faces scrolling on repeat across his tired mind. Teetarpur is a small place. It makes his job much easier, though suspects are sparse in this murder case. Chand and Balle Ram are both well liked in the district, men who avoid quarrels and controversies. When the panchayat meets, they rarely speak, but if work is needed, extra hands to help deepen the common well or fund an extension to the temple in the forest, they're the first to show up. Balle Ram's wife Sarita Devi is not known to be quarrelsome either.

The road that runs past their huts carries little traffic. A few trucks on their way to the factories further up perhaps, though most truckers prefer the more convenient main road on the other side. There are occasional visitors to Jolly Singh's farm, and a small number of devotees who find their way to the temple in the forest. Most of the devout prefer the large, gaudily painted temple in Teetarpur to the hushed shrine.

Narinder is the first person Bhim Sain and he interrogate. A known bad character, a history-sheeter, a man who had narrowly escaped conviction for holding up a goods train thanks to an incompetent prosecution lawyer. He runs a shop on the other side of the forest, quite a distance away from Chand's hut. The shop sells only a few items— biscuits, hair combs, tooth powder, paan masala, loose tobacco, odds and ends. Ombir and Bhim Sain know that Narinder's real trade is selling opium and chitta to factory workers and labourers looking for a temporary escape from their problems. They only raid him when he seems too prosperous, when the deliveries of bags of chitta— the synthetic heroin manufactured in Punjab, mixed with dubious ingredients—become too frequent.

Narinder's name is at the top of Ombir's list because of something that happened towards the end of March, about two months before this killing. He had received a curt phone call from the manager of Jolly Singh's farmhouse on his personal mobile number. He smooths out the windblown pages of the two newspapers that he has retrieved and replaced on his desk, the *Faridabad Daily Blaze* and the Hindi journal *Lalten*, recalling the incident.

～

'This has never happened before,' the manager had said to him. 'He banged on our gate for some time, and then lifted up his lungi right in front of the housekeeper and the guards, and relieved himself. Such foul language he was using. Even I didn't know all the words. What are the police going to do about this? I'll have to get the gate cleaned with Ganga jal before Jolly-ji returns this weekend.'

When Ombir rode out on his Bullet to investigate, he found Narinder staggering down the road, spewing a stream of curses that he listened to with admiration. The man had a rich and well-flavoured vocabulary. Narinder halted when he saw the Bullet, then regained his courage. He veered into Chand's fields at a fast clip, emerging with a rusty scythe that hung loosely from his hands. He made a wild swing, almost losing his grip, but managing to hold on to the scythe in the end.

'Be careful, Chand, he's not in control of his senses and he's armed,' Ombir called when Chand walked up to stand behind Narinder.

Narinder charged at the lantana bushes. Then he reversed direction and ran towards Ombir, switching from curses to war cries.

Chand sighed, returned to his hut and emerged with a blanket. Ombir parked the Bullet and watched with approval as Chand threw the blanket over Narinder, bringing him to the ground. The man struggled like a trapped pig. Ombir looked at the heaving tangle, then kicked at the man's arms with his heavy boots. Narinder screamed. Ombir whipped the blanket off. Narinder slashed at his face with the scythe, missing his mark.

'Wrong arm,' Ombir said to Chand in apology.

Chand grabbed a thorny branch from the weathered fence around his land, and used it expertly to deflect Narinder's flailing blows. Narinder lost his grip on the scythe, but he continued to fight, weaponless. Ombir circled the pair, waiting for Chand to step back. He landed two quick blows on Narinder's arm with his lathi.

The pain finally cut through the man's drug-fuelled haze. He screamed and fought them so hard that they couldn't get him onto Ombir's bike. They had to walk him all the way to the station, the two men dragging him along between them, his hands tied with Chand's rope. He glared at Chand, hatred in his eyes, and said as Ombir Singh formally booked him, 'I'll see you, maaderchod, I'll see you. You won't sleep in peace or Narinder is not my name.'

'It's not,' Ombir said mildly, locking the door of the only cell in the Teetarpur station house. 'My colleagues in Punjab know you as Babbu. They'll be happy to hear you're doing so well. Men can change their names, but not their nature.'

Narinder had an excellent reason to hold a grudge against Chand, but would he have taken matters this far?

❧

Ombir and Bhim Sain bring Narinder alias Babbu in for an unofficial interrogation. He has an alibi, but a thin one.

He was with friends, he says, naming four men. Ombir knows them. Small-time crooks and rowdies, useless louts who weren't even able to scratch up work with political outfits as hired hoodlums. Narinder is their pusher. They'll lie for him if necessary.

'Why so many questions?' Narinder finally asks.

Bhim Sain says, 'Only routine work.'

Narinder grins, showing his darkened teeth. 'It's about that girl, isn't it? I told Chand. I warned him, you do wrong by me, the gods will punish you. And they have. Karma is karma. Let him cry for the rest of his days, that bastard, laying his filthy hands on me. Let him weep over his beloved daughter, tasting the air high up in the branches, it's what he deserves. He brought it on himself.'

Ombir says nothing, watches the man.

'You think I'm the one who did it? You're wrong. Many sins are written in my life's book, but killing children, that's not for me. I prayed to the gods, give me justice, and they listened. But I didn't do it.'

Three denials, one after the other, but the man doesn't betray nervousness. He stands up, says to Ombir, 'It makes me laugh, you know? Chand looked at me like I was nothing, an insect he'd crushed under his chappals. I wish I'd seen his face when he found his darling daughter. You still doubt me? It's not my kind of killing. I don't go in for that, but I'm grateful to the bastard who did it. There's justice in this world. Everyone gets theirs in the end.'

Ombir Singh believes Narinder. Every man he has known with a taste for violence has had his own quirks, preferences, and killing a child does not fit with this man's particular appetites. But Narinder has a motive, and he had the opportunity. In his pocket diary, the pages warped by sweat, Ombir writes his name first on the list of prime suspects.

~⁀~

He falls into a doze, jolting awake when a lizard drops from the ceiling onto the desk. Ombir watches the lizard, its tiny translucent feet, the visible innards, and jabs it with the end of a stapler. It twitches and scuttles towards the edge of the desk. He uses the stapler to propel it lightly into the air, where it hangs for a millisecond like a diver about to plunge into the canal, before landing with a plop somewhere near the gutter.

It is a matter of great relief for Ombir and Bhim Sain that Jolly Singh has sent instructions to his staff to cooperate with the investigation. Jolly-ji is the biggest landowner in the area, and Chand's nearest neighbour, if such an unequal relationship can be considered neighbourly. The manager, Bhadana, has confirmed that Jolly Singh was away in Delhi on work the week of Munia's death, leaving his farm in the charge of a skeleton staff. All four of the staff have verifiable alibis. The CCTV camera footage shows that they were on the property at the time of the murder.

His second suspect will require careful handling. Dharam Bir, head foreman at the Sangam Soap and Heavenly Incense Factory, built on the lines of a prize bull—massive shoulders, lowered head—and as quick to anger as one of those creatures.

This factory's owners, the Saluja family, are the biggest donors to every local politician. Saluja runs several companies, and is rumoured to be in partnership with Jolly Singh himself, something to do with a new township. Ombir keeps the interview short, casual, takes care not to offend Dharam Bir with direct questions. But he has many questions, asked and unasked.

~~~

Some months ago, in spring, the daughter of two daily wagers had disappeared. The twelve-year-old was missing for a night. When the parents came to the thana, the mother could barely speak, choked by her fears. The father could not keep the tears from welling up. They told Ombir that they had searched the fields and gone down to the canal, and had finally received permission from the guard at the Sangam Soap and Heavenly Incense Factory, who said that they could return in the evening and look around the premises so long as the owners didn't find out. 'She's mute,' the father explained. 'She would not be able to scream for help.' Hesitantly, he asked Ombir whether the policeman would search on their behalf. They were nervous about getting into trouble with the owners, despite the guard's offhand permission.

The girl was discovered in a musty shed, dark and cobwebbed, in the empty lot near the factory. She wore only a pair of thin printed cotton panties, and when Ombir and Bhim Sain entered the room, she clutched her only other garment, a flimsy chiffon dupatta, to herself. The rest of her school uniform, her kurta and pajamas, was missing. Her breasts had not yet developed. She was a skinny child. Her ribs stood out.

Ombir could see no visible sign of injury, and after she was returned to her parents, the mother swore that the girl had not been raped. She used the word 'damaged'. Afterwards, Ombir searched the shed thoroughly. The only item of note he found was a crumpled list of machinery, handwritten on a torn page. He thought he could make out a signature in Hindi, a man's name in confident black ink. Dharam, just the one word.

The parents would not permit the girl to be medically examined. But they could not refuse Ombir when he asked if he might show the child some photographs, see if she could recognise anyone from the list they maintained in the station house of possible sex offenders.

He had found a photograph of Dharam Bir in his safari suit in a factory newsletter, slipped it into the pack of photos he showed the girl. When she saw it, she turned to her mother. Her thin hands trembled, but her mother gave her a stern look and shook her head.

'Do you recognise that man?' Ombir asked. Her father said, 'She can't hear you.'

The child went through the rest of the photographs, her face screwed up as if she was working on a difficult exam paper, but like her mother, she shook her head. No, she did not recognise anyone.

It was not his problem, he told himself. The parents insisted there was no damage. They left Teetarpur some days later. The girl should have vanished from his mind when they left, but she didn't.

When Bhim Sain and he had first walked into that stifling, damp space, she had flinched and tried to scrabble away from them. He soothed her, using a gentle, reassuring tone, and she calmed down. But she burst into tears when he covered her up, fetching the spare shirt he carried in a compartment of the Bullet. He picked her up gently and felt her body tense, and he knew what had happened to her.

It remained with him, lodged at the back of his mind, despite the long hours, the relentless cascade of paperwork, petty disputes and thefts, the days spent trudging around the district on foot when the Bullet developed some minor engine problem.

The memory became a hard pebble around which his anger gathered and grew. At the beginning of summer, barely two weeks before Munia's murder, he had a chance to inspect the Sangam Soap and Heavenly Incense Factory when he was deputed to assist a labour inspector. He waited for the opportunity to take a quick break, then made a small detour.

It hadn't surprised him to discover that Dharam Bir's personal quarters were close to the shed where they had found the girl. It surprised him even less when he unearthed a stash of magazines under the man's mattress. Nothing illegal, only borderline. The cheapest pulp. Magazines printed on paper so poor in quality that the women in them spread their legs in blurry smears.

The women were young. Almost teenagers.

What Dharam Bir did in his personal time was none of his business, Ombir told himself. If the parents didn't care, neither should he. But he could not stop himself from making a few discreet inquiries, from glancing at the timesheets that the guard maintained, logging every employee's arrivals and departures.

Dharam Bir seemed to have a solid alibi for the day of Munia's murder, but he had reported sick at the factory for two hours. That might have given him enough time to leave the factory, reach Chand's hut and return on his Yamaha—but barely enough.

Ombir Singh writes his name on the list of suspects, directly under Narinder's. Dharam Bir's private tastes are now definitely his business. He sets the hurricane lamp upright, lights it. The wick is encrusted with soot. The flame flares high, waking Bhim Sain.

'Suspects,' Ombir Singh says to his sub-inspector. 'We have two. That should keep the Delhi boy happy.'

Bhim Sain rubs his bleary eyes, achieving an even deeper shade of red.

'Sir, what time will the officer arrive tomorrow?'

'After lunch.'

'Sir, while you were out, I went to Chand's field and took a look around to see if there was anything Dilshad missed. We have a small problem.'

☙

The problem is stuck in the canal far beyond Chand's field, at the extreme boundary of the Teetarpur station house range. Ombir Singh shines his torch over her face. She must have been an attractive woman, but in the white glare, her features are livid with pooled blood, her skin like parchment around the neck.

Ombir Singh silently curses his gods. He and his gods have a long-standing relationship. He sends up his prayers and higher management kicks the file back, stamped 'Rejected'.

'It's that factory whore,' Bhim Sain says. 'She used to go with the sand-quarry truckers, the contractors, then she upgraded her clientele to politicians, small-time fellows mostly.'

'Her business is permanently closed,' Ombir Singh says. 'The last thing we need. Mr Delhi Boy arriving, the media flocking around like crows, and one more homicide investigation.'

'Her pimp must have strangled her,' Bhim Sain says with relish. 'Or a jealous lover. She must have cruelly abandoned the poor man for a richer customer.'

Bhim Sain's reading tastes run to Faridabad's more lurid magazines, gory stories about inept murderers who are always nabbed by brave policemen. These stories featured attractive young women, but they appeared mostly as unfortunate corpses.

'Any of the bastards she was fucking could have killed her,' Ombir Singh says. 'The inconsiderate bastard, if he'd offed her on the other side of the canal, she wouldn't be my problem and my headache.'

Bhim Sain says slowly, 'Then she'd be out of our jurisdiction.'

'Yes.'

A rustle and whirr as a startled black drongo takes off, flying away from the two men.

Bhim Sain steps into the water. Crouches by the woman's body, his hands gentle on her swollen ankles. Gives her an experimental push. A half-turn. In the flickering light of the torch, the woman seems to roll over on her side, the sodden green skirt spreading out in the water.

Ombir flashes his torch close to the woman's head. A silver ribbon floating free in the water, snagging on a branch. A tangle of twigs and long branches jamming the canal. He reaches in, clears the obstruction, and his head spins suddenly, the fatigue catching up with him. He takes a deep breath, closes his eyes, dark spots floating across his field of vision.

When he opens his eyes again, Bhim Sain is leaning forward, pushing hard. He should say something, he should tell the sub-inspector to stop, but his stomach lurches. He presses his hands to his temples, his aching head.

His vision clears just as Bhim Sain lightly presses down on the woman's left shoulder. Suddenly, she's free, the body shooting forward, the water picking her up at such speed that Bhim Sain stumbles in the mud. He climbs out of the canal, stands behind Ombir.

'Bhim Sain, what have you done?'

The sub-inspector says, 'But you cleared the twigs. I thought you wanted me to help.'

'Not in that way!' Ombir says. 'What do we do now?'

For a moment, he considers retrieving the body, but the thought dies swiftly. They can't bring her back, they can't return her to where she was.

Bhim Sain says, 'She was almost out of our area.'

Ombir looks along the banks from the canal. They are a fair distance from Chand's fields, too far away for anyone from that side to have seen or heard whatever had happened here. The violence of the whore's death implies a brawl, but there would have been no witnesses in this bare, lonely place. He tamps down his anger at Bhim Sain— he was to blame, the tiredness was to blame, the grinding hours they had already put in, and the hours ahead, all of that was to blame.

'Will we have to put this in the report?' Bhim Sain asks.

Ombir hesitates.

'No,' he says finally.

The problem has been carried a long way out of their jurisdiction. He tries to put it out of his mind.

A Sense of the Terrain

The Haryana cadre officer whom the police gossips call the 'Delhi boy' arrives in the afternoon. He wears an imported shirt with a clean collar unmarked by grime and sweat. The Delhi boy looks different from the local officers—his shoes and his brass buckles shine that much more brightly, he sports a city-smart haircut administered by a city-smart barber, a world away from the bullet-head haircut and shave Ombir and Bhim Sain get at the footpath stall. The officer will return at night to the guest house in Faridabad, sleep in a proper bed with the AC turned up full blast. No charpais, no summer sweat for him.

'The malkhana records are kept in these?' Senior Superintendent of Police Ashwini Pilania asks, eyeing the two frayed jute cement sacks incredulously.

'Sir, we have been issued one filing cabinet,' Ombir Singh says. 'Room only for the most important files. The rest are maintained here.'

In his first few weeks at the Teetarpur station house, Ombir had spent his mornings sorting out the store, the evidence room and its recalcitrant registers, passed on from the main station in Teetar Bani. Several blood-

stained clothes, lungis, saris, bush shirts and red-checked
gamchhas mentioned in the registers had disappeared with
a terse notation: 'Rats.' Some winters ago, the theft of sixty
bottles of Phensedyl cough syrup had been recorded, but
the station-house officer had not been formally apprised
of the incident, and no investigation had been launched.
Knives, gandasas and other kinds of scythes, iron-tipped
lathis and a mysterious sword had been stored on the same
shelves by date, rather than by category, and so on.

It has given Ombir Singh a small sense of pride, restoring
order to chaos, but he sees in his superior's expression that
his efforts have fallen short. A prickle of anger surfaces
through his tiredness.

This Delhi boy, this senior officer used to the comforts
of the capital—what does he know, what did he expect?
Computerised records in a place like this, where electricity
is available only for the richest factory owners, where even
Jolly Villa runs mostly on generators? Their malkhana is in
the second bathroom, the Western-style one that has never
been connected to plumbing. They had put in wooden
shelves, confiscating them from the medical packing
factory, stacked cartons in the corners, on the commode,
every box neatly labelled.

SSP Pilania inspects a stash of empty rum bottles, says,
'How far are your quarters?'

A snigger escapes Sub-inspector Bhim Sain, but he
quickly looks away.

'Quarters are under construction. We sleep here.'

'The crime registers are well maintained,' the SSP offers.

A pleased smile spreads across Bhim Sain's face. Ombir
catches the pity in the man's voice. A sop thrown to them,
like dry rusks to starving street dogs.

'This is an important case,' Pilania continues. 'For the Haryana police because it will get some media attention, for me because I dislike unsolved homicides, for you because it happened in your home territory. But it is also important for one more reason. The victim, this young girl. She deserves justice, and we will give it to her.'

Ombir Singh nods, less impressed than Bhim Sain. He is that type of officer then, the Delhi boy. Probably not one of the hard men, for whom joining the police is a relief because it gives them a chance to freely use commands, fists, lathis. Maybe not one of the corrupt men, using the power of their uniform to make lakhs in graft and bribes, and not a time-server. That leaves the last and smallest category. The ones who earnestly want to do good, who want to feel like potent gods, who want to see gratitude in the eyes of those they serve, who sprinkle goodness from above into the lives of people, as though it were holy ash. He can handle that kind.

Pilania insists on meeting Mansoor on his own. When he's through, he says, 'Give the poor bastard some chai and lunch, for God's sake. Bhim Sain, see to it. And some soap, and a wash if you're done fingerprinting.'

Bhim Sain says, 'Fingerprints are all in order, sir, also prisoner is breakfasted. I will arrange for the rest.'

Pilania surprises Ombir. 'How far is Chand's home from the station house?'

Ombir says, 'About 3.6 kilometres by the main road, sir.'

'Is there a shortcut?'

'Sir, if we cut across the fields, it will be a little more than two kilometres.'

The SSP smiles. 'Bhim Sain, can you manage the station on your own? If journalists show up, please request them to wait until I'm back. Ombir Singh, would you kindly accompany me?'

Ombir says, 'Sir, we only have the Bullet. But I can organise a car from the chemical factory in ten minutes.'

Pilania is striding out of the station house, whistling. 'On foot, if you don't mind. I'd rather get a sense of the terrain, can't do that on a bike.'

It's midday, the sun directly overhead. He had snatched an hour of sleep and he could manage, but this city officer with his clean collar, perspiration-free shirt and starched khakis?

Pilania gives him a sardonic grin. 'Don't look so worried, Ombir Singh. The heat doesn't bother me. I don't imagine it bothers you; in fact, I'm forming the impression that there isn't much that would throw you off course.'

'Sir,' he says woodenly, falling into step. It's annoying. He knows he's being buttered up, but the problem with flattery is that it's effective. He's beginning to like the Delhi boy after all.

～

'Your madman is a bit of a non-starter,' Pilania says as they cross the fields. 'It's perfectly possible that he's our man, but after our little chat, I'm not quite convinced that he's the murderer. I took a careful look at his hands, and I agree with you. Impossible for him to have committed the crime without any traces whatsoever from branches and bark adhering to his bandages. And if he was sane enough to kill the girl, he should have been sane enough to run for it. However, he was found near the body just after the murder. He's still our number one suspect, but is he the right man?'

They have reached the fields outside Chand's hut and the burning heat is radiating upwards through the thin soles of Ombir's shoes. He pauses, grateful for the blessing of a patch of shade under the jamun tree.

Pilania looks towards the hut. 'Is the father available for a chat?'

'Chand and his brother Balle Ram released the girl's body for the autopsy only the morning after the murder. The morgue is five villages away. Balle Ram spoke to me last night; he said they are staying with Sarita Devi's relatives for two or three nights and will be back in Teetarpur tomorrow.'

～

Ombir had made sure he was with Chand when the morgue van arrived. Chand's eyes were worn and blank and his shoulders sagged like an empty coat. Ombir escorted him into the van. Chand wouldn't let the attendant take his daughter, arranged her on the stretcher himself, drew the sheet tenderly over her still form.

Balle Ram said to Ombir, 'I've called his old friends from his Delhi days. He didn't want anyone here on that first day, but Sarita Devi felt it would be better for him to have Rabia and Badshah Miyan by his side for the rest.'

'You've done the right thing, Balle Ram,' Ombir said. 'Bhim Sain will let you know when the autopsy is done. He shouldn't be alone when he goes to collect the body.'

'I spoke to Badshah Miyan last night,' Balle Ram said. 'He was shocked and distraught, but he said that Rabia and he will be with Chand on that day. And I will make arrangements at the crematorium. My brother will not be alone.'

Ombir made a mental note to be at the morgue along with Chand's friends. He agreed with Balle Ram. No father should have to organise the funeral of his only child, and he would make sure that Chand had whatever support they could give him through this grimmest of parental tasks.

~

'I used to love fieldwork,' Pilania says. 'Don't get much of a chance these days to get out and about. Is this where she was found, hanged from this branch?'

'Yes, sir.'

The officer moves around, inspecting the tree, the broad fields, the track that leads to the canal, Chand's hut, and the approach to the highway.

When Pilania ducks into the hut, Ombir starts to follow, but the officer waves him away. He returns to the foot of the jamun tree. Something is different. The branches, the knot of rope on the ground—he squats, staring at the earth. The footprint is gone. He searches, shuffling around the roots, but there is no trace of the single footprint he is sure they had seen. Part of the earth seems too settled, and he inspects it closely, noting the light tracks that might have been made by a broom, or even a stick used to erase a print and smoothen the dust again. He straightens up, wondering whether to tell Pilania or not.

'The family are usually the first suspects,' Pilania calls from inside the hut. 'You have them on your list, but at the end. Why?'

'It's an unusual family, no tensions, no fights over land,' Ombir says. 'The brothers are close, and Munia was loved by Balle Ram and his wife as if she were their own daughter. Balle Ram used to say that God had blessed them with a child after all, only she was born to Chand.'

Pilania emerges, ducking under the low lintel, blinking in the sun's white glare after the darkness inside. Ombir walks over.

'Two photographs, black-and-white, taken at a local studio. Creased and dirty, but carefully kept in a tin box near his charpai.'

He holds them out so that Ombir can see. Munia as a baby, then Munia dressed up at about five or six in a sparkly ghagra and choli, bright bangles on her stick-thin wrists.

'They were close? Father and daughter?'

'She was Chand's whole life,' Ombir says. 'Everything he did, all the work he put into his lands, it was for her. He had big dreams for Munia. He went to Faridabad every few months to buy books, special books. He wanted her to study and go to college. He used to say, her mother knew nothing beyond the village, but he would give his daughter the whole world if he could.'

Pilania hitches up his trousers and sits down outside, sweat stains spreading across his shirt.

'Girls can be a burden,' he says. 'A father who realises that a growing girl might be a problem, even at—how old was she? Eight, nine?—it's possible, isn't it, that he could decide to take steps?'

'Not possible, sir,' Ombir says. 'He took her to the fields with him until the cane fires started. His face lit up when he was with his daughter. They were close. He disliked it when people in Teetarpur said that girls are a curse. He didn't agree with that kind of thinking.'

'I'll reserve my opinion until I've met the man, though the method of murder argues against Chand's involvement.'

Ombir frowns, not quite following.

Pilania says, 'It's improbable that a murderer who wanted to get away with killing his daughter would string her up from a tree in his own compound. Not impossible, but unlikely. If it was an outsider—was she raped?'

Ombir senses a trick question, sidesteps it. 'Until the autopsy results come back, we can't say for sure, Pilania sir. But after Chand found her, Balle Ram came running with his wife Sarita Devi, she also helped bring the child down from the tree. Bhim Sain spoke to Sarita Devi. She was certain there was no rape. Bhim Sain did not see any signs of assault on the clothes or skin, no visible marks, nothing to indicate a struggle.'

'That's useful,' says Pilania. 'Of course, we can't know for certain until we have the autopsy report, but let's assume that there was no sexual motive. Balle Ram, Chand, Sarita Devi—your notes say they have alibis. Sarita Devi was with two of her neighbours. Four witnesses say that Balle Ram was in his fields, and your report says that Chand was clearly visible to the family who owns the fields beside his.'

'Preliminary findings,' Ombir Singh says. 'Bhim Sain and I will fully investigate the alibis, but I know the witnesses personally. Teetarpur is a small place, sir. It isn't likely that they are lying.'

'The brothers—how far are their other fields from their homes? Could they have returned without being seen?'

'Not possible, sir. The distance is too great, and the fields are fully open to view. Someone would have witnessed their comings and goings.'

Pilania paces out the field from the jamun tree to the road and back. Once more, Ombir considers telling the officer about the footprint and its absence, but what will he say? That he noted the shape and size of the shoe, but forgot to tell Bhim Sain to take a proper rubbing or to ask Dilshad, the photographer, to make sure it was recorded?

'For the moment, let's assume that she wasn't murdered by her family, and that Mansoor is not the culprit. If he didn't do it, if he was merely unfortunate enough to walk through Chand's field right after the poor child was strung up, then who did? For what reason? If you understand why a murder is committed, you can practically slip a pair of handcuffs on the murderer. Tell me why you're not one hundred per cent sure it was Mansoor.'

'Sir, there were no signs of a struggle, and the girl was unmolested,' Ombir says. His decision is made—he will not mention the footprint to Pilania or even to Bhim Sain. 'Munia didn't know Mansoor that well. She would not have been surprised to see him, but she was shy. She used to run away if any of us stopped to talk to her, so how could Mansoor have approached her so easily?'

'No signs of a struggle. No signs of assault, rape, torture, any of the usual stuff that comes into play with a sex crime. That makes for a weak case against Mansoor or your other suspect, Dharam Bir. If the murder was committed as a deliberate act of vengeance against Chand by, say, your second suspect, Narinder, then why didn't he come prepared? Your notes say that the rope was part of an old scaffolding. The murderer used whatever came to hand, not his own weapons. Why didn't he—or her, let's not rule out other possibilities at this stage—dispose of the girl's body in the forest? Enough girls are murdered in this country, but there's always a reason. Sex, property disputes, revenge, it's usually clear. I don't understand this murder at all.'

He stares up at the jamun tree and shakes his head.

'It's the wrong shape,' he says. 'Perhaps the reports, the photographs, will tell us a little more, but this case isn't falling easily into place. You'll have to work harder, Ombir. We need this settled fast.'

Ombir agrees silently, and the words echo in his head later, after SSP Pilania has left for the guesthouse.

He slides the register over to use as a head-rest, finally closes his eyes. He dreams of a coil of frayed rope sliding into murky water like a grass snake, twitching with life, and Pilania's voice saying urgently, 'The wrong shape—the wrong shape', until the sharp rap of Bhim Sain's knuckles on the desk lets him know that the first TV crews have reached Teetarpur. Two uninterrupted hours of sleep, something to set down on the plus side of the ledger.

～

He stonewalls the TV crews, tells them they can set up on the main road, but forbids them from entering the crime scene. After they've gone, though, Ombir can't get back to sleep. He shifts on the charpai, takes a stroll around the compound, listening to the lowing of a cow as restless as he is.

They have a few other suspects, mostly outsiders. A child trafficking gang, nine women and two men, is known to be moving through the area, though the last reports suggest that the gang is on the other side of the Aravalli hills. Bhim Sain speculated that they might have attempted and botched a kidnap.

A gang of traffickers wouldn't attract attention to themselves. They would have concealed the body, or dumped the girl in a field, he'd said. He was gratified when the SSP concurred.

It comes back to him in that moment, that niggling seed of doubt. Ombir doesn't set much store by autopsy reports. Except for the big forensic centres, most autopsies in these parts are conducted by the doctors' assistants. They are under-qualified, knife-happy young men with rudimentary training, filling in because the doctors are upper caste and rarely want to handle dead bodies themselves. But the preliminary medical report, conducted by the local doctor, who is a decent man, was clear on one point. They hadn't been able to recover any useful fingerprints, either because of the dust that had settled on the child's skin, or because the killer had taken the precaution of wiping his prints off.

Ombir paces the narrow compound, ignoring the stink rising from the gutters and the cattle pound. He considers the footprint. Most of the villagers, including Chand and Mansoor, wear jootis, not city shoes—but the factory workers, and many of the pilgrims who pass on the road, might wear a proper pair of shoes. The doubt grows into questions. If the murder was committed with forethought, the murderer would have wiped his prints immediately, not risked discovery by returning at night or early the next morning. What kind of murderer came so well prepared that he wore gloves or wrapped his hands to conceal his fingerprints, but so unprepared that he brought no murder weapons with him?

Dharam Bir in his safari suit, his shoes always polished despite the dust that every step kicks up in these parts, a man who pays attention to small details; Narinder, a useless crook who acts on impulse, without consideration or forethought; Mansoor, his hands wrapped in gauze, who goes about life as though it terrifies him, who fears even the village children and his own shadow. Three jagged pieces. None of them fits perfectly into this puzzle.

Ghost Lilies

Chand is surrounded by the kindness of the village when he comes back. It suffocates him.

He would like them all to leave. Balle Ram and Sarita Devi, the pradhan, his neighbours, and other villagers whom he knows only distantly, he wishes they would all leave him alone. Instead, they bring him tall tumblers of fresh milk, a steel thali of fruit and roasted wheat, they argue with the television crews, keeping them at bay. He can hear the sound of their feet crossing his fields, the brisk whisper of the broom wielded by Sarita as she sweeps the courtyard, straightens the water pots, the cot he'd left outside.

He was not permitted to go into the morgue, had to watch from inside the ambulance as the stretcher was taken away. 'Sign the release form, over here,' the attendant said over his protests, and he scrawled his signature. When he looked up from the papers, she was gone.

It is four days since his daughter was murdered. He cannot tell his family and his neighbours to go, that he does not want them around him.

Chand turns to his left, and a band of sunlight flooding through the gap in the thatch hits his eyes. He has woken later than he can ever remember waking in his life. He looks across the floor at the empty space. Someone has folded the sheet and the thin mattress Munia slept on, folded them neatly and placed them on the shelf. His family whispers loudly outside his home, trying not to wake him. He makes himself get up.

⌇

It surprises and touches him when Jolly Singh brings him a giant bunch of white flowers at noon. Jolly-ji does not send Bhadana. He carries the flowers himself, stepping out of his big car to pay a condolence visit. Chand tries to remember how to greet such an important guest, pulls out a low cane stool, the only piece of real furniture in his hut.

'At least you know that the culprit is in custody,' Jolly says when he rises to take his leave. 'I pray that her murderer's soul rots in hell.'

Chand nods, thank you, Jolly-ji, thank you for taking the trouble.

He holds the bouquet of lilies awkwardly, unsure what to do with them. Later, he finds a steel bucket, shoves the flowers in, with some water to dampen the stems.

The next morning, he wakes at dawn. It is too early for anyone to visit, and he takes in the blessed silence. The ghostly petals of the lilies gleam in the scant light, unfurled, in full bloom.

Few of the big men, the landed men, are as kind as Jolly-ji. They are neighbours only in the loosest sense of the term. Their lands abut one another, but he is a small farmer. Jolly Singh is one of the richest men in the area. He is the biggest landowner in their village and will soon be one of the most important men in the district. Even Chand

and Balle Ram have heard about the plans for a Teetarpur township, whispers of recent land acquisitions by Saluja and Jolly.

Through the numbness of loss, it touches him that such a man had taken the time to care. The gesture of kindness means much to Chand in the swamp that has claimed him.

⌒

People don't like to look at the newly bereaved. They look down, or their eyes meet his and skitter away. He doesn't want to stay inside, so he has settled himself on a rush mat in the courtyard. Balle Ram and Sarita Devi answer the questions of those who're arriving to express their sorrow, to help him mourn. He has lost count of the days. Time moves differently now.

'In these fields?'

'No, behind. In that one.'

Chand hears Sarita Devi's voice catch, and then she breaks into loud sobs. His brother's marriage had been barren. After he came back with Munia, he'd said to his sister-in-law, she's ours, not only mine, she's your girl also.

Every morning, Chand tells himself, he will rise early and walk to his fields. He will sow some gourds, some cucumber. Prepare for the monsoon. He'll pace each part of his land, reach down to test the soil. He'll try to wear himself out with jobs he doesn't need to do.

He doesn't want to respond to anyone else's grief. Keeps his gaze on the dust, the cracked earth, listens to a troop of monkeys calling and whooping up in the forests.

He is at the far side of his field, rearranging the steel plates and khadi shirt that's hung up as a rudimentary scarecrow, when he hears Ombir Singh's Bullet slow down.

He doesn't want to talk, doesn't want to see the pity in anyone's eyes, so he pretends he's busy, waits until the policeman leaves.

He will keep himself busy, continuing to tend his land, returning as late as he can to his hut. His home is rarely empty in the evenings. His brother and Sarita Devi's relatives hover, finding pretexts to be with him every evening, and he cannot get himself to tell them to leave. But they do leave, eventually, and he takes the food his sister-in-law has carefully cooked for him, walks to the canal, gives it to the stray dogs or buries it in a shallow, rapidly dug hole, using the night as cover so that he does not hurt her feelings.

At dawn, he eats just enough to take him through the daylight hours, barely tasting the sharp tang of the rice he had left to ferment overnight for breakfast. He picks up his tools and walks to his land, to another day's emptiness. When he returns, he ignores the television vans, with their mikes and flaring lights. He ignores them, walks past them, his head down, and closes the flimsy door firmly in their faces.

The past is safe. He ignores the people outside, who glance timidly into his room. Locked into his silence, he lets his memories return to a time that is also safe, because it was before Munia was born.

◞

Chand had left home after a fight with his father, who had brought up his two sons with a stern rectitude after their mother's death from tuberculosis when Chand was seven, Balle Ram just five years old. He had wanted Chand to work on the land. When he hesitantly shared his dreams of studying in the big city, he was stung by his father's dismissiveness. It was not a serious fight, but his young blood was quick to anger.

'I will not be a farmer,' Chand had said to his father, who listened grimly. 'I don't care for the land, and it doesn't care for me. Do what you like with my share, give it to Balle Ram. I don't want to be tied to a patch of earth like your bullocks, going round and round and never getting anywhere.'

He was sixteen. Though he had never stepped outside his village, Chand thought he knew the country and the city from the shows on television that he sometimes watched at the Pradhan's house. When the rough narrow dirt track that he had known all his life widened into a black-tar road, when the highways came into view for the first time, he saw the veins and arteries of life itself spread out across the world.

Chand walked for a few kilometres in the heat—with each step, his legs felt the jolt of tarmac after years of walking on earth, taking him further away from all that he knew, closer to something he wanted, however blurred that want was. At a petrol pump, he stood and watched the trucks roll up. They were giants among the scurrying cars. Chand listened to the conversation of the truck drivers for some hours, until he had the salt-and-chillies cadence of their talk down. He stepped onto the road then, and hitched a lift from a passing truck.

He paid his way up and down the highways as a cleaner and then as a mechanic. He'd worked on tractors and carts most of his life, his hands understood machinery the way they understood tiring soil, eager seed, ailing trees. Trucks were not so different.

The trucker asked, 'Where are you going?' Chand had no idea. He stared at the mural painted inside the cabin, an ambitious vista of jagged snow-clad peaks against a bright blue sky, pointed at one of the mountains, and said, 'There.'

The truck driver chuckled. He said good-naturedly enough, 'I'll bet you've never seen the Himalayas in your life.'

'Are they far away?' he asked.

'Further than you can imagine,' the trucker said. Chand filed that away. This duniya was turning out to be bigger than he'd anticipated.

'I'll drop you at Delhi,' the man offered.

He nodded, as if he'd always meant to go to the capital, tried not to let the trucker see how his pulse quickened at the thought.

THE
YAMUNA
YEARS

Wellcome

For the first few months after Chand reaches Delhi, he shares a small room in Wellcome Colony with Khalid, who works as a loader for a trucking company. 'Small' and 'room' are euphemisms, just as 'Wellcome' is one of those fading Delhi colonies that does nothing to justify its name. 'Hope Building' is a grim, grey place; 'Sunlight Colony' is pressed up against a mass of industrial buildings and old mills; and Wellcome is a closed maze of narrow, rough-paved lanes, forbidding concrete sheds, open drains and half-installed electric wiring.

Their 'room' is a sliver of space about the width of the doorway. When one turns over in his sleep at night, the other perforce has to turn, as though they are roast chickens on a spit. But they come back so tired from their jobs as loaders that they barely speak to each other, just a nod, a muttered half-greeting in the mornings as they leave for work.

Chand learns that Khalid has a wife, Rabia. But this part of Wellcome is only open to single men, and the wife lives elsewhere for the time being.

The roll of rupees Chand had brought with him, and which he guards carefully from pickpockets and slum thieves, disappears at a rate that alarms him—on rent, and on as little food as he can make himself accept. He scrapes his needs back, searching for used razor blades, using sand and reetha nuts instead of soap, but the bundle that seemed kingly when he arrived at Wellcome dwindles and dwindles. His wages arrive in fits and spurts, and then at the end of summer, the foreman delays payment for over nine weeks.

He cannot go back, returning broke and worn down to lap from the bowl of his father's charity. And Delhi, filthy, crowded, brutal, a city where even the crows have a calculating glint in their eyes and will snatch a piece of bread from out of their fellows' beaks, has begun to exert its pull on him.

Chand has never seen so much being built so fast. He has never seen so many people flowing in and out of each other's spaces, never heard so many languages eddying around him. The air crackles with dreams. Most of them are doomed to failure, but as soon as one unspoken dream dies, a thousand other migrants arrive with theirs, filling the air with a current of unceasing hope and burning longing.

At home, he is Chand. Rooted to one spot, one way of living, the pattern of his years charted as surely as the path the plough takes across his field. Here, he hurries through the ITO crossing, breathing in air that has been breathed out by thousands of others, brushing shoulders with strangers he will never have to know or even think about again, connected only by their inhalations and exhalations.

Up on the footbridge, he looks down at the city, the swirling crowds, the puttering scooters, a trundling double-decker bus, motorcycle taxis festooned with passengers. He can feel himself becoming just one of many, at liberty to shape his life in any manner that he chooses. Anonymous, unknown, free. No, he cannot go home, cannot make himself do it, though the hunger has started to drive him to an edge he has never inhabited before.

One evening, Khalid returns to Wellcome early. He sees Chand squatting at the edge of the dump, sifting through the garbage, sees him retrieve a few onion skins, shaking off the papery peel, and a stale, tattered roti, sees how his roommate folds these discards together and eats them slowly.

The next night, he says casually to Chand, 'Heard of a job at a friend's shop. He's a butcher, Badshah Miyan, a Qureishi butcher. He's looking for a cleaner, sometimes takes a few Hindu boys on for that kind of work if they'll do it.'

Chand is startled. Kindness is a scarce commodity in the city, not to be squandered but to be handed out judiciously, traded for favours that he's in no position to offer. He tries to thank Khalid, but the man shrugs, says, 'We're not strangers,' and falls instantly asleep.

～

'I can cut meat,' he says to Badshah Miyan on his first morning at the job, intending to show that he is not a slacker.

Can, too. He has hunted partridges, wildfowl, slaughtered them, felt the tiny pulse beating hard in the creature's neck. He is used to the cries of dying birds, to the fading yelp of a stray dog caught in the wrong compound and beaten with the back of a gandasa till it is crippled or killed. Swearing each other to secrecy, he and his friends had once killed a peahen, the national bird. Killing one was a crime, which should have made the jungle curry they cooked all the sweeter.

This peacock ran for its life, and when it was finally cornered, it screamed like a child, and that brought an unaccustomed guilt into his carefree existence. The skinned peahen unnerved him. Its legs—shorn of the glorious feathers that had been so resistant to plucking, gripping the dimpled skin close—were long and dainty, womanlike. He had eaten his portion of the curry, the flames from the bonfire illuminating the faces of his friends. The meat was tough and uncured. He had made himself swallow each piece, but it had lost its savour. Still, he can slaughter. He knows something about meat.

Badshah Miyan says, 'You stink. You're a farm boy. You stink of it, of gobar and ignorance and stupidity. You can't cut meat, you don't know how. Most of you Hindus don't know shit about how to cut meat anyway. You can swab and clean, and empty the offal buckets. Touch one of my knives or the butchers' blades and I'll cut your testicles off and grind them with the rest of the keema.'

Badshah Miyan is a wizened man with bright eyes and a keen love of the radio. He sits on a rough-hewn high platform in a corner of the Qureishi butcher shop, supervising his employees with a steady stream of extremely polite requests and wildly impolite curses. The shift in pace tends to unnerve them and keep them on their toes.

The shop is in Mehrauli. Chand has to rise early to reach in time. This is a wealthy area, farmhouses sprawl across large acres of land, and the butcher's shop occupies an entire corner at one of the major crossroads. The recesses of Mehrauli are built for cars, and it is a long walk to the shop from the bus stand on the main road.

Chand does not mind the walk. The trees tower above him, fringing both sides of the road, and their entwined branches assuage the yearning for home that he cannot entirely suppress. In the cooler months, he slips his shoes off and walks barefoot, risking injury from a shattered bottle, shards of glass or stray pebbles, in exchange for the pleasure of feeling the skin touch soil.

He does the filthiest jobs in Badshah Miyan's busy shop. He cleans up shit from the goat's intestines, scrapes inches of it off the bottoms and sides of the coops stacked outside, where chickens pressed together wait for the door to open, for a hand to reach in and take them by a wing, a neck, off for slaughter. Cleans blood, cleans the various liquids that issue from the insides of bodies, some clear, some clotted. Cleans bone, in fragments and whole.

Thrice a day, Chand wipes down the tiled walls and countertops and cleans the gutters. He has been asked to do it only twice, but he dislikes the filth that runs non-stop from the butchers' blocks, so he adds a third round of sluicing. He swabs the front of the shop, the steps, ceaselessly cleaning away marks from customers' shoes, dirt from the streets. He sponges the butchers' blocks with vinegar and hot water, and he cleans the hooks from which the goats' carcasses hang. He slops out the pails, cleans the freezer, washes out the butchers' red striped gamchhas and towels. Feathers give him the most trouble, and he grows to hate them. He dreams of tiny feathers sticking to every bare surface, dreams that he wakes up and his hands have grown their own covering of small, yellow, shit-covered feathers.

He watches the butchers and realises that Badshah Miyan is right. He can't cut meat. Their skill is many levels ahead of anything he might hope to achieve. The best of them, aside from Badshah Miyan, is Hari. Whenever he can, he watches Hari's hands, his eyes, the way the man runs his eyes down a leg, a shoulder, seeming to see exactly how it should be cut, spotting the grain of the meat, where to gently persuade the blade to slice through muscle, where to use strength.

The flies that used to buzz around Badshah Miyan Meatwalla and Sons diminish in number. At the end of the first fortnight, Chand says, 'Give me more dusters and more vinegar.'

Badshah Miyan says, 'Your haramzada baap will pay or what?'

Chand says, 'I need more dusters and I need more vinegar.'

Badshah Miyan tells him that he can take the day off if he likes, search for his mother in GB Road, have her syphilis treated and suck her dick while he's at it.

Chand is unimpressed. He says, 'For the cleaning. To do it properly, I will need more dusters and more vinegar,' and returns to his work.

For the rest of the day, Badshah Miyan keeps up a steady stream of abuse, breaking off only to attend to customers, and Chand says nothing. But the next morning, he stands in front of Badshah Miyan and says, 'The shop must have more dusters and more vinegar, also bleach.'

'You stubborn bastard,' Badshah Miyan says. But he has noticed that they are drawing in more customers, fancier customers, memsahibs from the big farms who step into the shop, wrinkling their noses slightly, sit down gingerly on the bench that Chand has covered with a foam sheet wrapped in dark green plastic.

He turns away from Chand, ignores him all day. In the evening, he calls him over. Points to a jerrycan of bleach. A jerrycan of vinegar. Ten new washcloths. 'All right, Emperor of Hindustan? Satisfied?'

Chand says, 'Thank you. Also, the old brooms are worn down and we need two more mops and new buckets.'

Badshah Miyan's roar can be heard up and down the length of the broad road.

Chand waits till he has finished sputtering. He says patiently, 'See, the old buckets don't look right. The walls and the tiles look like new, don't they? When customers walk in, the first thing they notice is this cracked red bucket. Then they scratch their heads, because they're thinking, if the buckets are so dirty, the meat can't be that fresh.'

Badshah Miyan says, 'When you're done, please tell me how I should run my business and how I should wash my arse and how Hari should cut the pasanda.'

Chand says, 'All of that I don't know. But the mops, the brooms and the buckets don't look good. We should get some new ones. And if you buy a block of rock salt, it's even better than vinegar for cleaning the blocks.'

He goes off to finish mucking out the drains at the back. The next week, Badshah Miyan brings in a surly fourteen-year-old boy, Nakku, who takes over the dirtiest jobs under Chand's supervision.

'You're not fit to cut meat yet,' he tells Chand. 'You will continue to clean the blocks, the knives, and the tiled walls in the front of the shop. But you can start to learn an apprentice's work.'

～

He settles into Delhi slowly, the new routine of his life growing on him. At the end of his first month, he takes the fat wad of notes from Badshah Miyan with surprise and gratitude. He hadn't expected to be paid the same wage as the Muslim butchers. He pushes the money into an empty box of Mazdoor matches for safekeeping. When he attempts to give half his wages to Khalid, as his cut for telling Chand about the job, the offer upsets his roommate.

'I told you, we aren't strangers,' Khalid says. 'Keep your money.'

Chand casts about for some way of thanking him, chances upon a flute-seller, the sweet high melody winding in and out of the back lanes. He tells the man he wants only the best of his instruments, makes him play a dozen before he settles on one that has a sweet but deep sound.

Khalid is thrilled, and from then on, he treats Chand not as a friend but as a 'city brother'. They are bound not by blood but by sweat, dust, shared hardship. It makes them close kin.

One night, Chand returns late from the shop to find Khalid staring at rubble. The sleeping shape of a silent bulldozer is parked where their half-room had been. 'Beautification drive,' Khalid says. Their part of Wellcome has been neatly wiped off the map.

Chand asks around, finds them space at some distance, on an empty stretch of the Yamuna river where the city's claim on the land weakens, and the egrets, teals and storks stake their territorial and water rights.

They sleep under a wide bridge to one side of the rickshaw-pullers, waking to a view of broad, dark waters, buffaloes wallowing in algae-bright ponds, purple water-hyacinths, marshland and sand islands. Later, when Rabia joins them, they shift to a safer, more secluded part of the riverbank.

The river will become their home. They will discover the strange worlds and stranger people it draws to its waters, many of them security guards or factory workers and migrant labourers who can find no other place in the growing ferment of Delhi, but also the misfits, the ones who turn their backs on more ordinary ways of living.

Once a month, Chand stops at a PCO booth and calls the postmaster, the only person in Teetarpur village he knows who has a landline of his own. He always asks Lajja Ram to let his father know he is alive and thriving in the city.

His wages are riches to a man whose needs remain elemental. Even accounting for food, soap, tea, razor blades, blue-and-green gamchhas and bus tickets, there is enough for him to send a money order in Balle Ram's name every few months. These two things, the money order and the phone call, become the slender cord that holds him to family, land, the old certainties.

The City and the Friends

The three of them, Rabia, Khalid and Chand, have to learn two things when they arrive in Delhi from their villages: city Hindi and the habit of caution. Khalid and Rabia had picked up basic Hindi from families that had migrated to their village in Bengal, but living in the capital requires them to learn the language anew.

The city is a swift teacher. Khalid is cheated of most of his first month's wages when a gaunt, stumbling man clutches at his sleeve, calling him brother, swearing that he will die of thirst and hunger. Khalid rummages in the bundle that holds his work shirt and tools. He sets it down on the roadside, unties the knots. The dying man revives abruptly, plucks the roll of rupees and coins, darts away at a speed that even Khalid cannot keep up with.

Rabia's job at the oil mill is grinding work—long hours, few breaks, hard labour—but it is all that Khalid has been able to find for her. She had been happy enough to live apart from her husband for a while. His weak good nature, his inability to set his mind to the practical side of life, annoyed her when they were together. In his absence, she was reminded of his better qualities. The way he whittles whimsical toys out of twigs he gathers from the roadside, his kindness, the surprising gentleness with which he touches her, his hands light and questioning on her breasts, her face, when they do have enough space and privacy to have sex.

One evening, as Chand takes a shortcut through a slender alley, a policeman says something, swift, incomprehensible, to him. He shakes his head to indicate that he doesn't understand the man's accent. The policeman repeats what he had said and takes umbrage when Chand frowns, still not able to make sense of the sentence. He swings his lathi, aiming for Chand's forehead, breaking his nose. That, Chand understands. Rabia applies a poultice of turmeric and chuna until the swelling subsides.

Rabia's lessons in Hindi comprehension are harsher. She leaves the job at the oil mill to work as a domestic help in an ugly brick shoebox squatting on the illegal edge of Mehrauli. She doesn't understand when the mistress of the house says she is going to her aunt's place across the road. She nods, eager to keep the job. It is light work, compared to the grinding toil on construction sites or in mills.

The master finds her alone, clearing up cluttered rags and newspapers in the storeroom upstairs. The speed with which he waylays her, bending back her fingers so that she doubles over with pain, pushing her down so that she is splayed over a tin trunk, tells her he has done this before. She feels his hands push her sari up, hears it tear, feels him press into her. She bites savagely into his wrist, tearing a vein, the blood spraying across the bags of rice, the dusty Glucose biscuit tin, the marching line of ants, and squirms free under his arm, running for it before he can come after her. She is not clear in her mind whether he has managed to commit the rape in practice or merely in theory, but she tidies herself up, pulling her aanchal over her head, tucking her sari pleats back in, wiping small spatters of his blood off her neck and chest.

She doesn't mention the incident to either man when she meets Khalid and Chand that weekend. They have grown accustomed to life by the riverside, shaking off the rough brickwork of pure street Hindi like a jacket and hanging it up, sliding back into the shabby comfort of the way they used to speak the language in their respective villages. Khalid doesn't tell Chand about the thief. When Rabia exclaims at the blood on Chand's face and his broken nose, he only says, 'I was careless.'

They learn caution, they learn to pay their trust out in small change, they develop an instinct for danger. Within a year, they can negotiate the city with confidence.

～⌒～

It isn't possible for the men to continue living under the rickshaw-pullers' bridge once Rabia joins them. She has left domestic work, finding a job instead at a textile factory, but there are no quarters for women workers, and there is no place for a woman amidst the fleet of rickshaws. Their world is unabashedly masculine, aggressive and dangerous.

There is no room for them under Loha Pul either, the old Iron Bridge where thousands of squatters live in a state of cautious permanence. Each successive year that they are not uprooted by the government gives these squatters a wary sense of ownership.

'No more outsiders,' the men say, their eyes closed and hard. 'Already there are too many of us. More of you, and they'll notice, throw us all out.'

Chand says mildly, 'We are only three more.'

One man laughs harshly. 'Only one more, only two more, four more, ten more,' he says. 'We hear this all the time from you outsiders. Follow the river all the way down, past Sarai Kale Khan. Start looking after you cross Maharani Bagh. It's less crowded that side.'

If Loha Pul is in the centre of the city, this part of the river is at its outermost edge. The three friends walk down a sandy bank and enter a strange new world, the noise from the road abruptly cut off, the river ahead a broad, fat, silver ribbon, much bigger than they had imagined.

Rabia says, 'What is this?'

A wide pond shimmers before their eyes. On a long spit of sand that stretches like an admonishing finger into the centre of the water, a man clad in tinsel sits on a faded cot, shaded from the sun by an open black umbrella. Water spinach grows around him; a typewriter is perched on a broken cane chair. It is so unexpected a sight that they stand speechless and staring. The man sees them and waves a sheaf of papers at them angrily. 'Don't step on my island!' he calls. 'Did the police send you?'

Before Chand or Khalid can respond, he pulls out a steel ruler and shakes it at them. 'They're always sending someone or the other in disguise,' he says. 'The last time, they pretended to be goat-herders. Before that, rag-pickers. It's all lies. It doesn't matter what you say you are. Tell the police I'm not so easily fooled. I'll write them another letter of protest, wait and see. They can't have my kingdom back. This is all mine. Go away.'

When he stands up, Rabia examines his peculiar attire. He wears a long robe that reaches almost to his ankles, a pair of ragged and filthy green shorts underneath. His hair falls in thick tangles down to his shoulders, and his narrow eyes are filled with suspicion. The robe must have been made of some rich material once, possibly red velvet, but it is difficult to tell. Strands of tinsel are glued to every part of it, and lengths of unspooled tape, the kind used in old cassettes.

Chand says, 'The police are no friends of ours. We aren't here to trouble you, or to trespass on your land. We are only looking for a place where we can stay for a few nights, anywhere in this area.'

'You would say that if they'd sent you, wouldn't you?' the man says.

Rabia says, 'We're only workers. Chand is telling the truth—none of us has anything to do with the police.'

'The police are bastards,' the tinsel man says bitterly. He holds out a sheet of paper, his fingers trembling. 'Every week, every day, they send someone to try to kill me, do you know that? It's never worked. I have protection.' He points to the pond, and to the water buffaloes wallowing peacefully at the other end.

'Their spies,' he whispers. 'In disguise, but I can always tell. The water hyacinths let me know. There are spirits in the pond, you know? They speak to me. They keep me safe. They tell me what to write to protect myself properly. This morning, I finished a letter to them. See?'

Chand says, 'It's good that you have protection.'

The tinsel man smiles. 'Yes, yes. They take good care of me, the spirits in this pond. Here's the letter. Listen. "My beloveds, all of you gandus, all of you and your uncles and your sons-in-law and your mothers and your fathers, I challenge each and every one of you to a fight with my water spirits because why are you persecuting a good man like me? When I was in Tihar Jail, that bastard who hit me, who put me back in jail when I wanted to return to my pond, did he have any right? One inconsequential theft and you take a man by his ear and twist it and beat him? Wait and see what I do. I'll leave the corpses on your doorstep and you'll never know it's me, I'll commit a thousand murders and you'll still be scratching your paunches wondering who the criminal is, you and your uncles and your ..."'

'Thank you,' says Chand, hastily moving on. 'We won't trouble you any further. It's been very interesting to visit your kingdom.'

'Where are you going?' the tinsel man calls. 'I haven't finished, there are three pages more, addressed to the thana.'

'To see if there's a village or any place where we can find shelter for the night,' Chand says. 'Would you know of any such place?'

The tinsel man laughs. 'They are all bastards,' he says, 'every chutiya worse than the other. The village is useless. Filled with Gujjars. If you're not a Gujjar, why should they let you stay? You don't look like them at all. Find a pond. There's lots of them, only the police come from time to time and chase everyone away. Find a pond of your own, mind, you can't stay here, this one belongs to me. It's my kingdom, you understand? If I see you here again, I'll kill you. Then I'll cut up your corpse and feed it to the black kites. They would relish that. I think they would relish that very much.'

'Goodbye,' says Chand, hurrying Rabia and Khalid along. Khalid turns, unable to resist a last look at the Tinsel King. He lets out a roar of rage, bends down and throws a rock in their direction. It skips across the shining water and sinks.

'He's fully mad,' Khalid says when they are at a safer distance.

'And dangerous,' Chand says. 'Most lunatics aren't, but you have to watch out for the violent sort. Better to stay away from his side of the river.'

~

The Gujjar village is a sprawling, prosperous cluster of sturdy huts, edged by handkerchief squares of rich farmland that spread all the way down to the edge of the Yamuna. It is a place that has ample shelter for cows, goats and black kites, but not for wandering migrants. The only friendly soul they find is a marigold farmer, who offers them steel tumblers of cold water from his well and useful advice.

'You won't find a permanent home here,' he says. 'The police conduct raids to check that no one except the Gujjars has made a settlement on these banks. The Gujjars have a firm claim. Well, not a legal one, but it's understood that herders have always grazed common lands. If anyone else tries to build a home, it will be knocked down, no question. But you don't have to have a permanent home. Look around you. There's no shortage of reeds, or thatch, or river mud. Build your home where it can't be seen easily. Not on the banks. Inland, find a quiet place, and if they find it later and knock it down, you can just go further up or down, and build a new reed hut.'

They thank him, but he calls them back. 'For the time being, you can put up your hut over there, beyond my last field. No trouble from you, though, no brawls, no setting up hooch stills or matka games, no illegal activities, all right? The woman will be safe. Good people live here, but some peculiar sorts are also drawn to this place, to the tall grasses and the lack of company. It attracts all kinds of humans. You'll see.'

~~

The Yamuna is the city's watery border, a river that carries a memory of clouds and ice down from the Himalayas, of glacier-grey beauty and unpolluted waters the colour of storm clouds in a mountain sky, a dancing river before she reaches the plains. For the most part, Delhi turns its back on her, staining her swollen body with its ashes and garbage and sewage, choking her with the city's waste, its discards, its corpses and diseases. Most inhabitants notice the river goddess's turbulence only when she floods her banks, returning to the city all that it had discarded and dumped in her once-clear waters.

The river still exerts a half-felt pull on the capital's subconscious, infecting its citizens with watery dreams and silted nightmares from time to time. 'River of sorrows, river of tears, the river that swallows the world's poisons,' Khalid sings to Rabia and Chand, 'she bears them in her own flowing body until even her waters can carry no more.'

An invisible tide courses through the city, Chand knows. Every morning, the tide sends in a flood of people who work to build Delhi's roads and homes, to guard the factories and offices of the wealthy, sends in artisans and labourers, armies of domestic workers and clerks, mill workers and gardeners, and every evening, the tide ebbs, casting them back outside the city, strewn like human debris across the river banks, the floodplains, the unstable islands that appear in one season, and vanish or broaden in time.

Khalid has a riverine nature; he is ruled by his own mysterious tides. They pull him this way and that way, never allowing him to settle into one thing. He drifts in and out of several jobs, tiring of the rigours of the loader's life and taking up carpentry. He quarrels with the master carpenter and joins a road crew to fill in potholes, leaves that for a brief stint stringing cotton for a mattress-maker. Often, he quits working altogether, except for odd jobs here and there. He has a rare gift for coaxing fish from the murky waters, and trades his catch for a few handfuls of rice or red chillies or some cooking oil. He fishes, forages, plays his flute, whittles toys and startling, lifelike animals from bits of wood.

Chand learns to cook rice from Khalid and Rabia, easier than making rotis every day. One or the other of them will set rice, the cheapest unpolished variety, to boil at night. They flavour it with green chillies, salt. Sometimes they boil two potatoes along with the rice, or add wild greens foraged from the banks. They cook more than is needed and cover the rest with two finger-widths of water to make fermented rice, paanta bhaat, for the next morning. That dish sees Chand through his Delhi life.

Chand learns to love it all, the ebb and the flow, the sense of riding the tides, of being one of those who survives Delhi's harshness, and is rewarded by an immersion in a more urgent flow of life than he has ever imagined possible.

Their river life brings the most joy to Khalid. He scavenges ill-assorted planks of wood, patiently planes them down and fits them together to make a boat, gathers bundles of reeds and stashes them in hidden places. He does some rough work for one or two of the Gujjars, but turns his back on any kind of proper job at first. He prefers to walk or explore the river for miles, bringing back wild greens and roots for Rabia or fresh-caught puti maachh, tiny fish still swimming inside the tin pail he slings around his neck with a coil of rope.

Rabia understands that the wetlands and the river speak to Khalid in a way that neither the city nor his village did. At dusk, he lets his flute speak in turn to the land and the water, singing them wordless songs of love and praise.

Their hut is one of five that are spread out, far apart, around the inland lakes and pools. Their neighbours are almost as strange as the Tinsel King, but not as aggressive. One only returns to his hut at night. In time, they learn that he runs matka games in the slums that have started to spring up behind far-off Maharani Bagh, and also stores illegal gas cylinders behind a false wall in the Gujjar temple, giving the priest a cut of his proceeds.

Another claims to be a bastard descendant of the last emperor of Delhi, Bahadur Shah Zafar, while spending his days in an opium haze. He orders them to call him Alamgir, and startles Chand, who had naturally discounted his story, by showing him an old coin, which he claims is a silver rupee from the time of Zafar.

'I can read faces,' he whispers to Chand one night, when the full moon shines bright on the swollen waters. 'Yours is an honest one, maybe your friend is not so honest, he's a weak man. But neither of you will steal my treasures.'

From time to time, Alamgir sells part of his inheritance, eking out the money for a season or two. His wife visits once a month and holds one-sided arguments with him while he sucks on an opium pellet and talks to her languidly of the beauty of the night stars. Then she returns to the man she had left him for, after years of simmering exasperation, a hakim who peddles medicines of dubious origin in Daryaganj.

Some months, Chand and Khalid fish in waters that are almost clear, not the fabled sapphire-and-white marbled waters that the Yamuna was rumoured to have in the 1970s, but a gentle grey. They catch magur, whiskered catfish, and if they are in luck, even plump katla and rui. In those months, the golden light lies as sweet as palm molasses on the surface of the river. They have the orange-beaked Indian skimmers and painted storks for company, and the water-bugs that stride like landlords across the water.

Jackals slink out at night, shadows slipping by on the other side, beyond the water reeds. They are braver on moonless nights, and their call-and-response, *hukka-huwah! Kya hua?*, floats up and down the river, the skein of sound broken only when they make successful kills.

At the close of summer, Rabia takes to pausing her work for a few minutes at twilight to watch the birds return to Delhi. The skies thicken with the arrowhead shapes of migratory birds who land among the water hyacinths, splashing and cleaning their wings, wetting their bills exuberantly after the long flight.

But before the monsoons, the city's filth darkens the waters, strangling the river. The banks begin to erode. Rumours ricochet between the fishermen, vegetable-growers and flower-sellers that the year's crop of cauliflower and spinach are growing red for a reason, that the deep, vivid red of the watermelons is most unnatural.

A body in a gunny sack surfaces upriver, and for a few weeks, Chand, Khalid and Rabia sleep on the bare earth, unable to rebuild their demolished huts until the police finally finish investigating and leave them in peace. Some say this is the work of criminal gangs that transport their murder victims from distant parts of the city to lie in the Yamuna's lap. Others whisper that it must be a tantric, slaughtering some innocent soul as part of his secret rituals. The rumours die down in a year or two when no fresh corpses surface. The year comes to an end peacefully enough, and they grow used to the changing seasons, settling in so easily that they do not notice time slipping by.

～

By the end of the decade, the city's placid somnolence has been challenged by a new, restless, sometimes violent prosperity. Cement barons and property developers send their surveyors to walk the length of the riverbank. The men measure the land with assessing eyes, gazing at the border between Delhi and the state of Uttar Pradesh, where a new township is beginning to rise.

Rabia and Khalid argue about how long this life can go on. The river sings to her, too, but some days the heat, the uncertainty of their shifting lives, the difficulty of drawing water from the pond for every small and big task, the profusion of snakes and spiders that take shelter in the thatched roofs, drive her to anger at her husband's refusal to fix his mind on a better future.

'Concrete suffocates people. You can breathe in a hut,' Khalid says to Chand, looking around with pleasure at the keekar forest, the grace of the contemplative egrets. These elements soften the harshness of the air, make the filth in the water bearable, though the vilayati keekar, the foreign thorn tree brought into Delhi in the time of the British, has a way of strangling the rest of the vegetation.

Chand often says that it is funny how the illegal squatters have the best view of the river. Choked though it is with the city's refuse, the river seems to retain a faint memory in her depths of her earlier freshness, her unstoppable life.

He takes his turn at cooking and Rabia nods approvingly at his skill with the boti. He fillets and guts the fish so swiftly on it that his hands seem to blur, the scales falling in silver showers, the guts deposited in a neat, glistening pile by the side of the chopping block.

Standing by his side, Rabia gathers up the chunks of catfish, massages a thin paste of turmeric and red chilli into the flesh, and clears away the entrails and debris, burying the pile neatly in a deep hole she has dug outside. Chand wipes his hands, moves to the friendly crackle of the wood fire to start cooking the curry, one of the jobs he has silently allocated to himself over the years. He fries the fish first, then places the pieces on a battered tin lid. The aroma greets Khalid when he enters. Black nigella seeds sputter in the hot mustard oil. Chand adds seven green chillies, slitting them as he drops them in the pan, then a handful of coarsely ground cumin and ginger paste. The aroma makes Rabia feel better, he knows. It settles her stomach.

Chand puts in about two cups of water, using the cracked porcelain cup that stands by the side of the wood fire, lets the jhol simmer and thicken for a minute, then adds the pieces of fish. A simple curry; it will go well with the rice that Rabia has already boiled and mashed into coarse balls, salting each mound.

Sucking on the long bones, content with the evening, it comes to Chand that he might die in Delhi, an unexpected thought that he shares with Khalid and Rabia. He is not yet thirty, so death is a long way off for any of them. But when he tries to recollect the sparse dreams he had harboured at sixteen, he feels that he has stopped desiring either return or further exploration.

'You can live in a city for decades without knowing if you belong to it,' he says to them.

'So what do you think you were breathing in all these years?' asks Rabia, cleaning stray bits of fish innards and blood off the curved blade of the boti with a bit of coconut husk. 'The air, the floating grime in the air, the rain, the monsoon breeze, the water, the earth, everyone's sweat, the farts from the buses, the politicians' nonsense speeches, the dust in summer, the mist off the river in winter, what is this belonging–not belonging? At some point, what you breathe in is what you become. That's no surprise.'

Later, Rabia brings out a treat—pieces of jaggery for them to crumble and eat, as though they are children, a rare and welcome touch of sweetness. They rest in one another's company, the hurricane lantern casting a flaring, pearly light on the river's many night creatures, its multitude of small, rustling lives lived to the gurgle and slushy, sucking sounds of the water rushing through the reeds.

~

In the morning, restless from an unfamiliar ache to the right of her lower abdomen, Rabia walks down on her own, without the men, to the Yamuna. The clay brings her comfort, the sound of the water soothes her, and the river releases unexpected largesse, washing up a pristine earthen pot. She wades further in, a hand on her stomach. The water recedes, leaving behind more detritus. Two bird's wings, iridescent and beautiful, oddly joined by a thin frame of bone.

She runs her fingers over the wings, no longer surprised at the gifts of death that the waters often yield. Another twinge, like a peremptory knocking, in her belly. It comes to her that she is carrying her own gift, new life stirring in her womb.

~~~

Rabia's arguments with Khalid acquire a bitter tang. 'What's wrong with living here?' he asks, baffled by her restlessness, her constant demands that they look for a place back in the city, that he take up a proper job. 'The child can play by the riverside, learn the names of fish, birds, trees. It's a good life, no?'

'And school? And no drinking or bathing water? And where is the room here to bring up anything, a mouse, a cat, let alone a child? Even the beetles scuttle out because there's no space.'

'All right, all right. We'll talk about it later.'

'Later, later. Always later. I know your "later". When the baby's out of my stomach, later. When the baby's in long pants, then you'll have time to talk? You're going to be a father! Have you no sense of responsibility?'

Khalid gets up quietly and leaves the room. Rabia hears him push the boat out onto the river.

The baby isn't showing yet, it is only the fourth month. But Khalid's inability to understand scares her, and the fear salts her tongue, laces her voice with acid. Their quarrels, once rousing but infrequent, become the pattern of their nights. She tries to keep her voice down, but she knows that voices, however muffled, carry far over water.

Rabia gives Chand apologetic presents, sorry that some of their troubles have leaked into his life. He receives these in silence. A few baskets she has woven from reeds. Ferns, salted, sun-dried and pickled along with chillies and thin slices of haldi root. Sometimes he brings back scraps from Badshah Miyan's shop, and they make a rich soup with fat bones, splitting them later to get to the marrow. Or Badshah Miyan himself visits and cooks them delectable gurda-kaleji curries with the liver, the kidneys, the sweetbreads, the testicles.

In her ninth month, Khalid disappears after an especially ferocious argument. She feels responsible, bites down on her anger. Bites down hard, willing it to vanish and not harm the child, kicking and turning like a fish, ready to enter this world. Rabia waits for her husband to return, at first sure that his fit of temper will burn itself out and then less certain.

Her waters break the day they arrest the Tinsel King. The commotion brings them all out, the man screaming and kicking when the police finally capture him. He holds them off with his typewriter, curses, pulls a long pickaxe from the water. He had kept his promise. He had murdered four people in all, vagrants, beggars, homeless men. And he had left their bodies outside the police station, returned to his throne in the pond and written them taunting letters.

Rabia rushes over with the rest of the riverside dwellers. Unnoticed in the throng, she presses her hands to her belly, almost doubled over with pain. Then she feels the wetness, the sudden heaviness of her sari, the gush of fluid down her legs, and knows what is happening. The panic swamps her. She has not thought of how she will give birth without Khalid to take her to the government hospital. But Chand is by her side, his hand is on her arm as she buckles. He half-carries, half-walks her up to the main road, flags down an auto-rickshaw driver, and gets her to the hospital in time. He waits outside in the corridor, which is crowded with patients' families and wandering orderlies.

When Rabia sees the baby, covered in wax and white fluff, she forgets Khalid's absence. As her son is passed into her hands, she forgets that she shares a bed in the overcrowded ward with another woman in labour, puts aside the tiredness, the lancing pain where something, tissue, muscle, flesh, has torn. She looks into the baby's wrinkled, astonished face and tells Chand, her voice shaking with fervour, 'I swear I will give him a better future than a reed hut with murderers and madmen for company.'

The Cracks in This Changing World

In the months of Khalid's disappearance, Chand adjusts a few parts of his routine. He waits until Rabia falls asleep, then unrolls a light mat that he had woven from river grasses and goes to sleep outside her hut. He pulls a sheet of blue tarpaulin over himself as protection from the dew, silently lets the men who travel restlessly up and down the banks of the river know that she is not to be troubled by their attentions. Wakes at dawn, the birdsong soaring into a sweet sequence of ragas and rippling melodies, the sun touching the white feathery plumes of the tall kans grasses with its gold. He slips back to his own hut before Rabia rises, and goes over after he finishes work to help her with Arshad.

He has never handled a baby before. The weight of the boy, so light in his arms, makes him nervous. He holds the child tenderly, marvels as the weeks pass and Arshad turns his attention to everyday wonders, eyes widening in astonishment. Once, Rabia comes back from the pond to find him, eyes closed, smelling the baby's neck and hair. He is embarrassed.

'Such a new smell,' he says by way of explanation. 'I didn't expect him to smell so good.' Can't get enough, and is secretly delighted when the child flails his tiny fists and howls, wanting Chand to pick him up.

Khalid returns to his family when Arshad is five months old. Chand retreats to let the father claim his son. Khalid is enchanted with the baby when he's sleeping, or gurgling with laughter, or reckoning with the life around him, but shrugs and leaves to fish on the river when he is cranky or sick.

Chand steps into these gaps, walking up and down with the child held against his shoulder, feeling Arshad's tiny heartbeat like his own. He cleans Arshad up when the boy vomits from the first summer heat of his young life, tearing one of his own old gamchhas into strips so that Rabia can cool the child's forehead with water.

He does not leave Delhi after the riots that erupt when the Babri Masjid is brought down in Ayodhya by crowds of men swarming up its ancient stones, bringing their pickaxes to the past. It does not make sense to him, this business of bickering over temples and mosques, of picking at old wounds and letting the blood flow afresh. But he keeps a wary eye on the boiling rage that flames briefly, searingly, through the streets of the city. Badshah Miyan shutters his shop for two weeks, but their part of the river is not too badly singed by the fires and the bloodletting.

Chand respects the way Rabia faces the constant threat of violence or dislocation, the temporariness of their lives. It seems to him that, as the years have passed, she has discovered her strength, just as her husband lost his. She has let go of her fears, one by one, and Khalid has grown more timid, gathering up all the nervous worry his wife has learnt to discard. A crack had always run through him; it seems to have widened after the destruction of the mosque in a faraway town none of them know much about.

The police pick up Khalid one evening in one of their random sweeps. He is lucky. The jails are full of Muslim boys and men, and they only hold him for a week. They don't beat him much, but he returns from jail tremulous and fearful.

Rabia says to Chand in despair one evening, 'He is crumbling slowly, from the inside out.'

Khalid has begun to distrust sleep. He stays up for days at a time, wakeful, watchful, anticipating a mob that never arrives, an arrest that never happens, falling into a narcotic slumber only when he has worn his body out.

Chand finds him a job, a good one, as a part-time ambulance attendant, thinking that this might help his friend get his mind off his anxieties.

Khalid revives. Some of his old humour returns.

He tells Rabia, 'People are strange. So few want to go with their family members in the van. Some get in when we load the stretchers, but most say they will follow in their cars. I like to stay with the patients. On a stretcher, you're helpless. Patients can only look up at the ceiling of the van, so I hold their hands if it seems that they need their hands held.'

The work is tiring but well paid, and it seems to suit him. But he still cannot sleep, and over the months, the wakeful nights and his early morning nightmares seep once again into his days. Khalid starts to whisper to the patients. He holds their slack hands between his, and as the ambulance siren wails, he warns them to beware of mobs. Soon his whispers to the sick and the dying grow louder. He loses his job.

He finds another one, as a cash-box guard at a highway tollbooth, but that doesn't last either. He cannot stay awake for the last hours of the dayshift. He startles his fellow guards by shouting, 'They're coming! I can see them at the end of the road, they're carrying swords and kerosene bottles, can't you see them?' He is fired, again.

After a few months of this shuffle from one job to another, Rabia says, 'Why do you have to work for someone else? Go out on the river and fish, no? Keep the hut repaired, grow some vegetables like you used to.'

She is gentler with him than she has ever been, afraid of sending him into one of his long rages or silent slumps. He addresses the changing world, which he had once relished, with bitterness and fear.

Rabia has found a job working in one of the apartments close by. The family has two pampered children and a demanding, nagging mother-in-law who hovers around her, suspecting that she might steal if she isn't constantly under watch. But they pay her well, there are no predatory men at home during the day, and they allow her to bring Arshad along, a great favour.

'Don't they mind when he cries?' Chand asks her once.

She smiles. 'He's a surprising fellow, seems to understand that he has to stay absolutely quiet. I bought some opium syrup to smear on his lips in case he made a racket, but he never gives me any trouble.'

Chand says, 'Imagine that. Your son already knows how important a job is. He'll go far in life.'

❧

One day, when Chand makes his usual phone call to Teetarpur, the postmaster says, 'Wait, son,' and summons Balle Ram. His brother says that their father is grievously ill. He should come back soon if he wants to see him at all before the end.

Chand takes the night bus, walks the last stretch home, and by the next evening, has a miraculously revived parent and a new wife. Balle Ram and his father have conspired to trick him into marriage with a woman he has never met. Her name is Bihida. Her family lives two villages away, and the arrangement was settled between their parents when they were children.

More than anything else, Chand resents the deception. He sees no reason to return from Delhi to take up the chores of farming, the task of being a husband. He does not raise his hand to Bihida. But for the first ten years of their married life, she only sees her husband once every six months, for a few days at a time. Stubbornness runs in the family, a straight line connecting father and son. Neither finds it easy to turn from a course of action once it has settled in their minds.

What yawns between Bihida and Chand is not just the gap between city and village, but the distance he places between them with his resentment and neglect. On one of his visits, he overhears her confess to Balle Ram's wife that she fears she has crossed the years of childbearing, that her womb, once eager and ready, is no longer inclined to, or able to, nurture life. He steps away, not wanting his wife to know that he has heard, but the sorrow in her voice strikes his heart. It is a bitter moment for Chand. If there is one thing he has learnt from living with Rabia and Khalid, it is that he enjoys the company of children.

The Place of Knives

By the end of his first year at the shop, Badshah Miyan begins taking Chand with him to the abattoir at the Idgah.

He watches Chand closely on their first visit for signs of weakness. Brown-and-black kites wheel overhead, clustered in such large groups that Chand thinks their wings might someday blot out the sky. The stench announces the abattoir. It is a battlefield stench, a morgue stench, but it does not convey to him the full impact of what lies ahead.

The holding pens for the sheep, goats and buffaloes are overcrowded. The queues for the slaughter itself are long. The animals, even those stunned by terror into silence, find their voices when they sense that it is their turn to face the knife or the live wires that some butchers use in the buffalo market for swift, if illegal, electrocution.

Chand had not imagined so many animals, so much slaughter, could not have envisaged the blood-choked drains running the length of lanes, the mountains of offal and discarded entrails, that there would be no separation between the living and the dead. As the hour of closure approaches, the butchers pick up speed. They abandon caution and kindness, simply slaughtering a goat or a buffalo as it stands by its companions, instead of waiting for them to be brought up one at a time. The veterinary doctors, their skin strained and grey from long hours spent standing on their feet in the slush, blood puddling around their ankles as they stamp the necessary certificates, sometimes shrug as night approaches, and give up the pretence of inspecting the lowing, terrified, sometimes pregnant, animals being shoved ahead by their handlers.

The facts of death are familiar to Chand. What he grapples with is the scale, the lakes of blood and other fluids soaking into the ground, the feathers heaped in hillocks, the discarded hides, the pleading and fear of creatures about to lose their lives. But he holds his nerve, and he does not lose his stomach, and earns a nod of approval from Badshah Miyan.

Later, when he grows more familiar with the abattoir, he is troubled by nothing about it—not the death-saturated stink, not the cries of the animals, not the rolling eyes of the buffaloes or the shivering goats. It is Delhi's only slaughterhouse, and it attracts many communities, has a lively, busy buzz. It surprises him to see women among the men, briskly trading in the small cuts, the discards and the offal, but they are as much a part of the slaughterhouse world as the men.

The Hindu and Sikh butchers keep to their side. The Muslim halal shops keep copies of the kalima to assure the most devout of their buyers that they are in truth adhering to the norms of prescribed slaughter. He finds this as ridiculous as the memsahibs who come to the Mehrauli shop, anxiously asking, is the meat fresh, is it safe. The old and the infirm, the healthy and the sick, the young and the lively, the goats left to fend for themselves, grazing on wastelands, and the goats pampered by their owners, hand-fed, all come to the same end: a blade at their throats.

Some of the rigidities of the city fall away in the meat bazaar. Badshah Miyan and he often drink tea or eat a meal of brain curry and fresh-from-the-tandoor rotis alongside men of diverse castes and faiths, no one caring to ask another his religion, his place in the world.

Only one small thing edges its way into his dreams. The abattoir generates enormous piles of waste and offal. The scrawniest of cows feed at these heaps. They belong to nobody. They slink around the market like thin ghosts, much like the stray dogs that scrounge a living off the streets of Delhi. The eyes of the cows carry a plea that touches him greatly, an inarticulate lament, as if they dimly remember that life is not supposed to be this way, but have forgotten and cannot recover what kindness, or caring, or a full stomach, feels like any more.

Badshah Miyan undergoes a transformation in the lanes of the Idgah. He commands respect among the Qureishi butchers, among the Lals, Shaikhs, Suds and Khans whose families have been in the trade for centuries, and he discards the mannerisms of the shop. His language loses its profane edge. He speaks with seriousness, and when he clears his throat, those around him quieten down. He has helped settle many squabbles between the buffalo butchers and the goat butchers, gives advice sparingly and in a manner calculated to suggest that the others are under no obligation to follow his suggestions, though, as a rule, they tend to.

Chand sits quietly, listening to his employer with surprise. He files this away as yet another lesson he has learned from Badshah Miyan. A man can be many things at once, a learned authority in one place, a colourful character in another.

On their way out, that first day, they pass the chicken butchers who separate the heads of hens from their bodies at an almost supernatural speed. Badshah Miyan stops at the entrance to the abattoir and tells Chand, 'Breathe it in.'

Chand gives him a look of inquiry.

'This stench is not only the stench of death,' Badshah Miyan says. 'Every butcher who wants to know his trade must be willing to breathe in the souls of the slaughtered, and to take in each breath, each freight of souls, with due care. Their deaths feed our lives. You know how old the Idgah abattoir is? A hundred years ago, more or less, this place was called the Butcher Khana. The British started it, kept it outside the city, and now, long after the Angrez left India, the city has engulfed the Idgah. And though we are fighting to stay, in another ten or fifteen years, they will find an excuse to move us out to another abattoir on the outskirts. Then the city will grow around that one also, and refuse to face the blood and death that feeds its own stomachs, and that will also have to move in its own time.

'But Chand, remember this. In every lane, in every one of the closed gullies that even I would not go into without permission from the Qureishis or the Lals, death feeds tens of thousands of lives. The city's wedding feasts and the small comforts of their everyday dinners come from here. The pools of blood you've been trying to step around, they sink into the earth, become part of the water that cycles through the city's taps. Our livelihood, our security, comes from this place of knives. Breathe it in, with respect. Take it into your lungs.'

Chand takes a deep breath. He almost gags. But he lets the inhalation become part of him, feeling its sourness, its unmistakeable sweet stench, down in the pit of his stomach. Then he exhales the scent of slaughter back into this place of death, life and business.

He feels pity for the animals, the pity of kinship. All of them, humans and animals, constantly packed into spaces too small for them, spaces that make them cruel and hard to one another, always on the verge of displacement, never fully at home. You might feel that sharp blade on your neck someday, fate's axe cleaving your breath from your bones in one way or another. Or you might be the one to wield the knife. Those are the choices, and he is at peace with his choice.

～

Badshah Miyan's son returns from Dubai a few years later. He is a smiling man, bald, wears gold rings, a flashy suit.

'I meant to give you these this morning, Dad,' he says, bringing out packages of shirts in fancy wrapping, smart grey trousers wrapped in cellophane. 'But you had already left for the shop by the time I woke up.'

He lays his gifts out with a flourish, in front of everyone at the shop.

Badshah Miyan stares at the trousers, sets them aside. He says to the butchers and their assistants with pride, 'My son. Dubai-returned. Murshid.'

'Just call me MK,' Murshid says expansively.

'MK?' Badshah Miyan says. 'Where is this K coming from?'

Murshid laughs nervously. 'It's useful, Dad,' he says. 'These days all the big businessmen use their initials. Smarter.'

Badshah Miyan lifts the trousers up, using the long pole that he employs to bring plastic buckets and bowls down from the high shelves near the tin roof.

'Expensive material,' he says. 'Very fine tailoring. Thank you.'

MK brightens. 'Wonderful, Dad! You can put away your lungis, I'll have four more pairs made.'

Badshah Miyan glares at his son. 'I'm not going to wear these contraptions. I like a bit of breeze around my parts. Healthier. Have you ever heard of anyone who wears lungis having trouble in their parts? Men who wear pants, you go and see for yourself, the hospital wards are full of them. All kinds of diseases take hold when your parts are confined. Very bad for the system. Here, you take these pants back. Good tailoring, mind you.'

Before MK can say anything, he opens up the packet of shirts.

'Wah!' he says. 'These I'll keep. They'll look smart with my lungis. Such a good son you are. Thoughtful. But take those pants away. A man likes to breathe.'

⌒

But that is the only defeat Murshid suffers. He takes away the old signboard for 'touching up', the one that says 'Badshah Miyan Meatwallah & Son' in Urdu and in smaller English letters. He brings the new sign in two days later. On a midnight black background, planets and stars circle words outlined in startling gold-and-red dots.

This sign says, 'MK's Famous Meat Shop. BK, Proprietor. Cold Cuts, Chicken, Mutton, Fish. Guaranteed Fresh!'

Hari and Chand eye the sign, go back to sorting offal, their heads bowed. Badshah Miyan comes in late, humming an old Mohammad Rafi tune under his breath.

'What is this?' he demands.

MK says smoothly, 'Dad, you said I should take a greater interest in the business, and you're right. This is my present to you. Had it done at the new shop in Khan Market. By the way, we should move there. It's coming up quite smartly.'

Badshah Miyan says, 'We are staying put at this Mehrauli crossroad. It was good enough for my father, it is good enough for me, it should be good enough for my son. Where is my name on that damnfool fancy sign of yours?'

MK says, 'But, Dad, your name is here—"BK, Proprietor".'

Badshah Miyan says, 'BK? MK? Who are they? I don't know any MK or BK person. And cold cuts? What are cold cuts?'

MK says, 'Cold cuts are the future, Dad. Chicken salami, chicken ham, mutton and chicken sausages, we'll make a killing. I thought we could also put out our own line of kababs, pre-cooked, ready-to-eat, just fry and you're done. I've ordered two large deep-freeze units already.'

Badshah Miyan listens in horror. 'You want to sell our customers old meat? Stale meat? Some rubbish that's been sitting in the fridge God knows how long, stinking like a whore's arse?'

MK places a conciliatory hand on his father's arm. 'Dad, I came back from Dubai to help you out, right? I'm not going to do anything that will damage the business. Just let me handle a small part of it my way for three months, okay? That's all I ask.'

Badshah Miyan says, 'You put my name back on that signboard. This MK-BK nonsense I don't know. My old customers will think, he's sold his shop, they'll go somewhere else.'

'Right, right,' says MK, his rings flashing acquiescence. He has a smaller sign placed below the main board. In curlicued letters, it says, 'Badshah Miyan, Proprietor', a rocket ship sailing over the 'Badshah', a miniature astronaut trailing stars and suns over the 'Miyan'.

'Looks like the whole universe is coming out of my bum,' Badshah Miyan says, but he is pleased.

Badshah Miyan objects strenuously to the cold cuts once he knows what goes into their making. To take perfectly good meat, mix it together with who-knows-what scrapings from the mincer, put in some spices, do some hocus-pocus and slice it up into thin discs that are a world away from sumptuous kormas, delicate or fiery saalans, honest everyday curries—he doesn't understand what the point of it is. Then he tastes it.

'What do you call this?' he asks MK.

MK says, 'Chicken salami. You like it?'

Badshah Miyan says, 'You know what I call it? I call it sliced plastic crap. Go on, put that on a signboard. Come buy your fresh sliced who-knows-what plastic bird droppings here.'

But even he is impressed when his son ramps up sales. MK shrewdly markets the chicken salami and ham as 'Genuine US-style Sandwich Meat', showcases the chicken lollipops and kababs with the slogan 'As Sold in Dubai Supermarkets'.

The waves of liberalisation of the Indian economy have reached the high walls of Mehrauli's mansions. Businessmen and families have begun to travel, first gingerly, then with confidence, as stringent foreign exchange regulations are relaxed, though they are still careful not to bring too much in the way of perfumes or clothes or cheese in through

Customs. They dart Abroad, they inhale the air of Phoren. They like what they smell, and MK's Famous brings a whiff of far-off luxury into their ordinary Delhi lives.

Families that would not have dreamt of wasting money on eating out at the flashy restaurants tthat have sprung up in Connaught Place say to one another, 'I suppose we can give the cook a holiday, can't we? He can make parathas and go, and we can try out those MK Famous kababs.'

They feel a thrill when MK hands them 200 grams of chicken salami in rustling butcher's paper, as though they are picnicking in London or something.

Gradually, Badshah Miyan begins to take mornings off, arriving in the afternoon to oversee the important dinner orders. MK buys a gigantic Weston TV and a VCR for the house, and Badshah Miyan sometimes skips coming to the shop on slow days. He refuses to wear pants, but he swaps his lungis for pyjamas, tailored to his specifications, extra loose so that his parts will not feel too constrained. He is happy, and MK, sniffing the Delhi air, scenting big change around the corner, is happy.

The only one who isn't happy is Chand. His discontent steals up on him gradually. Salamis, kababs, chicken tikkas, chicken lollipops are frivolous items. They are not worthy of a butcher's skill. Unlike pasandas, which require an understanding of the grain and texture of meat, or chops, which require some rudimentary skill, or paayas or saddle of meat, or any part of traditional butchery, these are easy to make. He despises them, as well as those who buy them by the kilo.

And something else has begun to tug at him: the memory of land, specifically, the scent of earth fresh-turned by the plough, of woodsmoke, of last year's bales of straw. His thoughts turn often from the river to his village, and the first longings for a more settled life rise in his heart.

～

Left at home in peace, Khalid thrives. Rabia returns from work one day, pausing outside the hut when she hears the sounds of his flute, light, playful. It makes her smile. Inside, she looks around in wonder. He has plaited grass stems, hung them in wreaths around their hut's sparse walls, creating an odd beauty.

'What are these?' she says, pointing to a curious arrangement of whittled reed stems that run the length of the wall, snaking through a gap to the outside. 'Oh, look at the ants! So many of them!'

'It's a bridge for the ants,' Khalid says, putting down his flute. 'Do you like it? You've often said that the ants drive you mad, so I made them bridges ...'

Rabia kneels, peering at the bridges. Lines of red ants march purposefully across the bridges and out of their home. 'Where are they going?'

Khalid laughs, and the worry that has scored his face in recent times suddenly unmakes itself. 'Come and see.'

Behind their hut, he has set out small piles of food. Fishbones, ringed by a heap of pebbles. Crumbs of ragi, grains of sugar floating in water on an upturned tin lid. A generous buffet of assorted vegetable scraps.

'An ant dhaba!' says Rabia. 'But won't they come back into the hut for more food?'

'Why should they?' Khalid says. 'I've talked to them and explained everything.'

She stares at her husband.

'These ants are like the birds and the fish,' he says. 'They also have their own language. I've promised to feed them if they leave our hut alone, and they've agreed. Poor creatures. They also feel hunger, they also have to eat.'

He steps back into the hut as though he has said nothing unusual.

That night, after Arshad has fallen asleep, Rabia reaches for her husband. She holds his hand in hers, tentatively, feels the pulse fluttering under his rough skin. His fingers curl around hers, but he doesn't wake, nor does she want him to. But she feels a prickle of tenderness for this man who listens to ants, who finds comfort in the language of birds.

❧

A month later, Rabia returns from work, triumphant. There is something different about her, though neither man can tell precisely what it is.

'Here,' she says, putting a document with closely typewritten sentences in Hindi and English, purple ink on yellowing paper, in Khalid's hand.

'What's this?' he says.

'Our land,' she says. 'I've bought a kothi. In Bright Dairy.'

Khalid is silent, rubbing at the spot between his brows. 'How?'

Rabia says, 'Saved up. Did overtime. Sold a few things.'

Khalid looks confused, but Chand understands.

The delicate gold bangles that had given Rabia's sturdy wrists and small hands such character are gone, replaced by cheap green glass bangles. The necklace that had lent a gleam to her skin, which he privately thought had the sheen of the inside of a mahogany bark, is gone. Her throat is bare of jewellery. She has even sold her gleaming nose-pin. He feels that loss the most. It had flashed in the sunlight like a tiny droplet from the river held fast on the wide curve of her nose. He had watched the flash often, thought of kingfishers taking wing over running water.

Khalid says, 'But we'll have to leave the river?'

Rabia says, gently enough, 'We can't live here all our lives, Khalid. Bright Dairy is a proper colony. We'll have a home of our own, not a hut that can be knocked down or blown away any time. It's an open area, there are ponds around the colony. You can go there to fish whenever you miss the river.'

Khalid says, 'All right,' and turns away, his smile crooked.

The next day, he stays out on the river for three hours; the day after that, for five. Rabia grows accustomed to his absences, for he often finishes his jobs and takes Arshad out from morning till dusk when the weather is mild. It seems to both Chand and Rabia that he is saying goodbye to his river, a slow and long farewell to the fish, and the wading birds, and the bright ponds, and the marshy banks.

～

Khalid's worst times are during the police raids. When they first settled near the river, he had shrugged them off. Now they upset him so much that he walks around in tightening circles, muttering to himself in distress, at the first sound of the municipal trucks and police cars. Rabia soothes him afterwards, gives him the care and tenderness she might bestow on a terrified child. He cannot help her and Chand with the rebuilding of their huts any more. After a raid, he sits on the ground, rocking back and forth for hours.

'Go out on the river,' she tells him when the next raid begins. 'You'll feel better out on the water.'

He nods, and when he returns that night, he seems much calmer. A few days later, they hear the sound of the flute again, and they are relieved that his tremulous spirit has quietened.

The fourth of the raids that year happens in winter, just as the first of Delhi's fogs settles on the icy waters. This time, the police arrive early in the morning. Khalid trembles slightly as Rabia leads him to the boat, but he steps in and takes up the oar he has carved out of driftwood, gives her a smile.

She says, 'Don't worry, we'll soon move to Bright Dairy, there'll be no more raids. Tell your river birds that Arshad is growing up fast.'

He says, 'Look after my ants …'

Rabia goes back to survey the damage, listening to the light splashes made by the rise and fall of Khalid's oar cleaving through the waters. It softens the task of salvaging their possessions, the tedious necessity of rebuilding the reed hut from scratch.

There is a new officer in charge at the local station. New officers are zealous; this raid is a serious one. Under his direction, the policemen have not stopped at simply throwing out their belongings. They have smashed some of the pots, stepped on their dishes, stamped out their fires, and scattered the sheets and tarpaulins across different places. She sends a message to her employers through one of the other women that she will not be in that day, and resigns herself to further expenses. Much will have to be replaced.

She finds Chand contemplating the ruins of the ants' bridges and the shards of pottery that lie everywhere.

It takes them hours to sort through what is completely destroyed and what is still intact. They don't dare to rebuild even a single hut that night, in case the raiding party decides to return the next day.

Rabia sets up a makeshift fireplace in the open, by the side of one of the inland ponds so far from the main settlement that it is probably safe from the police. Chand fashions a temporary roof from a tattered sheet of blue tarpaulin stretched over two bamboos and a plastic drum. She swaddles Arshad in the warmest clothes she has been able to salvage.

The evening winds are knife-blade sharp. She peers into the darkness, realising how late the hour is, the moon riding high in the inky sky.

'Khalid hasn't returned yet,' Rabia says. 'He should have come home long ago.'

Chand says, 'He's afraid of the police. I'll see if he's hiding on the banks or in the fields. He did that one time, remember?'

But there is no sign of Khalid or his boat.

They are exhausted, but neither Rabia nor Chand can sleep well that night. Arshad catches their mood and cries for hours, stopping only when he has tired himself to sleep.

At first light, Chand rises. Rabia says, 'I'll come with you,' but he shakes his head.

'You can't bring Arshad out to the river in this cold,' he says. 'It's freezing out there, he could fall sick.'

He borrows a boat from one of the fishermen and heads out on the water. The river narrows briefly under the bridge, broadening after the sand bars into a wide, shimmering ribbon that catches the grey winter light. On one side, a straggling cluster of illegally constructed brick hutments comes almost to the edge of the bank, and in the distance, a few high-rise buildings loom, shrouded in the mist. After this, the river broadens further, casting off some of the sludge of the city and recovering some of its gleam.

Khalid loves this stretch. Chand had been out with him once or twice. It is a marvel, how swiftly all that they know as part of the river's life falls away. The farms of the Gujjars, the marigold fields that are cultivated by migrants further up, the clusters of huts, the low-roofed sheds that house machinery and cows, all that is human and known disappears, and the scrub, a floating forest of thin-branched green trees, takes over on both banks.

Few come to these graceful wetlands and wildernesses, but Khalid knows the names of most of the trees, and can boldly find a path through the thicket of vivid green grasses. Cows and buffaloes graze near the bridge, but not in these marshy grounds. Some whisper that the riverbanks are haunted here. Others swear that the real danger is not ghostly but mortal. Criminal gangs are rumoured to use this stretch as a dumping ground for inconvenient bodies.

It has an unsavoury reputation, but even though he shivers in the morning's bitter chill, Chand understands what draws Khalid back here. The black, sludgy waters weighed down by silt and sewage that flow past their huts change character here. The Yamuna dances, revealing a glimpse of what she might have been without the burden of the city's discards. For a moment, he forgets to keep an eye out for Khalid's boat, enchanted by the sight of skimmers rising into the sky, white egrets boldly flying past, unafraid in his presence. The mist lifts, and the sun sparkles briefly on the surface of the water.

They had rowed all the way down one summer morning, and discovered to their shared disappointment that the river only revived for this long stretch. A few hours out, they'd seen the factories rise up, the smokestacks and the tell-tale line of black where effluents were dumped into the waters.

But Khalid had stopped rowing and let the boat drift. He said, 'Can you feel it, Chand? Can you feel how joyous the water is, how free she feels over here?'

Chand replied, 'I can imagine it, but I can't feel what you're feeling.'

Khalid said, 'Imagine if some day all of the river was like this. It's possible.'

Now, Chand rows almost to the edge of the bank and lets the boat drift. He closes his eyes, giving his arm a rest. He listens to the river lapping at the boat's sides, feels the light spray of water on his skin.

He takes a deep breath. The air is cold, but sweet, untainted. When he opens his eyes and looks out over the shining, broad expanse, the river does not fail him. He is moved, once again, by the improbability of such astonishing beauty and peace, so close to the thronging city. He turns back. There is something in the reeds, to the extreme left of his vision.

Tangled in the roots of the hyacinth, a floating oar.

Chand locates the boat much further up the bank. It has drifted quite a distance, finally grounding on a spit of mud and wet sand.

An egret feather rests lightly on Khalid's shawl. The bottom of the boat yields a plastic jerrycan of drinking water, coils of rope, his worn chappals, neatly placed side by side, and nothing else. Chand brings his boat to rest.

He wades into the water, searching through the tall reeds for his friend. When he returns to his boat, he rows around in widening circles, but there is no sign of Khalid's body. The current flows swift in this stretch of the river, fast and treacherous.

He gives up when darkness hovers and begins to row back. He has to pull hard on the oars, the current cuts across, making his light boat weave and buck.

Chand will have to find a way to tell Rabia that the demons who have tormented Khalid's mind for so long are finally at rest, that the waters have carried her husband to a place far beyond their reach.

Khalid, his first and closest companion in the city: first the river comforted him, then it claimed him.

Emergency Ward

Over time, Delhi grows. The buildings draw closer and closer, lapping first at one bank, then at the other, finally squeezing the river into a sluggish, choked band of polluted water that runs between two sets of apartments, one a set of luxury high-rises, the other a set of unfinished, unpainted and illegal homes built by workers and migrants over the years.

Boys who dive for coins and tiny gold or silver statues of the gods deposited in the river by the faithful begin to slouch around the wetlands at night, when their work is done. Chand often finds the sandpipers and brown-headed gulls picking their way among empty bottles, razor blades, tell-tale tubes of adhesive squeezed for the last drop of glue and crumpled rags from which the boys had sniffed the hallucinogens. In the Gujjar village, locals have stopped sleeping out in the open and have begun to bar their doors at night against petty thieves, those roaming bands of men the police refer to as 'criminal elements'.

Bridges snap into place, connecting the city with bare lands that sprout apartment blocks like anthills, first only a few, then rapidly, like termite mounds, proliferating across the plains and the wetlands alike, startling the birds. The skimmers dwindle, the vultures diminish, the spoonbills thin out. The adjutant storks that picked their way across the reed-beds like absent-minded bureaucrats melt away so silently that it takes Chand a while to realise that they are gone for good.

Khalid's passing creates an awkwardness between Rabia and Chand. She moves to Bright Dairy with Arshad some months after. She has no reason or wish to continue their river life. Without her husband's presence, Chand and she are constrained in each other's company. She encounters the bright, hard stares of some of the Gujjar women in those last few weeks, and that also tells her it is time to leave.

Chand begins to spend more time in his village, returning for weeks rather than days. He and Bihida do not have much to say to each other, but a tentative, practical companionship sprouts between them. He grows to prefer the security of a home that is never under threat to one that is temporary, and now so empty.

More than Bihida, his land calls to him. The fields respond to his touch. Plants and crops flourish under his care, and bring another kind of satisfaction into his life.

Badshah Miyan is unsurprised when Chand says he will be returning permanently to his village.

He says, 'Don't forget us. Come back soon, come back often, and if you ever want to return, you'll find your mat and your knives waiting for you. But it's time for you to care for your own family. A man isn't a man unless he can take care of his own lands and his own home.'

Chand visits Delhi a few months later, after the harvest is done. He brings Rabia and Badshah Miyan sacks of green spring wheat, gleaming steel canisters filled to the brim with ghee and lassi from his cows.

That first summer, he brings Bihida along. She finds Delhi terrifying. The traffic makes her nervous, and she cannot cross roads. She freezes on the pavements, or she closes her eyes and lets Chand lead her across, her feet stumbling on the tarmac. The crowds, the elbowing roughness, the stares of the men, the gangs of women pickpockets at bus stops—she can bear none of it. Delhi's dust and pollution close her throat, make her eyes swell.

Chand takes Bihida to meet Rabia, but she has grown up with a set of insularities and customs from the village. She has never stepped into a Muslim home before. She meets Rabia's hospitality with frosty silence, refusing to touch any of the food brought in on platters and trays, or even to accept a glass of water. They board the bus back in silence. Chand would have preferred to ride down from Teetarpur on his Rajdoot 350cc motorbike. Because it was second-hand when it was given to him, it was the only item of dowry aside from kitchen utensils that he had been willing to accept from his in-laws. But Bihida is terrified of motorbikes.

'You could have tried to talk to Rabia,' Chand says when they are home. 'She and her husband were like my family in Delhi.'

It is the only time in their marriage that he has spoken harshly to Bihida.

She says, 'My parents would never let me make friends with Muslims.'

Much later, Chand realises she might have been offering an explanation. In that moment, his heart is raw from hurt and anger that his wife could not bring herself to be civil to someone of such importance to him.

He says, 'That's why I left the village, because of these narrow, backward views. You're nothing but an uneducated village woman, but I thought at least you would have some kindness.'

She says, 'Was it kind, to stay with strangers and call them family, to care more about a Muslim woman than your wife? Have I had kindness from you?'

He says, 'I should have stayed in Delhi. I made a mistake coming back.' He flings the words at her in anger.

For the next few months, he sleeps outside the hut, setting up a charpai in the fields on the pretext of guarding the crops from animals. His temper cools over time, and he returns to his home when winter sets in. But there is a fence of bitter words between them, and neither knows how to take it down.

Every year after that, he goes by himself to the city on his Rajdoot, gladness rising when he meets his old friends again. He spots the first streaks of silver in Rabia's hair before he realises that his beard is also greying. He never fails to bring gifts for Arshad as the baby he has known grows up, becomes a teenager. He smiles at the solemn boy, so eager to help his mother around the house, so impatient to step into manhood, and tries to bury his sadness at his own childlessness.

Bihida has stopped praying for a child long ago. She accepts her fate. Chand struggles to accept his. He often brings to mind one of Rabia's more tart maxims: Life is not a mithai shop, people should not imagine they will be granted all the sweetness they desire just-like-that.

⌒

Arshad turns sixteen. Chand gathers fresh marigolds from a neighbour's field, paying him in sugarcane. When he finishes with his decorations, the marigolds gleam like molten gold from the doors and steps of Rabia's home. Badshah Miyan and he bring in vats of nihari and roti to celebrate.

He returns to the village half a day earlier than he had intended, steps into the hut to find Bihida in tears. She brushes them from her eyes when she sees him.

'What is wrong?' He is stunned. He has never seen his wife crying. Then he spots the cloths on the ground, blood-stained. His pulse races with panic.

She says, 'I was going to throw them away.'

He says, 'What has happened to you? Are you injured?'

She shakes her head, pulling the end of her sari over her face. He used to hate this habit of hers, but has come to understand that it makes her uncomfortable to talk to him with her head uncovered.

'I thought I was carrying,' she says, 'after all these years. For some months, I did not have my usual—'

She stops. She does not have the language to discuss these matters with him.

He sits down, takes her hand in his. It is a small hand, hard-worn and roughened by the work she does around the house and in the fields, but beautifully shaped. He has never noticed the shape of his wife's hand before.

'You thought that you were expecting our child?' he says.

'Yes,' she says. 'I was so happy. I told nobody.'

The bleeding began the day he left for Delhi. It made her sick. She had told Sarita she was fine, just needed to rest, managed it herself. In his wife's sorrow for the lost child, Chand sees the mirror to his years of silent longing.

He soothes Bihida, tells her it does not matter, it is the will of the gods she believes so fervently in. He makes her rest when she would have got up to cook for him, orders her to lie down. He cooks a simple khichdi. Ignoring her embarrassment and her protestations that she can feed herself, he feeds Bihida from his plate.

That night, he talks for longer than he has in all the years of their marriage. It does not come easily to Chand to speak of his feelings, but he tries. He blows out the kerosene lamp. He speaks into the darkness of the night, shares his sadness that they have no child. He even shares his fears that there is something wrong with him. In the village, they always blame the woman. In the city, he has heard and read that it is often some lack in the man.

'But we have each other,' he says. 'We have made some kind of life. Could that be enough for you?'

His words are halting, his pauses long, but everything he says is salted with kindness.

At dawn, Bihida's pain eases and she finally drifts into sleep. Chand holds on to her hand. He will not let her go again. The next day, they do not speak much of her miscarriage, or of the sadnesses they have held pressed closely to themselves through the years, but they have both found acceptance.

She discovers a new tenderness in her husband. He has never beaten her, never raised his hand and only once raised his voice to her, but he has paid her scant attention.

He gives her the gift of his attention now, in large and small ways, and it brings her an unimagined comfort.

Bihida recovers in a matter of weeks. The night before the work of harvesting is due to start, she blows out all the lamps except one, which she places by their charpai. When he comes to bed, she reaches out, her tentative fingertips brushing his jawline. He is surprised by the depth of his own response. In the light of that flickering kerosene lantern, they slowly learn that there is much more to the pragmatic fellowship they have shared through the years.

He notices some months later that her belly seems to be swollen. She chooses to hide it from relatives and inquisitive neighbours, selecting ghagras with fuller skirts, tying her odhni to cover her belly. But she cannot conceal her pregnancy from him, not when they turn to each other at night. He says nothing, not wanting to set off her fears or risk disappointment if this ends in another miscarriage, but she feels his touch, his hands rubbing her belly before they explore further, and it calms her.

At five months, they finally tell Balle Ram, Sarita Devi and others, finally let themselves breathe freely. The time of risk is past.

Bihida sits outside, shelling peas and cleaning grain, with the special satisfaction of a woman who has been called barren too often and too long, the high curve of her pregnancy proudly displayed to all who pass by or visit. From the edges of the forest, the partridges run past, kicking up tiny clouds of dust. She smiles at the sight of their babies, the anxiety with which the feathered mothers scurry in search of those who have wobbled away from the flock.

At the start of the eighth month, she bleeds.

Chand only leaves Bihida's side once, to make two phone calls—to Rabia, and to the midwife from Teetarpur town. He comes back, sees that the bleeding has intensified. The darkness of the blood sends cold fear up his spine. The midwife arrives on the back of Ombir Singh's bike. The policeman hangs around outside the hut with Balle Ram, waiting to see if he can be of help. Sarita Devi is away, spending time with her ailing parents in their village.

When the midwife calls Chand in, her hands are stained with black blood. She says, 'Get her to a hospital. The big ones in Delhi. Don't waste time, it's a bad case. She's losing the child.'

'Bring her to the government hospital at the Delhi-Haryana border,' Rabia tells Chand. 'That's not far from you, and I'll meet you at the Emergency Ward.'

It takes a precious hour to get a doctor's attention, and by the time they are assigned a bed, Rabia has reached.

Bihida is in labour. Her skin, pallid from the blood loss, is stretched tight over her cheekbones. The bed is a shared one, and after just fifteen minutes, the other patient complains that the sheets are soaking wet. Bihida continues to bleed.

Rabia holds her hand, and Bihida grips her fingers so tight that Chand fears she will break Rabia's bones. He stays at the foot of the bed, obeying Rabia's instructions to fetch a nurse, to bring fresh sheets which he purchases from the shops outside the hospital, or some water, which they feed her in slow sips. The doctors are harassed, their young faces prematurely lined from lack of sleep and their gruelling schedules, but they are not unkind. The nurses are rougher, but even they soften when the seriousness of Bihida's condition becomes fully apparent.

A circle of young doctors discuss Bihida's case in low tones, switching to English when they see that Chand is listening. He does not let them know that he can understand a little of the language, that his time in Delhi has taught him some of its foreign rhythms. He passes over the words he doesn't understand. Haemorrhage. Disseminated intravascular coagulation. Listens for words that make sense—clotting disorder, yes, that he understands. Excessive blood loss. Falling heartbeat.

He sees the backs of the doctors' creased white coats. He sees his wife's body convulse, her feet drumming on the mattress. Rabia is assisting the nurse, her face drawn. The other patient is shoved onto a stretcher, taken off the bed. A doctor looks up, orders him out. He leaves, but sneaks back into the ward, hovering as close as he dares to the bed, wanting to be by Bihida's side. He catches a glimpse of her face. She is grimacing, her eyes rolled back in her head, unrecognisable.

One of the doctors shifts, and he stares, not able to make sense of what he is seeing, until he realises he is looking at the fuzzy crown of a baby's head. The nurse and Rabia catch her together as she tumbles from the womb. A river of blood floods the bed, the floor, the mother slipping out of life as the daughter draws her first breath. His child, yelling with a fury that takes Chand by surprise. Then the hospital staff gather around the bed, and the nurse firmly pushes him out of the room. He turns back once, glimpses Bihida's head, slack, dropping back. He does not need to be told that he has become a father, and a widower.

⌒

Once, he had almost stepped on a dazed bat, fallen to the ground in some nocturnal mishap. He had bent and picked it up, wanting to be gentle, and felt the creature curl and shiver in his careful hands.

He remembers that weight, the delicacy of it, the trembling bones, when he holds his daughter for the first time, taking her from Rabia. She weighs less than a paper bag of flour, less than a pillow stuffed with black mustard seeds.

She smells like the warm spring grass when he takes a scythe to it, like the first rains of summer falling on the hot earth, the scent of her neck like jaggery stirred over an open fire. She smells of her mother's blood, and her own sweetness.

If he strokes her forehead lightly, letting his fingers touch her miraculous skin, still sprinkled with the white down of birth, she curls her feet inwards and goes to sleep in his arms.

Through the numbness of his sudden loss, these things of sustenance.

~

Rabia keeps his daughter alive in the first week when he is still shuffling around like a sleepwalker. Arshad is old enough to take care of himself, and the neighbours have promised to keep an eye on her household. She goes back with Chand to the village. 'I'll stay until Sarita Devi can return,' she tells him. Rabia places a charpai for Chand outside the hut; she sleeps inside at night.

She makes sure that the child is warm and bundled up in soft cotton and wool, stays up to give her a feed every three hours, holds the girl to her heart when she seems fractious or restless.

Chand tries to remember everything she does and that she tells him to do, but he sinks back too often into tiredness, or fits of waking sleep. He drops into sleep like a man falling down a steep cliff, plunging into a bottomless abyss. He has no dreams, no nightmares. He wakes aching afresh with loss. Bihida's leather slippers with the frayed straps are still under the bed. Her altar with its cluster of terracotta gods gathers dust until Rabia notices, and then she takes a few extra minutes every morning to keep the modest shrine clean.

But his daughter draws Chand back into life. After a week or so, he begins to stumble up as well when Rabia wakes in the morning. He learns many small tricks and tasks of motherhood from Rabia. The naming ceremony will not take place until the mourning period is done, but he already has a name for his daughter.

'Munia,' he says experimentally one morning, and the baby bestows a wide, delighted yawn on him.

He feels the determined pressure of Munia's head on his shoulder, a slight squirming as she fits herself to him. He draws a ragged breath, unable to believe that this tiny human trusts him to look after her. He knows in that instant, smelling her sweet skin, that he will always keep her safe.

REASONABLE DOUBT

Outsiders

The high, spiked gates of Jolly Villa have never opened for Ombir before. Bhadana, Jolly's manager, sends messages if anything is required of the police. And once, Jolly Singh's Audi had stopped outside the station house, his driver relaying a curt message about goats that had strayed into the gardens of the villa through a gap in the fencing.

'This way,' Bhadana says, taking them along a stone path to the back. Ombir tries not to rub his eyes. It is humid, and the broiling heat sandbags him so thoroughly that he fears he might disgrace himself by nodding off in front of Pilania sir and Jolly Singh.

The gates slide open smoothly, soundlessly. The villa is three-tiered, like a layer cake, each tier a different colour—pista, strawberry, buttery yellow, the window frames picked out in spotless white plaster that reminds him of icing. Ombir glances at Chand, but the father walks with his head down, ignoring the bright flowers, the thick, waxy-green creepers in the gardens that surround the house.

Bhim Sain's jowls twitch mournfully. 'We won't get to see the mansion,' he whispers to Ombir. 'I wanted to see if it's true what they say, that all the furniture is gold.'

'Painted in gold,' Ombir whispers back. 'Not made from gold.'

'Ah,' says Bhim Sain.

Chand almost stumbles at the edge of a long, artificial stream that is glinting with carp. Ombir steadies the man. His cheekbones stand out like the curved bones of a fish, new hollows under his eyes, his skin grey and sallow.

He had said nothing when Ombir and Bhim Sain arrived to say that Jolly Singh had returned and was asking to see all of them. Chand's deep brown eyes were sunken, and white dust etched the grooves in his skin deeper still. His turban was soaked in sweat, coming loose. He had not changed his clothes for a full day. Ombir waited patiently. Finally, Chand had stood up, changed out of his vest into a fresh shirt, made a few desultory passes at the grey stubble on his face with an ancient cut-throat razor.

He walks with the shuffle of an older man. Answers any remark addressed to him by Bhim Sain, but after a pause, as if he has to cross a border from one country to another before the words find their way out.

'So many fish!' Bhim Sain says. 'How much fish can anyone eat?'

Bhadana laughs. 'These are for decoration, not for eating.'

The stream snakes like a black ribbon the full length of the garden. The gold and silver scales of the koi flash and gleam in the sunlight. A curious construction stands in the centre, something like the photographs Ombir has seen of Mughal tombs, but smaller, with a miniature dome and jaali work on the outer screens. When Bhadana opens the door, the blast of icy air banishes one of Ombir's fears. The powerful air-conditioning will keep him on his feet, awake.

Ombir waits for Chand to follow Bhim Sain in through
the low door. Chand, taller than either of them, has to
stoop. It seems to return him to the present, and he puts
his hands together in a shaky namaste when he sees Jolly
Singh rise from a massive armchair printed in brilliant
peacock blues and greens, its ornate arms clad in beaten
silver.

Jolly approaches in silence, removing his gold-rimmed
dark glasses in a gesture of respect. He surprises Ombir by
reaching out and taking Chand's rough hands in his own,
pressing them for a second.

'This should never have happened to you,' Jolly Singh
says. 'No father should have to suffer such a loss.'

He leads Chand over to a chair and nods at Ombir
and Bhim Sain to sit, but both men remain standing,
uncomfortable at the thought of sitting in the presence of
Jolly Singh and Pilania.

The room is larger than Ombir had imagined, round
but split into two halves. A curved wall of stone lattices
encloses one side, a curved bank of glass looks out on the
garden and the carp pond. He hasn't seen a floor like this
outside of the movies—white marble, with a small fountain
in the centre. Chand raises his head, registering the play of
water and light.

Gigantic silver pitchers, enormous brass statues of gods
and goddesses and potted plants crowd the room, but
Jolly wears the simplest of clothes, a starched white kurta-
pyjama rather than the flashy suits that Ombir remembers.

Pilania says to them, 'Jolly-ji has kindly taken a personal
interest in the case.'

Jolly shrugs modestly. 'I am nobody, Pilania-ji. I have
this small farm, I have my simple business. But we are

neighbours, you see? When my staff told me about this terrible crime, I felt if only I had been here, maybe it would not have happened. When I am in residence, then the road is busy, my Delhi office sends papers back and forth, people come and go. No chance for some outsider to commit this dastardly act.'

Perhaps it's the sleeplessness, perhaps the tension of working on this case with the TV channels demanding to know every evening at prime time why the police can't solve such a simple crime. Ombir knows he shouldn't open his mouth when his superiors are talking, but can't stop himself.

'Jolly-ji, why do you think it was an outsider?'

Jolly Singh's features are prominent, the nose majestically hooked, the eyes small and close-set like an irritable elephant's, matching his bulk. He looks at Ombir for the first time, spreads his wide hands, ruby rings flashing.

'You'll know better,' he says. 'But has to be an outsider. Everyone knows Chand in these parts. Who would harm his child? And excuse my saying so, but no man from the village would have dared to commit a murder so close to my place. You have a list of suspects? That vagabond fellow—Mansoor? He's under lock-and-key?'

Pilania says, 'Yes.'

Jolly Singh says, 'Chand, could one of our own have done this? Is it even possible?'

Chand lifts his eyes from the fountain, and suddenly, they are all aware of his presence. Ombir can't meet his gaze.

He says, 'My daughter ...' Catches his breath, continues, 'For years, she has played in our fields. She has always been safe. Who would have harmed her?'

Jolly says, 'You see? Mr Pilania, I asked your men to come here, I asked my poor neighbour to come here, to assure you of one thing. Whatever help you need, I will give it. Anything your men require to solve this case, to give this grieving man here the chance of revenge on the scum who killed his daughter, ask me. I am here to help.'

The SSP says quietly, 'Justice. What we promise is justice.'

Jolly says, 'Yes, yes. I agree. But what does Chand want?'

Chand appears not to have heard the question. None of them speak as the father stares out towards the carp pond, the light, playful splash of water from the fountain the only sound in the room.

The SSP rises, hands folded, to take his leave, and Chand says, 'I want him dead. The man who took Munia from me, he should die.'

Jolly looks away, smiles at Ombir and Bhim Sain.

'These policemen are good men,' he says to Chand. 'I've seen them at work. Early morning, late at night, in summer, in the monsoons, they are out in our village, doing their jobs. I promise you, Chand, this murder will be solved. You will have your vengeance.'

Ombir notes that, this time, Pilania does not correct him or speak of justice.

⌒

At the station, the SSP goes straight to Mansoor's makeshift cell. He comes out after a few minutes.

'He's in deep sleep,' he says. 'Have you been sedating him?'

Pilania is looking directly at him, so Ombir says, 'No, sir.'

It's not a total lie. He hasn't, though he avoids Bhim Sain's eyes. They have hosted few prisoners in their makeshift jail. Drunks, and once a tractor thief, but he knows that Bhim Sain prefers to crush Valium pills into their food rather than sit in the heat listening to their racket.

'He isn't our man, Ombir. I'm as sure as I could be without forensics to back me up.'

'Sir?'

'He was on the spot, and that always makes for a strong suspect. But it's the fingerprints, the lack of them.'

'Sir, Mansoor's hands are bandaged. He has had those bandages as long as I can remember.'

'Yes, and the cloth is old and frayed in many places. I hadn't noticed at first, because it looks as though his hands are fully covered, but that's not the case. He must have been wearing that filthy gauze for months, because his skin is exposed, even some of his fingers are exposed if you look closely.'

'You feel that some fingerprints should have been captured, sir?'

'Hanging is not like other kinds of murder. It's an intimate crime. You can shoot your victim or stab her, even beat her to death without leaving a trace, but it isn't possible to leave no prints if you choose to hang a child. Is it possible that, somehow, his loose bandages were sufficient cover to prevent him from leaving absolutely no prints, none, on the rope, on the girl's dress, on her skin? Technically, I suppose so. Probable? No. And look at the man, he's a trembling wreck at the best of times.'

'Sir, I will speed up investigations.'

The SSP laughs. 'I made a few inquiries myself, searched the database. Fascinating what you can find. Did you know, for instance, that the gentleman from the factory, your child porn enthusiast, had a case of assault and molestation filed against him seven years ago?'

'The victim in that case was also a young girl?'

'Clever man. He's done something like this before?'

Ombir nods. 'I had no proof, sir. But my suspicions were strong. Child was a minor, her parents refused to file charges.'

'A man of narrow tastes. The case involved a nine-year-old girl. A year older, or possibly only a few months older, than your Munia. Her father was a local well-digger, easily pressured into dropping the charges. Dharam Bir moved to this side of the state, far enough so that the talk wouldn't follow him here. Interesting, don't you think? Though it might not matter.'

'Sir, why not? It is not evidence, but it establishes possible motive.'

'Because if Jolly Singh believes that Mansoor was responsible, soon enough everyone in Teetarpur will believe it too. I have some good news, though. Faridabad says they can accommodate our prisoner soon. A space will be available in two days.'

'Thank you, sir. The sooner we can shift Mansoor, the better.'

'I have to be in Delhi tonight, for our annual batch dinner. I'll return on the weekend. Ombir, I'm relying on you to prevent any major disturbances in the village while I'm away.'

The Three Friends

Badshah Miyan calls Rabia to ask if he can come over from Mehrauli to Bright Dairy to pick her up in his van in the morning. She accepts gratefully. It would have taken her three to four hours, changing buses, to reach Teetarpur, and it will be a relief to have the company of a friend on such a journey.

'Have you had a chance to speak to Chand?' she asks.

'No,' he says, 'Balle Ram told me he is not himself yet. And you?'

'I called him right after Balle Ram spoke to me. But Chand did not answer. He has never liked talking on the phone, and after this, I didn't think he would take the call, but I thought at least he would see my number ...'

'And mine, and maybe he would know that we were thinking of him. Yes. I did the same thing.'

She says, 'I thought at first, it can't be true. She was his whole world.'

Badshah Miyan says, 'All he spoke of these last few years was Munia's education, Munia's future, Munia's happiness. I wish I could have been there that day itself. But we can be there for him now at least. No man should go alone to collect the body of his child. I'll pick you up at seven in the morning, is that too early? The drive might take two hours, maybe a little more.'

~

Rabia had not anticipated the television vans and the jostling crews. But of course they would be parked and waiting outside Chand's hut. She and Badshah Miyan face a score of journalists with their eager faces, the photographers forming a bristling posse around them.

They cluster around, blocking her entry. Badshah Miyan mutters, 'Don't tell them we're not Hindu.' Rabia feels a familiar mixture of shame and relief. She doesn't look obviously Muslim, she and most of her neighbours can pass unremarked as women of either community, Hindu or their own. It is a convenience, sometimes a necessity, that also feels like a betrayal. She pulls the pallu of her sari—hastily bought, cheap polyester with a severe pattern of black-stemmed leaves, sombre enough for the tasks ahead—over her head as protection from the invading eyes of the cameras.

'Sir! Madam! Did you know the girl? Can you tell us about her?'

'The father, you've heard the rumour that he tried to take his life last night?'

Rabia's eyes widen, she turns towards the reporter. Badshah Miyan shakes his head, not true, don't answer, he whispers, they'll say anything to try to get you to talk. Balle Ram had warned him about the reporters, swarming thick as flies on cow dung, he'd said.

In the reptilian eye of one of the camera lenses, she sees the reflection of her face, sombre. Touched with

the unmistakeable lines of care and tiredness. A middle-
aged woman like thousands of others. Her son, Arshad,
disagrees whenever she says this—he insists his mother has
the bright eyes of a sparrow, that it makes it easy for him
to find her in a crowd.

She quickens her step, trying to avoid the young reporter,
his face flushed and eager. 'The police won't confirm, but
was the child raped before she was killed? Is it true? Are
you her aunt?'

Badshah Miyan says to the reporter and to all of them,
'Please, give us some room to breathe. Yes, you can say
we are family. We have nothing to share with you at this
moment. Thank you.'

He uses his broad shoulders to clear a path, his hand
firmly on Rabia's elbow, not allowing the reporters to yank
her away. Pushes her through the door first. She hears him
swear at a cameraman who thumps him accidentally with
a heavy lens.

At the back of the hut, Chand raises his head. Says, 'I
wasn't sure you'd be able to come all the way from Delhi
with Badshah.'

His eyes are emptier than she could have imagined, but
he manages a small smile by way of greeting. She notices
a patch of white near the corner of his mouth. His skin
would dry out like that every summer if he had not eaten
for a while or had run short of drinking water.

She says, 'I was always going to be here.'

༺ஒ༻

Badshah Miyan steps in, frowning, shuts the door firmly
and secures it with a few bricks. He goes straight to Chand

and takes his friend's hands in his own, clasps them for a moment.

'I don't know how we can get you to the car,' he says. 'Two more of those misbegotten reporters' vans have arrived. Is Balle Ram coming with us?'

'Not for this,' Chand says. 'I sent him ahead to arrange matters for the cremation. Told the other villagers to stay away. I don't want anyone else with me when we take my daughter for the final rites.'

Rabia sees the faces peering in at them through the two small windows. She wishes there was something she could use as a curtain.

Chand and Munia had no need for curtains in this place where none of their neighbours would have breached their privacy. Before Arshad's wedding the previous year, when Rabia and he made the formal visit to hand over the invitation, Chand had insisted they stay the night, wouldn't hear of them returning the same day to Delhi. The morning light had woken her, a soft awakening, the way the light used to stream in when she, Khalid and Chand had lived by the river.

'All right,' Badshah Miyan says. 'Rabia, walk between us. It'll be a job, getting through this horde. Is there a way in from the back?'

'This is the only entrance,' Chand says. 'We might as well try. No point waiting around, they're hardly going to leave on their own.'

She braces herself, but it's worse than she anticipated. The crowd of journalists has grown larger. They surge around the three friends. Someone grabs her shoulder, tugging so hard that Rabia stumbles. She feels her grip on

Chand's hand loosen, but Badshah Miyan pulls her up and Chand clasps her wrist more securely.

'That's him, that's the father!' someone yells.

They are surrounded, hemmed in so tightly that none of them can move an inch forward. A bristling forest of mikes is pointed at Chand's face. He is breathing hard. She looks up and sees him shudder, his shoulders hunched over. Badshah Miyan swears again, loudly, and one of the journalists swears back at him, and just like that, it is a melee.

'Story's gone viral,' one of the reporters says, 'get a soundbite from the father, we need him on record.' She understands that word, viral. In the village she and Khalid had left, seeking the possibilities that the capital offered, fevers that went viral were deadly; memories of the cholera plagues stretch back generations.

She feels more hands pulling at her shoulders, her waist is pressed up against the back of a sturdy photographer who is expostulating with the crowd. 'Let them go, boys,' he says, and she realises that there are only one or two women among the throng of reporters, and that the fear she sees on their faces must be reflected on her own. She is not that short, but the men crowd in on her relentlessly. They are shouting their questions, pushing Chand and Badshah Miyan. Chand loses his grip on her hand, and suddenly, she is on her own, the men half-carried away from her. A flashbulb goes off in her face, blinding her briefly.

Rabia can't see clearly. But she hears the shot. Unmistakeable, the sound of a gunshot.

She whispers a prayer, a mindless prayer, not couched in formal language. Please, whatever has happened, spare

Chand, keep him safe. A space clears, the pushing and shoving stops.

Rabia breaks free of the crowd. Her vision swims back. The journalists are sprinting to their vans and cars. A tall, stocky man in an expensive grey suit stands on the road, rage darkening his face. His arm is raised, in the fashion of public statues at highway roundabouts, and he has a revolver in his hand, aimed at the sky.

'You bastards think this is your father's backyard? You can do anything you want? Slinking into our village like jackals, what is this behaviour?'

He fires another shot into the air. The last remaining journalists speed up, clearing the path before them.

Badshah Miyan says, 'It's your neighbour, Chand, the rich guy who owns half of Teetarpur. Does he always walk around with a loaded gun?'

Chand says, 'Yes, that's him, but I did not expect such drama. You're not hurt, Rabia?'

She shakes her head, no. Jolly Singh comes over to them, slipping the revolver into his waistband.

'My manager told me that these fuckers were crawling all over the place,' he says, then glances at Rabia. 'Okay, sorry for the language, Chand. But I can't stand journalists, swarming like cockroaches. They shouldn't have been allowed to come here. Ombir and Bhim Sain should have put a stop to it.'

'It's all right,' Chand says. 'Thank you for your help, Jolly-ji.'

Badshah Miyan says, 'We'd better get Chand out of here before those haramzadas catch their breath. They'll try to follow us, and my Maruti van can't handle fancy car chases.'

'Oh no,' Jolly says. 'They won't follow you. I'll make sure they don't.'

They climb into the van, Chand and Badshah Miyan in front, Rabia at the back. The seats smell of new plastic, and faintly, of meat deliveries. Their destination is some way off. Badshah Miyan had told her they'd take close to an hour to get to the morgue.

His eyes are on the rear-view mirror as he starts up the engine. 'Your neighbour believes in full action, Chand,' he says. 'I wouldn't bet twenty rupees on his sanity, he's not even a half-crack, he's one fully crack person, but he does know how to deal with this scum.'

The van pulls out onto the road. The sound of three quick gunshots fills the air, and Rabia ducks involuntarily. When she looks back, she sees Jolly standing in the middle of the road. The journalists are cowering inside their vans. He is taking out the tyres of each van, one by one. He takes aim at another tyre and they hear a fourth gunshot. She watches as the vans and the journalists grow more distant. Jolly Singh reloads his revolver. He waves at them, bullets clutched in his plump palm.

The House of the Living

The air in the van fills with the delicate fragrance of white lotus, startling Rabia for a moment. It comes back to her; she had placed two small bottles of attar in her bag on top of the other things they might need. The sandalwood was securely stoppered, but the tiny gold cap on the other blue vial must have shaken loose. Her aunt used to say that when the farishtey come for the souls of the newly dead, they announce their presence through perfume, a divine scent released for those who have left the earth with their souls and hearts still touched by the purity allotted to all humans at birth.

The scent reaches Chand. Neither she nor Badshah Miyan have said much on the way, out of respect for his silence. He rubs the back of his neck, his usual way of shrugging off fatigue, and says, 'Badshah Miyan, could you stop here for a minute?'

They have almost reached. A signboard says, baldly, 'This way to the house of the dead.' Chand takes five minutes to comb his hair and brush the road dust off his white kurta. He pours water out of Badshah Miyan's flask and rough-scrubs his face.

He looks at his two old friends, says, 'I am prepared to
see her now.'

～

He is not prepared. None of them is prepared. Rabia stares
at the broken slabs of cheap, stained yellow marble, the
rubble in the corners, while Badshah Miyan argues with
the two youths who appear to have been left in charge
of this morose place. The walls, distended from water
seepage, bulge outwards, plaster collecting in swollen
tumours. The filing cabinets, lined up in a row in the next
room, puzzle her. They seem much larger than any she
has seen in government offices in Delhi. She glimpses a
broom, propped up on one of the discoloured slabs inside
the other room, hears the rattle of a steel drawer, and
understands what the cabinets contain.

'Can't help you,' one of the young men says. He wears
his hair in a crude mohawk, never raises his eyes from
the screen of his phone, on which a dance video plays.
'Doctor's not here. Wait until he returns.'

'How long will he take?'

'Can't say. He has done his morning rounds. Maybe he'll
be back, maybe he won't. Usually, he doesn't come back in
the afternoons, but you can return tomorrow morning. Or
wait like the rest.'

'Listen,' Badshah Miyan says. 'This man has lost his
daughter, all right? The cremation is planned for today.'

'Everyone who comes here has lost someone,' the youth
mutters. 'Nothing special about people dying, they do it
every day.'

Badshah Miyan leans over the desk, places his hand
over the phone screen.

'What the fuck are you doing, boss?' the other youth says, standing up and glaring at Badshah Miyan.

'My job and your job are the same,' he says. 'I work with meat too. All day long, I deal with the dead, in my own fashion. The difference between us is that I have not lost my humanity. You know that word? Humanity? What the fuck is wrong with you two that you have no respect for the grief of a father who had his daughter snatched away from him by a murderer?'

'Achha, murder,' the youth says, his tone turning conciliatory. 'Why didn't you say so before? Parshu, take their details.'

Parshu puts his phone down. 'Okay, okay, this is the case that they were showing on television. I remember now. They've caught the murderer?'

'Yes,' Badshah Miyan says. 'He's in custody.'

'No rape,' Parshu says, addressing Chand directly. 'I did the autopsy myself.'

Chand flinches.

'You're a doctor?' Badshah Miyan says.

'No, I'm the refrigerator technician. It's a difficult job. Electricity here, you know what it's like. Comes and goes, comes and goes. But we have a good contact for ice, we manage. The doctor—he doesn't like that part of the job, touching the bodies, who knows who comes from where, so he trained us to do the work. He signs the certificates, let me see—yes, it's done. You're extremely lucky, sometimes people have to wait for a few days if the load is too heavy. Last week, there was a road accident, near the canal, and everything got backed up for days.'

'Can I see my daughter?' Chand says.

Parshu nods. 'Why not, why not? You have the police letter?'

Badshah Miyan and Rabia exchange a dismayed glance.

Parshu says, 'We can't release the body without police permission, no? It's a murder case. Actually, the police should have accompanied you, that's the usual procedure.'

'Can't you do something?' Badshah Miyan says. 'It's a long distance from his home, and his family are waiting at the cremation ground. Come on, boys, you two look like you have a heart, and you're in charge of this place, aren't you?'

Parshu confers with his colleague, and they both shake their heads. 'Nothing we can do without the proper permissions. But he and his wife, they can go in and see the body. It's in the cold room.'

Rabia glances at Chand. When he doesn't correct their mistake, she says nothing either.

Badshah Miyan says, 'No problem. I will return to Teetarpur and get the proper papers. It won't take long, I know the route now.'

Outside, a motorcycle draws up, the thud of its heavy engine cutting out slowly. When the two young men see Ombir, they stand up respectfully, and Parshu makes a fumbling attempt at a salute.

'I would have accompanied you,' Ombir says to Chand. 'But you had already left by the time I reached your home.'

Badshah Miyan introduces himself, and Rabia turns away from the men, leaving them to handle the formalities.

Chand is by her side. He says, 'Come with me.'

∽

She steps away from the other slabs, not wanting to look too closely at the unknown body in the corner, laid out like a heap of washing.

Parshu catches up with them. He has lost his air of indifference and speaks quietly.

'It is strange for everyone at first, though we've grown used to it. People call this the house of the dead, but for me, it is not a dead place at all. Some of the people who're brought in have no family. But most do. Day in day out, sister, we see one thing only. Whatever troubles people may have had, whatever faults or fights the dead may have had, once they are gone, everyone laments. Okay, almost everyone, some don't, but mostly, people break down, they cry, they are so filled with sadness that their tears flow in rivers. And where there are tears, there must be love in their hearts, isn't that the truth? So, this is not the house of the dead. They should have another sign put up, I would, if I was in charge. It would say, Welcome to the House of the Living.'

The slow, heavy rattle of the steel drawer. The smell of formaldehyde, and mould from the walls, strong in her nostrils.

Chand says, 'No, this is not her. Where is my daughter?'

Rabia knows what to do. She takes his hand, forcing him to meet her gaze.

'This is your girl, Chand,' she says gently. 'This is your Munia.'

He doesn't break down. He doesn't weep.

'I brought some clothes, a dress, a few other things,' she says. 'We can't take her back home because of the television crews. Parshu, if there is a small space, anywhere private, I'll take care of the rest.'

Parshu says, 'Yes, there is a room at the side. Small maintenance fee is there, okay?'

'Maintenance fees, after all that fine talk about the house of the living,' Badshah Miyan says, but stops Chand from fumbling in his pocket, slips the man a few Gandhis.

Chand waits in the cold room with Badshah Miyan. Parshu's stream of talk has dwindled, and the men say nothing. In a deep crack in the wall, a spider skitters, carrying a tiny, bundled fly across to a safer place.

When she brings the child back, Chand cannot wrench his gaze away from his daughter.

He says, 'Oh, my Munia. My beloved girl.'

Chand is like stone through all that follows. He mumbles his thanks to them, and to Ombir, but never takes his gaze off Munia, his eyes hard and dry through the drive to the crematorium, through the rituals, the mechanical droning of the pundit, through the cremation, until the moment when the fire finally blazes up, sparks scattering from the wood.

❧

Rabia and Badshah Miyan stay the night, but the next morning, Chand persuades his friends to return to Delhi. They have their own families and lives to tend. He does not want company.

On the road outside his home, afterwards, he hears Balle Ram uneasily greeting a camera crew.

They won't leave Chand alone.

'Was it here?' someone asks. A few of the villagers shake their heads, no, point to the field that Chand has not entered after he came back home. The crew, tramping through his land, his fields, without permission, their tripods sinking into the furrows as they struggle to set up.

Chand raises his head, listens as the cameras start rolling. 'Tragedy in the quiet village of ...' '... as more and more Delhi residents flee to the outskirts to escape pollution, returning to a life of the land, ugly reality intrudes on their dreams ... a young girl, her life cut short by ...'

Sarita Devi is answering their questions. Did she play here? Were these her toys? Why was she alone?

A tiny bomb of rage and pain explodes in his chest.

Because this was her home, he says silently to the television people.

Because Balle Ram's family was close by, and Munia could call out to them for help, which she only needed when she had climbed too recklessly, stranded herself on a high branch like a kitten, waiting for the rescue which would always come.

Because she'd always been secure here, away from the city's dangers. Every child knew that the daylight hours were theirs. The peacocks and monkeys would not harm them. The only fear, a minor one, was of snakes when they came out from their holes in the monsoons, seeking shelter.

Their voices are growing louder, harder to ignore, as the camera approaches, pans to take in shots of her sandals, their cooking utensils outside, near the brass tap. '...raises the urgent question, are India's girls ever safe? If a young girl, not even nine, is hanged from a tree right outside her village home where she was born and lived all her life, a village right near the planned Forest Dreams Villa project, what hope is there for us? Today, a simple farmer is left grieving; tomorrow, it could be one of you.'

Anger is good, anger is better than the heaviness he has been carrying. He lets it flare as the crew enters without asking for permission. They politely remove their shoes, the anchor's expression of concern and refracted sorrow perhaps even genuine. He looks up as they fold their hands, show respect for his state of bereavement.

'... Sorry for your tremendous loss ... if you have something you'd like to share with our viewers at this time ... heard that you brought your daughter up after her mother's death, you were mother and father both to her ...'

He raises his head, finally. Keeps the anger simmering in his heart but out of his voice.

'Have you ever lost someone you loved? Any of you?'

The team look at one another, the cameraman pauses in his recording of the girl's exercise books from school; the almost bare shelves; the precious hoard of glossy seeds and birds' feathers she had collected on her excursions; the small canisters that held tea, sugar, dal, bajra; the painted wooden mirror that she had held up every morning to his face so that its round surface contained both of them, father and daughter; a brightly coloured picture of mountains torn from a magazine, the ragged edges pinned to the rough plaster; the clean mud floor where she had helped her aunt lay down a fresh coating of gobar at the start of summer.

'After their funerals, did anyone come to your home, turn a camera on, and ask you how you felt? For their viewers? No? I didn't think so. Maybe you're only doing your job. But what kind of job have you chosen? What job is this that tells you to walk into a man's home when a death is still fresh? To take photos of her footwear, her books?'

They are backing out, apologising. He follows them, feeling the life-giving surge of anger pounding in his blood, wanting to stay on his feet. Otherwise, he'll turn his face to the wall and close his eyes, never open them again.

He has been more than a simple farmer. He has seen the world, been out in the world. Been a truck mechanic, a construction worker, a road builder, a part-time driver, a butcher. His daughter was born in a big city. She had been given life first by one woman, then another. Their lives could not be folded down so neatly, he wanted to tell the television people, not into these bloodless sentences, all the marrow sucked out of their experiences.

'Here,' he says. 'You want to show something to your viewers, show them this.' Picks up a yellow plastic sack, its fibres woven to resemble jute. The cameraman continues to film him, coming in for a close-up.

Chand opens the mouth of the sack, fetches out a handful of grey ashes from the brass urn inside. 'My girl. My daughter. Here she is. Record this, no? Had enough? Seen enough?' Unclenches his hand, lets the ashes flow into the sack, spilling over the lip of the urn. His palm as gritty as his aching eyes, the anger ebbing as suddenly as it had risen. He is left weak and empty without its bright fire in the wake of their departure.

The silence and the darkness grow as, one by one, the huts further down shutter their doors and their occupants snuff out the kerosene lamps. The night orchestra of crickets starts up, loud and insistent. Chand lies awake, staring at the thatch.

Good Arrangements

After the cremation, Ombir gets back to the station house and returns to his notes. Dharam Bir has produced an alibi, a tricky one to counter. One of the local dancers is ready to swear that he had gone to her quarters that day. As easy to take payment for a lie as for sex, to Ombir's mind, but it will be hard to disprove. He riffles through some of the forms that have piled up while he was busy with the investigation. His head throbs. A mountain of paperwork stands between him and the now urgent need for rest and sleep.

Bhim Sain and he should go back to the factory. Or perhaps he should go on his own, take a look around, talk to people who know Dharam Bir. He closes his eyes, just for a second.

And then Bhim Sain shakes him awake. Ombir touches the side of his face, feeling the mesh pattern imprinted on his skin by the fly swatter. The hazards of falling asleep at your desk.

'Sir, we have one more problem.'

He raises his head from the desk, his spine on fire. 'Now what?'

'The women are outside, sir. They say they won't leave until we hand Mansoor over to them.'

❧

The first of the pre-monsoon winds stirs the dust in the courtyard outside the police station. The women have gathered in front of the door. Sarita Devi sits in front, the pradhan's formidable wife by her side. The wind picks up speed. The drapes of the women's saris and lehengas flutter like a battalion's flags, screaming pinks and yellows, burnt orange and incendiary blues, deep-dyed ominous reds. Their silence worries Ombir, far more than if they were raising slogans or shouting.

Two days. That's all he needs, only two days, and they can get Mansoor out of here. It won't be his headache any more.

Bhim Sain says, 'Shall I order them to disperse?'

'No. I'll handle it.'

He steps out, sits cross-legged on the ground facing them, and waits.

They stir, whisper among themselves.

Finally, Sarita Devi speaks. 'Give him to us.'

He folds his hands respectfully. 'If it was up to me, he would have been in your hands on the first day itself. But I cannot release him without the approval of SSP Pilania and my superiors in Faridabad, in Delhi, much as I would like to.'

The pradhan's wife, Bimala Devi, says, 'This SSP–superiors business, we don't know anything about that. They are outsiders, they don't understand our ways. You told Balle Ram you wanted a week. That week is over, and it is time for us to decide what to do with this filth.'

'The law will decide, not any of us. We are not outsiders, sister. Bhim Sain's village is close enough, my in-laws live three villages away. We are on your side, but it is not in our power to release a prisoner after a case has been registered. You know that. All of you understand that we can't do as you ask. But I promise you, justice will be done.'

Sarita Devi says, 'The law, the law, what will we get from the law? I read newspapers, I'm not illiterate. The case will drag on in the courts for how many years? Five, ten, twenty? How long will Chand have to wait for this famous justice you promise? Already people are saying Mansoor will not hang because the crime was not so violent. The television crews are packing up and driving back to Delhi. What justice is this where a murderer lives comfortably in his cell while we die a little every day? Fetch him out, or I will go in and get him myself.'

'The SSP is returning tomorrow. Meet him and make your request. I also saw Munia every day, I also feel anger. It is not that our hearts are so hard. But before you go in—and you will have to get past Bhim Sain and me, I cannot stand around like a two-day-old calf while you break the law—let me ask you one thing. Are you so sure that Mansoor is the murderer? If you were aware there is another suspect, would you still go in? Or would you wait and let us do our job?'

'Another suspect? What new story is this?' Bimala Devi says.

It's an opportunity, and he seizes it.

'Bimala Devi, I am on duty. I am in my uniform, and this is a police station, not some chai shop. It's very serious to suggest to a policeman on duty that he is making something up.'

'I didn't mean ...' she says, wavering.

He sees a flash of doubt on Sarita Devi's face, doesn't let Bimala Devi complete her sentence. 'But you said it. You are all reasonable people. You know that neither Bhim Sain nor I can reveal details of the investigation before it is done. Will you trust me? We have to complete our work. Will you give us the time we need? Just let us finish, then you can do whatever you want. But don't take your anger out on the wrong man.'

For a moment he thinks he has won, then Sarita Devi shakes her head.

'Chand found Mansoor,' she says. 'Right there. That's enough for me. Will you give me the keys, or shall we break the door down ourselves?'

Ombir catches the sound.

'Wait,' he says.

Ombir has never been so relieved to hear a car coming down the empty road. He shades his eyes, staring in the direction of the sun. His spirits lift as he recognises Jolly Singh's Jaguar. The white dust swirls in tiny spouts, funnelling towards them, and Jolly steps out, crisp in his safari suit, wiping his dark glasses clean, Balle Ram behind him.

He nods politely at Ombir, says, 'All right. Bring him out.'

Bhim Sain looks at Ombir. It's his call.

'Sir, I cannot do that without the SSP's permission.'

Jolly looks around at the crowd, raises his voice. 'There will be no violence. No one will harm the man. Is that clear? I have your word?'

Silence, the women's eyes blazing with anger.

Finally, Sarita Devi nods. 'Yes, Jolly-ji. If you say so.'

'Ombir Singh, a request to you, a personal request. There are two kinds of justice, you know? The law is one kind. But the village has its own ways. If I give you my word that the murderer—'

'The prisoner,' Ombir says evenly.

'—the prisoner, if you wish, okay, that the prisoner will not be harmed, will you permit us to talk to him? I only want to ask him a few questions. Bhim Sain, please, bring him before us.'

He can make an enemy of Jolly Singh or make an enemy of the village, but not both, he can't afford that. And Jolly is too shrewd to allow open violence.

Ombir gives in reluctantly. 'Bring him out.'

⌒

Mansoor wishes they would stop talking to him so loudly. It bewilders him, scares him. When too many people surround him and talk to him, it makes his head hurt, his breath shorten.

That day in his village, three years ago, they had surrounded him. He had looked up impatiently from turning the claw feet of an imitation antique wooden bed, wondering why these strangers had come into his workshop.

'What can I do for you?' he had asked courteously.

His eyes ache from the sunlight. He is squatting on the ground, can feel the firm grip of someone's hands on his shoulders. Mansoor doesn't mind that so much, but he wishes they wouldn't shout. They are arguing, the crowd is growing, and he hunches lower as hands reach out to push him, as feet move too close.

He looks up, sweat and tears streaking a path through the dust on his face. The policemen, Jolly Singh and Balle

Ram are approaching. His fear forms a tight knot in his stomach.

'Bastard,' Balle Ram says. 'Why did you do it? Tell me that, haramzada, just tell me why you did it, that's all I want from you.'

The words take a while to reach him. Then he says, slowly, 'But I didn't do it. It wasn't me. Someone else must have.'

Balle Ram slaps Mansoor so hard he can hear the ringing in his head. He would have fallen over, but he is held up by many hands, and it triggers memories, swimming out of the darkness like malevolent fish. He starts to cry, the way he had when he had seen the poor child. He had been walking through the grove, his head down, the sweat trickling off his shaved head, and what caught his attention was her feet, the black string knotted around her ankle for good luck, the small silver snake-shaped ring around her second toe. He looked at her feet for a long while, dazed, unable to make sense of what he was seeing.

'You lying bastard,' Balle Ram says. 'How long did you watch her, you fucker? I used to see you walking on that side, mumbling your nonsense, and all the time, this is what you were planning?'

Mansoor feels the slap again, he feels something twang and sting, a bone in his nose, the sharp metallic taste of blood in his mouth.

'No,' he mumbles. He turns away from Balle Ram. 'Please, I didn't do it, I looked up and she was there. That poor little one ...'

Balle Ram raises his hand and Ombir says, 'Enough.'

Mansoor Khan closes his eyes, thinks of his home, his own daughter, running around barefoot, smelling often of wood shavings because she loved playing where he worked. And the day it changed.

The sound of a man screaming. 'This is what we do to bastards like you,' someone says. Pushed out into the light, blinking from the sun. The men kicking him into the street have their cell phones out. He feels his ribs snap. More screams. Dust on the ground blurring his vision. Someone is asking for water. He feels a patch of damp spreading under his back. Not his blood. The other man's blood. He turns his head. It looks like a bundle, a pile of clothes. The raised blade of an axe. The man groaning, 'Kill me, but give me water first.'

'Not a drop,' a voice says. 'We're not wasting water on you haramzadas. Okay, wait, focus is shaky. Yes. Fixed it. You can start now.' The axe, coming down. Again and again. The pile of rags jerking in the air. Then the screams stop. 'Bring in the next one.' Someone grabs his hair, turns his head roughly the other way. 'No,' he tries to say, but something is stuffed in his mouth. A shit-smeared rag. The stench, sickening. Gagging, trying and failing to spit it out. Then he sees her, understands who 'the next one' is. In his head, he is screaming at the top of his lungs, silent screams that no one can hear, as they drag his seven-year-old daughter out of the workshop into the street.

They left him and the others alive. Not as witnesses, none of them would dare to talk to the press, to file a case in the courts, but because they were not worth the trouble of killing.

❧

Jolly walks up to Mansoor, inspects the rips in his kurta, the bruises blooming on his face where Balle Ram hit him.

'Give him some water,' he says. 'Take it from my car. Balle Ram, you must remember that he won't be able to talk if you beat him so badly.'

He turns to Ombir, addressing him with respect. 'If I can ask him some questions? We are on the same side, no? It's my duty to assist you?'

Ombir says, 'Yes, Jolly-ji.'

Jolly says, 'Mansoor, do you often take that road? Don't worry, speak freely. No one here will harm you. All we are trying to do is understand what happened.'

Mansoor Khan stares at him.

'The track past Balle Ram's house,' Jolly repeats, his voice patient. 'Did you take that road often?'

Mansoor Khan tries to concentrate. 'Sometimes I go along the canal. I like the sound of the water.'

'It's a shorter route to Teetarpur town if you take the canal. Why did you take this road the day Munia was murdered?'

Mansoor Khan tries to focus.

'I don't remember.'

'Think, see if it comes back to you?'

Shakes his head, his eyes blank.

'All right. Did you see anyone else?'

'No. There was no one else.'

'There was no one else on the road outside?'

'Didn't see anyone.'

'Did you like Munia?'

Mansoor brightens. 'Yes,' he says. 'She ran around, she climbed trees. She didn't say much, but I used to like watching her.'

'You used to watch her?'

The crowd stirs, but Jolly Singh holds a hand up, silences their murmurs.

'When I was crossing that way.'

'You said you didn't go there often.'

'I didn't, only sometimes.'

'Sometimes, or often? Looks like you knew Munia well.'

'I saw the child sometimes.'

'That day, what did you say to Munia?'

Mansoor, bewildered. 'I didn't say anything to her. I looked up, and the little one was there, the life gone from her.'

'No, what did you say to her before she was hanged?'

The carpenter looks from Jolly to Ombir, puzzled.

'People I've spoken to tell me you often forget things. Is that correct?'

'Yes, my mind doesn't work so well. Sometimes the fog comes down and I can't remember.'

'Do you remember talking to Munia?'

Mansoor hesitates. 'I talked to her?'

'Have you forgotten?'

'I don't know. I forget so many things these days. Did I talk to her?'

'It doesn't matter. What did she say to you?'

'Nothing, I saw her feet—so small, and she was already—' His voice shaking as he remembers.

Jolly says, 'Not after. What did she say to you before she was hanged?'

Mansoor Khan says, 'She said nothing.'

'You came up to her and she said nothing?'

Mansoor, confused, says, 'She didn't say anything to me.'

Jolly says, to the men at large, 'So you did go up to her.'

Mansoor fumbles, tries to explain, 'She was already—I saw her in the tree—'

'And when you saw her in the tree, how did you feel? Horrified at what had happened?'

'Yes, I couldn't believe it.'

'You couldn't believe that she was dead?'

'Couldn't believe it. Tried to take the noose off the little one's neck.'

'You tried to undo what you'd done.'

'I didn't do anything. I tried to take the rope off.'

'Weren't you startled when you saw her? Why didn't you call out to Balle Ram? Why didn't you run to the house?'

Mansoor Khan brushes dried blood from his chin, stumbles into an explanation.

'I wasn't expecting—I saw her feet. So thin. My daughter, she used to climb trees too. They dragged her out. There was a riot. They brought her out of my workshop. Then she screamed, my daughter, she was so pretty, she was like Chand's daughter. I would never ...'

He closes his eyes. It's happening all over again. The mob. The sound of cloth tearing. Her hands reaching for him, before they pick up their axes, bring out the knives.

The women, silent, listening.

Jolly says, 'Chand's daughter reminded you of your own daughter.'

Behind Ombir, Balle Ram says with conviction, 'He's mad. He saw her and it sent him crazy.'

Jolly kneels beside Mansoor Khan, touching his shoulder, soothing him.

Asks, his voice gentle, 'You touched the girl?'

Mansoor Khan says, 'Yes, I wanted to bring her down. From the tree.'

'What did you do to Chand's daughter?'

Khan looks past them, returning to another time, another place.

'I lost her. She would have been alive today,' he says to everyone. 'If it hadn't been for me, she would still be alive.'

He starts to weep like a child, tears and blood dampening the collar of his shirt. Jolly stands up, triumphant, and Ombir Singh takes over.

Balle Ram says, 'Chand is exhausted from yesterday. He is resting, or else we would do it now.'

'Let Ombir and Bhim Sain take him back to his cell. He's in police custody, he won't go anywhere tonight. You please come with me in the car. I'll explain everything,' Jolly says.

He steers Balle Ram into the back of the car, murmuring his explanations. He has rolled down the windows. His words flutter into the heat, taken away by the wind.

⁓

The glare of the late evening sun hits the walls, the old blue bricks flaring into sudden beauty. A thin line of men at work seem like distant ants silhouetted against the arhar fields. They stand out against the treeless horizon, the dust and sunlight dappling them golden, like figures out of a myth. The black sparrows rise up, squabbling and complaining, over the low wall of the mandir that separates the thana from the vacant plot at the back, sown with wild, straggling stands of kadhbathua. A thirsty coppersmith calls plaintively from the cattle pond.

When Jolly returns, he is alone. He mops the sweat from his forehead with a handkerchief, crumpling it into a ball and shoving it into his pocket carelessly.

'Ombir, can we talk in private?'

The men walk outside and Jolly speaks for a while. Ombir listens and then finally nods. He can see no other way out, not after Mansoor's confession.

'I'll arrange it, Jolly-ji,' he says.

'Manage it right and there'll be no trouble,' Jolly says. 'Riots and unchecked mobs, they can damage your record. But if you make the right preparations, there'll be no tension and the papers will ask no questions. You can trust me. I'll personally speak to the SSP, and I have a few friends in the Delhi Police. I promise I'll tell them how well you handled this matter.'

Ombir walks to the car to see him off.

'You'll go far in life, Ombir,' Jolly says in parting. 'You make good arrangements.'

After Jolly Singh leaves, Ombir goes once more to the storeroom. He opens the outer glass windows to let in some air, checks the high bars, pats Mansoor Khan several times on the cheek, tenderly, as though he truly is a small child. But Mansoor has slipped into an exhausted sleep, so deep that he doesn't wake up.

Ombir Singh pulls the heavy wooden door closed. He runs the bolt across. Then he rummages in the wooden cupboard until he finds a cracked black plastic jar, full, kerosene spilling from its spout. He carries it outside, places it by the door of the storeroom. Next to it, a hurricane lantern, a packet of Bimco Cycle safety matches.

In the station diary, he makes a note that will cover the hours between midnight and the next morning: 'No disturbances.'

Then he sends Bhim Sain off to Lovely Bhojanalaya to get some proper rest for the night. An hour later, he quietly shuts the station house. He bolts this door too, but doesn't lock it.

Ombir walks some distance to a friend's field and settles down on the charpai outside his home, the stars casting their warm light on him. It isn't an ideal situation, but he's a pragmatic man. The murderer has confessed, the matter is out of his hands. He looks at his list of suspects, the notes he had compiled on Dharam Bir's movements and history, and puts them in his pocket, to be added to the working file later. He won't be needing them any more.

～

The men return after midnight. Mansoor is awake. The drugs are wearing off, though he is still groggy. He hears the scrape of the station-house door and raises his head.

Balle Ram and Chand are there, and Dilshad. They lift Mansoor with care, bring him out into the open. His legs are not functioning properly. He stumbles from time to time, once against Chand, who puts a guiding hand on his shoulder, helps him up again. There is something he wants to say, but he can't remember what it is.

'Can I have some water?' he asks when they reach the end of the field.

Balle Ram says, 'There's none here,' and he accepts that. But Chand says, 'It can wait.'

Dilshad is sent off, and Mansoor breathes in the warm air, looks up at the brightness of the many stars, the slivered yellow moon. His mind steadies. He sees the axe in Balle Ram's hand, the heavy wooden staff that Chand carries.

'I know why you're here,' he says to Chand.

Balle Ram says, 'Shut your mouth.'

But this is important to him. The rolling fog that blanks his mind is lifting. 'It doesn't matter what you believe. Your girl, she was the same age as mine, maybe a bit older. That's why I liked coming this way, Chand. I liked to watch her because she reminded me of my daughter.'

Balle Ram raises his axe, but Chand says, 'Let him finish.'

A fleeting smile touches Mansoor's bruised face. 'What does it matter now? Nothing matters. Chand, I didn't hurt her, I didn't lay a hand on your daughter. I would never have harmed her. We are both fathers. We have both lost what we loved most. But you don't have to believe me. It's all right.'

Dilshad returns with a jerrycan of water. Chand takes it from him, holds it out to Mansoor.

He tries to rise, but Balle Ram pushes him roughly back on the ground.

'Stay where you are,' Balle Ram says. 'Don't even imagine you can run away from us.'

'I wasn't going to run,' Mansoor says. 'It's my arms. The old weakness. Can't reach up that high.'

Balle Ram laughs.

'Acting won't help you. I told Chand everything you said to Jolly-ji today. What is to happen will happen, Mansoor. This drama doesn't impress us.'

'Wait,' says Chand. He looks at Mansoor's hunched figure, searches the man's tired eyes, moves closer to him, holding the jerrycan high so he will have to stretch for it, but within reach.

'Now try.'

The three men watch as Mansoor slowly raises his arms as far as they will go. His fingers uncurl, the bandages trailing as he attempts to reach the jerrycan. He can't. His arms will not rise above his shoulders.

'More acting!' Dilshad says in disgust. He roughly pushes Mansoor's arms up, grasping him below the armpits. But the man's arms are limp. When Dilshad lets go, they fall like the limbs of a tree when they are broken, attached only by peeling strips of bark.

Balle Ram starts to say something, but Chand silences his brother with a touch on the wrist.

'How long has it been this way, Mansoor?'

'That mob in my village,' he says. 'I don't know. Three years, maybe four this year. They kept beating me. My back, my arms. I couldn't raise my hands to help her. Then they took her. They took my girl.'

Chand sits down next to Mansoor. Gestures to him to lean back, pours water from the jerrycan into the man's parched mouth. He lets Mansoor drink his fill.

He says to his brother and Dilshad, 'I'll do the rest. Give me the axe.'

Balle Ram hovers.

'Go home. Both of you. Take the kerosene and the stacks of wood over to the old well. Leave them at the edge, I'll manage it.'

When his brother doesn't move, Chand says, 'This is my business to end, Balle Ram.'

'He has the right,' Dilshad says. Raises his camera. Takes a few rapid shots, click-click-click, of Mansoor and Chand, then he and Balle Ram leave.

The two men sit in silence, listening to the cicadas, the far-off throb of a tractor engine suddenly puttering into life.

'Are you tired?' Chand says to Mansoor.

'No. I'm at peace. Do what you have to, I'm ready.'

'Come.'

He takes a coil of rope, ties Mansoor's unprotesting hands together at the wrists. Leads him like a calf to the far end of the fields, to the unused, ancient well, so deep that it would take a man an hour, or more, to descend the pitted iron rungs all the way to the bottom.

'Here?' says Mansoor.

'Yes, at the edge. Sit, and lay your head flat along the stones. Do you want another drink of water?'

He realises he has left the jerrycan behind as he speaks, but Mansoor says, 'No, Chand. I am not thirsty.'

'All right,' Chand says. 'All right.'

He glances back. His brother and Dilshad are dim shapes in the dark, standing at the back door of the thana.

Chand unties the cord around the stacks of wood, keeps them ready. He lines up the tins of kerosense, the matches. Mansoor watches, his eyes glazed and peaceful.

'Don't raise your head,' Chand says. 'Lie still and look there, at the twisted babul tree, all the way across those fields. Can you see it?'

'Yes, Chand.'

'Good.'

He stands over Mansoor. Balle Ram and Dilshad are now faint shapes in the doorway. He gestures to Balle Ram, you can leave, it's all right. He waits, listening to the sound of their footsteps trudging away.

Chand says to Mansoor, 'Take your coat off, the collar is too thick. It will get in the way.'

He has to help the man. From the worn black woollen coat, two buttons dangling by their threads, the warm smell of Mansoor's body, unwashed but not yet pungent, rises between them. Chand waits until Mansoor has laid his head down again, then he folds the black coat, places it on the stone rim of the old well.

'Chand?' Mansoor says. His voice is soft, almost boyish.

'Don't speak,' Chand says. 'Keep your eyes closed.'

A dull sound. It is easy, clean, almost done. Only a few minor things to take care of; he works with precision. The doorway of the distant thana is empty. Balle Ram and Dilshad have left.

Down in the heart of the well, the wood finally catches, woodsmoke and kerosene fumes mingle. He is almost free. He has one last matter to sort out, then he can leave Teetarpur in peace.

Inside the Well

Ombir expected SSP Pilania to be thorough. He does not disappoint, goes through the prepared report with care, ignores the flaming high-noon heat as they walk to the well.

'Excellent report, Ombir,' the officer says, kneeling on the stone rim, his gaze fixed on the heap of ashes and the rubble of stones piled far down below. 'No detail omitted. Tragic but understandable that a man might go out of his mind with remorse after killing an innocent child in a fit of mental absence.'

Sweat pools under Ombir's collar. He glances at the SSP, relieved to see that the officer is not quite Superman. He perspires as well.

'It is also,' the SSP continues, 'entirely conceivable that he might have taken advantage of the precise hour—one hour, you mention in your extremely thorough report—when Bhim Sain was making a fine repast at Lovely Bhojanalaya, and you happened to be called away to a case of suspected theft, to return to his senses, make a cunning and indeed quite commendable escape. I see that he broke the door hinges? Indeed. The man was a carpenter after all, as you so helpfully point out.'

Ombir waits. He knows it's coming. First the honey, then the sting of red chilli, black pepper, can hear it in Pilania's smooth voice.

'Refresh my memory, Ombir, if you please. So, our man, recovering the faculties of his wandering mind, wakes up in the middle of the night, overcome by remorse after making a public confession. He breaks down the door of his cell. Staggers out into the sweltering summer night. Commits suicide by unknown means. Would he leap into the well, trusting that the fall is sufficient? Does he theatrically slit his wrists before he takes that final plunge, just to make sure? A waste of a life, but from our perspective—problem solved, case closed. Are these rungs safe?'

'Pilania sir, we have not tried them. You should not take such a big risk.'

But the SSP produces a coil of rope from his shoulder pouch, ties it around his waist, hands the end to Ombir.

'You can use that to haul me back, should such an undignified ascent become necessary.'

'Sir, please let me go into the well. Only tell me what is required.'

'Brave man, and I'm touched by your offer. But you wouldn't know what I'm looking for,' the SSP says, disappearing from view so rapidly that Ombir blinks.

The sun's glare directly hits the brickwork of the well. Inside, inky shadows obscure the SSP's form once he has climbed down ten rungs. Ombir can hear his deliberate, careful tread, the clink of his belt buckle from time to time on the rungs. After what feels like a long time, the SSP's voice floats up.

'It's rotten from here on,' he calls. 'The rungs crumble if you touch them. Can't climb down any further. I'm not yet at the halfway mark, but close. My torch—found it.'

The ghostly play of light on the mossy smooth stones of the well. Ombir grips the rope, secures it methodically under several bricks. He's sweating freely, his undershirt soaked through, not entirely because of the heat. It seems to take an age before he hears the sound of the SSP's returning footsteps. He tightens his hold on the rope, but it isn't necessary. Pilania balances for a second, one foot on the pitted rung, one on the arris of a brick, and swings back up, taking Ombir's outstretched hand to steady himself.

'Remarkable creations, these old wells,' the SSP says, brushing off the dust and moss that fingerprint his khaki trousers. 'If Bhim Sain is back, perhaps he'll rustle up some chai and we can have a chat away from this infernal heat.'

⌇

Ombir has kept the papers ready on the desk, all the forms that the SSP will need to sign. Bhim Sain stands to attention as they walk in. He pours out two cups of tea from their thermos flask, places one in front of the officer, one in front of Ombir.

Pilania says, 'A third cup, please.'

'There are only two cups,' Bhim Sain mumbles.

'Sorry, Pilania sir,' Ombir says, wishing he had thought to tell the sub-inspector to bring an extra cup back from Lovely Bhojanalaya. 'We receive few official visitors at this thana.'

The SSP locates a clean glass tumbler, takes the flask and pours out half a glass of chai for himself, pushing one of the thick china cups across the table towards Bhim Sain.

'I see you've organised everything already, Ombir. I would expect nothing less of you.'

Ombir hears it again, the touch of steel under Pilania's smooth phrases.

The officer leans back, addressing his remarks to Bhim Sain, though Ombir has no doubt that the speech is meant for him.

'So useful when a murderer does our job for us, isn't it? Saves us and the state such a lot of trouble, the long years of preserving evidence, ferrying the suspect up and down from the jail to the courts. Trials in this country do tend to drag on forever. It's a great deal of trouble, this business of proving someone's guilt beyond reasonable doubt.'

The ceiling fan, unstable at the best of times, hiccups and comes to a halt. Bhim Sain says, 'Sir, please excuse.' He climbs clumsily onto the wooden stool and pokes the fan with his lathi until it starts up again, the blades turning reluctantly, spinning gusts of hot air into their faces.

Pilania waits until he's done. 'Our job as police officers is to prove a man's guilt beyond any doubt. Of course, some authorities would consider that an accused who takes his own life after being discovered at the scene of the crime has settled all doubts. Perhaps it is enough to allow us to close this file. I have to attend some function that Jolly-ji has organised, some sort of evening dance programme featuring a lady called Reshma Bhabhi—ah, Bhim Sain, you've heard of her, I see by the smile on your face. The two of you are required to attend, so present yourselves at Bhoj Maidan at 5 p.m. sharp. It's a waste of your time, and of mine. I'd rather head straight back to Delhi after I sign these papers for you, Ombir, but the District Magistrate and the local MP and Jolly-ji will be there, and one must do one's duty.'

He signs the first document. His fountain pen hovers above the second sheet of paper. He smiles at Ombir.

'It did occur to me, while I was poking around in your well, that the late Mansoor was a man of rare abilities. He appears to have had the foresight to drag along bundles of wood, arrange them on top of his broken corpse, and somehow light a fire, all the while lying at the bottom of the well. I couldn't descend further. All I could see was ashes, and stacks of wood, partly burnt. Rather a lot of wood, I would have thought, for a man languishing in jail to arrange on his own, with no assistance.'

He signs the second sheet of paper. Reads the third, a small frown on his forehead.

'Have his body exhumed and buried in the appropriate place as soon as you can, Ombir. I'll leave the arrangements in your capable hands.'

Ombir takes a slow breath and decides to take the risk. Better for him to ask than for the SSP to grow suspicious at his silence and make it a formal order.

'Autopsy before burial, sir?'

When the SSP looks at him, he is ready. He doesn't look away, meets the man's gaze as directly as he can. Risks the second question.

'Or not required since cause of death is already established?'

'All right, Ombir,' Pilania says softly. 'I don't know what happened. Maybe I don't need to know. This is your terrain, not mine. I'll take your word for it that you, with your years of experience, left the station unattended with a prisoner in the lock-up. I'm even willing to believe that, in that tiny window of time, a suspect who seemed incapable of holding a glass of water on his own when I last saw him, magically revived and took his own life. It is only because Jolly-ji himself has taken a personal interest that I would like to close this matter as quickly as possible. And I have urgent work back in Delhi. However, I would like to understand how a man heaps stacks of wood on himself after he throws himself into a well. That little detail troubles my mind.'

Bhim Sain, who had been staring at the SSP in puzzlement at first, slowly comes to understand what the senior officer is driving at and clears his throat.

'Sir,' he says. 'Wood is my responsibility.'

Ombir avoids looking directly at Bhim Sain. He hasn't factored in a response from the sub-inspector, but he can hardly tell him to shut up.

'After my return from Lovely Bhojanalaya, I discovered the absence of the prisoner and informed Ombir-ji accordingly. We searched the premises and were led by footprints to the back of the thana. After investigation, we ascertained that the prisoner had jumped into the well. Some wood was also burnt, but not much. My thought was that he had first tried to set himself on fire and taken the final step while ablaze. This morning, sir, I felt that prayers were in order. After all, murderer or not, he was also a human being. So, on my own account, I did a small prayer. As part of the final rites, I took it upon myself to light a small fire. To his spirit, sir. Even though he was a Muslim, I felt he would not have minded.'

Pilania listens, his eyes closed.

'Thank you, Bhim Sain, most touching,' he says. 'Could I trouble you to arrange a fresh round of tea from Lovely

Bhojanalaya? I feel I need sustenance after that refreshing explanation.'

He waits until Bhim Sain is out of earshot.

'Ombir,' he says. 'I have two jobs to do in Teetarpur. The first involves the new township that Jolly and Saluja are planning—by the way, it might interest you to know that, if it gets the necessary permissions, your station house will be upgraded. The second job is simplicity itself. I have to close this case. They handed the mess to me when I had three other urgent cases in the capital, all of them involving bloody VIPs—anyway. This merely requires finding a murderer, and the late lamented Mansoor was so obliging as to present himself right in front of Chand's house. He certainly had the opportunity. Half the village believes he had a motive, that he was driven out of his mind with grief after his own sufferings. But was he guilty beyond reasonable doubt?'

Pilania touches a crisp, starched handkerchief to his face and Ombir sees the shadows under his eyes, understands that the SSP has his own set of problems back in Delhi.

'You had your doubts, didn't you?' Pilania says quietly. 'And so did I. No facts out of order. Just our instincts, telling us that something wasn't right. You interviewed Narinder and Dharam Bir. Maybe you'd have got somewhere, but then your prime suspect ever so helpfully kills himself. Everyone's happy. There's likely to be a promotion in this for you, especially if I mention that the suspect only managed to break out of the lock-up because of the poor condition of the current station house. Best not to mention in your final report that neither of you was in the station at the time. Ombir, you've kept nothing from me about this case?'

'No, Pilania sir,' Ombir says automatically.

He remembers the woman in the canal then, the rubbed-out footprint, but it's too late, the SSP is already moving on.

'The English word "doubt" comes from the Latin "dubitare", to hesitate, Ombir. Well, we both hesitated. But whatever happened to that poor lunatic last night, what matters most is that the father and the villagers believe that justice is done. Autopsy not required.'

He signs the rest of the papers swiftly, stands up, walks to the door.

'I'll see you at Reshma Bhabhi's delightful evening dance programme. By tomorrow morning, I'll be back in Delhi. This case will be over. The file will be closed. I won't give it another moment's thought, especially if you're right.'

Ombir sees him to the Ambassador, salutes the SSP formally.

'If you're wrong,' Pilania says pleasantly from the back seat as his driver starts the car, 'you have a murderer running loose and a case that can't be reopened without leaving a black mark on your record. It has been a pleasure working with you, Ombir.'

Dance Dance

Ombir's wife calls as they're leaving the station house.

'I'll drive,' says Bhim Sain. 'You've been so busy with the case, please speak to Bhabhi-ji.'

The breeze flutters in Ombir's ears. He can make out a few words, enough to hear the excitement in her voice.

'When are you coming home?' she says.

'I told you the last time, not until after the monsoons.'

'Because of the big case? We watched all of it on TV. They also showed the murderer, such acting, putting on a bewildered face, but you can tell he has a cruel heart. Your mother says they are all like that. It's good we don't have any of their kind in our village. Achha, can you come home earlier, only for one weekend, can you try?'

'Why, is there an emergency? I can't get leave until much later.'

'No emergency. Talk to your mother, she'll explain.'

'Hello?' Ombir says into the dead air.

'We're passing Chhotebhai's field,' Bhim Sain calls to him over the wind, which is swirling into a dust storm. 'Connection drops, but it will return once we've crossed the Shiv mandir.'

When the phone rings again, he puts it on speaker. Loses his mother's first words in response to his formal greeting, but catches the rest, the important part. Pregnancy. Four months. No fear of miscarriage.

'Are you sure?' he says.

'What a way to respond!' his mother says, laughing. 'I told her to tell you herself, but she's not like these modern girls. She felt shy to say it to you, so I had to give you the good news. After eleven years of marriage, God has finally blessed you. I knew it would happen. And don't worry, your brother is here for a few months, studying for his CA finals. He is making sure she has everything she needs. Can you come in two weeks?'

'Probably not,' he says. 'Wrapping up the big case. I'll try later.'

Bhim Sain whispers loudly, 'You take leave, I'll manage everything at the station, not to worry.'

He ignores Bhim Sain and says, 'Take care of her. Tell her she can go to her parents' house whenever she likes.'

He meant that to be caring, but it misfires. 'Why should she go anywhere? This is her home, you don't think we can look after her?'

Ombir listens to his mother, her words tinny and distant as she swears on her gods that she has always treated his wife like her own daughter. And he remembers the time, four years after their marriage, when she sat before her altar and lamented that the universe had seen fit to send her a daughter-in-law with a womb as barren as stones in the earth. Ombir lets his mother run on for a bit, then cuts her short.

'I have to go. On duty tonight. I'll send a money order tomorrow. Yes, it's the best news. Yes, better not to tell people outside the village until after the fifth month. Yes, do a special puja to keep the evil eye at bay; whatever you want, you do. I left her in your hands for a reason. No, no need to talk to her, tell her I'll visit soon. Next month, if I can. Okay, bye.'

'You're going to be a father!' Bhim Sain calls, rounding the last bend before they reach Bhoj Maidan. He is so delighted, he has forgotten to say 'sir', but Ombir doesn't feel like reminding him. 'One big case cracked and a son arriving in the same year! Or a daughter. It doesn't matter these days, that's what they say, a child is a child.'

'Yes,' says Ombir. 'I suppose you're right.'

❧

Pilania and Jolly Singh are seated in the front row on fancy sofas that he guesses are Jolly Villa property. The stage is made of wooden tables knocked together with jute rope, but the stacks of giant speakers on either side, the presence of bouncers, their muscles gym-rippled, their black jeans defying the summer heat, the strings of coloured lights and balloons painted gold and silver, give Bhoj Maidan an unaccustomed air of festivity. It usually sees only political speeches during election season.

To Ombir's surprise, Jolly gets up to greet him and Bhim Sain.

'The heroes are here!'

Bhim Sain's grin broadens when the crowd applauds, some turning to include the two policemen in their cheers. And even Ombir is pleased when Jolly's aides usher them to their seats. Almost front row, to the side of the stage. Plastic chairs, but clean, new, with a diamond design on the backs and arms.

He salutes the SSP.

'The highlight of your busy week,' the SSP says, smiling. 'I'm sure we'll all enjoy Reshma Bhabhi's performance.'

If he'd had a choice, he would have taken a two-hour nap on the charpai, he thinks. Bhim Sain likes dancers, but Ombir doesn't. He dislikes the loud music, he doesn't care for this kind of dancing, or the fever running high among the men, some of whom will get drunk on hooch and cause trouble for them all night. He says nothing, merely excuses himself and returns to his chair.

When Reshma Bhabhi strides on to the stage, the all-male audience cheers. They send up a loud whoop as Reshma begins her routine, the music blaring from the speakers, too close to where he is sitting. Bhim Sain is beating the rhythm on his thigh, out of time. Ombir's first impression is that Reshma is dressed too plainly—a shimmering white salwar kameez, high-necked, with demure long sleeves.

A revolving spotlight comes on, revealing that the sleeves and most of the top are diaphanous. The undershirt has been dampened to cling to her ample figure. Nothing she is wearing underneath is plain. Magenta lingerie, studded with gold.

Her backup dancers jump up and down in time to the music, and Ombir is suddenly reminded of the PT exercises he used to do in school. The bass thumps and he feels another migraine coming on. He closes his eyes as the lights change colour, scattering red and blue stars across the stage, across Reshma's high, bouncing figure.

❧

He had met his wife at the wedding, not before. The families arranged it all. Her uncle was in the Border Security Force, another uniformed service. They were of the same caste; their fathers and, more importantly, their mothers agreed it was a suitable match.

Kavita brought a sparkle into his life that first year. He had been assigned proper quarters, two small rooms, on the Rampur posting. She set out his uniform and belt neatly every morning, scrubbed the walls of their tiny flat, drew fat Laxmanrekha chalk lines around the doorways so that the cockroaches fled, pinned bright flowers she folded from sheets of cheap coloured paper onto the beige plastic window curtains.

He would come home drained, the crude facts of police work already beginning to grind him down at the edges. She would rise, no matter how late the hour, and silently emerge from the cramped kitchen to hand him a cup of freshly made adrak chai. One winter night, she brought out the bottle of cheap brandy he kept hidden at the back of his almirah.

'It will help you with the cold,' she said.

Her boldness thrilled him, though he said nothing, only grunted, waiting for her to leave before he poured a tot into the rough blue pottery mug. From then on, he listened to his wife, humming softly as she washed dishes at the broken cement sink, the way he listened for the sound of the few sparrows left in their concrete colony.

Then his mother fractured her hip. She requested that Kavita return to the village to help with her nursing and the household work. Ombir lost a decent posting because he fell out with his senior officer, a brutal man whose taste for violence found a ready outlet during the interrogation of assorted suspects. He stopped his senior when the man would have kicked in the head of a screaming drug pusher,

reversed his lathi and used the heavy iron tip to knock
the officer out cold. There were no witnesses. The officer
couldn't prove the assault, but he entered a false complaint
on Ombir's record, a permanent, indelible stain.

The years trickled by. Ombir was assigned to post after
post with no quarters available for married men. He saw
his wife infrequently, but frequently enough to understand
that the taunts she received for her continuing inability to
conceive a child were steadily draining her. The memory
of the early brightness that had touched their lives seeped
away. It seemed false, unreal, like something that had
happened to other people.

On one of his rare trips home, his mother-in-law
came over with boxes of mithai, other gifts, brass vessels
brimming with milk and thick curd from her cows. Ombir's
mother was inspecting glass jars of karonda pickle on the
veranda.

She said, acid lacing her voice, 'What a show! Anyone
would think your daughter had something to celebrate,
instead of the nothing she has given my son for so many
years.'

Those words, flung like hard stones, could not be taken
back. She continued the tirade, exorcising all the demons
of bitterness that had possessed her over the years, until
Kavita's weeping mother finally flared into anger.

'Don't be so sure it's my daughter to blame! I have
two sons, two other daughters. They have given me
grandchildren, every one of them. Maybe it's not the
ground that's barren, maybe the seed is bad.'

His mother stood up, her face reddening. 'Get out of my
house and take your daughter with you!'

'It's his house, and hers by right,' Kavita's mother said flatly. 'It's not in your power to turn a wife out of her marital home. And if you're so concerned about your lack of grandchildren, I'll have her tested, so long as you have your son tested too. Let's see whose fault it is. They can do the tests at the local hospital, you know.'

His mother faltered, then recovered herself. 'Such big talk!'

But she had hesitated, and Kavita's mother drove her advantage home, addressing Ombir directly. 'Please make sure my daughter is properly looked after while you're away at work, son. Our family is as respectable as yours, and I know many people in the local women's NGOs. I don't want to hear of any kitchen accidents happening to my child. We live in modern times, not in the old days. Forget what I said about tests. I spoke in anger, sometimes it takes time, that's all. And when you have so much tension and a bitter tongue at home, it's not easy. Trust in God. All will be well. He has a way of seeing our sorrows and hopes and addressing both.'

At night, Kavita said to him hesitantly, 'The tests don't cost much. Shall we get them done? If there's some problem with me, the doctors could help?'

He swung at her, the back of his hand landing flat across her mouth.

'Your mother mixes too much with those NGO women,' he said. 'They're troublemakers. I don't want to hear any talk about tests again, you understand?'

Ombir woke a few hours later. The edge of his bolster was damp with his wife's tears. He had long since overcome his initial reluctance to administer beatings to suspects; it was a necessary evil. But he had never hit a woman. This did not count as a blow, he told himself. He had put no force behind it, only firmness, some boundaries had to be maintained.

He put out his hand, touched her wrist, felt her jerk away from him. He said nothing, but he turned towards Kavita, stroked her back until she stopped crying. It was too dark for them to see each other clearly, but the silence between them softened, even though he spoke no words of apology. He kept his hand on his wife's back until he heard her breathing grow calmer, until he was sure that she was asleep.

When Kavita woke up, she found her husband in the kitchen, making tea. The kitchen was the size of a large cupboard. She hovered behind him, watching as he added finely chopped ginger and one fat green cardamom to the brew, brought the leaves to a boil, added milk and let it come to a boil a second time, poured out the chai. He motioned her away when she would have carried the tray out into the veranda, brought it out himself, stirred two spoons of sugar into her mug, a cheap but cheerful piece of pottery.

She did not take the mug from his hand. 'Don't become one of those men who brings their work home with them. I'm your wife, not one of your suspects down at the station.'

He said, 'It will never happen again.'

She nodded and accepted the chai when he offered it to her once more.

*

Reshma Bhabhi's back-up dancers warm up the crowd. In the rows behind, many of the men are already on their feet, clapping and whistling.

'Dance, dance!' One of the girls calls, her voice hoarse with an assumed seductiveness, as she whirls along the front rows. 'Dance, dance!'

The men roar back, Bhim Sain among them. She halts in front of Ombir, but he folds his arms and stares at the ground, refusing to meet her flirtatious eyes.

She says, delighted, 'I've never met a shy policeman before. You can look at me if you like. I won't bite.'

'There are many men here who would die for one glance from your eyes. Go and find one of them.'

'You don't like Chunchun?' she says. 'But everyone likes Chunchun. Okay, maybe you're married, maybe that's what makes you so shy. Don't worry, your wife's not here today. You can look. One teeny-tiny glance, yes?'

He raises his eyes and surveys her.

'You like what you see, Mr Oh-so-smart in your uniform? I told you. Everyone loves Chunchun.'

He smiles, beckons her closer. She laughs, triumphant, her hands held out.

'Chunchun has her rules,' she says, 'especially for such an important person. Either you dance with me, or you give me baksheesh.'

He says, 'I've seen you before. With Bachni. You know that name? The woman who was murdered? Okay, this is not the place or the time to talk about these matters. I will say nothing, and you will keep that simpering smile on your face as you go to one of the other men. Make him dance. Whatever you like. And you and I will talk tomorrow. How's that for baksheesh?'

Sullenly, the dancer turns away. He stops her with a touch on her elbow. 'Give me your number. Just say it quietly, once, I'll memorise it.'

She moves back to the stage, the crowd roaring as she joins Reshma.

'Dance, dance!' The men call, edging forward. 'Dance, dance!'

Bhim Sain says, 'She's a tight one, moves just like a film star.'

'I told her to get back up on stage. The men are growing rowdy tonight. She should know better than to stoke their fires; Reshma has more sense than that.'

'Reshma Bhabhi ...' Bhim Sain says, his voice swelling with longing. 'She's fully experienced.'

Ombir wishes he could leave, but he can't offend Jolly. If the SSP leaves early, he can make his excuses, but Pilania is deep in conversation.

The roar swells, and four young men rush forward, leaping onto the rickety wooden boards to join the dancers. The bouncers chase three of them back into the crowd. One remains, a bold youth with his hair dyed in dashing gold-and-red streaks. He grabs Chunchun by her waist, using her to ward off the last bouncer, spins her round and round, matching her steps so perfectly that Ombir decides he is not drunk, unlike most of the men in the crowd.

Jolly stands up, frowning, grabs a lathi from his personal bodyguard.

'Sorry, Pilania-ji,' he says to the SSP. 'These village boys don't know how to behave. I'll teach him some manners.'

'Don't trouble yourself on my account, Jolly-ji,' the SSP says. 'I've enjoyed myself—such an energetic performance. I have to be on my way, if you don't mind; early morning meetings. Bhim Sain, tell my driver to meet me outside.'

The bouncers are elbowing their way back, the crowd reluctant to let them through. Ombir glances at the stage.

The youth has outwitted the remaining bouncer by dancing between Reshma and Chunchun, using the women as effective shields. Jolly hesitates, the lathi half-raised in his hands, but the SSP is rising, making his way out, and he has to be seen to his car.

'Enough,' Dharam Bir says.

He is clambering up, on to the stage. The bouncer makes way for his bulky but agile figure. Dharam Bir grabs the youth by his belt and yanks him away from Reshma, who ignores the men and moves into a complicated set of thumkis. The younger man's hair gleams in the jerky stage lights, and he curses, headbutts his opponent. A swift move, and the youth is sprawled on the ground, Dharam Bir pinning him down with his massive hands, a knee in his back.

He swings the youth up on to his feet, using the boy's belt as a grip, and propels him to the edge of the stage. The bouncers grab the boy, frogmarching him away.

Ombir watches Dharam Bir with interest. The foreman lingers and Chunchun sketches a curtsey, pirouetting lightly until she is close to him. She has moved to the back of the stage, letting Reshma command the front. She continues dancing, but her eyes are on Dharam Bir, and he smiles back at her. She swirls closer in her peacock-blue costume, almost touching him.

Reshma laughs as the music switches to her most popular hit, '*Kasutta Swag*', raises her hands and shimmies. The men are stomping and whistling, holding their hands to their hearts. Jolly-ji is making his way back.

Ombir whispers to Bhim Sain, 'Make my excuses to Jolly-ji. I have to go.'

Bhim Sain gives him an incredulous stare. 'And miss the fun? Sir, take some time to relax after all your hard work. Case is closed, no?'

'It is,' says Ombir. 'I want an early night. I have some work of my own tomorrow.'

Another case. One that was closed too early, too hastily, one that they sent out of their jurisdiction. His promotion will finally happen, he knows that. But he doesn't like loose ends, and he will make sure these don't flap loose for too long.

The blare from the speakers follows him down the road. At the station, he doesn't go straight to bed. He walks through the station house, kicking a frog in his path back to safety, and spends some time examining the old well. Bhim Sain will return late, probably as drunk as he ever allows himself to be. He will sleep soundly.

At first light, Ombir intends to be up. He wants to settle a question that has been hovering in his mind ever since SSP Pilania climbed down the rusted rungs of the old well.

Loose Ends

Ombir is filthy by the time he reaches the bottom of the
well. He had chanced the rusted rungs, trusting they would
hold under his weight, and though he had to skip one or
two, the rest held. The bone-dry sand is specked with pools
of stagnant water, the sky a distant, blank oval far above.
There is a stink in his nostrils of old, dead things. Halfway
down, he had passed the carcass of a rat, wedged in the
brickwork, its eye sockets empty and staring.

He switches on his torch, the powerful Maglite that SSP
Pilania left him as a parting gift. A yellow light illuminates
the silent chamber. He moves meticulously around the
bottom of the well, flinching once when he steps on a
lizard so long lifeless that it cracks like parchment under
his foot. He plays the torchlight back and forth, pushing
aside stacks of wood, kicking through the ashes, until he is
absolutely sure of his discovery.

He climbs back to level ground, slipping and cursing,
wanting to get away from all of it, the stink of mud, the
eyeless worms that slip over the top of his boots, the slimy
handholds, the unreliable rungs. When he finally pulls
himself up the rope he had tied to a stanchion, he doesn't

bother taking off his uniform before grabbing the handle of the rusty tubewell nearby.

He pumps water rapidly, ducks back under the gushing spout. He washes the morning off him, the mud, the slime, the dust, the spiders' webs clinging to the back of his neck. Squints at the dial of the thick steel wristwatch he had left on the parapet of the well. He had started his exploration at first light; the descent took him an hour. One loose end, not tied up, not yet, but accounted for. He has the rest of the day to sort out the other.

⤳

Bhim Sain is wide awake. He is sitting at the desk, his expression dreamy as he strokes a half-grown rabbit that sits crouched on his lap.

'It's a gift from the villagers,' he says. 'It came along with the other things. Sir, will you try some kachoris? And some pooris with sabzi? I prepared a thali for you.'

Ombir squats down, eye-to-eye with a furious, caged mongoose. It rears back and chatters angrily at him.

'A gift for what?'

'They're grateful we found the murderer. The pradhan himself has sent bajra khichdi and malpua.'

'Have you finished your breakfast?'

Bhim Sain nods. The rabbit slumbers on his lap.

'Then kindly take this mongoose to the fields and allow it to live its life out in peace. The rabbit also.'

'Yes, Ombir-ji.' Bhim Sain puts the rabbit back in its cage, but he doesn't leave, hovering near the desk.

'What else?'

'Sir, while you were away, the SSP called on your phone. He said it wasn't urgent. And your family called. They also said there's no urgency.'

'Okay. I'll call the SSP back immediately. When they say it isn't urgent, what they really mean is that you shouldn't keep them waiting.'

He picks up his phone. Bhim Sain remains where he is. 'Yes, Bhim Sain?'

'Sir … I have rabbits at home. We keep them in a hutch. My children love them very much, sir.'

'My mother used to have a pair of rabbits. They eat their weight in vegetables and shit twice that amount. Their cages need constant cleaning.'

'Yes, sir. If you feel that the rabbit should be released, then no question, I'll set it free along with the mongoose. But rabbits are foolish creatures. Timid. They can't survive in the wild on their own.'

Ombir sighs. His uniform is still wet. The damp should be pleasant in this heat, but it only makes him feel stickier and unclean.

'If you want to keep the rabbit, Bhim Sain, say so. But it's your responsibility. And place the cage somewhere out of sight. This is a police station, not a farm.'

'Yes sir! I'll take care of the feeding and cleaning, you won't be bothered by any of it, I promise.'

Bhim Sain picks up the other cage. The mongoose lunges at the bars.

'Don't worry,' he says to the mongoose. 'You are one lucky prisoner. You will be released from custody without further delay. Sir?'

'What now?'

'Her name is Laadli.'

'Just deal with the mongoose, okay?'

'Yes, sir.'

～

The SSP's call is brisk, pleasant, but to the point. He wants Ombir to make sure that the signboard announcing the ban on Muslims entering the village is removed immediately.

'The TV crews will be all over that like a committee of vultures,' he says. 'If the pradhan kicks up a fuss, tell him I've given you direct orders. Report back to me tonight.'

'Yes, sir.'

'And congratulations. Bhim Sain informs me that you have two reasons to celebrate.'

'Sorry, sir?'

Pilania laughs. 'Your promotion will soon be through, Ombir. I signed the papers myself this morning. And your junior tells me you'll be a father soon. Well done.'

'Thank you, sir!' Ombir says.

'You should be proud of yourself, Ombir. Cracked a tough case in less than a week.'

Ombir catches a slight dryness in his superior's voice, waits. He understands the SSP well enough by now to know that he does not ask his next question out of idle curiosity.

'You're satisfied with the results of your investigation this morning? Bhim Sain mentioned you'd gone in for a spot of well-climbing. No surprises, nothing you'd like to share with me after your excursion?'

Ombir says, his mouth dry, 'Satisfied, sir.'

'What did you find?'

'Everything was as expected, SSP sir.'

'You're sure? This is your last chance to reopen the case. It would hold up your promotion if you did, but only by a matter of months. If there's any doubt, any niggling concern, this is the time to speak your mind, Ombir.'

'Thank you, sir,' Ombir says. 'No doubts. Further investigation will not be required.'

'That poor madman,' Pilania says. 'All right, Ombir. Take a few days off if you like. You've certainly earned a break.'

'Grateful for your support, sir,' Ombir says, but he's speaking to empty air. The SSP has, with his usual efficiency and speed, terminated the call.

He uses his sleeve to mop the sweat beading his face. If the SSP had asked a direct question, he would have had no option except to answer truthfully. A closed case reopened. There might have been another black mark against him in that file, until the many tangled threads of this case finally loosened and separated, revealing the truth.

But Pilania asked only, what did you find, Ombir? He did not ask, did you find a body?

He had found firewood and ashes, and the shed skin of snakes. He had found an empty wasp's nest. He had found the tiny bones of rats or birds.

Inside her cage, Laadli stirs, poking her soft nose between the bars in search of some food. He ignores the rabbit; they do not have a working relationship as yet.

He had not found a body.

This case, he thinks, is filled with inconvenient corpses. The body of the woman in the canal, with no explanation of how she achieved the fate of strangulation. Mansoor, whose shattered body should have been lying at the bottom of the well, has vanished into thin air.

Ombir takes a spoonful of bajra khichdi and offers it to the rabbit through the bars of her cage. Laadli gives him a reproachful look and retreats to the other side. He shrugs. She is Bhim Sain's problem.

And the village and its tangled troubles are his problem, not the problem of the SSP or any of the Delhi boys to solve.

He does not see any sense in holding up a promotion. Luck is luck. When it finally notices you, it is unwise to ask it to be patient, to take an appointment and come back later.

He contemplates the word that Pilania is so fond of. Justice. His years in the police have not convinced him that there is much justice in the universe, or that it is his job to commit acts of justice. But he does not like deceit. He does not like loose ends. Sometimes a problem seems insoluble until you find a tiny thread. And if it is the right thread, and you tug at it gently and patiently enough, the entire snarled ball of complications will unravel, all on its own.

❧

In Teetar Bani, delinquent flies buzz in dense black swarms, covering the dust and the trays of clotted milk sweets. They settle on the flanks of grazing cows in numbers so thick that the herds of cattle seem black, not brown, not cream. Clouds of midges dance and spin on the surface of stagnant waters. Mosquitoes fasten on to the thin underfed flanks of stray cats, tormenting rooftop sleepers, swarming up from the pits of squat toilets and the wide-mouthed wells.

At the roadside stands, stall owners can only raise squares of gauze muslin an inch before the flies duck underneath. The black cloud covers everything with indiscriminate zeal—piles of fruit, paper kites, stacked towels and rough khaddar bedsheets, plastic dolls, sweet pedhas, brightly printed copies of prayer books, gold-tasselled odhnis and scarves, all seen through a screen of moving, buzzing flies. Milkmen on their motorbikes ride with cotton dupattas wrapped around their heads and mouths, imperfect protection against the dust and the insects.

A daring bluebottle settles on Ombir's head. He ignores the creature crawling on his scalp and considers the new signboard. The lettering is well executed: bold, clear, the words 'Muslims Not Allowed' printed in ornate Devanagari script, twice as large as 'Outsiders Strictly Prohibited'.

The television vans have already reached. A small cluster of reporters are doing their earnest pieces to camera, pointing at the offensive sign. Bhim Sain parks the Bullet near the hardware store on Ombir's direction.

'Get two boys to take down the sign,' Ombir says.

Bhim Sain reads it slowly. 'What's wrong with it? The rule is for everyone's safety, isn't it?'

Everything is wrong with it, Ombir could have said. Because Mansoor probably did not kill the girl. Mansoor's wits wandered, but that did not make him a murderer. Even if he was, it wasn't right to take the anger of the village out on his community, when a Hindu murderer would not have received the same treatment. Also because the press-wallahs whom he dislikes—they are never fair to the police, always demanding answers—would enjoy the chance to point out the backwardness of Teetarpur, even though their own neighbourhoods in the civilised city carry out unofficial boycotts, rarely renting houses to Muslims, squeezing them out wherever they can.

City people are smart. They are as cruel and small-minded as anyone in a village, but they have more sense than to advertise these facts on a public sign.

'SSP Pilania's orders,' he says briefly. The fly perches on his shoulder and he measures the distance, swats it accurately, sweeps the black speck away. 'Direct orders.'

Bhim Sain grunts, returns with two men who can help him dig up the posts. Ombir finds a sugarcane stand, signals to the owner to bring him and Bhim Sain two large glasses of juice. Its thick sweetness is cut with a squeeze of lime and crushed mint leaves.

He finishes his juice and leaves Bhim Sain in charge, says, 'I have some work of my own, I'll be back at the station house late tonight.'

꙳

Five missed calls from his wife. The place he's headed to is at the edge of the town, according to his information, at the border of the keekar forests. Ombir calls reluctantly, irritated even before she says it is nothing urgent.

'I'm on duty. I'll call you later.'

'You don't have five minutes for me?' Kavita says, an unaccustomed sharpness in her voice.

'I have. So what is it? Is there a problem at home?'

'No, but you haven't called since—your mother said she gave you the news.'

'Yes, she did.'

He is climbing through a lane so narrow that he has to turn sideways, one of those roads intended only for people and animals, not for cars or even bicycles. The houses on this side of town are rustic, made from ancient bricks, with low, flat concrete roofs. Three children are playing with a flock of goats in a courtyard, goats and children spilling out through the open doorway and landing in a tangle at his feet.

'Okay,' Kavita says uncertainly. 'You aren't pleased? After all these years, no one can say anything to us again.'

He makes a non-committal noise, halfway between assent and a grunt.

'You have everything you need? I wired some extra cash into your account, you've seen?'

'Yes, the SMS came in immediately. Your brother has bought everything that is required. Will you be able to come soon? The big case is over, they won't give you leave?'

'I still have work to finish. Balbir is at home these days?'

'Yes, he's studying for his pharmacy finals. He's such good company, went to the market with your mother yesterday and even collected the new salwar-kameez sets from the tailor master. I had to order some clothes, the old ones won't fit any more. You don't mind?'

'Order whatever you want,' he says. Remembers the promotion, but says nothing about it—best to wait until the order is signed.

'I'm excited,' she says. 'I've waited so long to become a mother.'

He is silent, says finally, 'I've reached. I have to go.'

'You'll call later?'

'When I can.'

He is almost there, but instead of turning right into the last lane, he turns left, walks along the dusty track until he is at the edge of the forest. The branches of the keekar trees float like a sea of grass before him.

He had heard the hurt in his wife's voice, knew she expected a response from him. He had told himself to say something, but the words of caring, of congratulation, the excitement and the kindness she had expected to hear, stuck in his throat.

❧

Kavita's mother's taunt had buzzed in his ears, a wasp in his mind. He had been on temporary posting in Faridabad, assisting with a homicide. His duties were not exacting. He had time on his hands. One day, he gathered the courage, took leave and spent a morning at Shanghvi Urology and Pathology Labs, getting the test done. He went in plain clothes, hung around near the gates until he was absolutely sure none of his colleagues were likely to pass by, kept his head low like a criminal. The few other men at the centre wore the same look. Furtive, ashamed, they smelt of summer sweat and trepidation.

Providing the sample presented unexpected problems. Every time he tried to concentrate, images of his mother and his mother-in-law popped up. He leaned against the wall, wondering why they had chosen such a depressing shade of green for the smooth tiles. From the TV screen, bolted to an iron frame that made him think of hospital belts, a jerky stream of porn did nothing to solve his problem. In the next stall, a man groaned several times, long, deep groans that came from the back of the throat.

With an effort of will, he summoned up memories of every actress he'd watched and had the usual thoughts about, from Madhuri Dixit to Priyanka Chopra.

Nothing.

His wife, in their early years.

Nothing.

Then, finally, a memory he could work with. He had been fifteen. They were at a cousin's home for a wedding, every room of the sixteen-room house filled with guests. She had backed into the room, carrying a tray of phalsa sharbat in steel glasses, a middle-aged relative who had been pressed into helping. Even at fifteen, he recognised that she was not attractive. Her face had the resigned sternness of women who'd been told early, and often, that they lacked beauty, the planes square and uncompromising, and she was sturdy, her sea-green sari wrapped rather than draped around her.

She had glanced around the room with an expression of total contempt for the proceedings, assessing and dismissing all of them as nuisances, and her indifference flicked a switch somewhere in him. What nonsense all of this is, she seemed to be saying, this fuss over two people getting together, this celebration of something that will end up just like every marriage, equal parts dissatisfaction and endurance. She thumped the tray down on the centre table, handing everybody their glasses of sharbat as they wandered by. He went to collect his glass, said thank you loudly, hoping to draw a response, maybe even a smile, from her. There was a line of sweat under her tight blouse, beading on the tiny patch of bare skin above her petticoat, and two mosquito bites underneath, which excited him for no good reason. He stared into her apathetic eyes, let his hand brush her cold fingers, falling in something like love.

He was done. He tidied himself and zipped up, handed the sample to the technician.

The next day, he went back to collect the results. They said it might be fixable, that the low count was nothing to worry about, but the motility issue—that was the problem. They offered him further tests, this and that, courses of treatment, but he said, 'I don't need anything else.'

He paid and left, and tore the envelope with the results into the smallest shreds he could manage, dumping them into a stinking drain on his way back to his beat. He never told anyone about the test. It was one thing to fail at fatherhood because your wife was unable to conceive, another to fail because he was not man enough. He would never have children. Acceptance came, slowly, in time. The shame never left him.

And this is what the gods have engineered. His wife, pregnant. He does not know how it has happened, but a slow fury grows in him. It smoulders, burns.

INQUIRIES

A Hundred Fires

Rabia's eyes feel gritty from tiredness as Badshah Miyan's van rattles along the highway towards Delhi. None of them had slept much at night. The men had rested outside, leaving her in possession of Chand's hut. It was filled with reminders of Munia, and sleep eluded her. She got up in the early hours of the morning to take a drink of water from the clay pitcher, glanced outside and saw Badshah Miyan staring out towards the fields.

She takes a sideways look at him now as he drives, notes the tell-tale lines around his eyes, her exhaustion mirrored on his face.

'You seem so wide awake,' she says to him. 'Age is catching up with me, my bones ache more these days.'

'It's the grief, nothing to do with age,' he says. 'Sorrow will find its way out, one way or another. It affects me differently, makes me restless, but a cup of dhaba chai will settle that.'

The dhaba is no more than a glorified tea shop selling Maggi noodles, parathas and butter toast. 'The tea is superb,' Badshah Miyan says. 'He brews it strong, with ginger instead of cardamom.' The men sit outside on wooden planks and red plastic chairs. She is the only woman in the place at that hour, and it makes her uncomfortable.

'Would you like to wait in the car?' Badshah Miyan asks her. 'I'll bring you parathas and tea, you can eat undisturbed.'

She is close enough to hear the group of young men, their eyes lit with a familiar fire, their talk of pilgrimages and politics also familiar. The dhaba owner brews the chai over an open flame and the aroma revives her strength. The young men are saying, 'They've grown too bold, they have no fear of us any more.'

She listens.

'Why, just the other day, one of them murdered a young Hindu girl.'

'They can't stop themselves. It's like a curse, there is lust for our women in their hearts.'

'It's worse than that, much worse. I heard that the murderer was part of an organised gang. Usually, they pick up our girls and sell them off into prostitution, but sometimes their orders are to kill as many of our children as they can. They feast on our blood.'

Badshah Miyan, carrying the clay cups, is also listening.

'But that village did the right thing. The police caught the murderer, and I hear they finished the bastard off themselves. That's the way it should be. Instant punishment is the best way to settle these matters.'

One of the men sighs and says, 'It will continue until we've yanked them out of our soil, root and branch. Make no mistake about that, my friends. Until we've sent the last one of them out of our country, nothing will change.'

The boys murmur their assent.

Badshah Miyan and Rabia drink their tea in silence. She has no appetite for the parathas, but Badshah Miyan quietly wraps them up in a clean cloth and says, 'The man fried these with care, take them with you.'

~

Badshah Miyan says as the van crosses the border into Delhi, 'Are you and Arshad making proper provision for the future?'

'I sold the village land,' Rabia says. Khalid had left her half an acre in his village, which was in a part of Bengal prone to flooding, house collapses and mosquitoes. For many years, she managed the land herself, making the three-day trip in crowded trains, always emerging from the compartment with the names and phone numbers of her new women friends neatly written in a tiny Nimco Batteries pocket diary. She had kept a loose arrangement going with their tenant, a man who had squatted on the land for so many years that his gifts of mangoes and lychees counted as rent in her eyes as well as the eyes of the village council. 'Arshad and his wife are city people, and once they decided they would not be moving back, the council told us to sell it to our tenant.'

'Will that be enough for all of you to make the big move?'

'The big move?' Rabia says, not understanding. 'That money will go towards the final conversion charges for our Bright Dairy kothi. I made the down payments years ago, but every year, they change the tax rate and we've been waiting for seven years for them to make all those flats permanent under the law.'

Badshah Miyan is silent. Then he says, 'This is what Chand was worried about. We talked about you and Arshad a few months before Munia was taken from him.

He said to me, Badshah, you can see the signs. But she is stubborn, she will refuse to leave.'

'Leave where? Delhi? For what?'

'The country, Rabia. You can't have missed what's happening around us. Even in your own colony, the trouble at Arshad's wedding two years ago ...'

'But it's always been this way!' she cries.

'Some pushing and pulling, yes, some clashes between us and them, yes. We are used to a hundred little fires breaking out here and there, smouldering. Then people calm down and the fires go out, leaving only the memory of ashes behind. But this is different. When someone blows on each fire and sends the flames rising higher, when they bring fresh coals every time, when a hundred fires join together and become a thousand—I see it happening. We are in our middle years, Rabia, I am at the lip of old age. Too old to stay and spend the rest of my life fighting for a space to breathe.'

Rabia says, 'I've never considered leaving my country.'

'Arshad and his wife Sanam, they've never talked about it?'

She is silent. They have broached the subject. Many of her neighbours have already sold up and left for the Gulf, some have said they'll try their luck trading in Mozambique and other countries in Africa, a few have left for Turkey and Malaysia.

He sighs. 'Chand is in no shape to talk to you about this, but he meant to bring it up with you. My son Murshid made all the arrangements for us last year. We will leave for the Gulf in a month. My visa came through last week.'

'You'll shut down the meat shop? How can you speak so casually about leaving? What other home have people like us ever known?'

Badshah Miyan says, 'Business is down. They make us close our shops, all of us, every time there is a festival or even a prayer meeting close by. We are losing customers. The Hindus go to Hindu butchers or order online these days.'

'Is that enough reason to turn your back on the place where you were born? These are the games politicians play, in time things will go back to normal.'

'What is normal, Rabia?' he says. 'Thrice last year, my shop was raided by those gangs of young men who ride around the city looking for trouble. My boys have been beaten up, my freezers and equipment stolen, the bribes grow heavier each year. You've never met my mother. She is half-and-half, Hindu and Muslim. My parents had to move out of their village last year and come to stay with us because they were boycotted by both sides. If this is normal now, what will normal be for all of us tomorrow? You don't have to make a decision today, or next week. But take my advice and at least get your son and your daughter-in-law out of the country while you still can. What happened at Arshad's wedding was a warning, Rabia.'

～

Beginnings are the sweetest. Rabia distrusts the films and TV serials that end on a blaring note of happiness. Life has a way of dealing with happy endings, adding a few snakes, turning up unexpected nests of scorpions. But she had seen no shadows the day that Sanam and Arshad met, two years ago. That was the day when Bright Dairy was given its own Himalayas, when snorting machines summoned by the ifrit who lived deep inside the high hills of trash came galloping all the way from the main city to magically transform garbage into the most beautiful mountains.

Rabia had recognised Sanam on the bus. In Bright Dairy, Azizbhai's daughter was regarded with respect. She was one of the few to climb some distance out of the buzzing but limited world that the colony offered. She worked at an institute in Delhi as an interpreter of Urdu and Persian for corporate clients.

The bus was crowded, and Rabia was glad to find a seat. Sanam, across the aisle from her, had erected a border wall of bags and the fringe of her dupatta between her and the sweaty man who was sliding his fat, heavily ringed fingers into the gap between her thigh and his. She clenched the muscles of her left leg, creating a crucial extra half-inch of space, expertly holding off the invader's spreading thigh. Rabia knew that manoeuvre, had performed it herself so often, the careful shrinking of one's body away from purposeful invaders.

Under her breath, Rabia recited the names of the places they passed, ticking them off like beads on her favourite rosary. Khyber Pass, New Chandrawal, Wazirabad. The Yamuna glinted in the distance. They picked up speed on the Outer Ring Road. There was relatively little traffic here. Few visitors or tourists came to this part of Delhi. Nirankari Colony, where the Sikhs lived, Model Town with its speech therapists and urologists, the clean sprawl of Khusraupur with the neat, large-roofed houses she quietly coveted, Fuji Colony which was a corruption of 'Fauji', for fauj, 'army', and Jahangirpuri, named for a dead emperor who would have been dismayed at the thick cluster, wall glued to wall like ant nests, and finally, Bright Dairy Colony itself. It was more than fifteen years now, since Arshad and she moved here.

Rabia elbowed her way off the bus, and halted when she saw the transformation of their landfill. Growing hillocks of garbage surrounded Bright Dairy like a miniature mountain range. The landfill's colours were ink and earth, soot and dust, the waste from almost half the city mounded here. It rose, a reassuring, looming presence.

Massive JCB excavators were trundling past the entrance to their colony, bearing loads of fresh earth, and teams of men swarmed like bees on the slopes of their trash mountains.

꿈

Bright Dairy had one library, started by Azizbhai. Rabia's neighbours told her that he had found consolation in the printed word after his wife died from cerebral malaria. The library was housed in two small rooms, but Rabia had already discovered that a room could contain a universe. She polished her Urdu and her Hindi, and read the books that Azizbhai had donated from his own collection.

Book-buying was his sole vice. He would return from Ajmer or from the Nizamuddin Dargah with armfuls of books that, once read, found their way into the library— House of Treasures, Bright Dairy (All Are Welcome).

Rabia attempted to restrict her reading to discussions of the Koran and of Indian history, but she was drawn to the shelves filled with tales of djinns, marids, ifrits, shaitans who would lick your hands down to the blood and bone if you forgot to wash properly after a meal.

A few months after Arshad and she settled in, the top of the landfill had burst into flames, a slumbering volcano suddenly roused. They had swiftly packed their belongings into cardboard boxes and bedsheets and lined these bundles up on the road, ready to run if the flames spread. Smoke blanketed Bright Dairy, hovering above them in a thick, oily cloud, blotting out everything except the flowers of flame blossoming on the landfill's hide.

As fire engines tackled the fire, Rabia told Arshad tales of an ifrit, his arms and torso at one end of the landfill range, his sturdy hips and strong fairy legs at the other. The flames were his fiery breath, exhaling anger at his long imprisonment.

The queues at the hakim's and the local dispensaries lengthened, as though the landfill djinns had whooshed into everyone's throats and lungs, causing endless trouble. But people can get used to anything in time. They barely noticed the landfill fires after the second year.

⁓

Ahead of her, Arshad said to Azizbhai's daughter, 'As-salam-u-alaikum. You have dropped your water bottle.' He was carrying a parcel of books wrapped in rough twine, and Rabia saw her son through Sanam's eyes: a mohalla boy with a serious face, lightly muscular build, an air of tidiness to him. Rabia hung back, not wanting to disturb their conversation, which she heard in snatches over the roar of trucks carrying dozens of waving potted palms and shrubs up the landfill.

Even the Hindu boys from the militant shakha, trooping out after their evening exercises, their dark glasses identical, tilaks painted on their foreheads, blood-red scarves draped over their Western-style bush shirts, even they stopped to stare at the unaccustomed activity.

'A multinational is building a new office near Bankoli village,' Rabia heard Arshad say. 'They pulled strings in the municipal corporation to get this beautification done.'

Rabia winced. She knew that 'beautification' had a double meaning. The JCBs could turn, like malignant beasts, and as easily stamp their houses into oblivion as part of a 'beautification drive'. But today the beasts were benign. The vehicles wheezed like giant asthmatics, revving and reversing in sideways grumbles. As one deposited its load of mud on the landfill, another rolled up and tamped it down. Men swung down easily from the trucks, laying potted palms around the base of the landfills, which were steadily transforming into man-made hills.

Sanam said, 'Imagine how pleased the ifrit under the mountain will be!'

Arshad smiled. 'My mother also believes there is an ifrit trapped inside, a fire-breathing one.'

Rabia quietly walked past the couple.

Inside one of the transformed hills, the ifrit belched, sending ashes into the heavy summer air, a minor flicker of flame. Despite the swirls of black, plastic-laden smoke, its mellow blaze cast a benevolent light on the potted plants. Rabia felt ash settle on her lips, swallowed involuntarily. The powdery flakes carried a faint, promising warmth.

❧

'Ammi,' Arshad said, 'there is a job for me, right here.'

'What kind of job?' she asked, pouring out tea from the saucepan. 'Substitute driver?' The two of them had carefully saved the money for his driving licence and papers. They had to bribe the traffic department extra, the Muslim rate was substantially higher than the Hindu rate.

He'd had a steady job with one of the new cab companies for a while, and then the woman manager stopped taking their calls. When he went to the company office in Okhla with six other boys from the neighbourhood, they found a large brass lock on the door, dust and dead wasps piled up on the windowsills, a month's salary lost for all of them.

'No,' he said, 'much better paying than that, a courier's job.'

She handed him the tea in a black stone mug. 'Temporary?' Employment was not easy to come by. People were suspicious of anyone from their side, the wrong side, of Bright Dairy Colony.

'Permanent,' he said.

She sighed, closing her eyes, tracing the English syllables. They had weight. They locked into place, promising a solid future.

'Ammi,' he said, and she guessed before he said the rest. Mother and son had always been close. 'The permanent job, it's a generous offer. Made by Azizbhai.'

'Azizbhai,' she said. 'From two lanes down, near the wrestler's akhara. In the parcels and warehousing business, that Azizbhai.'

Arshad said with relief, 'Yes. That Azizbhai. Sanam's father.'

Rabia heard everything her son didn't say. She heard that he needed to say the girl's name. She heard that he would never go back to Bengal to tend Khalid's ancestral land. Above all, she heard the fever in Arshad's voice. The thought of Sanam, her delicate cheekbones, her determined eyes, already burnt like banked coals in his veins, and Rabia had long since learnt respect for the force of such fevers.

She had wrested years of peace from a troubled world, and hoped to return to a place less volatile than Delhi. A sour heat swept the city these days. Now here was fate, disrupting their lives. No return for them to Bengal, and maybe they would never have settled well in the village in any case. Rabia dropped that path, and resolved to arrange a meeting with Azizbhai and his wife as soon as she could.

∽

Sanam was secretly delighted when Arshad asked her parents for permission to meet her, with a view to marriage should they prove compatible. He turned to her and added, 'Only if Sanam herself is agreeable.' She told Rabia later, shyly, that she had made up her mind then to say yes, because he valued her agreement as much as her parents' assent.

Nothing was private in Bright Dairy, not even her son's romance. Rabia worked in the kitchen and the front room, and listened to her son and her future daughter-in-law, to their tentative, gossamer dreams, as they walked together near the entrance of the lane. Rabia had played Hindi film songs for Arshad on a tinny radio when they had first moved to Bright Dairy, those cracked, old-world soundtracks. She heard Sanam say, 'I love Madhubala and Nargis the most,' and smiled to herself. They already had that much in common, a few shared tastes that would become bridges in their lives together.

She still loved watching old films on their small television. Madhubala, leaning against coconut palms with Kishore Kumar on a moonlit night; romancing Ashok Kumar against painted flowers and trellises, offering to test him in the art of love. Nargis, in black and white, luring Raj Kapoor through fake frangipanis and tuberoses; perched on a staircase under a painted moon with clouds playing around her feet in a Dream Sequence.

She cleaned spatters of oil and grease off the kitchen tiles, scrubbed the brass tap until it shone with a handful of tamarind.

She looked out of the narrow window. Arshad was guiding Sanam around the puddles of toxic water from the dump, glistening with oil rainbows. A thin breeze stirred up the dust, which swirled in tiny clouds around their ankles, like a cut-price version of the Dream Sequence. Rabia prayed that her son, at least, would live his dreams.

~

Rabia spent a month in Khalid's village that spring, negotiating the sale of the land. When she returned, she brought a last sack of lychees from their trees for Arshad. They ate the fruit with enjoyment, setting aside the scaly red husk that reminded her of the skin of an al-ghul and other terrible monsters. She was sinking her teeth into the translucent, plump flesh when they heard a sudden shout in the lane outside, the roar of motorcycles.

A gang of boys, red flags raised high, swept past their home. Something crashed against their door. She jumped up, but Arshad said, 'Don't worry, I'll clean it up later.'

She stared at her son.

'Soda bottles,' he said. 'Or bricks. We usually stay indoors at this hour, no one's been hurt so far.'

'When did this start?'

'Shortly after you left for Bengal. They're young, hot-blooded, and they want to show off their power. Don't open the door, not now. We'll take care of it at night, after they've given up and gone home. Let's keep our attention on the wedding arrangements. It's nothing to worry about.'

~

As a special wedding gift, Chand and Badshah Miyan set up a tent where they prepared hundreds of skewers of kababs and giant deghs of biryani over fires of wood and coal. The aroma wafted temptingly through the lanes of Bright Dairy.

'You know why people are fools? Because they sniff after me asking, what is the secret of your masala, what spices do you use, what proportion—as if that makes a biryani,' Badshah Miyan told Rabia when she came by to see if he needed anything. 'That is not the secret at all.'

She gave him an inquiring look.

'Oh, it's important,' he said. 'It gives a biryani body and depth of flavour. Smell this—it has a delicate scent, you must take your spices from the aromatic side, not so much the pungent side. Mace and caraway, nutmeg and pepper, cardamom, cinnamon, a bit of cumin, cloves, the finest saffron, none of that fake dyed horse hair—that's your base. You don't drown a biryani in an ocean of rough, harsh spices, you don't. But the secret of a good biryani is—you tell me what it is?'

Rabia considered the meat, already marinated for several hours, and the rice set out to soak in salted water in a massive brass degh, the glass dishes that held food colouring and the fragrant water Badshah Miyan had extracted from jasmine flowers.

'The art is in mixing it, right?'

He laughed, pleased. 'Yes,' he said. 'Introducing the meat and the rice and the potatoes to one another, in the right order, at the right time. They must stay distinct, but come together in such harmony that they create something new. That, and timing, and learning not to disturb the different layers. The art of making a biryani doesn't end with cooking it. The true pleasure and the measure of your

skill will become apparent when you serve it—you must
lift it out just so, mingling the elements but not messing it
up, it's a biryani, not a khichdi.'

Rabia lingered, even though she had so much to do,
watched him mix the turmeric and food colouring with
a bit of saffron. When he raised the lid, the steam wafted
over the rooftops of Bright Dairy, a rich benediction.

෴

Rabia and Sanam laid out the plates for the special
guests. Together, they arranged the zarda pulao, sweet rice
coloured with real saffron instead of commercial food
colour, scented with the essence of jasmine and kewra
flowers.

Sanam scattered slivered almonds and candied rose
petals over the zarda pulao. Rabia impulsively caught her
hand, delicate, traced over with mehendi like dark lacework,
and said, 'So may all the sweets of life be scattered through
your future.' She felt a rush of welcoming love for her new
daughter-in-law. The dusty light fell on the young woman's
grave face, made more beautiful at the local parlour.

From outside, a hum of noise, ominous. It sounded like
a heated argument.

'Ayesha? Tabassum? Saira?' The girls came fluttering
up the stairs like a flock of parakeets, lipsticked, in high
heels, fine green-and-silver saris, dazzling pink-and-gold
lehengas, beauty that overrode the choked drains outside
the toilet block, the puddles, the smoke from the landfill
mountains. 'Stay with Sanam,' Rabia said. She went to
investigate, hoping that Arshad was far away from any
trouble that might have erupted.

෴

It was trouble, hovering in the summer heat. The maulvi and other elders had stepped in between the mohalla's boys and a swelling crowd of outsiders, boys from the new militant camp whose love of loudspeakers, marching and menacing displays of weaponry was in striking contrast to the far milder practices followed by the local Hindus.

Rabia saw the problem immediately. The maidan was open land, with the mosque on one side and, much further down, the Sikh gurdwara. It was used mostly by the Muslim boys. The women dragged their charpais out to the rim of the maidan on cool autumn evenings. Sometimes, the Hindus or the Sikhs from the next quarter played cricket matches or did vigorous stretching exercises out here, but there had never been any trouble.

Now the sect's crimson flags fluttered from high poles. Chand joined her, leaving Badshah Miyan in charge of the biryani. They walked to the end of the lane, Arshad and his friends closing in protectively around them. A banner rose above their wedding shamiana.

India for True Indians, it said in blood-red script.

The maulvi and the local priest were murmuring in dismay.

'They won't listen to reason,' the priest said, 'their function is tomorrow, but they say that the banner has been put up today and will stay.'

'We can't stop them,' the maulvi said, 'only request them to take it down, and they are not amenable.'

'But how can we proceed?' Azizbhai said. 'Our guests will feel unwelcome.'

'This is an assault on our customs. Who blocks a wedding in this fashion?' Rabia recognised Rafiq-bhai from the next lane. 'We make ourselves smaller and smaller, we move aside and we accommodate, for what? They want to grind us into the dust, they won't let us live in peace.'

The boys from the sect roared back at him in defiance. A neat man with powerful shoulders, Bulgari glasses, a thick foreign watch on his wrist, called loudly: 'See this? See this intolerance? This is public space, janaab, not your father's road.'

'Son,' Azizbhai said calmly, 'you are right, this is everyone's place. But traditionally, pujas and meetings are held in the other maidan, isn't that so? This maidan has never been used for functions—it's for everyone to walk, to play games. Even our wedding, as you can see, is being held inside.'

Arshad shouldered his way through to stand beside his father-in-law, sweating through the brocade of his sherwani.

The man with the dark glasses stepped right in front of Arshad.

'So this is the groom! Congratulations on your happy day,' he said. 'Your guests will come to your wedding, our guests will come to our meeting—you have no objection, mister? This is everybody's land. It doesn't matter how it was used in the past. This is a time of great change, you understand? The country must move forward. Why should only one side use public land and another side be pushed out?'

'Pushed out? But you are doing the pushing, not us!' Rafiq-bhai cried. The boys from the sect raised their staffs, the shiny swords that looked like children's toys, and shouted: 'India for Indians! India for True Indians!'

Chand stepped in between Rafiq and the throng of men. He said, 'This is a day of celebration. There will be no trouble.'

He raised his hand in a gesture of peace. Rabia whispered to some of Arshad's friends to escort Rafiq-bhai back inside.

'Your friend is looking for trouble,' said the man with the dark glasses. 'Mind it. If you start something, then we won't hesitate to hit back. You tell him to shut his big mouth.'

'We are all with you, Madan-ji!' a young man called.

Chand said, 'You are right, this land is for public use only. Please go ahead with your arrangements, there is no objection at all from the groom's side. You are neighbours, Madan-ji—that's your name, yes? Why should neighbours object to each other's celebrations? In fact, my friend and I are cooking a special lunch. You are welcome to join us. Please tell me how many of you there are, and we will gladly make the arrangements.'

'We won't eat with you,' Madan said bluntly. 'It is not our custom to have non-veg.'

'Plenty of vegetarian food too,' Azizbhai chimed in. 'As my friend Chand says, a wedding in the mohalla is a day of celebration for everyone, an auspicious occasion. Please join us.'

Madan looked at Azizbhai, said, 'I will remember you. My boys will remember too.'

'You're in our mohalla, Madan Chaubey. No need to start trouble in our part of Bright Dairy.'

When Azizbhai said the name, it jogged Rabia's memory. Madan Chaubey, 'Duffer' Chaubey. Also from Bright Dairy, but from much further away. He had a poor reputation in school, a reluctant student with a tendency to get into fights. The thin, insecure boy who hid his uncertainties behind a screen of aggression had grown into this belligerent man.

Madan said, 'Some day, this side, that side won't matter. It will all be ours.' But he signalled to the boys and they left without causing further trouble.

'That was smart,' said Azizbhai to Chand. 'Treating them like our guests will make it harder for them to start any ghapla. At least the immediate situation is diffused, thanks to you.'

'That Madan fellow is dangerous,' Chand said. 'He might have given in today, but watch out for him. He means to stir up trouble.'

~

As they surveyed the land, Rabia's heart sank. 'What will our guests think?'

'You can't change their minds or their hearts,' Chand said. 'But we can be smarter than them.'

Arshad, Chand and Azizbhai helped the boys take down the plywood gateway and its satin curtains. They carefully removed the flowers, the arches, and carried them across to the other side, far away from the waving banner. They turned the chairs and tables ninety degrees and shifted the temporary kitchen from one side to the other.

A small turn, a change of direction, and the wedding reception could continue without any fuss. The threatening banner disappeared from view, and instead, joyous yellow and blue saris, mango-coloured saris, pink and red saris—donated by the women in the Muslim mohalla, and by the priest's family and a few Hindus who didn't trust these outsiders, coming here to make trouble—filled the sky with a rainbow of hues.

Guests would enter through the second maidan, bypassing the sect's bristling preparations entirely, and come through a narrow lane into Rabia and Arshad's quadrangle.

Rabia stood with her son and his bride to receive their first guests. Her eyes were dazzled by the spangles on the dupattas, the road splashed with brilliant green, crimson and sky-blue, the colours refracted through the thin chiffon and cotton material. Rabia sent up a silent prayer of thanks for this precious gift of celebration, the damage so narrowly avoided.

~

But Badshah Miyan is right—that was only the first warning. In the two years since Arshad's wedding, there have been many more. Rabia is silent through the rest of the drive, but her friend's words have opened up the box of fears she has kept so tightly closed for the last few months. She has been living a day, a week at a time, not allowing herself to look too far into the future.

The talk between the young men at the dhaba, Badshah Miyan's plans to leave the country—perhaps she has been foolish to look away so resolutely as the flames and rising fires came closer and closer to her own door.

That night, sleep eludes Rabia, even after she says her salat-al-isha prayers. She can see a sliver of the moon, visible through the tarpaulin-covered planks. She sends up an extra prayer for Arshad and Sanam, for Azizbhai, for herself.

She can accept that Arshad and Sanam might leave the country, but what of herself? She cannot imagine leaving; she does not know how much longer she can safely stay.

Hisaab Kitaab

The woman who owns the maze of rooms rented out by Chunchun and others like her seems unsurprised that a policeman wants to see one of her tenants.

'Some of them say that they're dancers, but they're mostly shopgirls. Some work as cleaners, some will go with the truck drivers for less than Rs 2,000,' she says, unfastening the latch for Ombir. 'It makes no difference to me, so long as they do their dhanda outside my house. Which one of them is in trouble?'

'Chunchun. She's not in trouble,' he says, not wanting to cause difficulties for the girl with her landlady. 'We're investigating another case. She might be able to help.'

The woman says wearily, 'That one will end in trouble one way or another, just like her friend. But she pays her rent on time, what do I care? Her rooms are right at the back. Go through that door, turn left, and walk all the way down.'

Ombir watches Chunchun from the unpaved ground floor for a few minutes. Out of costume, in an ordinary peach salwar kameez, with her hair in pigtails and no make-up, she could be a schoolgirl. She appears to be going over some accounts in an exercise book, laboriously writing down figures, occasionally kicking away a young pup who wears a bedraggled pink ribbon round his neck in lieu of a leash. The pup yelps each time, but returns undeterred, an eternal optimist.

On impulse, he dials her number, still watching. He is mildly curious about her reaction to a call from him.

Chunchun picks up on the fourth try.

'I'm busy,' she says immediately. 'Can't talk now, maybe later.'

'I'm coming up,' he says, and disconnects.

'You can't go in there,' she says, standing in front of the door to one of the two rooms. He ignores her, ducking under her outstretched arm.

'Don't run away,' he says. 'I could take you down to the station house if you prefer, but better for you if we talk in peace.'

The room is tiny. An elderly woman sleeps on a low bed that takes up most of the space, her grey hair spreading over the pillow in ragged wisps. Bangles, stacked in a tower, hairpins, bindis, Ayurvedic tonics and empty, stained bottles of cough syrup stand in a straggling line along the windowsill. Dead marigolds droop in a flower pot, the soil stone-dry.

'Can we talk in the other room? I don't want my aunt to wake up, I managed to get her to sleep only an hour ago. She was restless all night because of this heat.'

'Was this Bachni's room?' he asks as they enter.

'Yes,' Chunchun says. 'The rent is paid till the end of next month. I can keep my possessions here until then.'

She tries to keep her eyes on him, but there's something he has noticed in previous investigations. If a suspect has something they want to hide from the police, they always betray themselves by looking towards that object.

'How well did you know her?'

She shrugs. Without make-up, her face lacks the softness that made her attractive on stage. The light falls directly on her, exposing twin lines of hardness and fatigue, furrowing her visage.

'We danced together sometimes,' she says sullenly. 'That's all.'

He settles down on a rug, cross-legged, blocking the door. A steady rain of questions; he refuses to let up, waits out her silences, her reluctant responses, her evasions. The women danced together, often for Reshma Bhabhi's troupe, sometimes for private performances. Chunchun swore she didn't do the other kaam, the extra work that had lent such luxuries to Bachni's room as a cooler, a mini fridge, a proper bed and furniture, a smart Godrej cupboard, the elaborate costumes that hang from hooks and hangers. He doesn't believe her, but it's unimportant.

When the pup wanders into the room, he pets it absently and asks, 'What was Bachni's relationship with Dharam Bir?'

'I don't know anything about that. She knew many of the local men.'

He says, 'That trunk behind you. Open it up, please.'

She stares at him, not moving.

He gently pushes the pup to one side. It settles down on a spangled purple dupatta and licks itself, content. Ombir locks the door, noticing how the girl flinches. He waits while she removes her kurta, lets her unhook her bra, a homely piece of lingerie gone chalky grey from repeated washings.

He says softly, 'Soojak and upadansh. That's what I see when I look at women like you. Diseases that I don't want. Put your clothes back on and keep them on. I didn't ask you to remove them.'

She is crying as she fumbles with her clothes.

'What I want from you is simple. I won't hit you. I'm not here to fuck you either.'

From the next room, a plaintive, wavering voice calls, 'Chunchun? Where are you, you lazy whore, it's time for my bath and massage.'

'No,' he says with the same softness. 'Tell her you're busy, and tell her to shut up.'

He opens the trunk himself, ignores the pouches and plastic bags filled with jewellery, the stash of pink two-thousand-rupee notes, and extracts the red accounts ledgers.

'Interesting,' he says, waving them in front of Chunchun's unresponsive face. 'Maybe they'll tell me more than you have so far. Stay there and stay quiet until I've gone through them.'

'Chunchun, you bitch! How long do I have to wait?' her aunt demands.

'Shut up,' he says, raising his voice so suddenly and to such a pitch that both the girl and the pup flinch. 'She is busy. She'll deal with you later.'

He ignores Chunchun's sobbing as he reads. The first ledger is illuminating, and he feels his pulse quicken with excitement.

'How many men was she blackmailing before she died?'

'I don't know. I had nothing to do with that part of her life.'

He laughs, sets the ledger down.

'I said I wouldn't hit you,' Ombir says. 'Don't make me change my mind.'

He listens as Chunchun babbles out the details. They are as sordid as he had expected. Bachni had an excellent business model.

'First she screwed the men, then she screwed them over,' Ombir says, shaking his head in wonderment. 'Some of the names and figures in this hisaab-kitaab—it seems that many of the men had been paying up for years. Did you help her?'

'I was the pick-up girl,' Chunchun says. Her eyes are blotchy, sore from crying. 'That's all. I collected the money from some of her clients, but not the big ones. Those she did herself.'

He opens the ledger, points to a section. 'These pages have been torn out. Four pages in all. Who were these clients? One man or two?'

'I don't know.'

'You do know. Was it Dharam Bir? His name isn't entered in the rest of the book.'

'No, Dharam Bir wasn't—he isn't interested in sex, not like that.'

'How much did she give you, as a matter of curiosity? Ten per cent? Twenty per cent?'

'Only a little,' Chunchun says. There's genuine grievance in her tone. 'She made me do it, okay? I needed to pay for my aunt's medicines, other things. I couldn't handle all of that by myself.'

'She minted money. How long did she plan to run this racket? The men, they would have run out of patience some day, wouldn't they? Did anyone threaten her? Did she ever come back with bruises, with stories of a fight with one of her blackmail victims?'

'Bachni was smart,' Chunchun says, wiping her eyes with the end of her chunni. 'She was saving up, said she was planning to buy land elsewhere, build a house of her own, she didn't intend to do this forever. You won't understand, but under her toughness, she was also kind. She was the only person who helped me when I moved here. She made the tailor give me discounts when I was starting out, showed me what make-up to wear, it wasn't like it was only dhanda between us. She was the one who rescued this stupid mutt. She took him off the street, and now I'm stuck with him.'

'Fights,' he prompts. 'Touching as the history of your friendship with Bachni is, it doesn't help me understand certain things about her case. Blackmail is not a joke, Chunchun. Blackmailed men are angry men. One of them was angry enough to strangle your kind-hearted, blackmailing whore of a friend and dump her body in the canal. Who was that man?'

'I don't know! Bachni didn't tell me everything.'

He grunts, goes through the next two ledgers. 'Household accounts, a few more victims,' he observes. He takes the trunk, turns it upside down. When he passes his hand across the rusted bottom, he smiles and uses his penknife to carefully cut the thin cords that bind a slender ledger to the underside.

Ombir doesn't tell Chunchun that she gave it away; she had looked at the trunk, but not at the top. Her gaze had gone immediately to the bottom.

When he opens the ledger, it tells him more than he wanted to know. He leafs through the pages silently, trying to control his anger.

'You bitch,' he says finally. 'You helped her with the children.'

She bursts into tears. 'I knew nothing about that! Please believe me, honestly, I was never involved with any of that!'

He holds the book open in front of her. She closes her eyes, turns her head away. He wrenches her head back.

'Open your goddamned eyes or I'll make you,' he says grimly.

Between them, the pages tell their own story. Pasted on each page, the photograph of a child. Young girls. Some as young as seven, some older, possibly just in their teens. Dates. Sums of money. At the head of each page, a rough notation in Hindi: 'Dharam Bir's Hisaab Kitaab.'

'How many, Chunchun? How many did you watch her sell to him? What was your cut? What did you get for each rape?'

There are at least twenty names, twenty photographs, twenty children recorded in the ledger, and the thought sends him into such a rage that he has to take a few deep breaths, control himself, or he would have hit the woman in front of him. She isn't Bachni, he reminds himself, whatever she has done, she didn't start this dirty business.

'What happened, Chunchun? Did she ask him for too much? Was that what tilted the balance finally? Did he realise that she would go on blackmailing him forever?'

'I don't know,' she cries. 'I don't know what happened, she didn't tell me everything.'

'Is there more? I want to see everything. Every exercise book. Every last piece of paper.'

'Only this. She had only these four, no other books.'

He turns the trunk the right side up, tries to choke down his fury.

'Was it worth it?' He grabs a handful of jewellery and shoves it in her face. 'Whoring yourself out, that's one thing. But you helped her sell children. For this?'

She raises her head then, finding a streak of defiance.

'Nobody was there for me,' she says, her voice harsh, 'when my aunt sold me to the first bastard of a man. I was eleven, and nobody cared. Why should I care?'

He would like to break every bone in her sullen, selfish face. It takes all of his self-control not to remove his belt and give her the beating of a lifetime, but he does not want to be that kind of policeman.

'You could have put an end to it, if you'd cared about anything beyond your own worthless self,' he tells her. 'You could have come to us, or told the pradhan's wife, just that much, and maybe some of the children would not have suffered. But you let them suffer. For money. And after your friend was killed, you took over her blackmail business, didn't you?'

She says nothing. In her eyes, a shrewd flicker. She knows now that he won't hurt her, and she watches silently as he scoops the jewellery, the cash, the hisaab-kitaab into an old, frayed rucksack.

'I know what you're thinking,' he says, turning back to her. 'He didn't hit me, he's a weak man, he didn't even rape me. But I'll tell you something, and you'd better listen, because your life depends on it. If you say one word to Dharam Bir, if I find out that he has been given even the slightest hint that I know, if you let a single word of warning escape, I will hunt you down and make sure that you suffer as those children did. I will break you in two, Chunchun, unless you keep your mouth shut.'

The fear in her eyes gives him a shaft of pleasure, the only pleasure he has derived from this meeting.

He takes the dog with him. On his way back to the station house, he stops at the sugarcane stall. Gives the proprietor a wad of bills, sets the puppy down, and tells the man, 'Make sure you feed him properly. I'll come back to check on how he's doing from time to time.'

He walks back, wanting to tire himself out, needing the time in the open air, instead of calling Bhim Sain to pick him up or accepting a ride from passing villagers.

At the back of the ledger, he had found four pages with children's photos, but no date, no amount. Three of the girls were unknown to him. The fourth girl was Munia.

Gifts

The bike gleams against the blue brick wall, the black metal pristine, factory-fresh. Ombir is inspecting it, forgetting the mild ache in his calves, distracted even from his migraine, when Bhim Sain joins him with two glasses of chai.

'Jolly-ji sent this over,' Bhim Sain says. 'It has its own name, look: Roadster.'

'It's a Harley-Davidson,' Ombir says. 'One of the most expensive bikes. Why is it here?'

'Bhadana dropped it off. Jolly-ji notices everything, sir. He said that it's lying around unused in his garage. We are welcome to use it until the other Bullet is sent back from the Faridabad repair shop.'

'Can't accept gifts of this nature,' Ombir says. He badly wants to try out the bike. It's a beautiful beast. He doesn't have to imagine the engine's low growl, or how easily it would slide around curves, handle the bumps in Teetarpur's roads, he has spent enough hours watching Harley-Davidson videos on YouTube, knowing he'll never save enough from his salary or from bribes to buy one for himself.

'Bhai,' Bhim Sain says, forgetting momentarily to call him 'sir', 'Jolly-ji is a sharp man, no? He knows everything that happens in the district. His boys must have already told him that you were unhappy about that sign. This is his way of saying sorry. And where's the harm in using the bike for a few days? We need two vehicles, Ombir-ji. Managing with one—today, you walked back all the way. The pradhan came by, he told me he saw you walking. It's not good for the reputation of the police, no? They won't respect us if we're walking here, walking there all the time. Even idiots like Dilshad have their own transport.'

Ombir says, 'Jolly-ji is acting like he runs this village. I don't like it.'

'Doesn't he, sir? Maybe he overstepped, but if we send back such a gift, he'll be annoyed. Is that wise?'

Ombir hesitates, trying to subjugate the lust in his heart for the beauty in front of his eyes.

'Jolly-ji shows off his power too much,' he says. 'But it may not be a good idea to antagonise him. Men like him feel insulted when their gifts are refused, that's true.'

'Sir, we could use it for just one or two days,' Bhim Sain says. 'I'll tell the Faridabad garage to hurry up. Only two days and then we can return it, how about that? The bike was purchased for Bhadana's use, but he is afraid of such a large vehicle. Rode it back from the showroom yesterday, prefers his smaller Kawasaki, says he can't handle such a powerful engine.'

'The engine's not a problem, once you get the hang of it,' Ombir says. Jolly's garage is filled with cars in any case, a Jaguar, two BMWs, an Audi, he knows that a bike doesn't mean much to the man. 'All right, but tell Bhadana the next time he passes this way that we can't accept any other presents. Only this for a few days, and the usual mahaprasad, but nothing more.'

The mahaprasad is a perk of the job. Every month, Bhadana hands them two unmarked envelopes plump with cash, as is standard in most police stations. It is expected that the big men in a district will send something to sweeten their lives. He doesn't want to go beyond that, to stray over the line that separates them from the men in Jolly Singh's squad.

Bhim Sain caresses the bike the way he would pat down a horse. 'You beauty,' he says. 'You beauty.'

Ombir walks into the station house, Bhim Sain reluctantly covering the Harley up with an old chadar and following him. He dumps the exercise books on his desk. Tiredness hits him so hard that he would have stretched out right there, taken a nap, except that the pradhan is crouched near the rabbit's cage, deep in conversation with Laadli.

'So you like the carrots, yes? I'll bring you more tomorrow, little one. Taste these, you won't find carrots like these in the bazaar, they're grown in my own field. Namaste, Ombir, I also brought some carrots and radishes for you.'

'Carrots,' Ombir says. 'And Harleys. We are blessed today, pradhan-ji. How can I help?'

The pradhan gives Laadli one last, lingering look, and the rabbit snuffles back at him.

'See?' Bhim Sain says. 'Being in the hands of the law isn't so bad, is it, Laadli?'

When the pradhan starts talking, he is his usual self—under the old-school courtesy, he is strictly business. It's the TV crews, he explains, and Ombir winces. The television crews have been a nuisance over the last week. They camped outside Chand's hut for days, outside the police station for a while. He had thought they would be rid of the mosquito horde after the murder was solved, but Jolly's ill-advised signboard had brought them back.

'They still have questions,' the pradhan says. 'After you left, they tried their best to get something out of me and Bhim Sain about the case. They kept asking, is it true that there was a lynching, that Mansoor did not die by suicide but at the hands of a mob? I told them the truth. They didn't ask about the women's gathering earlier that day—my wife was there, she told me all about it—but a gathering of neighbours is not a mob. If there had been a proper mob, if men had crowded into your station house later that night, I would have known of it, that's what I said. And I didn't, so there wasn't.'

He pauses, looking from one policeman to the other.

'That is the truth, isn't it? Bhim Sain gave a solid explanation, Ombir-ji. They asked if the village was anti-Muslim, and he said that the village had always welcomed Muslims, and that poor Mansoor had been fed and treated well by Chand and also by many other families. They asked if Mansoor had been the victim of a lynching, and Bhim Sain explained that Mansoor was mental, that it was not uncommon for first-time murderers to be overcome by remorse and attempt suicide. You weren't here, but they came briefly to look at the jail. Bhim Sain showed them where the hinges were weak.'

Ombir gives Bhim Sain a thoughtful look. The hinges had been strong enough, if he remembers rightly. His eyes rest on the top of Laadli's cage. Bhim Sain and he look at the screwdriver, and Bhim Sain hastily looks away.

'Pradhan-ji, if you have any doubts, let me clear them at once,' Ombir says. 'It is true that Chand and his brother came to visit Mansoor in his cell. It was late at night. I allowed it because tempers were running high. They met him. They spoke to him. And they left. Later that night, he took his own life. That is all there is to the matter. We were both perhaps too sure that he would not harm himself, but I promise you that there was no mob at my station that night.'

'You are a precise man, Ombir-ji,' the pradhan says. Behind his thick spectacles, his shrewd eyes assess the two policemen. 'I understand the case has been a triumph for you. Now, one of these TV fellows, he's an influential anchor, his talk show reaches lakhs of people every night, he will be here tonight. He has asked to speak to me. I hear you saying there was no mob after the women left that day. I believe you. Only Chand and his brother, two men, maybe three or four: that is not a mob. Achha, that is good.'

He half-rises from his seat, meeting Ombir's eyes squarely. His own eyes are much harder than they were at the start of the conversation. 'I can tell this anchor then that Mansoor was not lynched? It is one hundred per cent the truth?'

Ombir says, 'You have my word on this. Chand did not kill Mansoor. Nor did any other man from the village.'

'Good, good,' the pradhan says, settling back in the wooden chair. 'Sorry to take up your time. I see you have a new television set also?'

Ombir glances up, startled.

'It was installed this morning,' Bhim Sain says. 'The SSP sent it.'

The men look at the silent screen, the news scrolling by in big, bold, screaming headlines. Unrest in Bihar over reservations, four dead. Farmers block Haryana highway. Exposed: fertility scam in Faridabad private clinics.

The pradhan laughs. 'Our countrymen are such inventive rascals, every day a new scam.'

'There was a report in *The Lalten*,' Ombir says. 'But I haven't had time to read it. Munia's murder has kept us busy.'

'Of course, of course,' the pradhan says. 'But these people were so smart. One doctor used to run a sperm bank for bulls, that's where he got the idea. Men go to the clinics to be tested for their private marital problems. The results will show some problem or the other. It's like astrologers—if they don't find rahu-ketu issues, they'll find kaalsarpa dosha or pitra dosha, always some reason why your luck is not working. Same thing here.'

Ombir stares at the scrolling headlines.

'These Faridabad clinics,' he says. 'Their tests are not reliable?'

The pradhan laughs. 'Who doesn't believe a test report, printed and all? But it's a scam. Nothing's wrong with most of these men, only stress, overwork. They spend lakhs and lakhs of rupees on "treatment", but nothing's wrong with them. Sooner or later, their wives will conceive. Then they'll thank these scamsters for the cure. The government is closing down many of those labs. They were making crores, mind you, crores.'

'People are so gullible,' says Ombir. He feels a bubble of lightness expand in his chest. 'Only too easy to become a crorepati in our country.'

The buoyancy persists long after the pradhan has left. He finishes some of the pending paperwork, opens a new notebook and makes a start on entering his conclusions from his meeting with Chunchun. The burst of energy carries him some distance, but the fatigue, lurking in the background, finally asserts itself.

Gradually, his eyes close and he nods off, the exercise books near his outstretched hand. Bhim Sain clears the empty cups, settles down in the big chair to watch television. When he is sure that Ombir is in deep sleep, he stealthily brings Laadli out of her cage, lets her hop around the small room so that she can get some exercise, not good for any creature to be cooped up all day.

⌇

The next evening, with the first proper monsoon clouds amassing overhead and the heat dissolving into a dense, suffocating humidity, Ombir makes his condolence visit to Chand. He hesitates in front of the Harley-Davidson, runs his eyes lovingly along its shrouded curves, but takes the Bullet in the end.

Chand had returned from his daughter's cremation two days ago, but his eyes are still haunted. When Dilshad came by the station house on his weekly visit, he had told Ombir that Chand's friends had sat with him until the afternoon, fending off the last, stubborn machhars, his word for the buzzing, whining swarms of local television crews eager for a soundbite.

'I gave them a lift to the bus stop just now,' he says, unusually sombre. 'Rabia and Badshah Miyan said they could stay overnight, but Chand wanted to be left alone. He had visitors all day. The pradhan and even Jolly-ji went to see him, and most of the villagers. Such a tragedy, but it has brought out how much we care for our own. We're not heartless like city people.'

The pages from Chunchun's exercise book float in Ombir's mind, each child's photograph vivid. City or village or small town, it doesn't matter. The heartless drift through life like floating spores, evil spreading like mould wherever they land.

Radio Yesterday

For some time after the cremation, Chand leaves his phone undisturbed. It lies in the taaq, ignored until someone calls, and then the blue light from its screen briefly illuminates the bare bricks of the shallow niche.

After a week, he finally unplugs the phone from its charger, looks at the numbers. Distant relatives, a few calls from Bhadana, Jolly Singh's manager, six missed calls from Dilshad, some more from numbers he can't identify—perhaps journalists, perhaps inquisitive neighbours, he has no interest in talking to either kind. And two names that recur much more often.

He pours water from the goose-necked surahi into a steel tumbler, takes a sip, feels the dryness in his throat release its grip on him. He tries to remember to keep drinking water in this heat, even if he feels little thirst, but it sometimes slips his mind.

Rabia and Badshah Miyan, their calls form a pattern as distinctive as their personalities. Badshah Miyan has called often, scattering his attempts throughout his busy days, and Chand can imagine him reaching for his phone at spare moments, turning from the butcher's block, the thick red-and-grey accounts ledgers, the inspection of the gigantic walk-in freezers, whenever there's a lull at work.

Rabia, meticulous as ever, has tried his number in the punctuations and resting spaces of her day; before and after breakfast, once in the afternoon at an hour that puzzles him until he realises it must mark the end of her shift at the packing warehouse, twice every evening, and one last call, late at night.

Missed calls, reaching out to him like a breath of comfort. He inhales, and his own breathing sounds strange to him, a slight, shuddering rasp that seems loud in the silence of the hut. He has forgotten to fill the water tanks from the well at the back of the house. He finds the steel bucket instead. The lilies, Jolly Singh's gift, have wilted, their petals brown and drooping.

Chand carries them outside and scoops a hollow for them in the dry soil, returning them to the earth. He splashes some of the water left in the bucket over his face. It carries the faint scent of rotting petals and stems, not unpleasant.

❧

Chand doesn't bother to light the lamps, he'll do that later. He leaves the hut dark and lifeless, and walks up the road, taking the narrow path through the field that leads to the canal. The humidity has lifted and a hint of rain kisses the air.

The fields in Delhi's wealthier farmhouses are flat and featureless. He had sometimes delivered meat to those mansions, and glanced at the fields—no undulation, just one crop giving way to another. One of the pleasures of returning to Teetarpur has been rediscovering the secrets and surprises of the local fields. They are separate landscapes, entire in themselves. One might contain thorn thickets, peacocks and peahens bursting from the branches in their startled glory. Another might lead into a wilderness past the straggling lace of summer crops, to a tiny temple nestled near abandoned termite cities that house the occasional bed of scorpions, or a timid cobra.

He takes the track. It plunges downwards, and within a few minutes, the road is abruptly cut off, the darkness widening ahead to reveal glimpses of water and the broken concrete banks of the canal. At the end of the track, a man stirs.

'I didn't mean to disturb you tonight,' Ombir says.

Chand says, 'Look.'

Opens his hand, jewelled with three captive fireflies. They rest motionless, blinking points of light. He raises his hand to a tree branch, blows gently into his palm. The fireflies stir, taking off one by one like miniature helicopters.

'I'll leave you in peace, Chand. Dilshad said you'd had too many visitors today. I stopped by and saw that the house was in darkness, came down for a breath of air.'

'Peace,' Chand says. 'If it was so easy. Stay if you like, Ombir-ji. I don't mind your company. But let's not talk of sorrowful matters. My tasks are completed, there's nothing more to be said.'

'Your friends will be back soon?'

'They would have stayed longer, if I'd allowed them. But Rabia and Badshah Miyan have their own families ... That signboard. You ordered it dug up. I'm glad, I wouldn't have wanted them to see it. It's not right, this feeling in the village, it would not have happened before.'

'Mansoor was Muslim after all,' Ombir says. 'People grieve in many ways. Sometimes it makes them scratch at old wounds, that's all.'

'He was homeless, and a lunatic, and he did no harm in all these years. Is it so easy to forget what a man is?'

Ombir takes a breath and says, 'Is that why you spared him?'

Chand does not turn around, but his shoulders stiffen.

'You didn't kill him in the end, Chand. I checked the well. Thoroughly. There was no corpse, no sign of blood on the well rim, in the dust. Not a drop, and you were carrying an axe. You meant to do it. Why didn't you? Pity, because he is mad?'

Chand laughs, a hoarse, rusted sound.

'Pity. No, there was none of that. My daughter, laid out like a discarded sack in the morgue—it was not pity, not at all.'

'What was it, then?'

'I asked him to raise his hands, and he couldn't. His shoulder muscles are badly damaged. He could not have done it. Everything he said was true. I waited until Balle Ram and Dilshad left. I took him to the edge of the forest. I said, get back to your own village, Mansoor, or find somewhere else to beg, but never show your face here again. He understood. His mind clouds over, it wanders, but he is not completely out of his senses. Then he fell at my feet to thank me. Imagine that, a man tries to kill you for something you have not done, and you thank him ... He thanked me for believing him. He would not have harmed her. He said that over and over, and my last doubts melted, Ombir. Mansoor did not kill my child.'

Chand and Ombir walk back to the hut in silence. Chand bends down, lights the kerosene lantern.

Ombir waits.

'I'm tired, Ombir. It is a deep tiredness, it's settled in my bones. Shall we talk tomorrow?'

'Forgive me. There is one small matter.'

Chand looks at the policeman in silence. His gaunt face is more drawn than it was even on the day they found Munia, but he smiles.

'Don't ask me not to,' he says. 'You don't have that right.'

'All I ask is that you leave it in my hands. Will you do that?'

'The case is closed, Ombir. This is my business now.'

'It was my case. It is my business, not yours.'

'I carried her ashes home just the other day,' Chand says. 'My daughter's ashes have not yet cooled.'

Ombir can't look at his face too long. He says, 'Give me one chance to settle it. Just one. You are the father. You have a right, but not by law. I made a mistake. Allow me to fix it.'

'Tell me who he is. I can see it in your eyes. You know who killed her.'

'I'm not fully sure,' Ombir says. 'Give me a few days. That's all I ask. Please, Chand. Don't take this burden on to your shoulders. It is mine to handle.'

'A few days,' Chand says. 'After that, I will ask you again. And again, until I know his name.'

Ombir nods, accepting this as fair.

Chand says, 'Shanti. It was written on the walls of that crematorium. Peace, in big, sky-blue letters. The painter did a good job. But when I read that word, it burned in my heart, Ombir. It left ashes and dust behind.'

He picks up the lantern, carries it in, blows out the flame. The fireflies dance ahead of the policeman, darting across his path, pinpoints of light in the pitch-black darkness.

✺

The taaq lights up, casting a blue glow over Chand. He hesitates. A moth flies in slow, lazy circles overhead, briefly landing on the screen, the dusty gold wings flaring out before it leaves again.

Chand picks up when she calls a second time.

'Rabia,' he says.

She doesn't ask how he is, for which he is grateful. Too many people ask, and what can he say that is true and that will not make them flinch?

'I knew you would answer your phone when you were ready,' she says.

He says nothing, closes his eyes and listens to the sounds of her household. The clatter of a plate on the stone slab in her kitchen, boys whooping outside as they play a noisy game of cricket in the alley, the radio in the background, playing low music.

'You don't have to speak if you don't want to. This is only—' She breaks off, and he imagines her frowning slightly, trying to find the precise words.

'To be there,' she says at last.

'I know. I saw your missed calls, yours and Badshah Miyan's.'

'He said he would visit you this weekend.'

Chand says, 'The village is still closed to outsiders.' He tries to soften the word, not wanting to say it out loud—

outsiders, people of her faith, Badshah Miyan's faith, a sudden barrier between him and his friends that none of them had asked for. 'Balle Ram and I will talk to them again, and I'll call Badshah Miyan tomorrow, tell him myself. Maybe I'll visit him. Some day. Later.'

'Have you eaten anything today?'

He avoids the question. 'Sarita Devi sends over dinner every night. Too much food, but they are taking good care of me. I wish sometimes they would take less care.'

Her laugh makes him feel better.

'Do you want to talk?'

'No.'

'All right,' she says. 'That's all right.'

He doesn't want her to end the call, so he says, 'What are you listening to?'

'Some old songs on the radio, Naushad, Mukesh, Kishore Kumar. It's a programme called Guzrey Hue Woh Din. Arshad and Sanam are at Azizbhai's tonight, so I'm enjoying the pleasure of my own company.'

'I can't hear the music, it's muffled. Will you turn the radio up?'

'Is this better?'

'Yes.'

'I'll leave it on. You can listen for as long as you like.'

They spend the evening in each other's company, bridging the distance between his village and her home in Bright Dairy with old, familiar songs. Once, she forgets that Chand is listening, and he hears her humming along, as she used to do when the three of them, Rabia, Khalid and he, lived together on the banks of the river.

When the programme ends, he says, 'That brought me comfort, Rabia. The music, those tunes—they bring back the old days, a time when my village did not feel the need to separate us into insiders and outsiders.'

'I call these programmes my Radio Yesterday. But that time is long gone, if it ever truly existed. Bright Dairy has new gates for the first time, separating our side from the Hindu side. And barbed wire fences. They were installed last week.'

'Gates, and outsiders,' Chand says. 'How did all of us live together all these years?'

'We lived in the cracks outside the gates,' Rabia says. 'It was enough, for a while.'

'May I call again tomorrow?'

'Please,' she says. 'I'll find a good programme on the radio.'

'Yes,' says Chand. 'I like it a lot, your Radio Yesterday.'

He can hear her breathing. He nestles his phone closer to his ear, drawing comfort from this lightest of sounds, letting the easy silence stretch between them, until finally he says goodbye. His house is quiet, so still, so empty, without the light rise and fall of Rabia's breath.

❧

Rabia turns off the radio. The racket from her neighbours' homes pours in—the blaring televisions, the family conversations and squabbles, the clatter of someone washing stainless steel plates in a stone sink. The sudden quietness of her room feels startling in the middle of this friendly hubbub, the spell of the old days not fully dispersed.

It has been years since she thought about their last few days on the black river that had sheltered and housed the three of them. She had folded her memories into a tightly knotted bundle, shoved it firmly into the back of the highest shelf of her mind.

⁓

One word. Stay.

It changed everything between them.

Two months after her husband's death, a few of Khalid's friends from the ambulance crew took Arshad with them on a short trip to offer prayers for his father's soul at the shrine in Ajmer-sharif.

Rabia and Chand found themselves alone for the first time. It cast a constraint on their easy conversation. Her grief was ebbing, giving way to an underlying anger at her husband. Sometimes, when she was alone, she spoke it out aloud to Khalid, told him that he had committed not just a sinful act, but a selfish, thoughtless one. They had shared their lives, for better and for worse, and he had withheld this from her, this blackest of clouds, this dense fog of despair. 'If you had only told me,' she found herself saying to the whittled wooden toys he had left behind, to the silent flute he had left on their bed. 'What right did you have to keep it to yourself?'

The first two nights after Arshad's departure, Chand stayed away. Instead of cooking together, they lit separate fires. From her hut, she watched the light in his window, turned off her lamp only after he blew out his. On the third night, the rain poured down like sheets of glass, hard and unrelenting, and she was struggling to patch a bad leak in the thatch when Chand came in. He was soaking wet. He found an armful of straw, a few palm fronds left in one corner of the hut, and working steadily, patched the leak with her assistance.

He would have left, but she said, 'There is enough food for both of us.' They ate together, but in silence, neither able to break the awkwardness that hovered over them.

Chand helped her clear the dishes, as he had so often done. Thunder pealed overhead. Chand went to the door, and Rabia exclaimed when she saw the force of the storm.

'It's no matter,' he said. 'I'm already soaked, another drenching won't hurt me.'

He was at the entrance of the hut. She came up behind him and pulled the door shut.

When she placed her hand in his, he could not say a word. He felt her fingers clasp his, felt the firmness of her grasp.

Rabia said, 'Stay.'

She touched him first. She unfastened the carved wooden buttons of his kurta. She led him to the cot.

He made himself ask, so that she had time to pause, to change her mind, to say no, 'You're sure? You want this?'

Her mouth grazed his throat, travelled upwards. Her breath warmed the skin above his upper lip. She said, 'I know what I want. Don't you?' and he was lost, or not lost, he was fully hers in that moment before she moved to the bed, leaning backwards, bringing him home.

She was warm and ready, and she gave as much as she took, and she was so real, so present, shivering in the rain that leaked from the gaps in the roof, warming herself and him with her eagerness, her need, her delight.

Much later, she said, 'You have to know that this will never happen again.'

And he said, 'If you say so. But I am glad it did happen. I spent years hoping it would.'

Control

Ombir walks into the station house, and he knows immediately. Two men cannot work together for so many years, in such close quarters, without becoming closer than siblings, than any family. They can feel each other's ill temper, changes in mood, depression, anger. He can smell the change in the air even before he sees Bhim Sain at his desk, the exercise books open in front of him, the long rows and columns of figures next to the photographs of the children. Chunchun's childish scrawls accompany each picture. Even upside down, across the width of their desk, he recognises that face. Munia, her face blurred as she ducks away, the trunk of the jamun tree visible behind her.

'When were you going to tell me, sir?' Bhim Sain says.

Ombir hesitates. 'I would have told you soon,' he says finally. 'Only wanted some time to be sure.'

'We saw the woman's body together, sir,' Bhim Sain says. 'I was by your side when the SSP went down into the well. You knew then? That Mansoor wasn't the murderer?' The rabbit is sleeping in her cage. Bhim Sain keeps his voice low so as to not wake her.

Ombir says, 'I promise I would have told you. I interviewed this woman only two days ago, Bhim Sain.'

'You've spoken to the SSP? We're reopening the case?'

Ombir is silent.

Bhim Sain rises from the chair. 'Sorry, sir. Please take your seat. I sat down without thinking. Laadli was exploring after you went out. I let her out to take the air, it's not good for creatures like her to be cooped up all the time. She knocked the books over. I went to pick them up, and one of them had opened out, to the photographs. Their photos. The children's photos.'

Ombir says, 'I understand.'

'The case cannot be reopened?'

'It could have been,' Ombir says. 'But I gave Pilania sir my word that everything was in order. I assured him that the law had taken its course. It will be difficult now.'

Bhim Sain says, 'All right, sir. You can't do anything about this, I accept the situation. We can't ask for a probe, you are correct. This man, sir, what do we do about this man? The woman in the canal …'

'Bachni,' Ombir says. 'Her name was Bachni. She helped Dharam Bir with all that. The children, she helped him with those matters. Her friend told me everything. The dancer. Chunchun.'

Bhim Sain nods. 'Bachni. The children he raped. And Munia. What did he do to Chand's daughter?'

'I don't know,' Ombir says. 'I will speak to him myself.'

'No, sir,' Bhim Sain says. 'Not alone. You say we can't do anything, we can't bring in the law now, all right. We can't reopen the case, fine. We can't tell the SSP, that also I accept. But we can do what is right ourselves. If we are not the law, who is?'

He's striding out, still talking, before Ombir can stop him.

'I know where he'll be tonight,' he says. 'It's not that late. He's usually at the theka near the factory with his friends.'

'Bhim Sain, calm down,' Ombir says. 'Don't do anything in this state of mind.'

Bhim Sain is pulling the covers off the Harley, has the key in his hand.

'Sir, I'm a father. Maybe you don't understand what that means now, but you will, after your child is born. You ask the gods only for one thing. That nothing will harm your child. That's all any parent wants, that their children should not be hurt.'

'You're not riding now,' Ombir says. 'Give me the keys.'

'Yes, sir.'

'We are only going to talk to him, Bhim Sain. We'll make a few inquiries. That is all. This is a direct order, you understand.'

Ombir kicks the Harley into gear, and the sound of the engine swells into the night. Bhim Sain says nothing as he hops onto the back of the motorcycle.

～

The theka, a shabby booze shop, is located behind the Sangam Soap and Heavenly Incense Factory, near the squat rectangle of a cement tank that holds stagnant green water.

Bhim Sain doesn't waste time.

'Theka is closed,' he says brusquely. 'You lot, get lost. Not you, Dharam Bir. The rest of the men can go.'

Dharam Bir lounges on the rim of the tank, looking from one policeman to the other. Three of his friends are on their feet, their hands on their belts.

'Unusual time for a visit, Ombir,' he says.

'It is,' Ombir says. 'Best that we talk in private, Dharam Bir.'

'Or talk tomorrow, or some other time during the week,' Dharam Bir says. 'I have a busy schedule at the factory these days.'

'I think you'll make time for us,' Ombir says. He brings the ledger out of his backpack, holds it up in the air.

Dharam Bir doesn't change position, but he says to his friends, 'Go home. Anyway, it's late. I'll deal with these people myself.'

Ombir and Bhim Sain wait, Ombir patiently, Bhim Sain with palpable irritation, as the men leave. When Bhim Sain begins to speak, Ombir holds up a hand.

'Not yet, if you don't mind. Wait until their bikes have gone all the way up the road. Dharam Bir-ji, I would be most obliged if you tell your friends not to wait for you. Unless you'd prefer to have this talk at the station house.'

Dharam Bir glares at Ombir, but he nods his assent. 'Here is better,' he says. 'No problem.'

The man in charge of the theka glances at Bhim Sain and abandons the sorting of bottles and glasses. He locks the steel bars on the small window grille, pulling the corrugated shutter down with a jerky, harsh rattle, leaves as swiftly as his ancient Bajaj scooter will allow.

It's only the three of them now. Ombir waits, lengthening the silence.

'So much drama, Ombir?' Dharam Bir says. 'Chalo, I don't mind. Ask what you like.'

Bhim Sain moves forward. Ombir places a hand on his colleague's arm, gently forcing him back.

'I met a friend of yours the other day,' he says. 'What was her name? Chameli, Champa—no, Chunchun. Quite a talented dancer she was. Had a way with the crowd. Happened to stop by her home to ask for some information. I needed a few details, clearing up paperwork for one of our cases.'

Dharam Bir watches him steadily. The man is in darkness for the most part, but his face is well lit in the flare of the Petromax lanterns in front of the closed liquor store. His hands are near his pockets. Ombir guesses he has a knife, perhaps a gun, but probably no more than a country pistol.

'These signatures, if you'd take a look,' he continues. 'It seems like your handwriting to me. It is, isn't it?'

Dharam Bir does not move forward.

'If it is, so what?'

'Dharam Bir-ji, not to offend you or anything. But these signatures are next to the photographs of children, you understand? And against each photograph, there is also the signature of another person. A woman called Bachni. And one of these photographs is of a child, Munia. It so happens that within the space of a few days, Bachni was found floating in a canal, and the child was found—everyone knows where she was found. It makes me curious, that's all.'

Dharam Bir sits up, straddling the cement rim, and laughs.

'You cops,' he says. 'You think you own this place, blundering around with your useless questions. I thought you were smarter than the average village policeman, Ombir, but you're every bit as thick as the rest of your kind. If you want to ask something, ask it straight. Don't mess around with me.'

Ombir can feel the nerves jumping in Bhim Sain's arm. He tightens his grip a trifle, releases the pressure slowly, hoping that Bhim Sain can understand his silent signal: Don't lose your temper.

'You knew this Bachni well?'

'Extremely well,' Dharam Bir says. His smile is broad and reminiscent. 'She was an excellent businesswoman. Perhaps too ambitious for her own health. She knew too much about too many people in this village, and she was careless in her use of that knowledge.'

Ombir says, frowning down at the pages, 'What is the purpose of this ledger?'

Dharam Bir stands up, stretching lazily, takes a swig from his bottle of Thums Up. Ombir smells the battery acid tang of hooch.

'The purpose of this ledger,' he says, mimicking Ombir, 'is none of your business.'

Bhim Sain shakes off Ombir's hand, takes a few steps towards Dharam Bir.

'Everything that happens in this village is our business. If a cow farts and I make it my business or Ombir sir makes it his business, it's our business.'

Dharam Bir says, 'You two make me laugh. Bachni had three skills: she made powerful allies, she made powerful enemies, and she was expert at fucking them both. And sometimes she got fucked back by someone who was sick of being squeezed like an orange. I know what you're after. I was with Chunchun the day that Mansoor strung up Chand's kid.'

'Let me guess,' says Ombir. 'You were with Chunchun the night Bachni died as well.'

'I don't know when the whore died,' Dharam Bir says. 'But Chunchun and I spent a lot of time together this month. She started out as a common five-hundred-rupee randi, but she's improved over the years.'

The collar of Ombir's uniform is stiff with sweat. It makes his neck itch, and he's aware that his temper is beginning to fray.

'One woman, two alibis,' he says. 'That's convenient.'

Dharam Bir comes closer, facing down Bhim Sain.

'Tamasha over. If you have a warrant, take me down to the station. Saluja, my boss, would love to hear that you've called one of his top men in for questioning, but I have no problem with answering your questions. Once you have that warrant. And if you don't, I'm going home. This was amusing, but we're done here.'

Bhim Sain says, 'One more question. What did you do to the kids? To Munia?'

'Do? To Munia? Nothing. I just liked watching her when Chand was away. To the others? I'm a generous man, Bhim Sain. That ledger lists all the donations I've made to children and their families over the years, no? Chocolates, Coke, clothes, whatever was needed.'

He laughs in Bhim Sain's face. 'Charity,' he says. 'You ask around. Most of the parents take the cash themselves. They don't ask foolish questions. You shouldn't either.'

'Bhim Sain!' Ombir calls in warning, but he's too late.

Bhim Sain throws a punch. It should have connected, but Dharam Bir's ready for it, leans out of the way, something in his right hand glinting. An old-fashioned razor, a cut-throat, the blade slashing at Bhim Sain's unguarded face.

Bhim Sain screams, staggers back, blood seeping through the hand he uses to cover his ripped cheek.

'Fuck your questions,' Dharam Bir says. 'That's a warning, Ombir. Tell this thick-skulled dolt to leave me alone, don't poke your nose into my affairs, or next time—'

Ombir hits him. They hear the crack as the bones in his nose break. His head jerks and he grunts in pain, bleeding freely.

'Have you gone mad? When Saluja hears about this, he'll fuck you both so hard you won't be able to sit down for a month.'

Bhim Sain says, 'It's a small cut, Dharam Bir. You should have tried harder. Big mistake. I'm asking you again. What did you do to those kids?'

'You are crazy,' Dharam Bir says with conviction. Bhim Sain pulls out his favourite baton, a small, lead-weighted cosh, whirls it professionally, takes Dharam Bir down in two quick blows. The man is staggering despite his bulk, he's toppling, and Ombir can't hold it in any more. It comes up. The rage. The frustration. The long, sleepless hours and days. The tension that's been eating at him like termites taking a house apart from the inside, everything rises boiling to the surface. He kicks Dharam Bir in the ribs, choosing his spot so as to knock the breath out of the big man.

'You fuckers,' Dharam Bir manages to say, and then they're on him. Bhim Sain uses the side of his boots like a club to the back of his head. Ombir kicks until he is sure he has shattered a few ribs, then he shifts to the other side, for symmetry. They don't speak, they don't yell, they don't look at each other. They work in unison, a team, and when Dharam Bir finally screams, Bhim Sain kneels down, eye level with the man, stuffs an empty plastic pouch of

hooch in his mouth to stop the sounds, says, 'You should
have answered his questions and mine when you had the
chance. You should have.'

~~~

Ombir will always remember this with shame. It is Bhim
Sain who says, 'Sir, stop.'

He stops. The bloody mist clears from his vision. He
looks down at the man on the ground, motionless, broken.

'Sir, do you want him dead?' It's a clinical question.

He kneels down, takes Dharam Bir's pulse. Still beating.
Considers his choices as reaction starts to set in, tremors
racing through his body. It's the same for Bhim Sain, he
can see the sheen of sweat on the other man's forehead,
can see his trembling hands. They both have splashes of
Dharam Bir's blood on their uniforms. He feels soiled. It's
not a good thing, to lose control. He despises officers who
allow that to happen.

'No,' he says at last. 'He won't talk about this later.'

The theka owner and his friends will know, but that
won't matter. Bhim Sain forces a strip of wire through the
window of the theka owner's Maruti van that is parked
nearby, then fishes out one of the universal spare keys they
carry in their backpacks.

'With your permission, I'll leave this gaandu at the
hospital. They'll see to him. They owe me a few favours.'

'Is he only unconscious or in a full coma?'

'Doesn't matter either way, does it, sir? If Saluja makes
too much trouble for us, my father will smooth it over. I'll
tell him about the children.'

Bhim Sain is so comfortable in his police uniform that
Ombir sometimes forgets who his father is—one of the

area's biggest landowners, with hundreds of acres of land tightly controlled by his uncles, brothers and cousins.

'The kids,' he says. 'That got to you so badly?'

Bhim Sain looks at his superior for a moment, a considering stare.

'With respect, it got to you also, no? It's the worst crime. To hurt a child in that way, it is a sin.'

'Yes,' Ombir says. 'Yes, it is.' The adrenalin is wearing off, fatigue has kicked in. He'll talk to Chand tomorrow. Tell him it's sorted.

They load Dharam Bir into the back of the car. Bhim Sain, ever resourceful, uses gunny sacks and cardboard sheets from the theka to line the upholstery.

'It's done, sir,' Bhim Sain says.

'What?'

'Whatever you want to call it. Even if the case had been reopened, the evidence was not sufficient. Men who have this fault, they can't stop themselves. They don't wish to, and they can't. And who will stop them? The children? The parents? Who will bring shame upon their own children's heads, spend years in the courts fighting cases while the neighbours point to their daughter and whisper that there must have been something wrong with her from the beginning?'

'What was done tonight was not justice, Bhim Sain.'

'Please excuse me, sir. It was not as per the law, that is correct. You've seen what they do in jail to men like him, you've seen how other criminals—thieves, murderers, arsonists—treat a man who does such wrong things with children? We are human. Our blood boils in the exact same manner. What happened tonight, Ombir-ji, okay, maybe it was not justice. But it was right. You ask your heart, it will tell you the same. All right, sir, I'll bring the car back to the station. Maybe park it some way off. The owner can collect it at his leisure.'

'Goodnight, Bhim Sain.'

He does not say thank you, no need for that between them.

The Harley restores his sense of control. Ombir passes Chand's dark hut, slows down at the station house, and rides on. He takes a long detour, riding away from Teetarpur, the bike flying like a bird along the highway. He rides until some of the darkness clinging to him has shaken off, and then he turns back, the headlamps casting pools of golden light over the shadowed roads.

Trauma Ward

Bhadana comes by after lunch, when Bhim Sain is out on his rounds. He takes the only non-rickety chair without waiting for Ombir to offer him a seat, and pushes three envelopes across the desk.

Ombir says, 'Three?'

'The usual for you and Bhim Sain, and one for the extra work this month.'

Bhadana is a compact man, short and wide-shouldered, his roomy suit jackets concealing the muscle he carries, but Ombir's attention is always drawn to his toupee. A year ago, Bhadana had decided to tackle the galloping baldness that made him look more like one of Jolly Singh's bodyguards than his manager. He had ordered a custom-fitted toupee, which simulated hair with fair competence through the winter months. The heat was not kind to the toupee's glue, sadly, and through summer, Bhadana treated his toupee like a runaway hat, twitching it into place whenever it slid back on his head, so it crouched there like a fat rat. It looks damp and miserable to Ombir's judicious eye this afternoon; it has shifted too far to the right, and loose strands flop over the manager's ear.

Ombir does not reach for the envelopes. He will not give Bhadana the satisfaction of watching him count the notes, as though he and Bhim Sain are just two more employees on Jolly-ji's payroll.

'Two of us,' he says, 'and one extra envelope. This is to be shared between us?'

Bhadana shrugs. 'Up to you to decide who's done how much work. Is that a rabbit?'

Laadli returns Bhadana's interest, shuffling to the front of her cage to inspect him briefly.

'Yes, she belongs to the station house.'

'Rabbits and hares,' Bhadana says reminiscently. 'When Jolly-ji was a young boy, his father often took us out shooting in the forests. Only small game, but hares cook up well. If you partake of non-veg, that is. I became vegetarian later as per my mother's wishes, but at that age, I was fond of meat.'

'You've been with Jolly-ji's family for that long?'

'Most people in the village don't remember this, but my father served Jolly-ji's father in the same capacity.'

'Is the son like the father?' Ombir asks, leaning forward, interested.

Bhadana smiles. 'Singh sahib was a giant of a man in every way. Giant heart, a giant laugh, an appetite for all the gifts and pleasures of life, and a giant understanding of how this country really works. For every factory he built, every company he started, he also built schools, free clinics, shelters for cows, buffaloes, retired tonga horses— forty years ago, his business group was the largest in the area, bigger even than Saluja's.'

Ombir lost interest in the man's wandering wig. He was reluctantly impressed. Bhadana had managed to say that the son would never be his father without disrespecting his employer in any way, and he had lightly tossed the reason for his visit on the table with that casual mention of Dharam Bir's boss and benefactor.

'Factories and companies? But Jolly-ji's interests are mostly in land—farmland, stone quarries?'

A shift in temperature. Bhadana looks at him thoughtfully, he can sense the manager reassessing him.

'You have knowledge of Jolly-ji's business interests, Ombir?'

He shrugs. 'Only what everyone in the village knows. Your boss is a man of some importance, it's natural that the locals would talk about him.'

'Kripal-ji, Jolly's father, was one of those rare men who make their own luck. Anyone can start a business, become a crorepati—what is a crore these days? Nothing. But to set up a business house, you must have luck that will last for three generations. Kripal-ji took only thirty years to build up an empire that takes most people two generations of dedicated work, but in his seventies, he suffered a stroke. His younger brother had lived his life in Kripal-ji's shadow. He took over most of the businesses, ran some of them into the ground, though the oil mills are still functional, and he made sure that his nephew, his own brother's son, did not inherit very many of the family factories. Jolly-ji was only a youth then, perhaps a little bit high-spirited—you may have heard some stories?'

Ombir feels it again, that light prickle on his skin, the sense of being carefully evaluated, and stays silent.

'Like most boys, he settled down in time. They usually do, marriage draws the wildness out of them. And his father chose the right bride for him. Jolly-ji's wife, Neenaji, is a most godly lady. She is visiting her guru these last few months, spends her time between the ashram up near Satkhol in the Himalayas and the one in Haryana. Her prayers have helped greatly. I believe it is solely due to her faith that he has been able to restore the family fortunes. Once his land projects take off, he will become one of the most prominent men in this part of the state. You must have heard, he and Saluja are bringing a big development project to Teetarpur.'

'I only heard he's buying some parcels of land here and there.'

Bhadana says, 'It's warm in here, you don't have air-conditioning? I'll have one installed later this week, okay, an air-cooler at least. Yes, it will be a big project, our group has worked hard on getting the permissions, to explain that we are not building on forest land, merely on land that is close to the forests.'

It comes together in his head then. An inconsequential puzzle—it does not involve thefts or murders, it's not part of his beat, and yet it had tugged at the edges of his attention over the last few years. He had noticed as trees were felled, scrub cleared, in random locations on the outskirts of the village. The forests were given a haircut, land emerging bare from these ministrations, and he had wondered what purpose there might be to these apparently scattered efforts. He can see it now. You could push back the lines that demarcated a reserved forest from claimable land, one haircut and shave at a time, gradually convert forest land to useable land.

Bhadana was still talking, and Laadli snuffled at the bars, telling him it was time for her next meal. She would have to wait until the manager left. He did not feel it was dignified for people in the village to see him, uniform and all, feeding a rabbit. He had grown into the habit of talking to Laadli, telling her snippets of gossip, pieces of policing lore that he thought might be of interest.

'Jolly-ji has more patience than people give him credit for. He took his time and gained the confidence and blessings of Saluja and others in the area. The SSP came down for one of those meetings, you know, to discuss the possibility of setting up a proper police station once the project is completed. Teetarpur will need more than a station house, and of course you—and Bhim Sain—will also enjoy a change of status. Everybody benefits.'

His shrewd eyes read Ombir's thoughts with disquieting accuracy. 'You didn't imagine Delhi would send down such a senior officer only to solve a village murder case, surely? The SSP is a thorough man, he likes to spend some of his time in the field, of course. The case had to be settled, and you did well. Nothing for the television vultures to feast on when a murder is properly and promptly sorted out. I can tell you frankly, Ombir, Jolly-ji has been impressed by your abilities. There's room for a man like you to make his way up the ladder, especially if Teetarpur becomes the next Gurgaon. In a few years, no one will remember there was only a shabby village here, wait and see.'

Ombir struggles to conceal his sense of deflation. He should have realised that Pilania would not come to this small station house in the middle of nowhere only to take charge of an unimportant murder, the killing of a child from an insignificant farmer's family.

'But no more mistakes. Jolly-ji had to spend some of his time sorting matters out with Saluja. You hammered that man of his into keema. He was furious at the insult. What made you lose control to that degree?'

He says, 'It was a mistake. But Dharam Bir had to be stopped.'

Bhadana gives him a thin smile and adjusts his toupee, pushing the loose strands back into place. 'Most men have their extracurricular activities, and aside from that particular weakness of his, he was a useful man. You could have found a less bloody way to stop him. Anyway, since you are responsible for that mess, you can help with the clean-up. Jolly-ji made a deal. Saluja will take no action against you or Bhim Sain, his men won't target either of you. But the two of you will not raise a hand to Dharam Bir ever again without express permission from Jolly-ji or me. And make an apology to him when he gets out of hospital. Saluja is a big man, an important man for us. We can't afford to lose his goodwill.'

Ombir says, 'And the children? What about the children?'

The manager is already rising from his chair. He says, 'Take my advice, Ombir. You can rise high in life, do well for yourself and your family, or you can be the kind of fool who tries to do the right thing in this evil world. But in my experience, it is not possible to do both. I almost forgot— Jolly-ji is hosting a grand celebration on Saturday, a big party in Saluja's honour. He has requested your company that evening. Bring Bhim Sain if you like. Come after eight o'clock.'

After he leaves, Ombir feeds Laadli, though he skips his usual chat with the rabbit. She gives him an inquiring look, so he scratches the top of her head while she nibbles at her

carrots and greens. When she's done, he latches the door of
her cage and returns to the desk.

The light falls aslant, illuminating the dust under the
files. He touches the envelopes, finally opens them. Twice
what he had expected—in effect, a generous price for
becoming a company man. He'll share the extra money
almost equally with Bhim Sain.

His hand is resting on the investigation file. He opens
it and leafs slowly through Bachni's ledgers. He looks at
the photographs of the children carefully, stopping when
he reaches Munia's picture. Then he runs his finger down
the place where someone had pulled out a few pages,
leaving jagged edges behind. Pages that must have held
the accounts, history and name of one of the murdered
woman's blackmail victims.

꿍

The nurse is in her forties, scrawny as one of the village
hens, but with an air of iron toughness that Ombir has
encountered before in many of the local women.

'Patient is in the trauma ward. Upstairs, turn right,
you'll find him. Worst injuries in the whole of the hospital,
worse even than the boys who fell into the canal last week.
What to do with you policemen: first you beat up these
men, then you bother them when they're supposed to be
recovering from their injuries. Five minutes only, after that
you have to leave. He needs his rest.'

She glares at him, refusing to lower her eyes. The hospital
is little more than an abandoned cowshed, fitted with beds
and equipment. The floor is rough earth, not even cement,
the smell of stale blood and discarded bandages rises from
the overflowing trash can in the centre of the ground-floor

ward, and except for peeling posters singing praises of family planning and the need for vaccinations, the walls are stark and lack any form of decoration. She is the only point of neatness and order in the place, her crisp white sari a silent rebuke to the general air of disorder.

'Your name?' Ombir asks.

'Sister Sumanbala,' she says grudgingly.

'Do you know why your patient is in that condition, sister?'

'Since when have you cops needed an excuse to thrash some poor fellow?'

He is almost a foot taller than her. Looks down into her tight-lipped face, the fire of her indignation darkening her broad cheekbones.

He says, watching her closely, 'He raped children, Sister Sumanbala. Not one or two of them: many. He stalked them, and he lured them to his quarters, and he raped children as young as seven or eight. He raped them with or without the knowledge of their parents, and he would be out there, raping some poor father's daughter or son tonight, if he wasn't lying in one of your hospital beds. Make sure no one disturbs us. I won't hurt him, but I will take as much time as the situation requires.'

She does not speak, but he knows her eyes are following him as he takes the stairs. He pauses on the dusty landing. A heap of stained cotton waste lies in the corner, and a crow is tugging at a strand, yanking patiently until it floats free.

Dharam Bir is in a corner of the trauma ward. It is marginally cleaner than the ward downstairs, the six iron beds painted a dingy cream, light filtering in through four grimy but large windows. Ombir looks around. Two of the patients are shackled to their beds: either insane or so drug-crazed that they might be dangerous to themselves or to the hospital staff. A bored orderly stares up at the television set, snapping to attention at the sight of Ombir in his police uniform.

'Get me a chair,' he says, and waits until a rickety plastic chair is procured and placed by Dharam Bir's bedside.

The patient in the bed closest to them is unconscious. He will be able to speak freely.

Under the hospital sheets, faded grey from multiple washings, the big man stirs. His left leg is in traction and Ombir catches a glimpse of bandages strapped around his torso, remembers the sound of the ribs cracking. His hands are encased in plaster and his eyes are closed. Ombir settles into the chair, listening to the beep of the heart monitor, the steady bubbling from the oxygen cylinder, the sudden blare of a raucous pop song from a passing cart. He's glad that even in the full blackness of his rage, he hadn't touched the man's jaw or teeth.

He says, 'Dharam Bir?'

The man's eyes are closed, but Ombir catches the flutter of his eyelids, the slight turn of his head on the pillow. A rat scurries out of a hole in the plaster of the wall, skitters close to his boots, panics and darts back.

'I know you can hear me. I am here for two reasons. One is to apologise.'

Dharam Bir's head turns towards him, though he keeps his eyes shut. So easy to tell the difference between a man who is actually sleeping and one who is making a pretence of it—the slackness of true sleep is unmistakeable.

'On behalf of Bhim Sain too. I am sorry that we were the cause of such damage. I lost control. I should not have.

And I promise that we will not hit you again. May we talk?'

When Dharam Bir opens his eyes, they are baleful and unforgiving, as Ombir had expected.

The orderly says, 'It is time for his afternoon meal.'

'Give me the tray, I'll feed him.'

Dharam Bir stirs.

'It's no trouble. We can talk after he eats. Important for a patient to have his meals on time. What do you have for him? Dalia khichdi and lauki, okay, that's very nourishing. You can leave us alone.'

The orderly hovers nervously.

Ombir looks up. 'I know how to feed a sick person. Leave us and don't disturb me again.'

Dharam Bir waits until the spoon is close to his mouth, then jerks his head away, rejecting the food.

'That won't do,' Ombir says softly. 'No tricks from me. I promise. But this will go faster if we can talk while you're eating, and then I will leave and you will be rid of me, all right?'

He places the tray on the rough table that holds the patient's medicines and a change of bandages. Steadies Dharam Bir's head with one hand, gripping him firmly so that he can't turn away that easily, touches the spoon to the man's thick lips.

'Eat. One never refuses nourishment in this life. Eat without fear. You don't want to spill any of this on your chest, the orderly's gone off to attend to the next ward and it doesn't look like they have any other staff. If you make a mess, they won't clean you up in a hurry.'

Reluctantly, Dharam Bir swallows. His eyes blaze a message of hate.

'You're probably thinking that the moment you are fully recovered, you will come after us. I would want to, in your place. You're prepared to wait for the months it will take for your bones to heal; maybe not that many months, you're in your prime. And some day, no matter what agreements Jolly-ji or Saluja may have made between themselves, you're thinking that you and your friends will find Bhim Sain and me on our rounds, and somewhere —behind a tyre shop, in an abandoned field, out on those narrow canal roads—we will see the gleam of a knife and know that you are settling old scores.'

He waits until Dharam Bir has swallowed a second and a third spoonful of the thin, unappetising gruel. Uses a corner of his handkerchief to wipe a dribble of dalia off the big man's chin.

'That will not happen. Try the lauki, the vaids say it is the king of vegetables, a tonic for your entire system. Take a bigger spoonful—yes, that's better. Don't try to pull away, I'm not going to do anything to you this time. What was between us is over, done with, finished. From my side. From yours, too, if you have any sense.'

Dharam Bir speaks, his voice thick and slurring, but clearly audible. 'It will only be finished when it's finished.'

Ombir smiles. 'Don't get your heart rate up, the staff will come running to see what's wrong. A few more spoons of dalia and we're almost done, okay? This is between us. You, me, Bhim Sain. Saluja and Jolly have nothing to do with this matter, it's our personal affair. Dharam Bir, use your brain sometimes, not just your muscles. I'm in line for a promotion, and so is Bhim Sain. It's not so easy to get away with killing policemen, not even for you, but aside from that—you are not local. Your family is not from these

parts. Bhim Sain, on the other hand, his uncles and cousins
and nephews ... You will have a hundred eyes on you,
and if one drop of his blood or mine is spilt, your body
will be found stuffed into one of Saluja's factory chimneys
soon enough. You know it's the truth, so think it over, use
whatever God gave you in the place of brains, and calm
down. If you're smart, you'll ask Saluja for a promotion
and a change of scene. Word spreads fast around these
parts, and without Bachni, it won't be so easy for you to
indulge your hobbies. In a new place, you'll do better. We'll
let you leave in peace, I swear it.'

'Bastard,' Dharam Bir says softly.

'Call me whatever you like,' Ombir says. He puts down
the bowl of dalia, carries the tray across to the foot of
the bed, and returns with a hospital gamchha. He cleans
Dharam Bir's face and mouth with impersonal care.

'Which one did you kill, Bachni or Munia?'

'I don't have to answer your questions.'

Ombir places a palm on the man's ribs, presses down,
swiftly covers Dharam Bir's mouth to suppress his yelp of
pain.

'Which one?'

'Neither, you stupid bastard!'

'All right. Bachni disappears, she has been sucking
you dry for money for months, her body is found in the
canal, someone strings Munia up days after you've been
seen following the child, taking photographs of her. You're
saying there's no connection?'

The sheen of sweat on Dharam Bir's forehead, the pallor
of his face—he can't press the man too hard, but he must
push on for an answer.

'You understand nothing. Someone could drive a buffalo in front of you and you'd be peering at it, saying, it looks dark outside.'

'Bachni wasn't bleeding you dry?'

Dharam Bir makes a great effort, manages to raise his head slightly.

'We were business partners, you fool. I gave her money for some of her expenses, that's true, but I wasn't among the clowns and idiots she blackmailed. What she got from me was names, introductions, offers to dance. What I got from her is between her and me, but I had no reason to kill her. Plenty of other people did.'

'And Munia?'

'She was a juicy one, despite her shyness. I like them when they're that way—curious, bright, and it's more amusing when they're afraid of me. But use your goddamn brains, Ombir, if you have any left after all these years stumbling around playing at being a policeman. I never had to kill any of the others. Why would I kill her when I hadn't even fucked her?'

It slips out before he can place a bridle on his tongue. 'Why do you go after children, Dharam Bir, for God's sake? Why children, when there are so many women you could have had without any trouble?'

'You're vegetarian or not?'

He blinks. 'I don't eat chicken or meat at home, my mother would not like it and nor would anyone else in my household, but I'm not vegetarian. What does that have to do with anything?'

Dharam Bir says, 'Would you eat rotten meat? Meat that's old and stale?'

'No, of course not.'

'Neither would I. It's as simple as that. I can sleep with any woman, any age, but the older ones—it's like eating week-old meat. I like my meat fresh. Girls spoil fast as they age.'

Ombir takes a deep breath.

'If I were to believe you, not that I do, because you have every reason to lie, but if I go along with your statement that you didn't kill Bachni or Munia, who did?'

Dharam Bir says, 'You want me to tell you? Really? Work it out for yourself, Buffalo Brains.'

'Tell me one thing and we're done. Was it the same person who killed both of them?'

He sees a smile on the man's face, and more of those fat beads of sweat, standing out on his forehead.

From the doorway, Sister Sumanbala says, 'That's enough. You may be a policeman, he may be whatever-he-is, but you're making his condition worse. You must leave now.'

Ombir realises that the sound in the background is coming from the heart monitor, a long, warning beep.

He gets up, says, 'Thank you, sister. I was about to leave.'

From the bed, Dharam Bir says, 'You're such a genius, Ombir. You'll figure it out in a few decades.'

Finished Business

That night, after Rabia and he have spoken, Chand goes out into his fields. A full moon rides high in the sky, its indifferent light falling full on the jamun tree. He runs his hand over the bark, feeling each scar, tracing the rough patches. He presses too hard, grazing his palm, and looks down at the drop of blood. It brings him some relief, that brief, sudden pain.

He would have walked down towards the canal again, but he hears the sound of a car on the main road. The headlights blind him for a second, and the car stops.

Jolly Singh calls from the road, 'Is that you, Chand? I was on my way home, but I intended to come and see you tomorrow morning. Can I join you?'

He says, 'Yes, Jolly-ji,' unsure whether he is annoyed or relieved at the interruption.

'One moment,' Jolly says. After a while, Chand hears the car boot slam. Jolly carries two folding chairs, one under each sturdy arm.

'I keep them in the car for field visits, land surveys,' Jolly says, setting up the chairs so that they face slightly away from the tree. 'It's more comfortable, you don't mind?'

Chand says, 'Thank you, Jolly-ji,' and waits for the landowner to choose a chair before he sits down. In truth, he is as uncomfortable as he was on Jolly's previous visit. He would have preferred to sit on the ground in the company of someone like Jolly Singh, but a glance at his neighbour has told him that the man is slightly drunk. Not over the limit, but enough to explain this curious behaviour.

'How are you coping?' Jolly asks. 'I don't know how you must be feeling. Everyone says to someone who has lost one of their own, I know how you feel, but—how would I know?'

Jolly's rough speech is strangely comforting. In this week, too many villagers have said to him, you must feel like this, you must feel like that. He has wanted to say to them, ignoring their kindness and caring, you don't know how I feel. You have no idea how I feel. You wouldn't want to know if you did. But he has said nothing, only accepted their condolences with a nod of his head, his eyes shuttered.

'Losing your child ... I can speak to you, one father to another. My wife and I wanted a son. Every man does, I'm no exception. We tried for many years. She went to the best doctors in Delhi, she prayed to all her gods, but when the gods turn away, what can you do? I badly wanted a son. In my old age, everything I've worked for will go to her sister's boy, my nephew. He's a modern fellow, he has an MBA, but sometimes I think, why didn't my wife's gods give me a boy of my own? That pain I've carried for many years, but it is nothing to your grief. This is where it happened?'

Chand flinches.

He says, 'Yes, Jolly-ji. You were away that night on work. It happened here, outside my own home.' He stops, cannot say any more.

Jolly leans forward, his tiny, sharp eyes searching Chand's face. 'I'm a fool,' he says. 'A thoughtless fool. I'm not good at measuring my words, I speak too plainly. I did not come here tonight to add to your grief. I came here to ask how I can help.'

'It's kind of you to think of me, Jolly-ji. But Balle Ram and his wife do everything that is needed,' Chand says. 'My old friends call me often. I am managing.'

Jolly Singh shifts his chair so that the two of them are facing each other. They are almost of a height, though Chand is the taller of the two.

'What would we do without our families, without friends? By God's grace, you have both by your side. But Chand, I can help with something they cannot help you with. Something that, if I have guessed correctly, is much on your mind.'

He pulls out a newspaper clipping from his wallet and hands it to Chand, who reads it slowly. It is from the *Faridabad Daily Blaze*, dated from a few days after the murder.

Murder suspect takes own life

The chief suspect in the horrifying murder of a young girl, Munia Devi of Teetarpur village in the Teetarbani area, Mansoor Khan, broke out of his cell and committed suicide. Body of Mansoor Khan was discovered by local policemen near the Teetarbani station house after a short manhunt. SSP Pilania from New Delhi and a team of local policemen are to be commended for their rapid investigation and swift apprehension of the murderer.

According to police sources, the suspect had succeeded in breaking out of his cell and attempted to set fire to himself before falling fatally to his death in an abandoned well. The suspect had a history of mental instability. The murder, committed in broad daylight near a main road, had greatly disturbed many in Teetarpur village and police sources say that the case is now closed.

'Case closed,' Jolly says. 'As far as the police are concerned, the matter is finished. But is it finished for you, Chand?'

Chand is quiet, watching the other man keenly.

'It is not finished for me, you see. I keep an eye on Teetarpur. I discovered the truth of what happened with Mansoor some days ago. We are neighbours. Our homes touch, our lives touch. This murder took your daughter from you, it took my peace from me. Until you are satisfied that justice has truly been done, it is not finished for you either.'

Chand says, 'I don't know what to do with my time, Jolly-ji, and that is the truth. Without her, my love for the land itself seems to have been killed at the root.'

'What will you do with your fields?'

He had milestones in mind. He had planned to send his daughter to the school in the main town, which had an adequate headmaster, in another year. He had saved the funds for her to do a course at the polytechnic, or even for her to go to a Delhi college, if that was what she wanted. He didn't want her to grow up like her mother, marrying young, ignorant of letters and of the wider life outside their narrow world. He had already planned to sell this field for college, that one for marriage.

'The land has been in my family for many generations. But I want to spend some time away from Teetarpur, maybe go to the Himalayas, find some peace in a new place for a few years, away from my memories. Balle Ram will look after my home and the few crops I grow here. I'll leave the other fields fallow this year.'

'Would you consider selling some of the land to me? Maybe it's too soon to talk of these practical matters, but with you, Chand, I can open my heart. I have dreams for Teetarpur. Big dreams. I want this village to prosper, and the only way it can progress is if it becomes a township, the gateway to the Aravallis for so many city-folk from Delhi who are seeking a simpler life. I'll make no secret of this to you: I've been buying or renting many patches of land. Your other field is well placed. If you feel you can trust me ...'

Chand says, 'Yes, Jolly-ji, there is trust between us. You have been kinder than I ever imagined or had a right to expect from a man of your stature.'

'Well, then, I'll get Bhadana to speak to you. It's not right that we should discuss business at this time, when the mourning period has only just ended. Take your time, think it over, there's no need to make a hasty decision.'

Chand thinks of Munia, riding on the plough, building a mud village in one of the furrows of the earth, collecting the seeds and feathers that fascinated her.

'It's yours,' he says. 'I will not want to farm it again, not in my lifetime.'

Jolly Singh says, 'In a few days, I'll ask Bhadana to check with you again. If you still feel the same way, we'll sign the papers. I promise it will be a generous settlement. And ... the other matter.'

Chand says, 'You know who the murderer is. Tell me.'

Jolly shakes his head. 'If you knew, what would you do, Chand?'

Chand looks up at the jamun tree, at its highest branches. He says nothing.

'If I told you that the man who murdered your daughter has a shameful weakness, that he acted on impulse, out of fear, to protect himself? Would you be able to forgive him?'

Chand says, 'Forgiveness is beyond me. You do not forgive a man who has taken everything you loved from you, who took from her the years she should have had. You know his name. She was my daughter. Tell me who he is.'

'You would take matters into your own hands, and Ombir and Bhim Sain would have no choice except to arrest you. There would be a trial. Years of your life would trickle away in the courts, in jail.'

'My old life has been burnt to the ground, Jolly-ji. I do not care for that. He must die.'

'Will you promise me that you'll let me arrange matters so that he is dealt with, without consequences to either of us?'

'Why would you do that, Jolly-ji?' Chand asks quietly.

'Because sometimes the law cannot deliver justice, and the police cannot deliver justice, and then there is only us. If I tell you who he is, promise you will not take any action on your own, without hearing me out?'

'That much I can promise,' says Chand.

'He's in hospital. Ombir and Bhim Sain beat him to a pulp, but beyond that, they have no power over him. You know the man well. Saluja's right-hand man, Dharam Bir. His weakness is disgusting. He likes little children.'

Chand can't speak. His breath catches painfully in his throat, but Jolly Singh seems to read his expression.

'It is not what you fear. Dharam Bir did nothing to Munia. Though he watched her, he did not do to her what he did to the other children. He must have scared her in some way. Maybe he was afraid that she would say something to you. But a man who has his particular vices is a danger to the community, and to me, he is a business risk.'

'Jolly-ji, this is not your business to settle. A man like that, of those habits, in our village ... He is my responsibility.'

Jolly Singh steps away from the jamun tree. 'My father kept dogs. Hounds, hunting hounds. I grew up with them. He taught me how to shoot when I was ten years old. I could barely hold a gun. I disappointed him the first few times he gave me lessons.'

His eyes are almost black, despite the moonlight.

He says, almost to himself, 'I often disappointed him—but I made myself learn, because it was so important to him. When I was twelve, the hound I loved most went rabid. He had not been vaccinated that year, the servants were careless. My father sacked the dog-boy. He brought his revolver down from the gunroom, loaded it, gave it to me, and he said, "You will shoot Prince." My mother remonstrated with him, but he was adamant. He said I was old enough to know that if you fed a creature, if he depended on you, and then he went mad and became a danger to all around him, it was your duty to put an end to his life. No one else's. Mine. I shot the dog.'

Chand says, 'Dharam Bir killed my daughter.'

Jolly says, 'He was on my payroll as well as Saluja's. This is my business, Chand. Let me settle it. Give me one week, less than that. I have trusted you with this. Now it is your turn to trust me. Will you?'

～

When he speaks to Rabia about Jolly Singh's visit, he tells her about the land, and about the landowner's concern and his offer, but he does not tell her about Dharam Bir. He keeps that to himself, waiting to see if he was right to trust Jolly Singh. If he was wrong, he will settle that business on his own, no matter what Ombir or Jolly might say.

She picks up on what he leaves unsaid, not for the first time in their long friendship.

'Have you put it behind you, then? The question of who killed our Munia?'

He says, 'It died with Mansoor's arrest.'

'The papers said he took his own life. Is that true, Chand?'

'No, it isn't true.'

'Then what happened to him?'

'It isn't what you imagine, though it came close to that. I would have taken his life and thought nothing of it if he had done it. But he didn't. I let him go, and Ombir guessed. He has a sharp mind for a policeman.'

'You really would have killed him? An aged, half-witted man?'

'Yes. I would have.'

He wishes he could see her face. Wonders whether there is judgement in those eyes of hers, or understanding, or both.

'And the murderer, whoever he is? Will you spend your life trying to hunt him down?'

He says, 'No. That is not in my hands.'

'You have let it go? You've found forgiveness, whoever it was?'

He chooses his words carefully, not wanting to lie to her.

'I cannot forgive. I will never forgive, but it is out of my hands. There is nothing for me to do.'

'Chand, what will you do with your life?'

'I can't think of it. The years ahead, what use are they to me? Without her?'

'It's too early, I shouldn't have asked you.'

'You can ask me anything you like. But all I know is that I have a great desire to leave Teetarpur for a while. Maybe in the Himalayas I will find something to do, maybe I won't, maybe I will travel the way I'd once imagined I would.'

'I meant something different, Chand. I meant that, whether you like it or not, you have a life. Don't throw it away on vengeance, it's a hollow way to live. It may take time, it may take years, but find meaning for yourself. Life is precious. You have to fight for every inch of it sometimes. It is not to be thrown away so lightly, no matter how harsh our losses feel.'

'Tell me,' he says.

'Tell you what?'

'Whatever it is that brought so much sadness and pain into your voice just now, tell me.'

'It was a small thing,' she says.

❧

Tension has become a living creature in Bright Dairy, Rabia says to Chand, a vengeful spirit haunting the city, shorthand for all that is going wrong. People from their community pushed out of parks and told they can no longer pray in public areas: tension. Boys from nearby colonies rounded up and thrown into jail on suspicion of nameless crimes, never fully spelled out: tension. Small mobs of residents who let rumours ignite and flare into attacks on their own neighbours: tension. You never know when tension will show up at your door to become an unwelcome but permanent guest.

A year ago, Azizbhai had rescued a pup from some boys who were tormenting the creature, brought him home. His name was originally Brownie, but Sanam renamed him Sikandar, the Emperor of Bright Dairy, because he harboured grand territorial ambitions. At first, he was allowed to roam free, but of late, Sanam had begun to tie him up when she left the house, unwilling to risk a quarrel with any of their neighbours.

When she returned from work the day before, the boys from the shakha were massed in the lane. They had long knives and naked blades in their hands.

'Give him to us,' they said. 'We'll deal with him.'

She looked from one to another, bewildered.

'The dog,' said one of the young men. 'Bring him out.'

They pushed into the house with her and searched the rooms, scattering the family's belongings without care. Sanam showed them Sikandar's chain.

'He must have run away,' she said. 'See, he's chewed through the leather strap attached to the chain. We keep him tied up all day. But what's happened?'

Sikandar had staged his own revolt, breaking free of his imprisonment to run joyously in the maidan. He had bounded into the middle of the shakha, ready to play glorious games. When one of the boys threw a brick at him, he had whined in puzzlement; when a group surrounded him, he growled and fought his way out. Four of them had been bitten and scratched, and they were out for the dog's blood.

'He defiled our prayer meeting,' the boys said. 'If you're hiding him somewhere, all of you will suffer.'

Azizbhai shouldered his way through the growing crowd to stand by his daughter, and Rabia and Arshad joined him.

'Have some pity,' Azizbhai said to the boys. 'I will pay compensation for your injuries, but can you not find it in your hearts to forgive the animal? He is just a young dog, he was tired of being chained up.'

The leader of the group, Bunty, was a young man known to be one of Madan Chaubey's trusted aides. He turned away from them, addressing Azizbhai's neighbours.

'There is a limit to our patience,' Bunty said. 'Don't test us. This man and his family cause too much disruption in this mohalla. If the dog has run away, we'll let the matter drop. We could have destroyed Azizbhai's house, you understand. We could have taken badla after these savage bites our brothers have suffered, but we are not petty men. But if the dog returns, he must be handed over to us immediately. Vicious beasts are a danger to all. They must be destroyed. We'll be back tomorrow at noon. If you see the creature in any part of Bright Dairy, catch him and bring him to us.'

Sanam did not cry until the boys had left. She stayed dry-eyed when their neighbours came in to tell Azizbhai that Sikandar must be found and given up to the shakha's boys. She only cried when they were alone, and then she sobbed in Rabia's arms like a child.

⁓

'Was he found?' Chand asks after a long pause.

'Yes,' Rabia says. 'Sikandar came back at three in the morning. He did not bark. He slipped in through the storeroom window that doesn't close properly, and went straight to Sanam. He had injuries too, though they were not serious.'

'You can't keep him hidden forever,' Chand says. 'That would place you all in grave danger, and your neighbours will be dragged into this khichdi too.'

'People are saying that if Azizbhai and all of us go away, Madan Chaubey will leave them alone. I don't believe Madan's encroachments and bullying will stop after we leave. But that's what our neighbours are saying. Azizbhai told everyone this afternoon that he, Sanam and Arshad will be leaving for Oman soon. That is what Madan and his boys wanted all along. Our poor Sikandar was just an excuse.'

Rabia continues, her voice dull, 'At five in the morning, before the shakha opened, Azizbhai and I fed Sikandar leftover keema and rice. We brushed him till his coat shone, and we put more medicine on his cuts. Sanam wouldn't let him go at first, but Arshad made her understand—it had to be done. We smuggled him out of the colony.'

She falls silent for a while, then continues.

'Azizbhai and I drove him far away, to the animal shelter on Dhauj Road. We left him outside, chained to a tree. And we left his bowls of food and water, his favourite ball, the toys Sanam had bought him, so that they would know he was loved. Azizbhai wrote a note asking them to open their hearts to Sikandar and give him a home. Then we left. He watched us go, wagging his tail. He was sure it was a game. He was sure we would be back for him.'

Chand clasps the phone tighter in his hand, listening to her sobs.

'He trusted us, Chand,' she says. 'And we broke his heart.'

'Rabia, will you meet me next week?' Chand says. 'I'll be leaving soon. I'd like to see you before I go.'

She hesitates. 'It's not safe for you to visit me in Bright Dairy,' she says. 'It has become as segregated as your village.'

'Come to the riverside. There's a road, under the bridge, it's a proper paved road. I'll meet you at the end of it, on the banks of the river. It's close to our old home. Will you come?'

She says, 'Of course I will.'

RECKONING

Scorpion Grass

Ombir and Bhim Sain sit stiffly in Jolly Singh's sumptuous office, facing Saluja.

'Good men make mistakes, Saluja-ji,' Jolly Singh says. 'It takes a better man, a big man, to accept an apology and move on.'

Saluja raises a hand, gesturing that Ombir may speak. He doesn't look at the policemen. He loosens his tie, an eye-hurting yellow that stands out against his light grey summer suit, and stares over their heads, his ringed fingers drumming a light beat on his host's gilt desk.

Ombir has practised his apology, knowing that it will have to be made, but the words are surprisingly hard to say.

'We got carried away, Saluja-ji,' he says. 'We should not have taken such a step without your permission.'

Saluja takes a sip of water from the burnished copper tumbler in front of him, says to his host, 'I don't hear him saying he's sorry. Not a real sorry.'

The back pain that had been plaguing Ombir for the last few days feels like spears of molten fire digging into his spine.

'Bhim Sain and I are sorry for the inconvenience caused,' he says. 'Please accept our apologies for our thoughtlessness.'

Bhim Sain crosses his arms and looks down at his shoes.

Saluja nods, says to Jolly Singh, 'The other one won't apologise, haan?'

Ombir stirs in his uncomfortable, ornate chair, trying to find a position that will bring him some relief, and delicately nudges his colleague.

Bhim Sain says like a schoolboy addressing a particularly stern teacher, 'Sir, we are sorry for this lapse. It won't happen again.'

'Dharam Bir was the factory's most valuable man, okay?' Saluja says. 'Screw his personal life, that's his business, not yours or mine. Saluja wants you to understand what you've done. We had two big deals coming up this month, and you put him out of commission at a time when Saluja needed him. Listen, you two. One call from Saluja to those fancy-pants officers in Delhi and fuck your promotions, you won't get a job as a wiper of goats' arses, okay? If you ever touch one of my men again, Saluja will destroy your miserable, shitty, inconsequential lives, is that understood?'

Jolly smiles at Ombir.

'They are good fellows, actually. They got carried away by their emotions.'

Saluja snorts.

'Who gave them permission to have emotions? What nonsense.'

'They've apologised, Saluja-ji. They won't do it again. And we have your promise that Dharam Bir will not go after them when he recovers, yes? We have that assurance?'

Saluja says bitterly, 'Two more weeks in hospital, that's what the dried-up stick of a nurse was saying. My best man, in my busiest season, but okay, Saluja accepts your apology. Because of Jolly Singh's intervention. You can thank him later. Now get out of my sight. And don't fucking investigate anything in Teetarpur, even the theft of a newspaper, without express permission from Saluja and Jolly Singh, is that understood?'

As they get on their bikes, Bhim Sain says, 'I had a bastard principal just like that. Talked big, died of acidity before he was sixty.'

'Fuck him and fuck these fucking apologies,' Ombir says. 'Anyway, it's done.'

The Jaguar roars past them, and the policemen have to hurriedly swerve to the side of the road. Jolly Singh is at the wheel, Saluja beside him, gesturing with his bejewelled hands as he talks.

Ombir stops the Harley-Davidson, parks it, stretches, and feels the spikes of pain spread from his back upwards to his neck.

He turns his bike around.

'Station house is that way, sir,' Bhim Sain says.

'Fuck their express permission,' Ombir says, hopping back on the bike.

'Where are we going, Ombir-ji?'

'To do what we should have done in the first place, when we found Bachni's body. To investigate. Bachni and Munia—they were not separate murders. They were linked. I'm sure of it.'

⌒

They've left it too late, he thinks. It's been too long since Bachni's corpse was found in the canal. The search area is considerable. One path snakes up towards the main road, another reaches a dead end — a brick wall that rises too high for him or Bhim Sain to see what's on the other side — and the third winds through thick scrub and brush towards Chand's fields.

'Nothing, sir,' Bhim Sain says, coming back from the dust track that leads to the main road. 'But after all these weeks, maybe there won't be anything for us to find. What exactly do you want me to look for?'

He doesn't know. Footprints would have been brushed away, impossible to find fingerprints, he cannot imagine what other evidence there might be.

But he says, 'Was she killed in the canal, or was she brought here after she was murdered? I just want a picture in my mind, Bhim Sain. Some idea of what happened that day. Is it possible that she and Munia died on the same day? The body had already been in the water for a while when we found it.'

'All right, sir,' says Bhim Sain. They are both covered in dust, and his hands are scratched from pulling back the thorny keekar that lines the path. 'I'll do my best.'

'This path is also a dead end,' he calls. 'There's no way to reach Chand's fields from the canal.'

Bhim Sain walks ahead of him, circles around.

'Sir, there's no path, but if you push through the lantana—see, the hedge is broken and trampled, it's low enough for a cow or a goat to leap over—yes, there is a way. It leads directly to the back gate of Chand's field.'

Ombir follows him. Bhim Sain is thrashing about, swearing because he's walked into a patch of scorpion grass. Ombir kneels, using a twig to push back clumps of the prickly weed. He straightens up, frowns, drops back to peer at the lantana bushes alongside.

'You have a pocketknife?' he asks.

'Swiss Army knife, Ombir-ji,' Bhim Sain says proudly. 'It may be fake, but it's a tip-top quality fake. What have you found?'

Ombir works at the roots of the lantana bush, frees a ribbon of cloth. A strip of green patchwork, the thorns puncturing its length. And half a bedraggled silver ribbon.

'Her skirt was green, her blouse pink-and-silver, you remember? She was carried here,' he says. 'Either she was knocked out by the murderer or she was already dead, but he brought her through these bushes down to the canal.'

Bhim Sain says, 'Sir, if we can't reopen the investigation officially or take any action, how will we bring Dharam Bir to justice?'

Ombir is at the rickety bamboo gate, near a stand of dhak trees. He stares at the field, at the jamun tree.

'We won't disturb Chand, he'll be resting indoors,' he says. 'We'll have to be careful about making inquiries, and I don't know about justice. All I know is that the murderer was definitely not Mansoor—he couldn't have carried or dragged a grown woman all this way, not with his physical weaknesses. It was probably not that drug-pusher Narinder, because his broken arm never did heal properly. He wouldn't have had the strength for this. It may have been Dharam Bir. But it was someone who felt he had a good reason to kill Bachni, who chose this spot because he thought he wouldn't be seen, who killed Munia—why?'

Bhim Sain says slowly, 'Munia was usually in the top field with her father, wasn't she? She spent most of her days there until the cane fires started. Chand's hut and his field here were usually empty during the day.'

They are silent, retracing their steps until they can take the path back to the main road. A peacock bursts from cover, startled, and a peahen takes flight over their heads, her stubby wings brushing the air near Ombir's head.

'The man who killed her was someone who knew enough about Chand's household to expect that she would be away, but not close enough to know that they had changed their routine, that Chand was leaving her behind all day.'

'A neighbour,' Bhim Sain says. 'Someone in this locality.'

The pain in Ombir's back has gone; it seems to have left his spine and climbed upwards. His head feels like a nest of angry bees, and he can feel a pulse of blood beating at his temples. He doesn't want to give voice to his thoughts, not yet.

'Bhim Sain,' he says, 'let's get back to the station house. I'd like to take a fresh look at the case files.'

He looks at his colleague. They are both covered in cobwebs, soil and dried leaves.

'And we could both use a wash. Bhim Sain, we can't take this further officially. But someone killed that woman. Someone killed that child. Someone would have left Mansoor to rot in jail, or be lynched by the villagers, without mercy. We'll be careful not to let either Jolly or Saluja know that we're still investigating this crime, but for my own sake, I want to know. I just want to know.'

By the next morning, Ombir's mood has soured. His headache seems to be worse, even after two aspirins, and

Bhim Sain's heart and stomach troubles are equally bad. They have made no headway with the files, though he has stared at every photograph, squinted at every note the two of them have made. When Kavita phones, as she does most nights, he is unable to give his attention to her plans for the baby's arrival in a few months, but he does his best to sound enthusiastic.

He spends an hour trying to focus on the security arrangements for the upcoming panchayat elections, on wards and booths and coordinating with the larger police stations in the area. There is also the paperwork that the head office has sent him to fill in for some cases of breaking and entering from last November. Even Laadli, who hops towards him when Bhim Sain lets her out for her morning constitutional, can't cheer him up.

Ombir pushes the files away roughly, and tells Bhim Sain that he is heading out for a ride to clear his head.

Bhim Sain says, 'Sir, I'm also feeling restless. Chand is leaving Teetarpur soon, he'll be making his pilgrimage to the mountains. Shall we say goodbye to him?'

A twist of shame in the pit of his stomach. He could not have prevented Munia's murder, but the summer is almost over, the monsoon is hovering over Teetarpur, and he hasn't been able to give Chand the closure that is the man's right. Still, he says, 'Yes, let's go.'

⌇

Dilshad's bike is outside. He is seated on the ground, Chand on the charpai, both of them examining photographs.

Chand brings out tall steel glasses of chhachh, the froth on the buttermilk flecked with jeera and black mustard. 'Balle Ram brought over an ocean of chhachh, I won't be able to finish it on my own,' he says. 'And Dilshad has brought the only parting gift I could have asked for.'

He hands Ombir a stack of black-and-white photographs of Munia, peering at the camera with an equal blend of curiosity and shyness.

'I took them at the village fair last year,' Dilshad says. 'I'd forgotten about them, but I was clearing out an almirah and thought that perhaps Chand would like them.'

Bhim Sain holds the photos gingerly, by their edges, so as not to smudge them.

'I have so few photos of her,' Chand says. 'I'd meant to take her to the studio in Teetarpur town, but these are better. I'll treasure them, Dilshad. I'll take them up to the Himalayas with me. I'll leave in the next few days, maybe tomorrow, maybe the day after.'

Bhim Sain passes them back, fumbles, and the photos fall on the charpai, scattered like a pack of cards.

Ombir says, 'This is from another set.'

Only one of the photographs is in colour. A close-up of Munia's dress, coloured purple by jamuns. Her face is not visible. Chand touches the photograph, his fingers brushing it gently.

'You've decided what to do with your land?'

'Balle Ram helped me to make my decision,' Chand says. 'He will take care of my home and this field, and with his blessings, I will sell the rest of the land. Teetarpur will see a lot of change. Maybe it'll become more like Delhi in the next ten years, you never know.'

'Saluja says there'll be malls soon,' Dilshad says, brightening. 'It'll be good for me and my friends. We can start businesses, set up shops for the city people. Saluja's in a bad mood today, though, I heard on my way over.

Bhadana says he's upset after what happened to Dharam Bir last night.'

Bhim Sain and Ombir glance at one another, then at Dilshad.

'I guess he's not eager for the news to get out so soon, he must have told the hospital staff to keep it quiet. Dharam Bir was making a strong recovery, but some mix-up happened with the oxygen supply last night. The line was blocked, the power went out, something like that. I heard from two of his friends this morning. They said the hospital staff fixed it quickly, but by then he'd spent an hour off oxygen, and his brain had gone phut, kaput. He's alive, barely, on the ventilator. That man was like a bull, he could survive anything, even the thrashing you two gave him, but this has finished him off. He'll never recover his mind, even if he emerges from this coma.'

Chand closes his eyes. He says, 'It is done, then. It is over.'

Ombir says, 'Chand, I must take your leave. Have a safe journey.'

Bhim Sain walks him to the road. 'I am at peace,' he says. 'Dharam Bir ... I am at peace. It makes no difference who did it. But are you at peace, sir?'

Ombir says, 'I will be. Soon.'

～

'It's you again,' the woman says, sounding bored. 'I knew she was in serious trouble. She's packing, mister, but she's cleared my rent for the month, what do I care? She's on her way out, so you'd better hurry if you want to catch her before she leaves for the railway station.'

The tiny rooms have been cleared. Four trunks stand like a tower in the corridor. The bangles and bottles, the costumes and film magazines have all been packed away.

'I could hardly let you leave without saying goodbye,' he says.

Chunchun's eyes harden. 'You have a warrant? I won't say anything unless you have a warrant.'

He steps inside. On one wall, a torn poster of Priyanka Chopra sags to the ground. A clutter of old lipsticks and discarded scrunchies litters the floor.

'I won't—' she begins, and his fingers dig into her wrist. He drags her into the room, shuts and latches the door.

'I'm only here for a social visit,' he says. 'And to clear some minor questions. I won't bother you after this, I promise. Be civil, Chunchun. Where's your aunt?'

'I made her daughter take her back,' she says. 'I won't have time to look after her the way I used to.'

He says, 'That's a fine satchel you're carrying. Roomy. Much larger than your usual handbag.'

She glares at him, and her hate warms him suddenly, makes him feel better, like a proper policeman.

He opens the satchel and brings out thick wads of money, letting them fall back into its leather depths.

'You're taking over Bachni's trade?' he says. 'You'll do well at it, but mind you don't make the same enemies she did.'

'I wouldn't do that work for twice this amount!' she says, stung. 'I'm setting up my own business, okay? That's not illegal, is it?'

'What kind of business, Chunchun?'

She says, 'Men like you will never understand our lives. Women like me, we get into the dance trade because it opens some doors, you know? We're not whores, we're respectable women.'

'For a while,' he says softly. 'Until you make a few compromises. Not much. You look away when someone makes children the target of his evil, you take his cash because you don't have to witness their pain, and because you're already losing dance gigs, aren't you? New girls, younger dancers, they elbow you out. The first wrinkles appear and the first grey hairs show up, and then you'll do anything you can to keep making money, won't you?'

She has no make-up on except for thick lines of kohl rimming her eyes. The light streaming in through the stained window is strong enough to illuminate the tiny crow's feet, the lines on her neck.

'Easy for you to judge. I never meant to spend so many years dancing. I wanted much more from life. Men are scum. Dharam Bir, there are so many Dharam Birs, their sins are allotted to their account books, not mine. Why shouldn't I take his money, or any other bastard's? I'm setting up a store for dance girls like me and Bachni, even Reshma Bhabhi. It'll turn a big profit. You need costumes and wigs, make-up and good shoes. You need jewellery on rent, or the solid fakes, the ones that look like the real thing. You need different outfits for different occasions, what you wear for a public performance won't do for a private mujra. Even the bindis and bangles, the hairpins, the flowers. All of that costs a lot. That's my new dhanda.'

'I wish you luck,' Ombir says. 'You don't believe me, but I do. Give me your phone for a moment, please.'

She hesitates, eyes the closed door, and reluctantly hands over her mobile.

'Password.'

'4321,' she says.

He shakes his head, marvelling at the idiocy of someone who would use such an obvious password, keys it in, goes straight to the videos.

'What are you looking at?' she says. 'Give it back!'

When she snatches at the phone, he bends her wrist back until she cries out, and continues scrolling.

'Chunchun, I don't care who you sleep with or if you record all of your encounters with all of the men you fuck, all right? I'm looking for—here it is.'

'I only recorded it because he liked to watch himself later,' she says sulkily.

He holds the screen out to her, and they both watch a jerky video of her and Dharam Bir. He lets it run through, the volume turned up.

'Any fool would know that you were faking those moans,' Ombir says. 'He couldn't do it unless he watched child porn, am I right?'

'What does it matter?' Chunchun says, her sulky face scorched with anger. 'What difference does it make? He's finished anyway, his number has been called.'

He says, 'I don't care about what you two were doing. But the time at which you took the video, that interests me. There are three more videos. You were telling the truth. He was with you that day, all through that morning, and he left after 3 p.m., that's correct?'

She says dully, 'Yes. I told you this before.'

Ombir says, 'I should have checked your phone earlier.'

He makes a quick note of the times in his notebook, transfers copies of the videos to his own phone. Dharam Bir was indisputably with Chunchun the day that Munia died. There are gaps between the videos, but none of them long enough to allow the man to drive to the other side of Teetarpur, commit a murder and return.

'Why do you care?' she asks him suddenly.

He gives her an inquiring look.

'About the children,' she says. 'That kind of dhanda, it happens all the time, everywhere. Why do you care? They're nothing to you.'

Ombir says, 'Because no one else seems to. Not the men who run Teetarpur, not their parents. Someone has to. Why not me, and Bhim Sain?'

Chunchun shrugs, bored by this sentimentality. 'Can I go now?' she says. 'I'll miss the train.'

'One last thing. Just for my own curiosity. Who gave you that money?'

Her eyes slide away from his. She says, 'It's Bachni's stash.'

He says in the same calm, easy tone, 'No, it isn't. These are new notes. The newspapers they are wrapped in are dated the day before yesterday, Chunchun. Let me make it easier for you. And I promise you won't be arrested. Who paid you to cut off Dharam Bir's oxygen supply at the hospital?'

'You have no proof,' she says. She watches him closely, her broad hands curled into fists.

'I spoke to Sister Sumanbala on my way here. She sent me the CCTV footage from the camera in the corridor outside Dharam Bir's ward. It is poor quality, but you can see a woman, with a swept-up hairdo like the one you have, wearing the same kind of clothes you have on, walking in. I'm sure that there'll be more footage from other cameras.'

Ombir prays that she can't tell it's a bluff, that she hadn't the sense to notice what he had on his visit. The hospital's

CCTV cameras are either broken or stolen. He'd bet his life that there isn't a working camera on the premises.

'I can't tell you,' she says. Her voice is high and strained. 'He's ruthless. He'll kill me if he comes to know you were here, that we spoke about this. He'll finish me like that, if he ever gets to know. I can't tell you anything except that I didn't know what it would do to Dharam Bir. He said, just switch it off from the main supply and unplug the machine so that it doesn't beep, then switch it back on later.'

'You're a liar and a coward, Chunchun,' Ombir says. 'You did know. You knew exactly what it would do, and you knew why that satchel was given to you, why this job was worth so many Gandhis.'

'Take it,' she says. 'Take it all.' She is trembling.

He unlatches the door, holds it open. 'No need. I would not touch that bloodstained money. You've been helpful, Chunchun. Everything you said is recorded. I'll find you if I have any more questions, and I'll find you if you dabble in murder ever again, wherever you are.'

'You're going to let me go, just like that?' she asks in bewilderment.

Ombir smiles. He says, 'Yes, I am. Goodbye, Chunchun. Don't ever come back to Teetarpur. Let's hope we never meet again.'

Black River

These days, Rabia waits at the bus stand to meet Sanam every evening. She is uneasy, senses danger in the air.

Bright Dairy has changed with the influx of the young men. The women used to retire to their homes by nine every night, leaving the streets to the men by tacit agreement, stepping out in groups for necessary trips to shops, or the toilet block. Now they retreat by seven and stay indoors, bearing with the inconveniences, the lack of toilet access through the night hours, as best as they can.

She feels the prickle of the men's eyes on her this evening. And on Sanam, when her daughter-in-law alights from the bus. They walk back, exchanging small details about Sanam's job, a new colleague, Rabia's day at the warehouse where she did the morning shift, six hours of bubble-wrapping cellphones and other goods that rich strangers had ordered over the Internet.

Rabia sees them before Sanam does. Two lanes before Azizbhai's home, hemming them in, a group of lounging boys who look up at their approach.

Since the trouble began, she has taken to carrying a small kitchen knife in the pocket of her kurta. She touches it for reassurance, but it is talismanic. Neither of them will stand a chance if the men choose to close in.

For the first time, she notices how many of their neighbours keep their doors and windows closed. Some have run up plastic curtains across their balconies. All that can be seen are their dim shapes moving behind those makeshift screens. This hour, the bridging hour between day and night, used to be the time when people used to come out, perch a rickety wooden chair on the edge of the road, or sit on the steps or on their charpais, when chatter would light up their lives. No more; people come home and seal themselves away.

'Don't let them see that we're nervous,' she says to Sanam.

The men slowly move out of their path, waiting till the last moment. One of them holds out his cellphone. He's smiling. Then another, then the rest. They hold the screens towards the women, so near that Rabia accidentally brushes one man's hand with her elbow. She flinches away.

Lynching videos. Rape videos. Each man playing a different one. To walk past the men, they have to walk through this wall of screams, through the sound of the pleas and lamentations, through the last dying cries of those who've been hunted down by vigilantes far more viciously in the last few years than Rabia can remember ever happening before. The men are silent, though she feels the hands of one or two of them lightly flick against her thighs, her breasts, as she passes, as a reminder of what they can do if they wish.

Rabia holds Sanam close, her arm around the young woman's waist. 'Keep your head down,' she whispers. 'Try not to look.' But she can tell that Sanam has already seen too much. Her daughter-in-law is crying soundlessly, her tears damp on Rabia's wrist.

Up ahead, she can see a streetlight. The entrance to Azizbhai's lane, and to safety, at last.

She almost screams when the last man reaches out, grabs her by the shoulder, turns her around to face him.

'We know you,' he says. 'Tell Azizbhai from us that he should take better care of his family. These are evil times. Anything can happen, at any time.'

~

Arshad and Azizbhai work swiftly towards their date of departure. Rabia examines the passports, those all-important booklets, while the men talk. Passports signal their importance: every other form of identification that matters to them, ration cards, identity cards, are small rectangles of plastic, pieces of cardboard. The passport has its own cover. It is meant to be carried around with the same care as a miniature sacred book. Arshad's passport and Sanam's passport, carefully placed in ziplock bags, have the sheen of newness and hope.

It is taken for granted among the three of them, Azizbhai, Arshad and Sanam, that she will join them in Oman later. Rabia does not contradict them. She does not want to hurt them, and she is touched that they had thought to include her. So she says nothing, only listens as Arshad and Sanam warm to the subject of Oman, and the wonders and relief of living in a country where they cannot so easily be singled out because of their religion.

Outside, the boys roar by on their motorbikes. She hears them chant:

'Madan Chaubey, Bright Dairy's star

Vote for him, wherever you are!
Madan Chaubey, Bright's brightest name
Join us and spread his fame.'

Chaubey is standing for the municipal elections and is likely to win, her neighbours say. Bright Dairy will be transformed even further. She turns back to Sanam, tries to concentrate on her daughter-in-law's excited chatter about their future in a new country.

∽

Another notice, another offer for the houses on Rabia's street. This time, it is hand-delivered. Sixteen boys, knocking at the door. When she lifts the hook, they push the door open with such force that she is almost knocked off her feet. 'It's a good offer, sister,' they say. 'We'll be back tomorrow night with your letter of acceptance. Everyone is signing.'

They say the same thing to all her neighbours. Salma tells her that she and her husband have packed already and will leave soon. Bright Dairy is no longer the right place for people like them, and you cannot spend your life fighting the tide. Because, she says, that is what it is, Rabia. It is coming at us like the tide, and it will sweep us away if we are not careful.

The boys saunter through her home. One taps his lathi on the cardboard cartons that Azizbhai has left in her keeping. He delivers two taps of approval. 'Good, good,' he says. 'We aren't looking for trouble. It's better if you're leaving on your own.'

The neighbour across the road shouts, 'She's going to live with her son and his family in Oman, the lucky woman. Not all of us are so blessed.'

'Oman, it's in the Gulf?' he says. He is younger than Arshad, and already adopting the postures and tone of one of their leaders—dark glasses, gold medallions around his neck, a studded wristband letting the neighbourhood know that he has made his bones on the street, can handle himself in a fight.

She nods.

'A Muslim country,' the neighbour yells, coming up to the doorway. 'She can say her prayers in peace, without any kind of disturbance.'

He is unruffled. 'It's a good thing, to be with your own kind. You can eat your non-veg if you want, any time you like. Pray five times a day to your God without feeling out of step with us. Be with others like you. Why be a minority here, when you can be part of the majority there? That's what I cannot understand. Why would anyone not want to live alongside their own people?'

Her patience snaps. She says, keeping her voice steady, 'I am among my own people.'

He eyes her, lazily twirling the lathi in a long, slow circle, letting the tip come down softly on her shoulder.

'No,' he says. 'You are not. But you will be soon.'

～

The shabby, makeshift huts that fringed the banks of the Yamuna are gone, though the wallowing buffaloes and the hyacinth pools remain. The Tinsel King has been forgotten; a ring of carts stands by the pond where he once ruled, and vegetable-sellers wash bunches of carrots and spinach in its waters. Boys play cricket where the ground has been cleared.

The skeleton poles for an open-air stadium are planted in the earth like a row of sentinels, and a large billboard proclaims, 'For Three Days, Let God In. With Baba Muktisagar, The Truth Shall Be Revealed. Entry Free.' A towering cut-out presents Baba Muktisagar, a clean-cut man with impressive abs and pectorals striking an advanced yoga pose, wearing a tight gold leotard. Rabia turns her back on the bulging Baba and finds the track that leads down to the river.

There are no wading birds, though convocations of black kites have gathered on the power lines overhead. The waters have lost the shimmer she remembers. The river flows like tar, sluggish and heavy, and the deep clay of the banks is almost lost to sight, covered in plastic, in trash, from edge to edge. The air stinks from foulness further down where the drains discharge into the Yamuna everything the city has no use for.

A prosperous farm has come up where their huts once stood. Rabia walks the length of the fence, and when she reaches the end, she sees Chand. He is waiting for her on the bank, talking to a boatman.

～

'I told him we would row ourselves, and he said he'll charge double if we tip over,' Chand says, pulling at the oars.

'You still remember how to row,' she says. 'After all these years.'

They are leaving it all behind, the clusters of concrete, the plastic shrouding the banks, the cars, the cricketers. He has turned the boat towards the far side of the river, moving out into clearer water. Buffaloes wade through the chars, the clouds mass overhead, carrying the promise of rain, and the water shimmers silver, flows more freely.

From the road behind them, a driver in a passing car turns up the radio. They catch the first notes of a familiar tune. Then the car whizzes by, the song is lost. Khalid used to play it often on his flute, he had taught Chand the Sanskrit words.

Muraari kaaya kaalimaa lalaama vaari dhaarini,
trnni krta trivishtapaa triloka shoka haarini
Manoanukuula kuula kunja punja dhuuta
durmadaa
Dhunotu me mano-malam kalinda-nandinii sadaa ||

Salutations, O Goddess Yamuna
your river waters carry traces of the beautiful,
blue-dark body of the Lord Murari
the waters of your river remove all impurities,
your river's waters are filled with sweet nectar.

He falls silent, letting the boat float out, borne by the current.

'When we first came to Delhi, what dreams we had for our lives,' he says. 'Did we ever imagine the losses ahead of us?'

'But we lived some of our dreams, Chand,' she says gently. 'We had friendship, and we made lives for ourselves in the city, and for a while, we had enough. Your losses are the harshest, but who goes through life without their share of sorrow? Weren't we given love as well, along with the rest?'

'Badshah Miyan wrote to me to say that he has settled in well, that he misses India but is teaching his useless new boys how to cut meat properly. Arshad and Sanam will find their footing in Oman. It seems it's only us who've been left unmoored.'

She trails a hand in the water, says, 'They want me to join them in a few months.'

'Will you?'

'I've accepted the offer Madan and his boys made all of us for my house. It's a low price, but it will be enough for me to rent something small near Rafiq-bhai. He and some others have moved to Samaypur Badli. I'll move there for a few months, see if I can make it work. I might visit Arshad and Sanam, but I don't want to leave, not yet. Will you make a life for yourself in the Himalayas?'

'I don't know, Rabia. I've never been to the mountains. Maybe my heart will feel less burdened if I'm in places that carry no memories for me. What about your job at the warehouse?'

She laughs. 'I've already given it up. Can I tell you a secret?'

He looks at her. Age has touched both of them. When he saw her, he was struck by how much smaller and frailer she seemed compared to the wiry, strong woman he remembered. But her eyes still sparkle the way they used to, fearless and curious about all of life itself.

'I've learnt how to drive! Arshad began to teach me last year, so that I could drive the car in an emergency if he was away, and I love it. People treat you differently when you're behind the wheel, Chand. They get out of the way of your car. I have some savings, not much, but I thought— maybe I can start a small driving school for other women who want to learn how to drive. Even if we only go to the market and back on our own. Is it a foolish idea? You're laughing at me.'

He picks up the oars and rows again, directing the boat to the middle of the river, an unpeopled world with just the two of them and scattered skeins of egrets overhead.

'I'm not laughing at you, I'm delighted for you,' he says. 'And maybe some day you can drive up to the mountains to see me.'

She is smiling, but her smile fades at the seriousness in his eyes.

'Come with me, Rabia,' he says. 'I mean it. We can see the Himalayas together. We can travel as much or as little as you want. We might make another kind of life together.'

She says quietly, 'You never did forget, did you?'

'Never. But neither did you.'

She does not deny it. The clouds are thick and dark overhead, blotting out the sun, and the wind picks up, cooling the air around them as the first fat drops of rain fall on their boat.

Rabia says, 'You had Bihida, and then Munia, and I had Arshad to look after. And I grew used to being on my own, to managing on my own.'

'Is it too late for us, Rabia?'

As always, she speaks her mind with the honesty he admires. 'I've grown used to my own ways, to being alone, taking my own decisions. I've become a friend to myself, Chand. I treasure my own company.'

'Is there a place for me in your life?'

'Was there ever a place for us to even meet? To spend just one afternoon together, to talk with one another as we did in our days on the banks of this river, without whispers, gossip, questions? Some days, I wonder whether there is a place in this city, this country, for me to breathe freely without this Hindu–Muslim, Hindu–Muslim trouble, a place where I can rest and be myself. Then what space is left for a Chand and a Rabia? The mountains are infected with the same prejudices and terrors as the plains. I am tired of battling these tides of hate.'

'I meant it,' he says. 'I will always mean it. And I will come back and ask you again, after a few seasons.'

She says, 'Later. We'll think about all that later. It is too soon for you to know your own mind. Maybe after some time you will know for sure if this is what you want, but at least get to the end of the first season of grieving.'

He rows their boat back to the waiting boatman.

When they are on land again, he says, 'I want you to have this.'

He hands her a battered blue suitcase. She looks at him, frowning.

'Just something I thought you would find useful,' he says as they walk to the bus stand. 'Don't open it now. Promise me you'll open it only after I leave for the mountains. I have one last task to finish before I start my journey, but once that's done, I'll send you a message.'

The streets are empty, people sheltering under flyovers and under the awnings of shops because of the rain. Chand opens his umbrella and holds it out over her head, so that they can walk together.

'That question you asked,' Chand says as they reach the bus stand. 'How would we live together, yes?'

She nods. 'I meant it, Chand. I cannot see a way.'

His smile is the most genuine one she has seen in a while.

'Let them have their high walls and their barbed wire fences and their gates,' he says. 'We'll live in the cracks outside the gates, and it will be enough. It can be enough. If you want it to be.'

She laughs, her own words turned so neatly against her, and boards the bus.

A Night at Jolly Villa

The lights blaze forth from every window and every wall of Jolly Villa, diyas clustered in the alcoves, lanterns strung high on tree branches, chains of twinkling fairy lights festooned like ropes above doorways, red lamps in the shape of a giant heart fastened on gates, candles and oil-soaked torches on the wide parapets.

Bhim Sain and Ombir walk past the troupe of welcoming dancers, most of them well-muscled youths hired for the night from the local akhara.

'It is exactly like a fairy tale,' says Bhim Sain.

'The villa looks like a birthday cake with a thousand candles stuck in the icing,' Ombir says, brushing a shower of rose petals off his trousers.

They stand awkwardly to one side, Ombir assessing the cars that drive in, mostly BMWs and Range Rovers, and a few Volvos and Porsches. Mostly local licence plates, but quite a few industrialists and politicians from Delhi. He nods at a thickset man he recognises, the head of a well-known security firm, one of the best in the area. No expense has been spared tonight. Even by the standards of Jolly Singh's lavish parties, this is a big bash.

Ushered in, the two policemen wander timidly through the villa.

Bhim Sain sniffs the air. 'It stinks of flowers,' he says.

'Khuskhus and jasmine,' Ombir says. 'My wife's uncle is in the attar trade. The zamindars used to do this, spend thousands of rupees just to perfume the air around them. Don't drink too much tonight, Bhim Sain. We may not be in uniform, and we are here as guests, but it's better to behave as though we are still on duty. Too many VIPs around.' The staff usher them out onto the vast lawn.

The stage is massive, done up in blue lighting and glitter, with artificial snow and disco balls twirling from the steel beams overhead.

'Reshma Bhabhi!' Bhim Sain says, smitten. Perched on a swing suspended from the arm of a crane, the dancer looks like a resplendent parakeet. This evening, she wears a spangled crimson strapless choli, and under its transparent gauze, a green conical brassiere, a skin-tight lehenga. She's singing one of her old hits, and Ombir hums the words absently, *main apne nanhe nanhe kapdon mein is nanhee nanhee duniya mein sirf ek nanhee nanhee ladki hoon.* I'm just a teeny tiny girl in this teeny tiny world in my teeny tiny clothes.

'She was a state javelin champion, you know,' he tells Bhim Sain. 'Before she discovered cabaret. That's why she has such fine muscles.'

Bhim Sain is in heaven. He edges up to the front of the stage, joining the hordes of raucous middle-aged men, many of them already several pegs down. Ombir glances around. The carp have an even more polished gleam to their scales, a trick of the Japanese lanterns that cast a mellow glow on the water. Above that artificial stream, the garden slopes upwards towards a boundary wall, creating the illusion of a steep hill.

Guests are thronging in, and he counts six kinds of cuisine from Awadhi to Thai, pasta stations to chaat stalls, even fish fry from one of the most famous dhabas in Amritsar. Gigantic lights strobe upwards, creating dazzling patterns in the sky, but when he walks up the slope, it creates an unsettling effect—the concentrated blaze of light has the effect of throwing the forest into even deeper darkness and gloom.

'Ombir, there you are,' says Bhadana, resplendent in a strawberry-pink suit. 'I thought you'd be near the stage. Jolly-ji has requested that you meet him in the house. On your own, without Bhim Sain. If you don't mind.'

'Is that a Lucky Dip stall?' Ombir asks as they walk back towards the house.

Bhadana grins. 'Yes, the boss thought his friends from the city would find it amusing.'

The crowds, the laughter, the buzz of conversation, the music, the band, Reshma Bhabhi's whirling firecracker figure, the glitter, the sumptuous silk streamers fluttering in the artificial breeze from massive mobile air conditioners set up everywhere to combat the heat—for a moment, all of that fades from Ombir's mind, and he thinks of Dharam Bir, sinking as his oxygen ran out, the lights dimming one by one in his brain, and he wonders whether Jolly's friends would find that amusing too.

༺༻

The waiting room outside Jolly Singh's office is twice as large as the station house. Ombir moves around, restless, studying the shelves of books on law and investments and taxes, picking up a heavy glass decanter and marvelling at such a fancy container for sharab instead of the plain, thick bottles in which the local theka sells rum and imitation whisky.

Out of force of habit, he is a policeman after all, he leans against the wall, listening through the gap where Bhadana did not fully close the door.

'... I told you I would settle it within one week. It's finished, Chand, the matter is closed. Dharam Bir will never harm another child again. Is that enough for you?'

Ombir hears Chand's slow voice. 'As you promised. It feels hollow, empty, but it is an ending.'

Bhadana says in a murmur, 'The signatures.'

'The other matter. I promised you would not lose by it. I hope the signing amount is to your satisfaction.'

'It is a fair price for the land. Thank you, Jolly-ji.'

'Sign here and here, and it's done.'

Ombir hears the chairs scrape back, and walks quietly to the bookshelves, taking out *The Handbook of Real Estate Tax* and skimming through its pages.

Chand comes out, saying, 'I will take my leave, Jolly-ji.'

'You must stay on for the fireworks. I had them shipped over from a company in Japan, it'll be a spectacular show.'

Chand says, 'Thank you, but I'm not comfortable with crowds. If you don't mind, Jolly-ji, I would rather go home.'

'But you must at least have some dinner,' Jolly-ji says expansively. 'No one leaves Jolly Villa on an empty stomach. I'll get my staff to make up a plate for you.'

He has an empty whisky glass in his hand. Bhadana takes it from him, says, 'Jolly-ji?'

'Fill it up. Ice, no soda. Bhadana, take Chand out to the garden. I'll join you in a while.'

He raises his glass to Ombir after Chand has left.

'Time to celebrate!' he says. 'You're not drinking?'

'No, Jolly-ji. It's against the rules.'

Jolly tugs at the collar of his shirt, laughs. 'Screw the rules. Only fools follow the rules ... you'll be celebrating tomorrow anyway.'

He pours Ombir a stiff drink, hands him the glass. Ombir takes it without protest, but sets it down near a potted palm when Jolly moves to the window.

'I told them, start with the rockets, then bring on the bigger ones, but they never listen. Good, no? Good to see people enjoying themselves. So, your promotion is confirmed. Bhadana heard from his contact in Faridabad. Congratulations, Ombir.'

'Thank you, Jolly-ji,' Ombir says.

Jolly Singh fishes inside his glass, takes out a cube of ice and crunches it with relish. He tops up the whisky from the decanter.

'Sad about Dharam Bir,' he says. His eyes are slightly bloodshot, but Ombir can tell that he is being closely watched. 'You haven't heard yet?'

Ombir says carefully, 'Why, what happened?'

'An unfortunate incident at the hospital. The power went out on Dharam Bir's floor for an hour or so. Seems that the outage affected the poor man's oxygen supply. He's in a coma, not likely to survive. Saluja asked me to let you know that he doesn't blame you or Bhim Sain. These things happen in rural hospitals.'

'They do,' Ombir says. 'We have power cuts all the time at the station.'

Jolly comes up, leans close to him. He can smell the alcohol on the big man's breath. He says, 'Ombir, I have nothing but admiration for you. Teetarpur will prosper, and you will prosper with it.'

He feels Jolly's hand slide into his shirt pocket, and has to stop himself from pushing the man away.

'A small present, that's all,' says Jolly, grinning. 'You reacted like a shy village girl. It's just a tiny gift. To the good times ahead.'

He removes the envelope from his shirt pocket and says, 'There's no need for this, Jolly-ji. You've already been most generous.'

Jolly says, 'Take it, take it. It's only the start of bigger things. You don't want to miss Reshma's next song. I told her, do a cabaret number, she said, no, no, Jolly-ji, I don't do that any more, and I said, but you must, no one says no to Jolly Singh. Come on, Ombir. Have some fun tonight. Everything is as it should be, and you have a promotion to celebrate.'

~

The bass rocks the speakers. Ombir sees Bhim Sain dancing wildly, right up near the stage. The press of guests and dancers is massive, the chatter and the music head-pounding and loud. He presses on through the throng, looking for Chand.

Ombir finds him in the only quiet spot in the garden, sitting behind a statue of the Buddha.

'Are you all right, Chand?'

'I sold Jolly-ji my field. Our land. Munia's land. He's been kind through this time. I wanted to leave, but I thought I'd wait until the crowds cleared.'

Another round of fireworks goes off and the two men look up at the sky, where brilliant Catherine wheels chase intricate coloured lights that explode like wildflowers over their heads.

'I wish this was over,' Chand says. 'I wish I was leaving Teetarpur tonight. Jolly-ji has helped me a great deal, but this noise, this press of people ...'

Ombir says, 'It will be over soon. These Delhi people always head back after dinner. Bhim Sain is enjoying himself, but I'd be happy to leave early with you. I will just inform Jolly-ji or Bhadana that I can't stay on.'

They don't have to search hard for Jolly Singh. An amber spotlight plays on the dance floor, and fireworks in the shape of a lion's head light up the sky. Ombir tries to guess how much more he has drunk from the well-stocked open bar; Jolly has a full glass in his hand again. His eyes are bloodshot, his fancy shirt soaked in sweat, and he's attempting to match Reshma's moves by jiggling his belly in time to the music and jerking spasmodically.

A tall man, well built, cuts in front of Ombir. He recognises the intruder from the advertisements in the papers—one of Delhi's biggest contractors.

'Got to say, Jolly, you know how to throw a party. Everything is fucking perfect. I love ice fans. I love Reshma. Awesome kababs, yaar, and the—Reshma's costume change, the second one. Fantastic party, yaar.'

He staggers, holding on to Jolly for support. Ombir and Chand move out of the way as the men stumble towards them.

'Only one thing is not perfect,' the big man says, slurring. 'Only one small thing.'

Jolly snaps back into near-sobriety. 'What is it? What's wrong?'

'It's the carp pond. I like fish. And Reshma, I love Reshma ... I collect ornamental fish, you see? And your guy, whoever, the chap who put in the pond—he's overstocked it. Too many carp.'

Jolly says, 'Too many carp.'

'Yes, but that Reshma—fantastic. You have her number? She gave me her number. Right here. No, I've lost the card. Must have dropped it.'

He gets down on the floor, with care, and begins scrabbling around on all fours, making his way through the legs of dancers and revellers like an elderly dog.

Jolly gives Ombir a twisted smile and says, 'Only one moment.' He leaves the floor and disappears into the villa.

'Maybe we can find Bhadana,' Ombir says, looking around. Some of the dancers cannon into him, and he takes Chand's arm, steers them to a less crowded spot.

He hears a gasp from people at the extreme edge of the dance floor. Jolly is walking out of the villa, a Glock 19 in his pudgy hand. Guests scatter out of his way. Ombir propels Chand behind one of the gigantic bass speakers.

The big contractor rises from the dance floor, waving triumphantly. 'Found it!' he yells. Then he sees Jolly, walking in his direction with the handgun, and freezes. Dancers stumble as they push one another, frantic to be out of the line of fire.

Jolly walks right past the contractor and down to the edge of the water.

Someone's shouting, 'Turn off the music, bhenchod, turn off the fucking music!'

Jolly takes aim and fires six shots with careful precision into the stream. He fumbles a bit on the reload, but manages it in the end, walks up the hill and fires six more, then a final six.

He slips the gun back into his belt, and calls to the big contractor, 'That's all right, no? Not overstocked any more?'

The man says, whimpering, 'It's fine, Jolly-ji. It's perfect.'

Jolly's forehead and neck are coated in a thick sheen of sweat.

Ombir weaves through the crowd, following Jolly up the hill.

'He has a loaded gun,' he tells Chand. 'Stay out of the way.'

But Chand does not leave his side.

Jolly waves at him, unaware that he's waving with the gun still firmly in his grip.

'Best view in all of Teetarpur, Ombir!' he shouts. 'Come up and take a look. If you tilt your head back, you'll see the fireworks properly. Unbelievable.'

Some of the carp have flopped out of the water. The golden fish twist on the grass, blood seeping from their gills and sides.

Chand stops, takes a skewer from the kabab stall, sliding the chicken tikkas off it. He kneels by each wriggling fish, finding the right spot, despatching them swiftly and cleanly.

Jolly says regretfully, 'What a mess!'

Ombir says, 'Sir, will you let me take the gun, please?'

'What?'

'The gun, sir.'

'It's a fantastic handgun, one of the best. Bought it last year.'

'Yes, Jolly-ji. Please give it to me.'

'You want it? Okay, but you have to give it back.'

Below, the guests are streaming out, pushing and shoving. Jolly hands Ombir the handgun, smiling widely, and the policeman takes the Glock, shoves it into his waistband.

Jolly picks up speed as he lurches down the hill. He stares at the musicians, and at Reshma's back-up dancers, cowering behind the drum set.

'Did I tell you to stop playing?' Jolly bellows. 'What kind of party is it where the dancers stop dancing?'

Ombir takes a deep breath and turns away for a second. He looks up the hill, over the low boundary wall.

It's not that low. On the other side, a steep drop. The wall is much higher on the outside than on the inside because of the hill. He picks up one of the lanterns that Jolly had kicked over on his way down and raises it above his head. It illuminates the scrubland on the other side of Jolly Villa, the wilderness that leads on one side to the canal and on the other to Chand's fields. He hadn't seen it before, because of the particular construction of the garden. Jolly's mansion is much closer to Chand's home than he had realised.

Chand has come up and the two men stand side by side, looking down. Chand says, 'I can see my home from here.'

They hear a thud and look back down the hillside. Jolly Singh has stumbled over a set of footlights. The whisky seems to have finally caught up with him. He drops to his knees, waving Chand away when he walks over to offer help, collapses again. Ombir picks his way carefully down the slope.

Jolly fastens his arm around Chand's neck, pulling him closer. Ombir has a clear view of Chand's face, illuminated by the sparkling lights of the fireworks display. The two men, one sprawled on the ground, the other crouched beside him, are staring into one another's eyes. He strains to catch the next words Jolly says.

'Chand. I'm sorry for all of it …'

Jolly slides further down the slope, releasing his grip on Chand. Ombir reaches them and helps Chand lift the man to his feet.

Jolly blinks, rubs his eyes with both fists. 'I slipped,' he says. 'Told the bloody landscaper he'd messed up the slope, but he'd already pocketed his cheque. Who the fuck turned off the music? Got to—got to say goodbye to my guests.'

His voice is surprisingly normal. Ombir notes that his progress down the hill is steady, as if the fall has unaccountably revived him. He joins a group of men. Ombir recognises the District Magistrate, Saluja and a few other prominent businessmen.

He turns to Chand, searching the man's face keenly. 'Why did he apologise to you just now?'

Chand says, 'I don't drink myself, but many men are like that when they have a bit too much of the bottle. They talk a lot of nonsense.'

Ombir says, 'Men like Jolly Singh can get away with nonsense. Powerful people usually can.'

'Yes,' says Chand. 'They can go fully out of control, but they never have to face what they've done. I will take your leave, Ombir.'

'I'll walk with you,' the policeman says.

The music comes back on as they're leaving. Someone turns the speakers up to full volume.

'Let's get this party rocking again!' Jolly Singh yells at his departing guests. He's propping himself up with the help of the mike stand, bumping into Reshma's back-up dancers. 'The night is young, the show has just started!'

Behind them, the staff at Jolly Villa clean up the mess. Ombir glances back and sees the tiny gleaming bodies stacked neatly on the grass, their dulled eyes staring at the rust-orange moon and the last of the fireworks.

The Quarry

Ombir finds Chand in his field, peering at a tangled knot of baby mice, their eyes unopened, in a dirty nest of plastic shreds and straw. The policeman parks the Harley, watching as Chand picks up the largest spade, shifts the nest onto its blade and moves the mice out of the furrow to a safer place.

'That's a good way of bidding farewell to your land,' Ombir says.

'As good as any,' Chand says.

'I came to give you a lift back home,' Ombir says. 'If you like.'

Chand smiles, hops on to the back of the bike.

Ombir waits while Chand changes into his travelling clothes—a checked shirt and comfortable trousers, socks and proper sneakers for the road ahead. Bags of dal and rice, sesame laddoos, jars stuffed to the brim with mathri and other savouries are stacked neatly on the rough floor.

'You look so different after your shave and in those Angrezi clothes,' Ombir says when he emerges. 'Like a man from the city. If I saw you on the road, I'd think, that man could have come from anywhere, a small town or a big city.'

'I'll take a few kurta-pyjamas along,' Chand says, 'but I'll have to leave behind all of this. It would take a lorry, not a Rajdoot, to carry everything Balle Ram and the others have given me for the journey. Ombir, please take the rest. I can only manage one small bundle. They are very kind, but I'll get enough to eat at the dharamshalas and dhabas along the way.'

Balle Ram enters, touches his brother lightly on the shoulder. He says, 'May you find peace. Come home soon.'

'I'll accompany him to the main road,' Ombir says. 'Don't worry. We'll give him a grand send-off.'

He glances at the rear-view mirror when they're on their way. Balle Ram and Sarita Devi are still on the road, waving, sending Chand off with all the love they cannot put into words. Ahead of him, on the Rajdoot, Chand does not look back, not even once.

When they stop at the main highway, Ombir says, 'Chand, will I see you again in Teetarpur?'

Chand glances at him keenly. 'I have no reason to return to the village.'

'None?'

'Did you come to say Godspeed as a friend or to see me off as a policeman?'

'A man can be both, can't he? You are truly leaving Teetarpur?'

Chand says, 'The case is closed, Ombir. You said so. The big officer said so. Everyone says so. There is nothing to hold me to our village any more. I must be on my way.'

'You are at peace? I'm asking as a friend, not as a man in uniform.'

'You will always be in uniform, you can't help that. No. Not yet. But I will be soon, I hope.'

Ombir lets him go without further questions. He watches the receding figure on the bike, growing smaller and smaller, lost in the traffic.

The case is closed, everyone knows. But as he rides back to the station house, he thinks, you can close a file more easily than you can find your way to the heart of a matter. Men stay true to their nature; he will never fully be out of uniform, that he acknowledges. Some men are ruled by their weaknesses. Some have the freedom and the power to act impulsively, recklessly, not once, but over and over again. Those men might escape justice, not once but every time, leaving others to sift through the wreckage. Even his uniform does not give him the power to change the past, or to reel in those who are beyond the reach of the law.

Chand rides only a few kilometres up the highway, the rain battering the back of his neck. He parks on the other side of the high-rises, the meandering grid of apartment buildings and cubes of glass, impractical in the summer, that houses a few offices, a gleaming hospital.

He crosses plots where the foundations for new complexes are being sunk in giant pits among the high grasses, the scrubby straggling trees. When he sees guards, or nightwatchmen, he holds back, not wishing to be seen, and he avoids the well-lit roads, where the risk of being photographed by a random CCTV camera is high. The air sizzles with the last of the summer's heat; the deep stillness before the rains.

He crosses two more fields. He catches a flash of neon
signs, some words missing—'Great', '—vana', 'Business
Park', 'Tech Haven', 'Supermodern City'. He takes a sharp
right, off the road, through a narrow thread of a lane, and
plunges into a different world, as abruptly as if he has
travelled between two planets. He had said to Ombir that
he would not return to the village, but he had not said
where he would go instead.

～

The darkness is so absolute that, for the first few moments,
he feels his way along the narrow road, letting his feet
sound out the descent, down into the patchwork of fields.
This side is hilly, in the lap of the Aravallis. A massive
signboard in neon announces: 'Royal Villas: Live Like
a King. Enjoy Forest Dreams, Clean, Green, Luxurious
Living. Project by JS Developers.'

Ahead, a lone tubelight sparks and sizzles—
gnnnnnnnzzizzz, gnnnnnnnzzizzz, like the buzz of a
helicopter-sized mosquito—and swarms of flying ants hurl
themselves at its hot white glass, falling in dying heaps to
the earth. The sounds of traffic cut off as the road dips
down. He avoids the scrubland and thickets, taking to the
tall fields of thickly planted foxtail millet and wheat.

Up ahead, mustard bushes grow to waist height, left
unpruned before the monsoon. They stand as high as a
short man. In the next field, sugarcane is clustered in thick
stands. He walks by the light of a solar-powered lamp,
styled like an old-fashioned hurricane lamp. He pauses
when he sees the figure looming up ahead, a scarecrow in
the middle of the cane.

It is a poor apology for a scarecrow, a cross of four twigs, two long, two short, bound by wire, with a matka tipped over the top, but someone has clad it in a ripped dhoti, a discarded, faded shirt, swung a curved sickle over the end of one of the shorter twigs. In the flare from the lamp, it bobs its head in his direction in a clumsy, life-like greeting.

In one lot, three abandoned tractors have been partly reclaimed by the curving tangles of wild vines, and leaning against them are the shapes of discarded wagons, old tyres, rusted pickaxes and mattocks.

The silence stretches across the land. There are no birdcalls at this hour, and those who farm this area won't be here before dawn. He picks his way through the fields, through the soft, humid night, to the lip of the cliff where the land plunges into a deep ravine, the stone-crushing machines scattered far below.

Between the fields and the cliff-edge, there's a half-constructed ten-storey building swathed in green netting, the walls and floors in rough grey cement. There's nothing else yet, no wiring, no fixtures, no windows or doors. He rolls out a light rush mat at the edge of the last field, drops into an untroubled sleep.

The smell of the rain wakes him, the rich scent of mud and air, water and earth and clouds. He dresses, in no hurry, lets the rain soak him to the skin again.

Chand checks once that the papers and photographs he has carried so carefully inside two plastic bags are dry, then leaves the fields to shelter in the empty building near the ravine for the day.

He thinks the man will come that night, perhaps the night after. He listens to the rain's soft whisper, watches the fields turn to a vivid green, unbelievably beautiful against that purple- and gold-flecked sky, the Aravallis plunging down to the stone-crushing quarry.

He settles in for the long wait. The man will come. He is sure of that. Most likely, he will show up alone, but if he doesn't, if he brings his driver, bodyguards, friends, Chand has gone over the possibilities and settled on a plan for each eventuality.

⌇

The newspaper cutting is damp. For weeks, he had kept it in his pouch, not needing or wanting to read the news item in the *Faridabad Daily Blaze* again, but not able to let go of it.

He had reached home after the evening at Jolly Villa, taken out the clipping: 'Murder suspect takes own life'. And that was when he finally read the smaller news item below:

Body of unknown woman in canal killing identified

District police have identified the body of a woman found in the canal as Miss Bachni, 32. The discovery of the body near the canal had sparked fears of safety among the locals. A source in the police stated that Ms Bachni had been strangled by an unknown assailant. There were no signs of a struggle and no evidence of rape, indicating that the murderer was known to the victim. The case is closed for lack of witnesses or further evidence.

There was a smudged colour photograph. The pink-and-green blouse splashed with dark bloodstains, a cloud of butterflies hovering above the green, gaily patched skirt.

Something had fluttered in his mind. The laughing woman he had glimpsed at the outer edge of his fields one day. The sound of a car door slamming, the sleek expensive vehicle backing and turning, carrying its passenger back to the big city. A man's drunken apology.

The last of the pieces came together. The way he could look at pieces of meat scattered on a steel tray and see the whole limb, the living animal, they fitted like that in his mind. He knew then why his child had been murdered, strung up like a kid goat shivering in the slaughterhouse.

~

He had thought about sending the message by phone, and rejected the idea. He didn't want to leave any traces.

On a trip to the main market in Teetar Bani, Chand located a busy photocopy shop. It took him no more than a minute or two to photocopy a leaflet he had carried in ('Having Fatigue? No Energy? Dark Circles? Lack of Joy in Life? Ayurvedic Japani Massage Revives All'), just in case someone looked over his shoulder, and the newspaper clipping about the unfortunate demise of Bachni.

He bought some envelopes and postcards at the post office. It was easy, when he was back in the village, to wait quietly until the ration-shop owner had to go on an errand. He used the rusty Godrej Prima to type a few lines in Hindi on the postcard.

'I saw you and Bachni. I saw everything.
Royal Stone Quarry. After 11 p.m. on Friday or Saturday. Don't bring anyone with you, come by yourself.
We will talk.'

Delivering the message presented no difficulties.

∽

Chand waits patiently. He has chosen his spot with care. The moon is a yellow half-circle hidden behind clouds, and a mizzling rain dusts the muddy track, the fields. Far down below in the ravine, he glimpses the sodium-vapour glow of the lone security light outside the Royal Stone office.

It's almost midnight when he sees the headlights, swinging from side to side as the car bumps down the narrow road, illuminating patches of crops, their black shadows. Only one car then. Chand watches carefully as he comes down from the building and walks across the mossy mud to the fields, but the car has no escorts.

The man in the car has his lights on full beam. The ghostly shapes of the tractors spring into sudden relief, the scarecrow's tattered shirt lit from behind, as a gust of wind sets it spinning.

Passing the spot where Chand stands unnoticed, the car stops at the barrier he had pulled across, taking rusted, corrugated sheets of iron from the junkyard, piling lantana branches on top of them. The man gets out cautiously. He's alone. His right hand hovers at his waist, and Chand guesses he's carrying a gun.

The wind is rising, and the purple sky cleaves in two as lightning strikes; moments pass, then thunder peals, loud in the open, rolling across the fields and over the ravine. The mustard plants sway and bend, curving almost to the earth.

Chand rises silently from the ditch, skirting the car, barefoot. He freezes when the man half swerves in his direction; then his target turns back, searching for movement beyond the barrier. Chand crouches low, and it's only when he's right behind that he stands, pushing something into the man's back.

Says, 'If you'll raise your hands in the air, Jolly-ji. Above your head. You won't need your gun. All I want is to talk to you.'

The headlights are still on. Chand reaches inside the car, turns them off. Jolly Singh blinks, momentarily blinded by the plunge into darkness. Chand, standing so close that they're touching like old friends, lovers, pulls the gun from Jolly's pocket, sends it spinning into the far distance. It isn't visible in the dark, but he imagines it arcing high, sinking deep into the mud.

'Now neither of us is armed, Jolly-ji,' he says, stepping back. The man turns around to face Chand.

'What are you doing here, Chand? You surprised me. I came to check on some papers in the quarry, some urgent business ...'

Chand says, 'I sent the postcard.'

'I don't understand.'

'Jolly-ji, I understand. I understand everything. You were expecting someone else tonight. You thought it would be Bachni's partner, or her manager, or maybe one of the policemen, anyone who was smart enough to see that the only person who had reason to murder her was someone she was blackmailing. She was blackmailing you, wasn't she?'

Jolly Singh flinches when Chand flicks on a torch, a heavy, old-fashioned model. He sets it on the ground so that it shines on Jolly's face, but far enough so he can't reach it.

'This is quite a story, Chand,' Jolly says, his face registering only wounded surprise. He's wearing a black tee shirt and jeans, not his usual suit. He moves towards the car, but Chand puts a restraining hand on his chest.

'No,' Chand says. 'I sold you my land in good faith. I trusted you. It touched my heart that you cared about people like us, inconsequential neighbours who lived at the foot of your big mansion. My girl, the girl you saw growing up these last five years, Jolly-ji, she would have trusted you too. She would have let you get close to her, and she would not have called for me or my brother.'

'You couldn't have seen anything. You weren't there, Chand. You have no proof. If you did, you would have gone to the police.'

'None.'

'Then we have nothing to talk about. You're still grieving for your daughter. You're not in your proper senses. When you return from your pilgrimage, we'll pretend that none of this ever happened.'

Chand smiles. The rain pours down, a cloudburst that soaks both men.

Jolly puts one hand on the car door and Chand slips the knife from his belt, slashes a long, fine line across the back of the man's neck, barely breaking the skin.

'You're not going anywhere, Jolly-ji,' he says.

'Are you out of your senses?' Jolly says in disbelief, touching the light scratch on his neck.

'All my life, I've addressed men like you, big men, important men, with respect. I've never asked for anything more than to be left alone to live my life with my daughter. You pretended to be a friend. You pretended to care about my Munia.'

He takes Jolly Singh by the shoulder. The man is tall, taller than him, heavier too, but Chand has worked all his life, lifting bricks, cement, stones, ploughing the land. He has more muscle on him than this man from the city. He slams him against the car, once, twice, using only his left hand, the knife in his right.

Jolly, the knife at his throat, says, 'Chand, you're making a big mistake. Don't do this.'

Chand slides the knife half an inch forward. Jolly screams as he feels his blood trickle from a small cut, no more than a tear in the skin.

'It wasn't planned,' he says, his breath coming harsh and fast. 'None of it was planned, I swear on God.'

Chand twists the point of the knife.

Jolly starts to talk, gabbling, 'It was Bachni's fault. She got greedy, couldn't be content, no matter what I gave her. She wanted more, property, company shares. The bitch threatened to tell my wife, to go to the press. I made a decision to kill her and dump her body in the canal. Chand, I swear, she was a common whore, cold-hearted, money-grubbing. Bachni was trash. She's no great loss.'

'My daughter. What harm did she ever do to you?'

'I thought she was away with you. She's not usually home at that hour.'

'She saw you and Bachni,' Chand says. 'When she was gathering jamuns.'

He does not take his eyes off Jolly for an instant.

Jolly nods. 'She was up in the tree. She saw everything that happened. I panicked. It happened in a moment of weakness, Chand. I couldn't take the risk.'

Chand holds the knife steady. 'And Mansoor? He wasn't a witness. He was no risk to you.'

'It wasn't my fault that the police thought he was the killer.'

'Wasn't it? Ombir had another suspect in mind. You didn't want him to ask too many questions, isn't that the truth? You weren't in Delhi that day. You were in Teetarpur, in my fields, meeting Bachni. If Ombir had pressed on with his inquiries, he might have found out about your relationship with her. Bachni, my daughter, Mansoor, and then Dharam Bir—all those lives, Jolly-ji, all those lives.'

He takes a breath, tasting the rain, remembering Mansoor, the carpenter's wandering, confused mind, his slow wits. Mansoor, with his look of a mongrel who had strayed, unsuspecting, into the path of enemies, his eyes asking why me, why me.

Chand raises the knife and Jolly says, his voice wracked by sobs, 'Wait. I can't change the past, you understand? I never meant for any of this to happen. Please, Chand. I didn't come empty-handed to this meeting. Let me give you what I've brought along. You can start a new life, make a donation to the temple in her memory. Let me make amends.'

He scrabbles at the car, at the door handle.

Chand says, 'You're trying to buy me off? You think I want your God-cursed money? Men like you should be wiped off the face of this earth.'

Jolly raises his head. His face is unmarked by tears. His eyes are dry.

'But not by you. You're not a murderer, Chand. You don't have it in you to kill me.'

He kicks viciously at Chand, catching him off balance, drops to the ground, rolling away from the point of the knife. Chand lands sideways, in the mud, scrabbles for purchase. Looks up, and Jolly is standing over him, pulling a long rubber baton out of the open car window. One end of the baton is covered with barbed spikes.

'You fuckers are all the same,' he says, grinning. 'You are all so easy to fool. Can't see what's right under your noses.'

Chand dives to his right, flopping like a gutted fish. He can hear the swish of the baton, missing his cheekbone by inches. His knife is gone, he can't see it in the dark. In desperation, he scoops up a handful of mud, throws it in Jolly's face.

He is backed against the barrier, the makeshift hedge he had built. Chand scrabbles to his knees, his eyes fixed on Jolly, who's advancing towards him. He feels behind him, searching for something, anything, he can use as a weapon.

'Ombir had his doubts,' Chand says. 'He must have asked himself why you were so eager to step in for such an insignificant matter.'

'Ombir! He's only a brainless fool, an unimportant village policeman. I'd have dealt with him.'

He's circling Chand now, weighing his chances of getting in a blow.

'How many more people will you kill, Jolly-ji?' Chand asks.

That long-preserved habit of respect, 'ji', is hard to drop, even now.

Jolly laughs. 'You should have left this alone, Chand.'

It takes a great deal of strength, but Chand manages to lift the jagged piece of corrugated iron up and out of the barrier, the branches trailing over his head, leaving a deep scratch across his left temple. He slams it down on the baton, knocking it from Jolly's hands just in time to block the attack.

Jolly staggers back. Chand is up, scrambling over the barrier, sprinting into the mustard fields. The rain makes the earth under his feet slippery and treacherous, the tall plants clutch at his shirt and whip back across his shoulders. But running steadies him.

This is his terrain. The land gives him an edge. He knows the shape of the field, the depth of its furrows, the surprisingly tall ridges, where to place his feet so that he doesn't stumble or sink into the mud. He takes a zigzag route, running by feel rather than sight, listening to the heavy rasps of Jolly's breathing, his curses as he clumsily follows.

He should have killed the man. Chand knows that. He meant to, but the cold rage that had descended on him in Jolly's garden and spurred him this far was not sufficient. He could not do it. Jolly was right; he is no murderer. He cannot murder so easily, not with cold head and heart.

He takes a sharp right through the cane field, hoping he will not tread on a sleeping snake. The glass-edged leaves rip his skin. He risks a glance back. There's only the rain, its fury lessening, drumming softly on the mud banks. He moves silently, glimpses the clearing where the scarecrow sways, dancing in the wind, lit by the solar lamp he had placed by its side. A rustle from the left. He pauses, resting his weight on one foot, listens.

He can't make sense of the sound at first. A scraping, like metal on stone. Chand turns, searching in the dark. The clouds part over the slivered moon, slipping away. In the thin thread of light, he sees Jolly's glaring eyes, his bared teeth as he comes at him with a rusted pickaxe—that sound, the tractors, the tools leaning against them—and he shrieks, the man is close, so close.

He's pushing his way through the cane. Can hear his own breath, he's gasping like an asthmatic. Just as he stumbles out into the clearing, Jolly grabs his elbow, jerks him back. He frees himself, punches Jolly in the face, deflecting the pickaxe—though he catches a sidelong blow from the handle. The pain in his ribs is sickening. He shakes his head like a dog to clear his sight, hears the other man grunt as he stumbles back on his feet.

Jolly catches up with him in the clearing. Blood runs down his face from his broken nose, but he holds the pickaxe with a steady grip as he edges forward.

'It ends here,' Jolly says. 'No more running.'

Chand shrugs, holds his hands out, palms to the sky. The wind ruffles the fields, rippling through the stalks and leaves. There is another bright flash of lightning. He sees it all so clearly, the two of them, facing off in the stretching emptiness of the fields. Chand turns towards the man who had killed his daughter, is about to kill him.

He moves into the light of the lamp, still standing.

Jolly raises the pickaxe for the final stroke. 'Kneel.'

Chand slowly sinks down, half-kneeling. As Jolly starts to swing the axe, he reaches out, grabbing the scarecrow's sickle, diving, slicing at his adversary's ankles, aiming for the tendon. Jolly stumbles forward, his leg collapsing under him. He screams, losing his balance, falling forward, and Chand strikes upwards, cutting at his hands, his wrists. The pickaxe drops from Jolly's hand and Chand kicks it out of reach. He rips a strand of wire from the scarecrow and roughly ties Jolly's bleeding hands behind his back.

'They mattered,' he says to Jolly. 'Munia, even Bachni. Even Dharam Bir, for all the evil he did. The gods know that their lives meant something.'

He holds the sickle to Jolly's throat, studying his face in the glimmer of the lamp, smelling the acrid stink of the man's fear.

'Anything you want,' Jolly says, his voice breaking, 'anything at all, I can give you. Land, as much farmland as you need. Five crore, ten crore, all of my wealth. I'll leave Teetarpur forever, only spare my life, please. I beg of you.'

Chand says, 'At night, did you ever stay awake? Did you think about the lives you've taken?'

He watches Jolly's face and says, 'I didn't think so. I am no murderer. But I am a butcher. It was my job for many years before I returned to Teetarpur.'

He has moved behind Jolly. He takes his head in his hands, gently forcing his chin up.

'Look your fill at this world. Take your leave from it.'

The line he slices with the sickle starts just below one ear, curves across the throat, cutting from one carotid artery to the other. It's a clean line. He has pressed deep, breaking the skin easily, letting the blood fountain forth. He waits without emotion, as Jolly Singh spasms, jerks, gurgling and choking on his blood. Holds him upright, cradles the man slumping into death. Waits for the final stillness, then he lifts the body onto the four sticks, ties the hands and legs securely. A new scarecrow for the field.

～

Chand rests for only a short while, shaking off the deep fatigue crawling up his bones. Dawn isn't that far away, and he must clean up before he goes.

There is no record of his fingerprints. Officials were supposed to come and take them for some government identification scheme, but the man with the machine had not yet visited their village. He wipes his fingerprints off the sickle handle and elsewhere as best as he can, to be on the safe side.

Chand leaves the pickaxe where it lies, but wraps a gamchha around his hands, takes a jagged stone and smashes in the windows of the car. He has no use for the murderer's money, but he can't leave bundles of cash in the car if he wants the police to assume that it was a dispute between rival developers, settled by a carjacking, a struggle, a murder. Ombir will guess, but Chand does not think the policeman will share his knowledge with anyone.

He stuffs the cash into his rucksack, checks one last time to make sure he has left nothing behind that might identify him. He walks back to the abandoned building where he'd left the Rajdoot and changes into the clean set of clothes he had kept there, washes his face, folds and packs the bloodstained clothes he was wearing into a small black bag. He can smell fresh rain riding in on the early morning breeze. The land will soon stir to life.

One more life taken, a life for those lives. It will not set the balance of the universe right, but it tilts the scales, a little.

Ascent

He sets out at dawn, the black wings of night turning to indigo. Red headlights glare from big saloons that move aggressively into the empty spaces of the highways, racing one another and honking impatiently at the buses and trucks that refuse to move into the left lane to allow the swift, the powerful-engined, to pass. Chand weaves through, the Rajdoot's throbbing pulse becoming part of his own heartbeat as his muscles remember what it's like to ride a bike.

The Rajdoot surges up flyovers, skimming past Ghaziabad. The fog rises from the steep drop below the highway, a carpet of grey cloud around his feet. At the crossing, a blare of horns, the red lights stab through the early light of dawn, and every motorist around him ignores the traffic signals. He spots something strange to his right, takes a closer look. About a dozen solemn-eyed monkeys are crouched silently inside a blue tempo, the back open but covered with wire to make a cage. When they see him looking, their sad eyes meet his, their paws curling around one another's fur and tails, but they do not bare their teeth or change position, just meet his eyes with that incurious, steady gaze.

At Hapur, he glances at the half-built flyover, a broken concrete wing jutting into the sky, iron rods dangling like deadly serpent ropes. Welders are perched precariously at the end of concrete beams, on the tiny cement square of the top of uncrowned pillars, sending showers of sparks down onto the road.

Securing his helmet, he sights down the line, takes a calculated risk, veering off the road where traffic has slowed to an endless crawl, bumping down the sand and scree of the verge. It takes an hour to cross a six-kilometre stretch, even with the shortcuts. Schoolchildren sprint across his path. A farmer drives a pair of bullocks up onto the road, forcing the animals, their eyes rolling, to take the sheer vertical climb from the fields. Rickshaws and bicyclists swerve into his lane.

He revs up, cutting across two lanes, ignoring the drivers who roll down their windows, cursing at him, and fits the Rajdoot into a gap like a minnow darting between bigger fish. He notes the vacant faces of the passengers in the back seats, their shoulders hunched as they concentrate on their cellphones.

Chand stops the bike near Garhmukhteshwar. Below, boatmen row mourners out into the middle of the river, where they throw more ashes into the swirling muck. Families behind him are buying balloons flecked with gold and tinsel. He buys a green coconut from a seller whose sad eyes have the same flicking, fatalistic gaze as the caged monkeys, lets the coconut water refresh him, clearing some of the road's dust from his throat.

At the bridge, he drops the bag containing his stained clothes into the river. It bobs on the surface in the middle of a floating island of marigold garlands. He follows its progress until it sinks slowly to the bottom.

On the opposite side of the road, there is a swell in the number of cars, trucks, carts, buses returning to Delhi. A tempo driver cuts out of the traffic jam, takes his oversized tyres over the divider, and the tempo wobbles for a dangerous second, almost overturning. Like a beetle recovering its balance, it makes the steep climb, disrupting the flow of traffic on Chand's side. The tempo driver pulls up on the pavement, facing the wrong way, catches Chand's eye as he climbs down from the cab.

'Nothing to do, brother,' he says. 'Full-on traffic jam building up. If you're going up to Rishikesh, you should turn back.'

'Accident?' Chand asks.

'Bad one,' the man says. 'A Delhi SUV lost control, ploughed into a pilgrim convoy. Must have killed four–five people. A big crowd is gathering, they've cordoned off the highway in protest. Won't let anyone through.'

Already, cars and bikes are beginning to stream down this side of the highway, the wrong side, carving one lane out of the three taken up by vehicles heading from Delhi up to the hills.

'You'll join them?' Chand asks, pointing at the wrong-way cars.

The driver laughs. 'Not on your life,' he says. 'This jam will make a mess of everything. I'm going to take my tempo down to the river and give her a bath, rest for a few days. I'll tell the malik I got stuck for a day or two. He won't believe me, but he won't be able to complain, no? Where are you going?'

Chand says, 'I thought I'd go to Rishikesh, a bit further up from there, but actually I have no fixed plans. Just wanted to go to the hills.'

'You're a lucky bastard if you can go up to the hills just like that, whenever you want. Take the right before the traffic gets totally fucked. The Corbett road should still be open.'

Chand says thank you, doesn't want to ask what this Corbett road is or what it leads to, but after he has cleared the traffic, leaving the loud horns, the arguments and the rumble of overheated engines behind him, he stops under a banyan tree. He studies the map on his phone. It marks a path through a jungle, then a rising, winding road, and a river. The Ramganga, winding through the mountains. He checks the distance and realises that, for the first time in his life, he will be leaving the plains and the city for a completely unfamiliar landscape.

The trees stretch further into the sky than he had imagined, standing together like close family. At first, he rides down the Corbett road at a clip. Then he slows, brings the Rajdoot to a stop near a fruit-seller's stand. Canopies of sal trees rise up over his head, the leaves as broad as platters. Baby monkeys dart onto the road, playing nervous games of tag with the cars. When they grow too bold, their mothers or the older bull monkeys cuff them back.

Further on, some distance from the hotels and lodges, a short line of cars and vans has stopped, for no reason that he can see. There are no barriers or checkpoints. He rides up, drawing level with the car in front. The driver signals to him to keep quiet. He doesn't spot it until it is almost in front of them—an elephant, majestic, uninterested in the humans, crossing the road. He watches the beast, his engine idling, letting the traffic start up and go past, watches for its grey shadow long after it has melted back into the bark, the leaves, the trees.

He sends her a message from the roadside.

'Please open the suitcase now. Don't be too angry with me. It's from the sale of my land. You refused to let me give you anything all these years. Accept this at least. You and Munia are the only real family I ever had. Say yes to a gift for once.'

Chand smiles, thinking of Rabia. She would open the battered blue suitcase. She would glare at the money, she would curse him, she would be angry and annoyed. But maybe she would see sense. Maybe she would buy a home, buy some cheap used cars, start that driving school.

He can feel the shift, the change in the air as the highway starts to curve upwards, the first whisper of the mountains ahead. The rush of vehicles has eased, most of them dropping off at the luxury resorts and villages below, but he keeps going, fascinated by the intense green, rolling hills, the steep curves and sharp bends of the mountain roads, each one beckoning him like a temptation.

Far below, he sees the shape of a river curving, silver water shimmering like a sky mirror. He watches a flock of goats leaping up a hillside so steep they're running along a ladder of air. He has to take his eyes off them to concentrate on the hairpin bends coming up. He has never ridden the Rajdoot along such twists and turns. After the third bend, he starts to get the hang of it, hugs the edge, taking the bike almost parallel to the road, leaning as far as he dares, his body shaped by the wind.

A lone shop is perched át the edge of the road, clinging to the hillside like a pebble. Chand stops, his attention caught by the disparity of the goods spread out in front. Bicycle chains, wood-burning stoves, frying pans and kadhais, mattresses, even a carved wooden door hangs askew from its hinges. The sign, painted in Hindi and English, announces: 'Pandit-ji's Shop. All That Is Broken, We Undertake to Repair.' Below that, a welcome list, hand-lettered on cardboard, with blue and gold birds painted with such loving skill that he feels they might fly off the sign any moment. The items on the menu remind him of his hunger:

Maggi masala
Maggi cheese
Samosa-chhole
Maggi tomato
Poori-aloo
Chai

He needs a short rest. A man in a black weathered coat, a bright embroidered cap on his head, leans against a log, cleaning the inside of an ornate hurricane lantern.

'Pandit-ji?' he says politely.

'One moment,' the man says. 'You see this brass? It's older than you, and even me. It has to be cleaned with love, my friend. Sit, drink the air, the tea will soon be ready. You want tea, no? One plate poori-aloo?'

Chand nods, looking for a place to sit. Pandit-ji says, 'If you take that end of the log, it will balance well. Beedi? You don't smoke? Very good, very good, it's bad for your health.' He finishes his work, pats the lantern gently, the way he might pat an obedient dog, fishes out a beedi from behind his ear and lights it.

'One of these days, He will knock on my door in any case, right or wrong? Right. I gave up smoking for thirteen years, didn't miss it for one single day. Then my friend Bisht got married. What a fine wedding. I ate pooris, ten, fifteen, and then I felt, something is missing. You know that feeling? Like an itch. Doesn't go away so easily. Just at that moment, my other friend Chimwal walked by, smoking like a lord. I said, Chimwal, you give me that beedi. You cough too much these days. Tobacco will be the death of you. I will take that burden out of your hands. He stopped smoking, I restarted. If my wife had been alive, she would have thrashed me. Good woman, but what a temper. However, she departed some time ago. So here I am. You have a wife, children?'

Chand says, 'I don't have a wife or a child.' A kind of truth in that.

Pandit-ji takes the blackened kettle off the ring of bricks in which a small fire of twigs and leaves is smouldering, pours out two cups of strong tea, thick with twice-boiled milk, adds generous measures of jaggery.

'Travelling from far?' he asks.

'From Delhi.'

'I thought so. Many Delhi people visit in summer. They rush up in their cars, drive along until they get to a viewpoint. Look at this place. Everywhere you turn, there's a view, but that won't do for the city folk. They must find a proper signpost saying, this is a viewpoint, before they can see what's before them. You like our hills?'

Chand takes a deep breath, the sweetness of the air like a blessing. 'I've never seen the mountains before. They are far more beautiful than I had expected.'

'You haven't seen the Himalayas yet,' Pandit-ji says. 'Then you'll know what real beauty is. Sit in front of those mountains for a few hours and your mind grows completely still. Like a pond without ripples. When the sun sets over the snows, they blaze with pure fire, and you can't look for too long, and you can't look away. But don't stay out after dark.'

'Is it dangerous?'

'Not so much for us, but you people from the city aren't used to living with animals. And even we latch our doors fast at night out of respect for the tigers and leopards. These hills and forests are theirs, not ours.'

Chand sips his tea. 'I'll remember.'

The old man presses a bottle of water and some crumbly mithai into Chand's hands when he leaves.

'For the journey,' he says. 'Follow the road for a few kilometres. You'll come to a point where it's burnt from the summer fires. Stop there. You can see the river on one side. If the light favours you, you may even glimpse the Himalayas, if they are in a gracious mood.'

The rushing song of the river accompanies him, growing louder and more melodious. He rides slowly. He is riding higher and higher into a realm he could not have imagined. There are new marvels at each bend—the soft line of grey mountain ridges in the far distance, the scent of herbs, ferns curtaining the walls of rock, the forests thinning out.

Chand stops at the edge of the road, his eyes filling with the sight of the Himalayas in the distance. A line of austere ice and snow, rising to meet the sky, cloaked in ancient grandeur. The river far below reflects the shimmering diamond sunlight. The valley below is verdant, except for a massive burnt patch that spreads inky shadows across two hills and this side of the mountains, the legacy of summer forest fires. The porcupine shapes of scorched pine cones and ashy branches snake like broken vertebrae across the forest floor.

Something is knitting together in him, something is breaking, he doesn't know which.

Overhead, two griffon vultures soar through the brilliant blue sky. He never thought a sky like this could exist.

From the saddle bag, Chand pulls out the yellow plastic sack that he has carried all this way. Holds it against his chest, his eyes following the griffons as they dip and weave, chasing one another across the valley, into the forests, and spiralling up again, silhouetted against the Himalayas.

Prayers don't come easily to him, but he recalls an old one. He closes his eyes as the light icy breath of the mountains touches his skin and his hands start to go numb in the unaccustomed cold. He stumbles at first, can remember only 'lead us', but where? Then the words come back to him.

From untruth to truth. He says it quietly, the sun beginning to set. From darkness into light. From death into immortality. Let there be peace.

He opens his eyes, takes a slow breath and releases all of it. The cold-blooded act that changed his life forever, the emptiness he had descended into, the grim deeds he had witnessed, the ones he committed, the love he was given and that he gave in return. He breathes these out into the silent valley, the towering uncaring ranges.

The massive birds swoop lower, curious about this lone human in their territory.

Chand unties the silk cord with which he had fastened the mouth of the sack. He kneels at the edge of the road, where a muddy hillside track plunges straight down to the river. He tilts the sack, shakes out the contents, the cinders, all that remains. The ashes cascade down to the forest floor, settling around the black scorched stumps of pine trees.

He upends the sack, shaking it until there is nothing left. A few lazy plumes of ash drifting in the wind, a scatter of grey on the surface of the charred earth. The white mountains blaze before his eyes, painted in liquid golds and shimmering reds, the river like molten silver far below.

He lets go of all that he has carried for so long.

He lets his daughter go, into the light.

Acknowledgements

I have spent half my life around reading and writing, and I believe that no writer ever truly works alone. *Black River* and its companion novels owe a debt to many friends, editors and others; if the books fall short, that's on me.

Friends
Prem Panicker, Karthika Naïr, Rahul Bhatia, Meenakshi Ganguly and Baba Kapoor steadied my hand, helping me to shape, discard, and return to draft after draft.

Anita Roy, Ruchir Joshi, Priyanka Dubey, Kamini Karlekar, for the constant support and great advice.

Gauri Gill, for the thoughtful conversations, the shared love of dogs and the incredible gift of author photographs taken on a sweltering monsoon day.

Kiran Desai, Sonia Faleiro, Jeet Thayil, bless you for taking time out from your own writing to send love and blurbs.

Mohit Satyanand, Premi and Kanika; Malavika and Hiranmoy Karlekar; Anuradha Roy and Rukun Advani— for the gift of days of tranquillity and time in your mountain homes when I most needed it.

Gratitude to my family for giving me the space to write—especially to my sister, Nayantara Roy, and to my parents, Sunanda Roy and the late Tarun Roy.

Editors and Agents

David and Heather Godwin, agents, friends, companions who share the love of books. For keeping the faith, for championing authors, for pushing me to do better, again and again.

Karthika V.K., for your wise counsel and unshakeable values, your fierce editor's eye, your indomitable calm through all storms, for knowing my novel as well as I do.

Ajitha G.S., for teaching me through your edits what a novel owes its characters, and for the devotion as well as the skill you bring to those crucial final reading sessions.

Gautam Padmanabhan at Westland, for the warmth you bring to the business of encouraging writers.

Daniel Seton and Adam Freudenheim at Pushkin Press, for opening your doors wide.

Alec Russell, Laura Battle, Rebecca Rose, Frederick Studemann, Lorien Kite at the *Financial Times*, thanks for being such wonderful and supportive colleagues.

Key research

Delhi's Meatscapes: Muslim Butchers in a Transforming Mega-City by Zarin Ahmad (Oxford University Press, 2018)

What the Eye Does Not See: The Yamuna in the Imagination of Delhi by Amita Baviskar, *Economic and Political Weekly* (Vol. 46, No. 50, December 2011)

River of Love in an Age of Pollution: The Yamuna River of Northern India by David L. Haberman (University of California Press, 2006)

Places
The seed for *Black River* and other fiction took root at The Rockefeller Foundation Bellagio Center—that grant of an Arts & Literary Arts Fellowship in 2013 changed my writing practice.

To Sangam House, for the gift of a residency and evenings of readings and laughter in Tranquebar in 2016.

Designers
Neeti Banerji, who imagined Black River perfectly, and Saurabh Garge, for your care and vision.

Typesetter
Jojy Philip, for his meticulous work.

Always, Devangshu Datta, best friend and first reader, for seeing me through messy drafts and the years of loss, for babysitting our boisterous posse of cats, for saying ever so gently, keep going.

AVAILABLE AND COMING SOON
FROM PUSHKIN VERTIGO

Jonathan Ames

You Were Never Really Here

A Man Named Doll

The Wheel of Doll

Sarah Blau

The Others

Zijin Chen

Bad Kids

Maxine Mei-Fung Chung

The Eighth Girl

Amy Suiter Clarke

Girl, 11

Candas Jane Dorsey

The Adventures of Isabel

Joey Hartstone

The Local

Elizabeth Little

Pretty as a Picture

Jack Lutz

London in Black

Steven Maxwell

All Was Lost

Louise Mey

The Second Woman

Joyce Carol Oates (ed.)

Cutting Edge

John Kåre Raake

The Ice

RV Raman

A Will to Kill

Grave Intentions

Paula Rodríguez

Urgent Matters

Tiffany Tsao

The Majesties

John Vercher

Three-Fifths

After the Lights Go Out

Emma Viskic

Resurrection Bay

And Fire Came Down

Darkness for Light

Those Who Perish

Yulia Yakovleva

Punishment of a Hunter